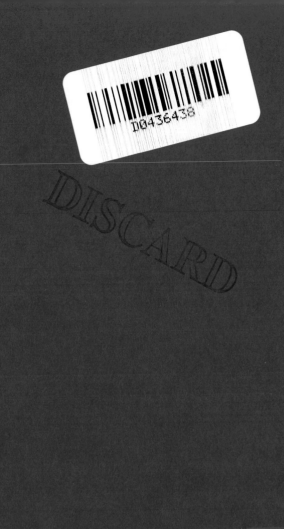

D0436438

CRY UNCLE

CRY
UNCLE

Alan Michael Parker

UNIVERSITY PRESS OF MISSISSIPPI
Jackson

www.upress.state.ms.us

The University Press of Mississippi is a member of the Association of American University Presses.

13 12 11 10 09 08 07 06 05   4 3 2 1
∞

Library of Congress Cataloging-in-Publication Data
Parker, Alan Michael, 1961–
  Cry uncle / Alan Michael Parker.
    p. cm.
  ISBN 1-57806-727-8 (alk. paper)
  1. Victims of violent crimes—Fiction. 2. Corporate reorganizations—Fiction.
3. Separated people—Fiction. 4. Amnesia—Fiction. I. Title.
PS3566.A674738C79   2005
813'.54—dc22   2004013731

British Library Cataloging-in-Publication Data available

For Tom McGarey, Joe Morse, and Mark Willhardt;
good friends and brave men,
who have all begun anew.

CRY UNCLE

CHAPTER 1

With his good hand, Ray reached down to pull up the overalls. Wait. Was that—? How had he gotten here? Whose overalls were these?

Huh?

He was sitting in the dirt, a pair of overalls pooled around his ankles. He had walked, naked, from a road to a house and then down to a barn, in pain, but then more had happened than he could remember: somehow his body or his internal clock or whatever kept track hadn't registered a chunk of time, as though a few frames of film had been surreptitiously snipped from his life.

What had happened to him? Had he been good? What had happened that might get worse? Was this like being dead? Or maybe he was dead. Not that Ray believed himself dead, but the loss of time felt ominous, like waking to night sweats and a numbness in the left shoulder—and now he was sweating and his left shoulder was sort of numb.

"Oh god," Ray swore aloud; he was only forty-one years old. He looked down at the overalls, looked up, then looked around. No, no corpses. But something did smell awful, something rotten, some kind of meat or animal. He thought that the smell came from a pile of wood to his left. And the smell smelled dead.

His name was Ray. He told himself his full name. Twice. Then he tried to pull up the overalls, shimmy down into them—and in response to the pain searing his chest as he pulled one-handed on a strap, his left arm cradled, limp against his stomach, Ray was afraid, the fear everywhere in his body.

Wait. Right. He had taken the overalls from the barn. Of course. Ray exhaled—he had been holding his breath—as the memory filled itself in. From the road he had seen a few unfaded letters still legible on a barn wall, illuminated by a floodlight, fuzzy in the humidity: O-L-S-E- A-N- -O-N. Olsen and son. And a date: 1889. A gray cultivator had stood rusty in the weeds. The yard had been posted—that yard, back there. Up the untended drive to Ray's right, under a wide giant elm, stood a boarded-up two-story house, its red brickwork the color of old blood. Definitely an elm, one of the few kinds of trees Ray could identify.

He remembered: he had seen the house from the road, and had wanted to get closer. He had told his body to move, but it had refused. Ray had pleaded, and his body had relented, just this once. He had been naked. He had needed clothes, and to strap his left wrist to his torso so that he could use his right arm more freely, all without setting off those blinding neural fireworks.

And then part of the memory was gone again. Another skip.

The windows of the Olsen family mausoleum had all been nailed shut, the front door had been sheeted with tin. Ray remembered standing on a crumbling stoop. He remembered thinking that the Olsens might have moved but this was still their house, and their dogs and cats were probably buried out back, their tiny bones six inches deep in a dusty yard ruled by the various wrecks of a Rambler, a Dart, and a John Deere.

Ray had identified, but he wasn't sure with whom or what. He still didn't know.

Would there be anything in the barn? He had remembered turning—in pain—to consider the barn, which despite its dilapidated sign, had looked somewhat kept, rented or leased.

Then he stopped remembering: he acted. And as he acted, he knew that all of his actions, from this moment on, would be different.

Ray pulled himself up to a standing position, only half-surprised to discover that he had been sitting on a railroad tie in the grass—how had he arrived here?—and then he waddled back down the drive, stepping as lightly as he could between clumps of spiky weeds and a smattering of sharp stones. Ouch. Hey. The stones hurt more than they should have hurt.

He opened his eyes. He had closed his eyes to remember. He was dizzy. He hung his head: but keep the eyes open, he told himself. Ray looked at his feet, torn up, raw. That was why the stones had hurt so much. In the ditch to his left, two glassy and feral eyes caught the light, gleaming. A wild something just half the size of a sitting, grown man. "Scram!" Ray tried to say, but his voice cracked. "Shoo," he cleared his throat. "Beat it," he managed. "Go on."

He had broken into the barn—wedged the creaking door open and squeezed through, scraping the hell out of his stomach—and had found a pair of boots that almost fit and a pair of overalls that reeked of manure. He had taken the clothing.

Now that he knew about the overalls and boots, or really, now that he remembered, it was time to move. Ray pitched forward, hoping to rock onto his right arm, pitch back, and then surge to his feet. The pain blazed through him. Not easy. He bent his legs and then fell more than clambered upward into a kneeling position. He rested. He breathed. The pain seemed to fill every inhalation, sizzling in each lung.

He stood up as though climbing his own body from the inside, wobbly, his left shoulder caved in, curled, his left wrist pressed weakly across his hip, and standing up, he was impressed with himself. Even still, his shoulder hurt too much for him to feel impressed for very long, especially now that he was standing, sure that his shoulder must be separated.

Now that he was standing, which way should he go? That way; a decision. With his left wrist tucked into the bib of the overalls, to keep the bad shoulder from being jostled, Ray turned around and began walking that way, back down the road, or back up the road, whichever the hell way it was.

The night seemed colder, the stars farther away. Once, Ray had owned a dog, but the dog had died. Was that true? Yes. He was telling himself stories to keep going. Once, Dad had played catch with Ray, and thrown a ball through the neighbor's window, father and son standing there, their mouths open. No, that story wasn't true. Dad had liked baseball, but only to drink to, on television.

Once Ray and Dad had been driving to Nana's house, and Ray had felt carsick, and Ray had said, Dad, I'm going to throw up, and Dad had said, Ray, just don't, and Ray had said, Dad, please, and Dad had said, Oh Christ, don't do that, for godsakes, Raymond, I just cleaned the car.

C'mon. All this pain and all this feeling were making Ray into a sop. He had never been so pathetic, trudging along in stolen floppy boots, one good arm hugging one bad shoulder. What a pitiful sight. But no one would pity Ray, not even the people in that oncoming car, its headlights searing across a line of poplars—the driver wouldn't take pity on Ray, brake to a skidding stop and swing wide an inviting passenger door.

He was standing alongside the road. Standing here was not a good idea. Ray should hide from that car. Could he walk nonchalantly? Run? He had to make it to that tree. "Wait up," he heard himself say.

Wait up? What? Stupid.

Clearly, as Ray hunkered down behind a tree until the car passed and drove on, the fingers of his right hand wriggling to wedge themselves deeper into the furrowed bark, being stupid meant more in the country than it did in the city. More people were stupid and more people did more to hurt stupid people, or something like that. The car passed, whoever it was: Ray exhaled loudly. Not asking for help had probably been a stupid decision. But he was not from here, and he couldn't stay here.

Ray was walking again, slowly, holding himself up in his newfound, stolen clothing. He was being held up by his clothes, he thought. Stitched together. His neck and his shoulder and his arms and his heart were all coming apart, unraveling, and only the clothes were keeping his body from doing so completely, from falling to pieces.

Left, right. Left, right. Why did he always start on the left? He stopped, to start again with his right foot. Right, left.

There was a breeze. It was cold. He was cold, he realized, which seemed worrisome—and he realized that he had been walking with his eyes closed again, and that he had no sense of for how long. Not good. He stopped. He looked at the sky. Stars. Don't worry, don't think, he told himself. Don't even think about it. He had been walking and walking, there was nothing but walking. Time stopped or started, no matter. He told himself his name. Ray. He told himself to walk. Screw the traffic.

Had there been more traffic? Ray couldn't remember. There had been a building, he remembered a cement building. Ray had walked past, his head bowed, as he watched his feet make their own decisions. There had been noises. More animals or something. And then he looked up: the sky glowed just ahead, an ionized corona of carbon monoxide and ragweed smearing the air above Brighton, Ohio, population fourteen thousand, home to the world-famous Windy Oaks combed cotton Oxford shirt. Ray knew what he was looking at, which wasn't helping.

He could see a line of streetlights blur a mile or two or three away, and beyond that, to the west, he could just about imagine the subdivisions and rolling four-acre estates of the country club set, their lawn jockeys newly painted white, their inground sprinklers synchronized to bloom in the predawn mist. Ray knew the town already, sort of—since how much of Brighton could there be to know? Fourteen thousand seemed an awfully generous figure, from what he had seen already. One country club in a dying town. Lots of gun clubs, probably.

He knew where he was: lost, where he shouldn't have been, on the outskirts of Brighton. No, wait: Ray wasn't lost, just not found. So he stopped to readjust the strap of the overalls. There was something foul on the button. Or was that a rivet?

Ray surprised himself: he cared, briefly, and wiped the rivet clean and then his hand.

They better not see him, he realized. And then, whether prudent or terrified or some combination of both, Ray made a decision: to sneak undiscovered and unrecognized through town to his leased house; to stay off the main streets, avoid the light, keep his head down. Then once he was safely inside, he'd get a damn doctor to make a damn house call. With them probably still out there, cruising, Ray had more to worry about than Velveeta or Livingware or the grass browning on the devil's strip where the neighborhood dogs liked to piss.

He wasn't making sense, that he knew. But he was walking, and they were still out there—and they had rammed his car in the parking lot, grabbed him, and thrown him into their truck. They had done unspeakable things, Ray thought, not knowing really what he meant. Three vicious boys.

There. Parallel to the road ran a ditch of sorts, a trough of water, weeds and the occasional sumac stand. He skidded or fell or both—down the embankment and into the ditch. He stood. He walked again, which was more like slogging or wading.

And whatever it was he was doing, through the muck, became dangerous, as Ray's one-armed flailing rendered his balance wildly unreliable. He could step where he wanted, but he couldn't keep himself from falling—nor could he catch himself when he fell, aside from twisting to land on his good side or his ass. His stolen boots made sucking sounds in the mud, Saturday morning cartoon sucking sounds. Ray could be sitting here and watching this on TV, he thought, cuddled with his son, Tom, still in pajamas. We are Animaniacs, Ray thought.

Feet, move.

Breathe.

Inhale. Deep breath.

Wipe your face, right hand.

Come on, exhale. All of it.

He moved. But the closer he came to the streetlamps, the harder it seemed to draw a breath. He had no idea of how late it was, but the thought of some guy driving home from third shift and catching in his headlights Ray's vacant gaze made him shudder. Keep low, he told himself.

At the first street sign, where the speed limit dropped from a rural fifty to a municipal twenty-five, Ray came up from the ditch, clawing his way up the incline until he stood in the gravelly break-down lane, the rank overalls newly dripping with field runoff and roadside filth. He leaned against a useless metal pole. Ahead, in the glow of a streetlight, stood the Welcome to Brighton sign. It occurred to Ray that he should stay on the sidewalk, rather than sneak through various backyards and alleyways, banging into trash cans as the police sirens wailed closer and closer.

They were out there. Who were they? Three guys, one in charge. A mealy shit of a guy, cruel and wide-eyed, someone who seemed to know what he was doing, the effect each demeaning gesture would have on Ray.

A streetlight turned yellow then green: it made no difference to anyone, for no one was here. Up the block, at McKinley Boulevard, another light flashed red, red, red in time with the pulse pounding Ray's left temple. Red. Red. He put his hand over his eyes to regain his equilibrium. He lowered his hand again and opened his eyes: nothing had changed. Ray had yet to walk more than fifty yards into town and already he felt that much closer to dying.

What the—? Wait.

It had happened again: his consciousness had skipped, his memory useless. Ray was standing on the sidewalk in front of an A&W. Fink's A&W. And the Fink's dumpster offered shelter from no one, for no one else could be seen, but now Ray had to get there. He had no ambitions, he had only the present, small as it felt. He had no future: the pain had stuck him in the moment, a fly on a glue strip.

Bzzzz, Ray told himself, as he realized that there were flies all over the rotting garbage in the dumpster. But he knew what the smell was, too. He was the smell.

He abandoned the dumpster. To hell with that. Left on Reston, near the Buick lot. Head down. Walk, walk, walk, walk, walk. Right on Eighth, the block after Seventh. Eighth to Bine, then east to the river. Ray's body had a plan, but his body wasn't sharing. He heard a car horn; he didn't look up. Again, a horn, and Ray began to walk a little faster. Faster, although it seemed that his feet were dragging their weight, the stolen boots even heavier than before.

Whose overalls were these?

Maybe he was running: to the tree over there, to the sign, to the car. But the flies wouldn't leave him alone. And now he knew he was running, his good arm swinging, his left elbow cradled inside the bib of the overalls. Pain hurt but he was running. He had a song in his head: *Doo-doo-ba-doo-doo, is give peace a chance. Doo-doo-ba-doo-doo, is give peace a chance.*

East Bine, a street he knew. The car horn sounded louder, and a metallic voice rang out. There must have been a fire somewhere, or something: Ray could see the whirl of the lights as the hose sprayed his way, almost knocking him down. Hose? There was no hose. What was he thinking?

Stumbling forward, he could no longer run, but the house must be just ahead, it had to be there, please? Because Jeannie and Tom were coming to Brighton and he had to warn them—stay back, kids, this place wasn't safe. I'm your father and I say so.

No, Ray pleaded. Damn you, he swore. Then, leave me alone, Ray told the horn and the flies, although he doubted whether either would listen. But there was the door—was it locked? Oh god—and he could get there any time, and it would open, please open, and he could lie down for a week and feel better and then leave this goddamn goddamnable place.

Ray arrived at the screen door and stopped himself by leaning there. He was soaked with sweat, and the pain in his shoulder raged. He heard something, and turned his face back around: a cop was stepping from a cop car in a driveway, hat in hand, and inserting a billy club into a loop on his belt. Ray could hear the club's soft tick as the club slid where it slid. He had never heard a sound so perfectly.

But the cop was mad. No! Ray roared, and it may have been aloud. Then the door opened, with Ray plastered to the screen, and it was Mrs. Reeves, the black lady next door with the azaleas and the roses, and she wore a housecoat which she held closed, pinched between her fingers. She was wearing a pin; he wanted to remember her pin. It was something to remember. Would he remember?

He was standing at the wrong door, he realized.

And she asked, "Mr. Stanton? Is that you?" and Ray wanted to answer, but he looked at her and that was all.

CHAPTER 2

Perched on a gurney in the emergency room, alone, Ray was trying to decide whom to call. When his dad had died, Ray's mom had called from the ER—she had called Ray, her son, but not Fran, her daughter. Fran, always in trouble, drinking or not, wouldn't have handled Mom's crying. Mom must have known; she had called Ray.

What do the doctors keep in those drawers? Which drawer had the blood pressure stuff? Was there a Bible in one of the drawers? From where he sat, Ray could see himself in the mirror above a tiny sink. Yes, five feet eleven inches tall and with his own brown hair and a monster shiner, and still in okay shape, usually, not in danger of going fat yet, like his friend Bruce.

With a ringing swish, the curtain of Ray's little world was opened. In walked a doctor, two nurses, a clean-cut youngish guy—a plainclothes cop?—and Mrs. Reeves.

Ray was surrounded.

"Mr. Stanton . . . What's on your arm?" The guy was talking. Must be a police officer.

"What?"

"That. On your arm. How'd that get there?" The police officer pointed to Ray's arm, then glanced at the doctor, an older black guy who wore a stethoscope like a gym towel. "Right." The cop seemed to remember something. "I'm Detective Shaw from the Brighton police." He flashed a badge. "Mr. Stanton."

Badges always flash, Ray thought.

Ray looked down: on his arm was a drawing, a bluish blur beneath a smeared layer of muck. The drawing was of a lightning bolt. One of the three guys who had dumped Ray, naked, into a ditch had drawn a lightning bolt on Ray's arm. He looked at his arm, and felt a shudder come. What were all these people doing here?

Mrs. Reeves sidled forward, and took Ray's good hand. "Oh that silly thing." She was Mrs. Reeves, his neighbor, and she was smiling. "My godson was playing with Mr. Stanton, why, just yesterday." She almost giggled.

What was she talking about? What godson? Ray tried to turn, but his body wouldn't go that way. He couldn't look at his neighbor more directly; the angle was wrong. Someday, Ray thought, Tom would be Mr. Stanton.

"Hmph," the policeman said—then he picked up a long-handled clamp or something, which the older of the two nurses immediately grabbed away.

"Any ringing in your ears?"

Ray was glad to respond to the doctor. "A little," he winced. "This ear." He pointed to the right. Turning back and pointing had hurt too.

"Blurred vision?"

"Some. But not—"

"And how about dizziness?" The doctor shined his light into Ray's eye.

"Some."

"Well, well." The light shifted left, right. "Look up. Good." Then the other eye. "Again, up. Good. And now I'd like you to walk a bit for me."

Mrs. Reeves squeezed once more before she let go. He had forgotten she was holding his hand. Now, with the help of a nurse, Ray slid down to the floor, wobbly but standing. He held shut the loose hospital gown in back, took a few shaky steps, turned, and then returned to the bed a bit more steadily. If Ray closed his eyes, he might see the face of the ringleader, the main thug, that nasty redheaded guy. So Ray kept his eyes open. But he was still thinking about Mom. Dad. He pictured Mom holding up Dad, on the way back to bed.

"Good," said the doctor as he nodded to the younger nurse. "Please make sure to clean that laceration, Beth." And then, eyes narrowing, the stethoscope looped around his neck once again: "Okay, Mr. Stanton, I'm going to send you up to X-ray, for head and shoulder series, and think about a CAT scan once I see the results."

The doctor squinted at Ray. Why? They squinted at each other. The doctor had never introduced himself, Ray realized, and he didn't wear a name tag. Was he a real doctor? Ray tried to squint back, to win. In a curtained cubicle far away, some-one gave a little moan.

The doctor extended a hand, politely demanding the clip-board from the older nurse. He took a pair of half-glasses from a case, flicked the frames open, and put them on; then he clicked a fancy pen and quickly scribbled something. It occurred to Ray that the doctor seemed like he was playing doctor, tending to Ray, who was playing a patient, someone kidnapped.

They had been in the back of a pickup, the three kids and a naked Ray. They had insisted that he see their fingers plucking his chest hairs and tweaking his nipples, and if he didn't watch, they did it again. Nothing hurt too much, but that hadn't been the point: he was theirs and they had paraded over him, with all their preening and conquest and beer-chugging bravado. Of course, the redhead had spewed abuse, too: fag this, and asshole that. So Ray had lain there, and he had felt like he was watching his body be tortured and he hadn't fought back, and no one had said anything about why they were there—although they had known his name all along, when they had first bashed his car and grabbed him.

The doctor leaned forward, looked in Ray's ear, then whis-pered: "I can help."

What? Ray glanced at Mrs. Reeves. Her first name was Mae, wasn't it? Ray was pretty sure. Mae with an "e."

"Doc?" Detective Shaw had taken out his notebook.

"Okay. I think there's been a transient loss of consciousness, consistent with findings of moderate head trauma. The X-rays will tell us more, but I'm not expecting any surprises. The tinnitus worries me; he took a nasty blow to—"

"Transient ... ?" Scritch, scritch, scritch. As he wrote, Detective Shaw bit his lower lip.

"Loss of consciousness. I'll put it all in my report."

"That'd be great, Doc." The policeman flipped shut his book. "Mr. Stanton, do you know where you got these clothes?" He pointed with his pen at the overalls heaped on the floor.

"Not really." Ray told the truth, sort of. People around him seemed to be deep in some kind of game, the rules a secret. But Jean was safe, right? Yes, Ray reminded himself. His daughter, Jean, and his son, Tom, were still in Medford with Jilly, Ray's ex. He could picture Jilly's angry face, frightened when she found out what had happened. The veins in her neck. Ray's kids weren't due in Brighton for another six weeks or so, the arrangement awkward but most workable during the summertime. His kids were safe.

One of the nurses gave a little wave and left. Ray wanted to wave back.

"Hmph," said Detective Shaw, writing something.

"You poor man," chirped Mae Reeves.

"How 'bout the boots? They yours?"

"No."

"Hmph," said Detective Shaw, the blood rising in his cheeks.

"I mean, sort of."

"They're yours or they're not yours. That's the way it works. Let's get this clear."

"Well, no. I don't think so," said Ray. "They're not mine."

"Right," said the policeman. He paused, writing. He looked at Ray. "What do you do, Mr. Stanton?" Shaw asked.

"Hm?"

"You know, 'do'? For a living?"

Ray liked the change in topic. "I've been in middle management and sales," he said, not telling all. "I've worked in industrial relations. . . ."

"Worked? And now?"

Too many people were looking at Ray. "Now, I've moved
here. I'm at Windy Oaks."

That was true, Ray thought. He was now, technically, at
Windy Oaks, his first solo reorganization and retooling project
on behalf of Riggs International—insofar as someone who practiced corporate and industrial makeovers, trimming fat and even
bone and then bringing technology up to speed, could be considered "at" a site. Ray was in BPR, business process re-engineering.
He fired people and replaced them with smart machines and
computers, which mostly meant that he never felt at home anywhere in particular, at least he hadn't so far, in his three years
with this division of Industrial Management. But even without
being in charge, as he was in Brighton, Ray had been one of the
permanent outsiders, a guy who fired people to save jobs, Ray
Stanton, employed by and for the greater good.

Ray realized that he had stopped speaking, and that people
were waiting for him to say more. But it was only space, and Ray
had nothing to put there. You're fired.

Detective Shaw smiled. "You're the guy at the plant." Which
meant that he knew. "You're the guy from the Puzzle Palace."

The what? Ray gestured with his right hand to ask, just
as Mae Reeves approached the bed again and took his out-
stretched hand. "Detective?" She kept her face turned from
Shaw. "Can we continue this later, or even tomorrow? I'm sure
Mr. Stanton could use his rest. Couldn't you, Mr. Stanton?"

Ray understood. He only had to nod his head, and let his
body agree. "I think I need to lie down," Ray said, although
he hadn't meant to say that. Oh no, now what was happening?
Something wasn't right. "I'm dizzy," Ray said, because he was.
And then: I'm passing out, he tried to say.

Ray could only remember the dream in flashes: an elevator to the twentieth floor of some building, the backlit 20 aglow above a door; rain, and lots of it; the sleeve of a blue bathrobe wiping a bit of spilled jam from a glass table; his errand shoes, the Topsiders, next to a cardboard box marked LR. And a serrated hunting knife. Maybe the knife woke him up, or how bad he felt, the pain and soreness. Whatever it was that had awakened Ray, he was conscious before he noticed, the parts of the dream tumbling together even as he knew himself to be exhausted but alert, the 20 and the LR blurred into one image, still there, just behind his eyes.

In the front seat of Mae Reeves's car, Ray had slept, or done something like it—but he couldn't have slept; the trip was too short. Regardless, now he was awake. Had someone called? Ray remembered a telephone ringing—or he didn't. Maybe it was another dream.

From across the front seat, he watched her get out of the car; then she came around and opened his door. She was still wearing the pink sweatsuit that she had changed into before accompanying Ray to the hospital—and Ray's head was resting on some other pink top, maybe a matching cardigan, that had been balled into a pillow.

Clothes could do so many things, Ray thought, as an image of work flashed through his mind. The job. He thought about Anderson's advice, Anderson from Windy Oaks, a nervous guy who ran scared of the CFO but nonetheless knew his people: never wear a tie to a management meeting you call, Anderson had recommended, or everyone will think they're fired. Ray thought about how he had disconnected his cell phone when he moved here, so as not to seem the corporate slick.

He missed his cell phone. Everyone was fired.

She was either younger or older than he had originally believed, but she no longer seemed to be about forty or so, his age, which had been Ray's first guess. Okay, she was older. Around Mae Reeves's neck lay a simple strand of turquoise beads, each the size of a pecan. She reminded him a little of his sister, Fran, although Ray hoped for Mae Reeves that she had better taste in men. She was thin but not skinny; attractive in a cheery sort of way. Comfortable.

She helped him inside, into his leased house in Brighton, Ohio, into a chair he had brought to town, an overstuffed beigeish armchair picked up a year or so ago in Medford, to furnish Ray's bachelor pad. Ray liked the chair; the chair felt comfortable, Ray's chair—though the room still didn't feel his, what with the curtains and the semiabstract wallpaper daisies all in a garish 1968 yellow. He knew the color too well, that sixties yellow, from a curled and water-stained poster he had discarded the day he moved out of his and Jilly's Medford house: Not To Decide Is To Decide. That's right, Ray reminded himself. After almost two years of internal exile, he had officially been separated from his wife what, a year ago? Fourteen months, he counted, although Ray had mostly stopped counting; he had thrown out the poster a year ago March. Now the divorce papers would be ready soon enough, the decision even more right—which didn't matter, really, unless you were Jilly and still angry at Ray for throwing out the Not To Decide Is To Decide poster, on the day he had moved out of their house.

He had decided, and thrown out the poster. The kids had been staying with friends the weekend Ray moved out, but they had been told. Jilly had stood in the hallway, furious, kicking her heel back against the laundry room door. It wasn't going to be his job to repaint that door; she'd get the house, he figured.

He should clean up. He got up, shuffled to the kitchen. "Sorry about the mess," Ray said to Mae Reeves, in this foreign kitchen in this foreign town on this alien planet called Ohio.

"How do you feel? Can I get you anything? I'll put a kettle up? Would you like . . ."

"A little better, thanks." Ray needed to lean on something. Nope. He sat. He had answered only one of her questions.

"How about some tea? I know, a cup of clear soup. Beef or chicken? Maybe a bite of toast." She dragged a chair across the room, up to the table, and joined him, her entwined hands holding one raised knee. "Lordy, I'm tired. . . . Dr. Gates wants me to wake you every three hours, and try you on fluids. If I can stay awake." She laughed. "But I'm sure you'd like to start by taking a shower, if you're steady enough. I can get towels for you—would that be okay? Do you need help?"

He did. Please, he wanted to say. Instead, he nodded.

She was up again: "Oh dear, you look so tired." Then from the hallway, she added, "I'll get you all set." And then, from the stairs: "I'll be right there. Maybe you'd like to call your wife. She must be worried to death."

Ray looked at his hands. One hand was cleaner. What time was it? A shower seemed a good idea.

On the kitchen table next to his briefcase was a piece of paper he didn't recognize. He picked it up. The note was scrawled, as Ray instantly knew it would be, in block letters, on a scrap of grocery bag.

The note said, "GOT YA."

In the bedroom, scared, Ray was naked again. All those people had seen him naked, which changed what naked meant: the doctor, the nurses, Detective Shaw, and even Mrs. Reeves. And although Ray had managed to steal the filthy overalls and make them filthier—to do anything, it seemed, to keep himself covered—people kept taking his clothes away, and with the loss of his clothes, something changed. Everyone had seen him.

The night was still hammering at him, little fucking hammers hammering at him. Fuck! Ray thought, not so surprised by his anger this time. "Fuck you," Ray said to someone. To whom?

And where were the towels? He stripped the top sheet and wrapped it around his waist, one, two, three, four times, his good arm doing most of the work. His left side felt less sore than stiff, really—and, as Dr. Gates had explained, while Ray might have suffered a posterior shoulder separation, both the negative X-ray and the quick improvement indicated that if the thing had popped out, then it had also popped back. Spontaneous reduction, Gates had called it. But the concussion was more troublesome. Anytime you lose consciousness we worry, Gates had said. There's always a chance . . . Of what? Ray had asked. Oh, you know, Gates had answered as he gave Ray an information handout entitled "Head Injuries." Of complications. Then Dr. Gates had waved his hand: or not coming all back.

He had lost the handout; it wasn't here. Looking in the mirror in the bathroom, as the shower steamed, Ray unwound the bedsheet and then fingered the mound on his head—just like a little kid, he realized, to see where it hurt. There. It hurt. Superficial scratches scored his ribcage, from one side to the other; his thigh was painted with a yellowish iodine soap, and his left eye was partially swollen shut, rimmed with dark blue and a trace of violet. He was a sight, as his mom would say. Plus they had drawn on his arm, for chrissakes. Ray sat on the lip of the tub, and then he sank slowly to the floor. Why was he crying? Why was he shaking and crying?

"Mr. Stanton, are you okay? Mr. Stanton? Is that you?"

He was unable to answer. He tried.

"Mr. Stanton, I'm afraid." The knob turned. "I'm opening the door. . . ."

Ray made a sound he had never made before, a noise he didn't recognize. Curled on the cool tiles, clutching himself, the bathroom steaming and the exhaust fan humming, Ray made a noise so small that it almost didn't exist. It was a plea, he knew, somehow, but it wasn't anything, too. It was all Ray was.

"Oh, Mr. Stanton." Mae knelt beside Ray and cradled him in her arms, her cheek pressed to his hair. "You poor man. I'm so sorry. Oh. Oh. Oh." She began to rock. "Hush now. It's over." She began to hum, but stopped when his sobs deepened.

He was shaking and sobbing. That he knew. That was it. "They hurt me." Ray gulped. "I didn't even know them and . . . they hurt me."

"They're gone. Hush now. I've got you."

Got you? GOT YA? Oh god, oh god, oh—

"Shh. Shhhh."

"Oh god, oh god, oh god, oh god."

At some point Mae had turned off the shower, and sometime else she had handed him a cup of something hot which he had shakily gulped down, spilling some onto the bathmat. She had also handed him a towel to cover himself. A box of Kleenex sat in his lap. He had been thinking of his kids, in a random sort of way: Tom's new haircut, the sides short, almost shaved; Jeannie's driving lesson, grinding the gears in the Nissan as Ray gritted his teeth; Jean flopped on her bed; Tom's always dirty fingernails; Tom and Jean at the table, punching each other playfully, and then not so playfully until they began to fling the Chinese takeout, which had made Jilly holler. Maybe Ray had hollered too. When had that happened? Eons ago. He thought himself an okay dad, a little too quick to judge, maybe, but better than some—and better than Jilly was as a mom. He knew that the kids loved them both, even though his daughter Jeannie couldn't love Ray, not now: she was sixteen, and her parents were getting a divorce.

So what would Jeannie think of all this? Ray wouldn't tell Tom, though, right? Ray looked up. Mae Reeves sat primly on the toilet seat, her hands on her knees. "I . . ." Ray couldn't think. "Um, I . . ."

"Don't mention it. You're welcome."

He smiled. He had been trying to apologize. "Mrs. Reeves . . ." He blew his nose.

"Oh." She fidgeted. "Just Mae's fine."

"And Ray. I'm Ray."

"Ray then. I'd like that."

He considered shaking her hand, but instead Ray reached for the wastebasket and began to collect the used tissues from the floor. He couldn't remember when last he had cried, not to mention bawled. Crying was his sister Fran's job. Ray was responsible for not crying. But wow, was he ever tired: "I'd like to go to bed, Mrs. Reeves. Um. Mae. Ten hours of sleep."

"Yes," Mae said. "I mean no."

"Excuse me?"

Mae smiled. "I'm supposed to watch you, Ray. The doctor wants me to wake you every three hours, remember?"

He hadn't remembered.

"Mom?" From the front of the house, someone began to call. "Are you here? Momma? Where are you?"

"Oh. That'll be my April." She called back: "Up here." And then to Ray: "You okay?" And then: "I hope you don't mind."

"Sure," Ray said. He was trapped here. Another trap. Call the fucking Chamber of Commerce, Ray's naked. Call the Associated Press. He exhaled. Why did he notice exhaling but not inhaling? And Mae Reeves. Mae and April, mother and daughter. She had named her daughter April? Oh come on.

But there was the note: GOT YA. Holy shit, he couldn't stay here. GOT YA.

When the guys had grabbed him from his car, and dragged him up into the bed of their pickup, Ray had wanted to scream. But someone had punched Ray, hard, in the face, and he had gone quiet, terrified. The biggest of the three had hit Ray. Now, he tested his bruised eye. Ouch.

She was back in two minutes: Ray hadn't moved. "If you're feeling up to it, you might want to take that shower now." Mae smiled from the doorway. "And I thought I'd send April to my place for some food, since I'm your assigned nurse—I asked her to drop by, if that's okay, since I need to stay here. . . . Right? I mean, you understand? If you don't . . . I guess . . . Well, doctor's orders!" She laughed lightly. "Would that be okay? Ray?"

The tissues were all collected. Ray looked up. "No. I mean . . . it's . . ."

"What is it, Ray?" Mae had turned, and come back to stand in the doorway. She pushed the button-lock in and then turned the knob to pop the button. Click. Unlock. Click. "Ray? What happened? What did you say? You know you can tell me, if you want. . . . I'm a good person to tell." Unlock. Click. Unlock. Click. Unlock. Click. "You're a nice man," she added.

Why had she said that? He tried to make words come out of his mouth. There's a note, he tried to say.

"Momma?" The daughter's voice from the hallway.

"I . . . "

Unlock. Click. Locked. "Yes, Ray," Mae said. "Okay."

"There's a note," Ray said. "On the table downstairs." There. It was said. And then: "I have to leave. Please help me. I have to get out of here. We can't stay here."

CHAPTER 3

By early afternoon, having showered somewhat painfully and then slept again—his sleep roiling with dreams and fragments of dreams and nothing he could remember clearly, but each fragment like something torn—Ray was hungry, a good sign. A TV blared in another room. Occasionally, Mae's easy laugh could be heard, and then a deeper laugh, which must have been April's. Ray rolled himself slowly to the side of the bed and stood, stiffly, his muscles tight with pain, as his left eye and the left side of his head throbbed. Even though moving hurt, he did feel better. He unzipped his travel bag and found a pair of Jockeys, a pocket T, and his black sweats. Then his rubber Rio sandals with the waffled soles. Getting dressed hurt too, but he discovered that sitting on the bed improved balance—when sitting, Ray could bend to the Velcro straps of his shoes without having to set his jaw against the soreness and dull pain. Dressed in his own clothes, Ray looked around for his wallet. Oh hell. The credit cards, the driver's license, the whole rigmarole. Gone. Or maybe . . . He pictured the incident in the Food Town lot: groceries in the trunk, shut the trunk, keys, bang, there were the boys—hey, what the? Right. They had smashed into his car with their truck, grabbed him when he got out, and he had probably left his wallet on the seat.

He would join the two women in the kitchen, Ray thought. No problem. Mae's house was identical to Ray's house, cookie cutters in the same development, with the apparent exception of her backyard solarium as opposed to his cement patio. Wait. What? Right, he shook his head. He looked around. This wasn't

Mae's house, it was April's apartment. And even though Ray knew where he was, he couldn't remember getting here. A head injury. A blackout, he told himself. Don't be scared. He almost remembered getting here, in pieces of a memory, and being awakened, and hearing voices, and lots of rolling over, going back to sleep.

Ray could hear April and Mae in the kitchen. He waited, then he tapped lightly on the two-way kitchen door just as he pushed it open.

"You're up! How are you feeling? Come, sit here." April pulled out a chair and patted its cushion, for which Ray nodded in gratitude. Ouch. Nodding hurt. "Thank you," he said. "This is a nice place, April."

Kayla grinned. "Momma!" She pursed her lips at her mother. "I'm Kayla," she said. "Kayla Reeves. With a 'K.'"

Ray hadn't followed. "So where's your sister?"

Mae twinkled. "Ray, this is my only daughter, Kayla Reeves. Kayla Reeves, Ray."

"Pleased to meet you," she said.

"How are you," Ray replied. He still wasn't following.

"Why, I'm just fine." Kayla laughed. "My Momma . . . when I was twelve, Ray, I called myself April. But Miss Mae gets a thought in her head—"

"Don't you start now."

Both Mae and Kayla laughed, laughter that seemed uneasy. Then Kayla hoisted herself onto the countertop to sit. How old was she? Thirties, Ray thought, which made sense. She had very short hair, a big smile, and noticeably large ears accentuated by enormous hoop earrings. Her smile must have mattered to the white guy Ray had seen with her in all those photos in the hallway.

He had noticed another picture too, Kayla looking grim in army fatigues. She looked kind of tough, Ray thought. Now too. Bet she works out.

"Are you hungry? You're looking better—"

"This is better?" asked Kayla.

"Oh my, my," answered Mae. "He was something, banging on my door and shouting like Death itself."

Kayla was in motion, which meant that her earrings were moving against her cheek and neck, the earrings going one way while her body went another. It made the earrings noticeable, Ray thought. That's why she wore those earrings, Ray supposed.

Mae looked at Kayla too, then offered: "Would you like a little tuna salad, Ray? It's got celery and Miracle Whip."

"Yes, please. And is that coffee . . . ?"

"Oh sure! Kayla, honey, give the man a cup. The blue one."

"Mom!" Kayla growled. "You're doing it again. Remember? My house?"

"Am I? I suppose I am!" She tilted her head toward Ray. "We've just decided that I won't order my daughter around, and especially not here. Aren't we mature? As though we weren't related," she laughed lightly.

Kayla handed Ray his coffee. "Sugar? Milk?"

"Just black, thank you."

In the ensuing quiet, Ray could hear a shampoo commercial promise everything to the empty living room. Ray didn't need everything, but he knew without thinking further that he had to stop the kids from coming to Brighton. He'd have to call— which reminded him that his calling card was probably still in his wallet. Maybe the three thugs had his wallet? His torturers. Ray had been tortured.

Kayla placed the sandwich and the washed fruit on a plate nestled in a straw placemat. The smell of the food made him reel with a hunger that bordered on nausea, but Ray told himself to eat slowly and chew each bite five times, since his hostesses were watching. Then Kayla returned to her countertop, where she nursed a can of diet something. Ray ate, and that was all: then he ate another sandwich almost as soon as it appeared on his plate. Then he took a deep breath and a long swallow of coffee.

"What's this?"

"Advil and a multivitamin," answered Mae. "Doctor's orders."

"Right. Dr. Gates. What's that guy's story?" Ray asked.

Mae's eyes flashed: "Now what could you mean?"

"He . . ." Ray stopped himself. Oh, what the hell. "He told me I could trust him, and when people say that, I always think they're lying."

Kayla smiled. "This one's trouble, Momma."

"Don't I know. But you're still the most trouble, Baby Girl. Number one trouble. Ray?" Mae topped off her own cup. "More coffee?"

"Yes, please."

"Right. First, maybe Ray can tell us what happened, since everyone wants to know, and I mean *everyone.* . . . Ray?"

He didn't answer.

"Momma." Kayla almost smiled at Ray. "I think you killed him."

Ray didn't move.

"Ray . . ." Mae tried again. "We're here for you."

"And you can't trust us," Kayla added brightly.

"We?" Ray asked. The coffee smelled good, kind of smoky. He sipped. The coffee did its job; Ray kept his own counsel.

"Yes, Ray. We." Mae was serious.

"I don't understand," Ray said. He didn't. "What's this have to do with you? I mean, nothing personal, but—"

Mae Reeves interrupted him by reaching over to pat his wrist, near to where the drawing had been scrubbed away and a red swatch persisted. She seemed to move gingerly. "Ray. Even if you had banged on your own door that night, we'd all still be involved—" She looked at her daughter.

"That night?" Ray looked at Mae, then Kayla. "What do you mean? How long was I out? Oh god. What day is this? I have to—"

"Ray," Kayla said. "Today's Saturday. You slept for two days. First at Momma's house"—she looked at her mom—"then here.

Once we could arrange it," she added, which meant something. "Two days, Ray. And yes, everyone wants to talk to you. I've got the messages from your machine"—she waved a pad of paper. "A burglar alarm company and a Mr. Rivers and that nice Detective Shaw." Her voice filled with something. "And your mother," Kayla smiled. "She said she has big news."

Saturday? Where was Friday? GOT YA.

Rivers, the Windy Oaks CFO, had to be Ray's first call. Rivers had a cell, Ray thought, bitterly.

"Rivers."

"Hi, Mr. Rivers, this is Ray Stanton."

"Ray! I've been worried sick about you. Everyone has. Are you okay?"

Ray twirled the telephone cord around his thumb. No. "I think so," he lied.

"Well! That's a relief. We wouldn't want to lose our top gun, would we?" Rivers laughed a laugh Ray didn't like. "Gotta keep our noses clean, or nothing goes to the grindstone, you know?"

Ray didn't. Kayla peeked into the kitchen, waved "hi," then ducked out.

"So you see . . ." Rivers was still talking. Uh-oh. Pay attention. "You're going to have to bite this bullet, Ray. I mean, if the papers pick this up, we won't be able to move forward. We won't be able to make any move at all!" He laughed again.

"Mr. Rivers . . ."

"Call me Jim."

Uh-oh. "Jim . . . what would you like me to do?"

"I knew you'd be accommodating, Ray. Just knew it. You gotta keep this one to yourself, know what I mean? Take a week or two to yourself. Maybe go somewhere. And no telling, of course. I mean, it's a secret, you see? No police, too. We're in such a small town . . ."

A secret? Ray half-listened, as he began to understand. No complaints lodged, no charges filed, no press. No heart-to-heart with Detective Shaw, or Ray would be out of a job—and although Rivers wasn't threatening, both he and Ray knew the gravity of the situation. No scandals. Ray understood. GOT YA.

"Hi, Mom."

"Ray! I'm so glad you called. I can't tell you how excited I am."

"What's up?" He got out of his chair and sat on the floor, then lay there. Better.

"Oh well, I have just the best news. You know . . ."

Ray was having trouble concentrating. Mom was saying something about her neighbor, another member of Kimberly Downs, her retirement community; a pure gentleman with a moustache and a nine handicap, and . . . Ray was thinking about a visit to Mom, when he had brought the kids a few years back, Jilly elsewhere. In the pool in Mom's complex, Ray had taught Tom—an early, happy swimmer, thrilled to be underwater—to do a rudimentary crawl. Tom in his goggles, coming up from the pool bottom, all toothy and excited, sputtering, *Daddy I can did it*, his swimming better than his grammar. Jeannie pouting already for some reason—how old was she, ten? No, twelve. An early pouter. Ray could picture Tom with a stripe of sunburn across his lower back, where either his swim trunks would pull down or the waistband would rub away the sunscreen, or both. Ray's big hand on the small body of his son, applying a smear of gooey aloe from one of Mom's plants. Then later, some sort of fancy dinner at Kimberly Downs, Jeannie actually having fun, another girl there to play with, as Tom fell asleep, head in Ray's lap. Or had the dinner happened another night, maybe during a different visit altogether.

"What? Mom!"

"That's right, Ray. I haven't felt this way since . . . or . . ." She was crying. She blew her nose. "Excuse me. The wedding's in September, and I hope you and the kids can make it."

"The wedding?"

"Yes, Ray. Haven't you heard a word I said? I'm getting married! Randall and I are engaged."

Three hours later, at the moment when Detective Shaw had rung Kayla's bell, Ray had been lying down, almost watching ESPN on TV. His head had been hurting, and the TV hadn't been helping, but he had found that he couldn't concentrate enough to hold a conversation.

A smell was still with Ray, too, his own smell, he guessed. He figured that he had crapped himself two nights ago, even if he were clean now. The memory of the smell was almost a smell.

"Mr. Stanton." The cop was standing in Kayla's living room.

"Hello," Ray said. He didn't get up, but gestured.

"No, thanks," the detective said. "I understand that you've had some rest?"

The statement had ended like a question but Shaw wasn't asking. "Yes," Ray said.

"Great. If you could throw on some shoes—are these your sandals?—I would like to show you something."

"I don't think I'm up to that," Ray said. "I mean I—"

"Mr. Stanton," the policeman bent to the sandals, picked them up, and then stepped closer, deliberate, his polo shirt crisp and his hair neat. "I wasn't asking you, sir: I was being polite. Let's go."

The police officer did his TV cop bit, Watch your head, as he ducked his prisoner into the little cell that was the unmarked car's back seat. There were three panels, some sort of Plexiglas—bulletproof, Ray supposed—between the front and the back. Detective Shaw turned down the radio and the police scanner, or whatever it was that emitted regular beeps and flashed green lights.

Two nights ago, the redheaded kid had known Ray's name. Raaaaaaay, the kid had crooned, adding syllables. More like a bully's chant. Now Ray and a police officer were driving over train tracks. The bumping up and down hurt, another kind of rhythm. They went past a lumberyard; Ray saw Shaw give a chuck of his chin to two utility workers. Hello, guys, the gesture said. Behave yourselves. Just doing my job.

There were fewer trees here. Where were the trees? Ray didn't know why trees grew in one place but not another. The car slowed. A dog had come out from a driveway and wandered into the road. The policeman didn't hit the horn, he merely waited, which seemed in character. Throughout the drive, Detective Shaw said little, and what he said and asked were all meaningless. Chat.

Holy shit, Ray's mom was engaged. Randall someone or other. Would she give up her condo? The kids liked visiting her there, what with the pool and the short drive to the ocean. Tommy really liked it—and Jeannie always seemed to get a kick out of her grandmother's eccentricities, the brightly colored muumuus and enormous handbags. Mom had become such a different person, Ray thought. Free of Dad, years after his death, and maybe, now, free of her adult kids, Fran and Ray.

He had to focus. The officer had light blond hair. Very cop-like. He was a little shorter than Ray, maybe an inch, five feet ten or so, midthirties. He had a birthmark or a mole on the back of his neck, the mark large enough to be visible from where Ray sat. Ray's hair was brown; he couldn't be a cop, then, right? Cops had blond hair.

"Bingo," Detective Shaw said. "Here we are."

"What?" Ray looked around; they were parked in an empty lot. How far out of town were they? Or had they left town and then circled back—or were they in another town? "Where are we?"

"Let's get out."

As Detective Shaw came around to open the back door, Ray slid to his left, out, stood, and shaded his eyes. The sun hurt. No sunglasses. But the day was nice, the season not too hot, a nice time of year for this part of Ohio.

"What is this?" Ray asked again. "What do you want to show me?"

"Show you?" The cop smiled a tight smile. "Oh, nothing. That's just something to say." He winked.

"I beg your pardon? You mean there's nothing—?"

"Oh, there's something, Mr. Stanton. But you need to tell me." The policeman turned, leaned against the car, nonchalant. "What the hell did you do to piss them off?"

Time to be careful. Ray liked his job. "I don't know," Ray answered. "Truth."

"I see."

They were both leaning against the cruiser, the engine still running. They both had their arms crossed. The car was very powerful, Ray knew, although he wasn't sure why that thought had occurred to him, just then. He had given up shielding his eyes. In the distance, beyond some sort of field—soybeans? the green of the crop was luxuriant—ran a line of small hills, a ridge or maybe a bluff. The right word came to him: escarpment.

He could smell the exhaust. He could smell, in his memory, himself. Crap.

They waited. Ray waited for the policeman to stop waiting. A minute felt like a long time to wait. Inside that minute, Ray could feel his anger begin to rise. Five minutes seemed interminable. They waited beyond five minutes, Ray thought. Longer than that. Maybe twelve minutes, a whole quarter of a professional basketball game, twenty-five or so points scored by either side, fast breaks and slams and layups and steals. They were waiting for Ray to tell on himself, to confess or something.

Ray could wait. He was patient, and he was furious, but he could wait. "My mother's engaged," he finally said, for no reason.

"That's great." Shaw give a quick snort. "Congratulations. Who's the guy?"

"Dunno," Ray said.

"I see." Detective Shaw nodded. "Consider this one a freebie," he added meaningfully. "Got it? You'll be talking to me, Mr. Stanton." The cop seemed to be agreeing with himself. "Okay," he said, when he was ready. "Let's go."

CHAPTER 4

"That's it? He drove you out there and then nothing?"

"Yeah," Ray said.

Kayla laughed. "That son of a bitch," she laughed harder. "I always liked that son of a bitch."

"Kayla!" Mae said. "Language."

"Piece of work, that one." Then Kayla began to say something else.

"Shush," Mae told her daughter.

The kitchen table was full of groceries along with grocery bags in various stages of unpacking. Ray had arrived, escorted, and stepped out of the police car just as the two women had opened the door downstairs; he had helped Kayla carry the bags, two bags with his one good hand, but only one trip. He was tired.

Ray folded a supermarket flyer, which hurt to do, pain through his shoulder. No one said anything. And then Ray admitted. "But I . . . that detective . . . I don't know. . . . I'm supposed to be moving here," Ray said. "I mean I live here. My kids are coming this summer, and . . . " He turned his palms up on the table.

"You need help, is that what you're saying? Right?" asked Kayla.

On the counter were a box of granola bars, two bottles of salad dressing of a brand Ray didn't recognize, and a little green container of beef bouillon cubes. The perishables had been put away. Tommy liked to take a granola bar in his lunchbag. "Maybe," Ray almost agreed, which wasn't what he had wanted to say. "Can I use the phone again? I'd like to call my kids."

The number dialed, Ray stretched the cord into Kayla's hallway and sat on the floor.

"Hello?"

"Hey, Tommy. It's Dad."

"Dad! What's up? The Red Sox won again, and I broke my bike jumping Sam's ramp, but I fixed it good. Where are you? Are you at the office? It's just the sitter, a new one but she's nice. School was fine."

Ray listened. He was listening for what he, Ray, would say.

"I'm in a meeting, T . . . I just wanted . . . I love you." That was hard to say.

"Love you too. Hey, that's Sam at the door. Gotta-go-see-you-soon-bye." Tom hung up.

"Bye," Ray said to his son who wasn't there. "No message."

The ramp in Sam's driveway wasn't a good idea, Ray knew. The ramp was in Medford and Ray was in Brighton. Nothing was a good idea. You're fired.

Ray returned to the kitchen, as Kayla hopped back up onto the counter. She liked to sit on the counter. He wished that she weren't so happy. Mae didn't look happy. "You okay?" Mae asked. "Sit down, you poor thing. You look a bit green around the gills. Oh my."

"Mm."

"Momma, you know he's not okay. Someone messed him up, and it was only a warning. You need us, Ray." Her expression flared, and then looked grim. "He's got to stay somewhere safe, right? Till he's better."

Mae didn't answer, so Ray spoke: "I . . . I'm not supposed to have help. Or talk. I mean, I. . . . What do you mean, it was only a warning?" Then he understood. Okay, he thought. "But I can't . . . " Can't what? Could he trust these two women? Did he have a choice?

He had a choice: he chose, blindly. "I can't call the police. I mean, I can, but I'm not going to," Ray almost explained. Then he told them about Rivers.

"Oh my," Mae shook her head. "That's a horse's ass!"

"Momma! Mr. Stanton, if you can make Mae Reeves swear, then you must be in trouble. She won't even say 'breast of chicken' in a supermarket."

Mae wasn't smiling. Kayla slid down and pulled out a chair, to join them at the small kitchen table, three chairs all together. "Mr. Stanton, Detective Shaw's no dummy."

Silence. She and her mom had the same voice, sort of.

The women looked at Ray; they were waiting for Ray. What was he waiting for? He couldn't talk to the police, and he couldn't go back to work. But he had to go back to work: this was his first solo assignment, and Ray just had to get it right. Work was what he had, after all, most of what still mattered. No, he wasn't going to leave; he wasn't going anywhere . . . except to a hideout, some place to lie low, or something like that. To wait and see, until it was safe to go back to work.

So what about these women? Ray didn't know what to think. Okay, Ray told himself, looking at their faces, mother to daughter. He was waiting and they were waiting. Everyone was waiting for Ray. "I don't know why this happened to me," he admitted. "I . . . Some creeps hit my car. Then they hit me, and took my clothes. And they did stuff to me—the lightning bolt, and . . . other stuff. And then the note—"

"That note you got? Isn't that scary?" Kayla wasn't asking. She bopped a little in her chair. "That drawing on you, and that note. But it's possible, Ray, that we know who they are. They did this more than once. Not just to you."

Mae gave a sigh. Kayla looked down. "Sorry, Momma. I know."

They had done this more than once? Oh god. But what was the daughter sorry about? Everything was happening too fast. "What do you mean you might know who?" Ray asked. "Who are they?" And then, quietly: "I'm not sure I want to know."

Looks were exchanged, then eye contact broke. Even in silence, Ray and the two women seemed to be constantly in motion, as they danced around each other, a little family dance. "You want to know, Ray. You know it's important. But as for understanding, you're—" Kayla touched his hand, stayed, then moved hers away once more. "Shit, Ray, you're white. Of course you don't understand." She had angered instantly.

"Baby Girl—"

"I'm sorry, but the man needs to know. Full disclosure. Look, Ray, just ten days back Nathan Mapes was jumped. Those white boys drew on him, too, and I don't know, but maybe they left him a pretty little note at his house. Think Detective Shaw hasn't heard about Nathan? Telling Shaw won't help. Think he's out there serving-and-protecting? Then how come this shit happened to you?"

Ray toyed with a package of little boxes of raisins. Now Ray was waiting for Ray. "But who's Nathan . . . ? I mean, what does this have to do with me? And why—if you don't mind my asking— why do you care? We just met, right? So I'm white, but you don't even work for me, or used to." Ray took a deep breath; he began to think aloud. "At the plant, I mean . . . I . . . um, I fired a few people so far. Six or seven, I think." He was being coy. He knew the number was seven. "It's what I do. I can't be very popular around there. My attackers could have been anyone. . . . But I don't get it. Seems to me they needed only the slightest excuse . . . I mean, it could have been personal. It felt . . . it feels"—his voice dropped— "personal."

"You're white, Ray. You don't understand. This gets personal."

He agreed. "I don't get it. Who cares? They were white, and I'm white and Nathan's black—" Ray guessed. "I'm white. That doesn't add up to a hate crime or whatever. Plus it's not like I'm gonna live next door to your mom permanently—" He looked at Kayla. "So what does it matter? If you think it's a white thing, and I'm on the wrong side of these tracks, then . . . what are one white guy's problems to you?" He was done; he tried not to unclench his fist so that anyone would notice. He didn't want to be in this conversation, or even in Brighton.

Kayla's eyes were shining. She shook her head, argued with herself. Then she looked at Mae. But it was Mae who spoke first, which surprised Ray. "That doctor, he said something to me. He called me out to the hallway and he . . . he . . . Well, my, my! Lordy," Mae laughed at herself. "He asked if you were my new special friend."

"Bastard!"

"Kayla . . . " Mae drew out her daughter's name, a reprimand. "Language."

"Well he is, Momma, and you know it."

"I don't understand," Ray said. "Please?"

There was something almost comical in Mae's expression, her jaw set. Then she seemed to feel it; she shook her head, "Lordy. You can't see what we see. It's a small town."

Ray was losing his poise: "These guys, and this doctor, and . . . I don't understand! I mean, screw it, let's just go to the police."

Silence again. Kayla was thinking hard. Ray looked at her hands, which were kind of sleek. Nice. "Is that what you want, Ray? Screw the job, and whatever?"

"No," he admitted.

"What do you want?" Mae asked. A mom question.

Kayla had taken a can of mandarin oranges, turned it on its side, and was rolling the can on the table. Away and then back: Ray and Mae watched, something to watch. No one spoke. A stranger might have walked into the room, just then, and thought that none of these people knew each other.

Kayla wanted to be involved because she was crazy or angry or both. Mae wanted to help him because of some insult he couldn't understand and she wouldn't explain, something involving the doctor. So actually, they weren't really helping him; they were doing something else for themselves. What did Ray want? A good question. He wanted to do his job, hug his daughter. No one but the police knew he was here. That was good. He wanted to call Dr. Gates, and give him a what for. Damn. Imagine that. The thought scared him, because of its appeal. Ray wanted to do something. He wanted to call Dave Peterson, his boss, and say, Get me the hell out of here.

But Ray wanted Windy Oaks to work, most of all. So he convinced himself: it would be fine to hide here. It would all be fine. He needed to be unknown, somewhere. Here would be good. These women weren't a threat, if he kept an eye on them. There's a decision, Ray realized. Just then. He had made a decision to let them help so that he wouldn't have to deal with them anymore.

It was a bad decision. You're fired, he told himself. But he had chosen to make this bad decision, his own bad decision—which was why he was here in Brighton, for godsakes. Ray's job was to make other people's bad decisions his own. He worked for Riggs International, after all. Tough decisions save the bacon, Rivers had said.

"Okay," Ray said. "I mean, is it okay? Can I stay here a little while, get back on my feet? I mean, I work in town and I can't very well stay at my house." He paused. "The note." He looked at Kayla. "No police," he offered.

Mae looked to Kayla until Kayla nodded, her nod an agreement to calm down. "Okay," Kayla said. And then to Ray, "Okay. But you've got to do what I tell you."

"Kayla," Mae said. "You're placing conditions on your grace."

Again, Kayla rolled the can away, then back. Her hands stopped; she looked up. "I know, Momma. I am," she said.

Mae's expression changed to something lighter. She would change the subject. "Now, Mr. Staton—"

"Stanton," Kayla smiled. "You're tired, Momma. Let me begin." She stretched backwards, to open a utility drawer. Kayla was wearing a button-down shirt, not tight: Ray let himself watch her torso and the curve of one breast. He looked at Mae, too, for a second, who was wearing a sleeveless orange top, nice. How old were these women? They were all three in jeans.

"Notes," she waved a pen and a pad of neon orange paper. "You're a white guy and white boys did this to you. And it's on account of black people."

"How do you know?"

Kayla looked to Mae, and Mae nodded her assent. Yes, the nod said. Tell him.

"Let me put it this way: Momma and I live here. Which means, contrary to what you said earlier—not that I have to be contrary, at least not all of the time, Momma—we *are* at the plant, in a way. This is a mill town, Mr. Stanton. Or it used to be, so it still acts like one. I mean, just picture the Fourth of July, starring Norman Rockwell." She scribbled quickly. "On the Fourth of July, or actually, the week of the Fourth, the whole town closes for the week, and everyone goes somewhere, like to a lake or even the beach. That's a mill town, one town, one horse.

"But more important, to say that this is a racial incident, or a bias crime, would be to fit it into what we know. You don't know. You've never lived here. I'm telling you, this is the way it is. On Nathan, it was because he's black. On you, that same boy—three boys, right?—did stuff to you because you are on the wrong side of something. You earned it, hear? You've done something to earn your place. So those kids and Dr. Chicken Breast both think you're on the wrong side, which may seem like a contradiction, but it's only more bullshit."

"Kayla . . . please . . . "

Mae reprimanded Kayla and simultaneously requested both pen and pad. Mae didn't want anything written down or she wanted to write something herself. The pad was slid across the table. Kayla had only been doodling. A loop, and then crosshatching. Nothing that meant anything.

Ray exhaled. "Well, that seems simple." Please don't write anything down, he thought. No paper trail.

"Simple? You think that it's simple when a white boy has done this to you—"

"Kayla . . . "

"So who are they?" Ray pointed to his shiner. "The Klan?"

Both Mae and Kayla stared at him, and both of them smiled a little, and almost, maybe, laughed, Kayla more so. But there was anger, too. Then Kayla, still sputtering, held out her hand, three fingers pointing, deferring to her mother: you tell him, the gesture said. You convinced him, you tell him.

Mae put down the pen: "Not the Klan, Ray, not really. We're in the present and there's no Klan in town—that we know of. Just white people and black people and a not-so-nice African-American doctor and the two of us and you in between."

"Shit," said Ray. "Oh. Excuse me, Mae. Language."

Rivers wouldn't like it. Anderson, the plant manager, wouldn't like it. The Windy Oaks brass. Ownership wouldn't like it. Dave wouldn't help. Trouble. And Ray didn't want more trouble. He was scared: the note. What the hell was happening?

Holy shit, his mom was engaged.

CHAPTER 5

Another day in bed, and then three more days to lounge around Kayla's apartment doing nothing. His seclusion had begun to feel so ridiculously Hollywood—except that in the movies actors only act like they've been beaten, that's why it's called acting. And up there on the screen, the two black women and one white man who have to deal with the hate crime would probably be one black, one white, and one Hispanic. Someone should be Hispanic, Ray thought. Of course, near the end of the film the victim-hero would learn that the nasty boys worked for a crooked real estate agent—Ray was pleased to cast his soon-to-be-ex-wife as the shrill woman in the lamé blouse—and a quick trip to the county records office would uncover the scam, a development deal where a highway would be built, and a body buried in the concrete beneath a public fountain. Ray liked those kinds of movies, although they usually ended with a car chase and a shoot-out. But this wasn't the movies, and Ray's concussion wasn't the work of someone in Makeup; and car chases and shoot-outs kill real people.

Ray's head hurt. His shoulder too. The scratches stung. His head hurt a little less than it had, he thought, but hey, it still hurt.

Kayla and Mae. Ray hadn't done anything, and he already regretted getting involved with them; he regretted already the future, the developments he didn't know enough about to regret yet. That's right, okay, he still didn't feel rational, and not because of the blow to the head. Normally, he never would have agreed to such foolhardiness, to hide and not to let the police help with crimes—to listen to Rivers—but this wasn't normal. Or, maybe what he believed to be normal had changed.

Ray had always thought that what happened truly happened. When he talked to someone, he talked to them, no matter their skin color, or how they thought of themselves, really, because one person was talking to another person, and that's what was happening. To people like the Reeves women, what actually was happening wasn't happening. Something else was happening. In that regard, since skin color always mattered to some people, Kayla was right, when she had said—yesterday? They had been talking a lot—that he did think differently. Quite often, each day, Ray's jaw ached from breathing, just from the effort to keep his teeth unclenched. Was that thinking differently too? He had never been particularly naive regarding others and their motives, or his own motives, for that matter, and he was in Human Resources, in a way, but the past few days had taught him a new suspicion: events, too, weren't what they seemed.

He called his mom. "Hi, it's me."

"Hi," she giggled. "Hold on a minute. . . ."

His mom giggled? Oh wow. After that, the rest of the phone call almost didn't matter: Mom had been chatty, she had told Fran the news this morning. And Randall's kids (three girls, one adopted) would all come to the wedding. One of Randall's grand-kids had a broken nose; he had been pushed into a lamppost while playing Capture the Flag, and Randall was sending the boy some kind of spectacular electronic toy, quite a generous present. Ray listened, but more to the tone of his mother's voice, the singing under the words, to her happiness, instead of to what she was saying exactly. He couldn't believe it: if Mom had ever been happy before, Ray didn't remember. Not like this. She sounded wonderful.

"I love you, Mom," he had said, suddenly, in the midst of her monologue.

"What? Why, Ray. Of course you do." Then on she went, into a little story of her neighbor, another widow, who must have had designs upon the unsuspecting, sweet, sweet Randall, and who was considering selling so as not to live next door to the newlyweds. "Oh, Ray. He's so sweet."

So Randall would move in: Ray wondered if it had happened already.

Where was Ray moving? To Brighton, he thought, at least for the duration; to get Windy Oaks back on its feet, a project that could easily take two years. If the whites and the blacks would have him, Ray scoffed—still unconvinced that racism had caused his troubles. Just three malicious hicks who weren't smart enough to have invented a motive. Don't do it again, they had said, which had no racial overtones. Do what? Ray knew even less than before: what had he done?

After talking to Mom, Ray had decided not to call Bruce, his fishing buddy who had offered to take Ray up north, where they would fly in somewhere to a fish camp, drink themselves into a puddle, and chow on char. Bruce could wait, even though Ray should have called him yesterday.

The drunker Bruce and Ray got together, the more they would talk about women, or at least the women Bruce wanted to talk about, the ones with whom he had slept. Bruce was a nice guy, divorced ten years or so, nothing steady since. Bruce who said he worked out because he had to. Lonely, Jilly had said, even when Bruce and Kath had still been married, although Ray hadn't seen it. When fishing, Ray and Bruce would talk about fishing, a sport that Ray found just challenging enough to occupy his thoughts, but never too stressful, thank goodness. A busy, boring thing to do. Better still, Ray liked to fish when he could eat what he caught, as catch-and-release seemed kind of unfair, merely sporting, the fish played and then let go—so the fly-in sounded fun, flying back with big whacks of fish on ice. And the trip would be fun: Bruce was a good guy with whom Ray liked to do things.

What day was it? Ray read a magazine and he watched TV at the same time, and the disconnected images rolled across a screen at the back of his memory like weird outtakes, as he tried to ignore them. No way would Ray pay attention; just let the bad times roll. So what if he had been linked romantically to Mae, by way of town gossip and Dr. Gates. Who cared? Really, Ray told himself. Come on. It was a little ridiculous to care about, wasn't it? For anyone to care.

Apparently, Kayla cared. He was in Kayla's bathroom, whatever magazine and TV show abandoned. He knew that he was having trouble concentrating, the images of the three punks still there. They were all Ray could think about, or so it seemed; he kept coming back to his memories.

The boys had stopped, at one point, to chug their beers together. Ray was hugging his own knees, and the third kid, the one who seemed mostly the lookout, had taken a handful of sand or something and let it sprinkle slowly on Ray's head. Laughing like a lunatic. Oh god.

A little later, who knew what time it might have been, the same kid had brushed something off Ray's forehead, when the other two guys had turned to piss in a ditch. Had the gesture been kind?

Ray stood at Kayla's bedroom window, pulled back the eyelet curtain. Her room was tasteful, a Van Gogh poster on one wall, another poster, a collage thing with African-Americans, on the other. A small set of free weights, different sizes, lined up in one corner, at the foot of a mirror. The top blanket looked home-made. On the dresser, a little tree made out of wire—maybe eight or ten inches tall—was festooned with earrings, a good twenty pairs hanging in the branches, the whole arrangement atop a shiny tray. Nicely done. She was a careful person.

Was someone coming down the street? Yes. Now Ray felt like the lookout.

These Reeves women were certainly something. They lived in Brighton, and they stayed in Brighton, and they seemed totally embroiled in Brighton, the racial politics and the small-town gossip. So much invested in—what? How could they be happy, feeling this way about their own town? Or being so deep in it?

His mom was happy: she met the right guy, at age sixty-eight, and boom. Was it that easy?

Ray could handle being the lookout, so long as no one was looking in. From here on the second floor, just off Watson Street, he could see a pinched corner of Brighton's main drag. The town was gray, or too many shades of gray, sidewalks and tired awnings and the sky full of fall and winter both at once, even today, on a sunny May day. Ray had first visited Brighton last November just as the local government changed hands, the race for mayor hotly contested between a former school principal and a lawyer. Their faces and slogans were everywhere, one mayoral sign to every three for the next high school football game. Ray had arrived in town hungry, had lunched somewhere along the seven blocks of Main Street, a dry hamburger and weak coffee, and then had stepped outside to a new smell. Sulfur, maybe, although there was no pulp mill nearby. Windy Oaks? He hoped not; that might be costly. Ultimately, he hadn't been able to identify the smell; it had smelled bad, something not quite sour. Wet wheat? Maybe that was it, he thought now. Some sort of wet grain or mildewed wheat.

There was a tree fully green outside Kayla's window; somewhere a dog barked. Was the dog happy? Ray could never tell about dogs, at least not from the sound of their barking. Ray liked dogs. But if something were capable of happiness, wouldn't that mean it had a soul?

Where the hell did that thought come from? He brought his thoughts back to what he could see. Focus. The sky was blue, the tree green, the town gray—the natural and the unnatural simmered together in Brighton. The contrast only reinforced Ray's impression that the town didn't belong here, or anywhere for that matter, and that Ray couldn't belong in a town that didn't belong.

He was looking out Kayla's window. If he wanted, he could count the telephone poles strung together—as they were by conversations and solicitations, people picking up and hanging up, how are you and no thank you. When he drove, and he was usually the driver, Tom or Jeannie and their friends misbehaving, Ray didn't think about telephone poles. Until the ride in Shaw's car, Ray hadn't even sat in a backseat in a very long time, which might have let him look out the window and count telephone poles. It was true, too, that he never really thought about telephone poles when he called his sister or someone—he would just dial and there was Fran. Or there he was, for her, as when her first marriage had broken apart, and the booze had poured in through the cracks, and Fran had called Ray to shout. Not that he had understood, but he had never hung up as she wailed and screamed and blamed Ray for Dad's death and Mom being Mom and the goddamn hole in the ozone.

Those were bad nights, listening to Frannie drink. Ray would take the phone into the bathroom and sit there and listen, while Jilly covered her head with a pillow to go back to sleep. Sure AA helped, but Ray was the one; Fran's patient baby brother at thirty-two on the other end of the phone, as the telephone wires sizzled with years of fucked-up rage. Those nights, he had learned a lot about himself, too, not all of it nice and very little of which he wanted to admit. He was capable of patience, but not when it came to most members of his family. He had told Fran, one particularly tough night, No, I don't forgive Dad either. Fuck him.

Thank god Ray wasn't susceptible, he believed, to addiction, no matter the drunk gene or whatever the researchers called it. He hadn't become an alcoholic too, had he? Why not remained a small mystery: the motives were there, including the question of a questionable career that increasingly involved making difficult choices that inevitably affected a lot of people adversely, and he did like his g-and-t's, but something else had prevailed. In truth, as Fran had once said in a less-than-kind tone, her self-hatred magnanimously extended to include him, Ray was probably just too boring to drink.

More to the immediate point, Ray realized that he wanted a drink. It was late enough. Sadly, Ray shook his head. Sad? He almost wanted to talk to Jilly, but only the old Jilly. He and his almost-ex were beyond communicating, for good, mired in the havoc of the past three years. Done. Sure, they had been kids when they met—seventeen years ago this New Year's—but they had somehow kept working until there was nothing left to work at, no meeting ground. They had stopped agreeing.

Her silence had confused him, as Jilly was a talker. Still, there had been something else, too, some mystery in her silence that Ray had found a little bit intriguing. Ray knew his wife better than he knew anyone else, and when she had stopped talking, she had become kind of mysterious in a really frustrating and kind of sexy way. But if she had wanted to be mysterious, she should have said so.

Okay, so he wasn't making sense. So? And yes, he was condescending, Jilly was right, he was still ignoring what she felt. Sometimes, Ray suspected that the job had done this to him. You're fired.

No, that was a cop-out. Of course, their marriage hadn't ended because of how Riggs International had turned Ray into a monster, or because of his workaholic commitment to the job, or Jilly's to hers in real estate, or some act of lust inspired by middle-aged hormonal panic. Once, five or so years back, he had had an affair—but it hadn't been male menopause, my god, who's middle-aged at thirty-six? Marsha had been needy and available, he had been horny and working too hard, the whole illicit arrangement had fallen into place like the little tumblers of a little lock, click, click, click. And just as precisely, predictably, it had ended with a click: Marsha a mess, his marriage shaky, his conscience like an ever-present, high-pitched dog whistle only Ray could hear; unrelenting, disapproving, never leaving him alone. Ray hadn't told his wife, but he hadn't denied anything either, and she had seemed to have known the truth, for she hadn't trusted him again for a year or two, if ever again.

So the affair wasn't worth its consequences or its costs, but Ray knew that it wasn't an event in his life that he wholly regretted either. The sex had been fun, just as Ray had always understood—even then, as it was happening—that anyone can have sex with anyone. But the excitement had been the point, really. The living. It had seemed at the time and maybe more so now in retrospect, like really living, or living again, or maybe for once.

Their marriage had ended because it had ended, Ray thought. Right. Because when the silence had stopped being mysterious, punctuated by fighting, the marriage hadn't been able to take the strain. The marriage just wasn't good; they had outgrown each other.

Okay, so Ray couldn't list all the reasons why their marriage had ended, he admitted to himself. The thought didn't make him upset.

He had been at Riggs for almost ten years. The job meant plenty: his team's reputation for successful industrial makeovers was well established, enough so that some individual team members would be assigned the occasional solo project, like Ray to Windy Oaks, which was even beginning to make him think that maybe he should go it alone, form a company, a start-up. Although with the divorce his capital would have to come from loans. Stanton Consulting. Stanton, Inc. Stanton Management. Ray smiled to himself; maybe he could get Jilly to invest her share of the settlement in Stanton International. President's office, Ray speaking. You're fired.

"Expecting someone?"

Ray turned around. She had startled him, but he hadn't jumped. A good sign. "Maybe," he shrugged. "Don't know," he added.

Kayla opened her closet, took out a blouse. "Excuse me," she said. "Do you mind?"

Ray turned around, to look out the window again. "Can I ask you something?"

"Sure," she said. "Let's talk in the kitchen."

Kayla poured Ray a cup of coffee and set it down, then she put her hand under Ray's chin and tilted his head toward the light. She was holding his face: he let her. "Your eye's looking bad. Can you see?"

"It's a little blurry. . . ."

"How's the head?" She let go.

"Better, thanks."

"You know . . ." Kayla pulled out a chair, swung it around backwards, and then straddle-sat. She had changed her earrings when she was in the bedroom. Ray waited. With her left index finger, Kayla traced a line on her right palm. "I mean. . . . I'm not trying to lose it, you know? But I get so fucking mad." She looked up at Ray and smiled. "I'll try not to put my shit on you. . . . I mean . . . you know what I mean?"

"I think so."

"Good. I'm glad. 'Cause Momma is just too nice and she doesn't have a clue. Shit." And then to herself, softly: "She's too nice."

"She is nice," said Ray.

"Good," Kayla decided. "That's right," Kayla reasoned. "Okay," Kayla declared.

He swirled his mug, content to watch Kayla. She still seemed abuzz with Ray's troubles, or with her workday, the day manager of the King's Plate, a restaurant out on 21, where Ray had never eaten. Ray thought he should say nothing, leave her alone. He didn't consider himself very good at sorting out other people's problems. What could he say that Kayla hadn't already asked herself? In truth, Ray believed that he had a tendency to say the wrong thing, and to ignite even more emotional fireworks, especially when he meant well. He did mean well.

"Want some pie? Ellard's strawberry-rhubarb. . . ."

"Well, all riiiiight," he slurred his response. "Twist my arm. But a little piece, or I'll have to add another mile to my run." When he could run again, he added to himself.

"You run? Yeah, that makes sense."

Ray looked up. She was smiling, although her remark hadn't been a compliment. "What do you mean?"

"Oh, I don't know. . . ." Kayla turned her back to Ray. The light from the open fridge seemed to hold her in place. "What'd you want to ask me?"

"Nothing that won't wait. C'mon, Kayla . . . " And then he imitated her voice, just a little. "What'd you mean?"

"Don't you flirt with me, Mr. Stanton." He could see only part of her face, and maybe a tight little expression.

"All right, I won't. But you were gonna tell this white guy why he looks like a jogger."

"Shit, Ray!"

"Yeah, yeah. Shit. But I want to know why everything you think about me you think because I'm white."

"You can't say that."

"I know."

"Damn!" She grabbed a fork and served him his pie; the fork clattered against the plate. "Put the man in the room, and he acts like—"

"Like what?" He took a bite; the pie was good. "Good pie. Thanks." Crumbs fell onto his lap.

She half-laughed. "Rude. You're just rude."

"Maybe so. But I think I need to know this. I'm white and probably stupid about it. And I must be saying nasty racist shit to you all the time because I don't know better. . . . You think it's because I'm white and I think it's because I'm white but no one ever says that." He wiped his mouth, a little embarrassed with himself, grateful for the napkin, a prop. "I'm telling the truth, right? Plus, you talk about me like this when I'm not around."

Her eyes were shining. "Mr. Ray, don't you think you know me. You don't wanna know me. . . ."

"Hey." He raised his hands, leaning back and backing off.

"That's right. You eat your pie."

He had done something smart. That's how she worked: she needed proof, the world in front of her. He smiled. She returned his smile, sort of. She was rattled. He was having fun.

"Okay, white man. You think you want the truth. Black people work and white people jog: it's called 'plantation economics.'"

"Whoa—"

"Oh no . . ." She smiled but it didn't look like a smile. "You took off the lid. Black people rent and white people buy; black people wash and—" For a moment, Kayla stopped looking through him, her gaze lingering on something behind him. "White people bathe. And black folks love but white folks have lovers. You know—white folks *have*, like, they own. It's not like it *is*, you know, but you say it is and it is."

"Jesus," Ray swore. "Sorry I asked." Neither he nor Kayla spoke, for a long enough time to be too long. He looked down: he had shredded his napkin and balled the shreds. He looked up, and then he reached forward to touch her shoulder. He couldn't reach. She might have been crying. "I'm sorry. Really," he said. He was.

"You don't know shit."

"You're right, I don't know shit."

She paused. "You're a clown." Kayla stared at him and then she shook her head: she had not been crying at all. She looked like her mom, April and Mae. "You're nuts."

"White nuts."

"Shit. There's no such thing as white nuts," she smiled. "I'm boarding a sorry-assed lunatic."

"That's me," Ray said.

"Shit. You just shut up."

Ray smiled a big smile.

"There. See? You're a clown."

Ray took his time. "Kayla . . . You don't have to answer but . . . where's all this from? I mean, this whole mess is more than me, right? For you, I mean. This isn't about me." She didn't answer;

he tried again. "You've got something you're working on. . . . If I can help—"

"You can't," Kayla said.

"If I can—"

"Don't try." She pushed away from the table and stood, her earrings tinkling like a sound heard far away.

"Hey . . ."

"That's right. Don't try."

Ray toyed with the napkin shreds on the table: all you guys go over here, all you guys go over there. Now you guys line up and you guys watch. All right. Touchdown. Ohio loses on the last play.

"—and don't go thinking I'm Nation of Islam either."

"I don't. I mean, I know." He didn't know. What?

"You don't know shit," she correctly surmised. Kayla took his plate and fork to the sink, rinsed, and then opened the dishwasher. "Damn . . . ," she muttered, then turned back to face Ray. "Remember your doctor friend? Dr. Gates? Andy Gates? The one who wants to help? He's a cousin by marriage, Momma's dumb cousin Gabby's husband. And he was only the second African-American doctor to move here since . . . well, shoot, since a president had polio. And let me guess, he was real nice to Miss Mae Reeves when they were in public, right? Like he was polite and all? Only he doesn't speak to her on the street, or at the grocery, on account of my dad. And when she was in the paper for saving that kid, a billion years ago, when they went to take the photo, Andy Gates sat on her bed and put his arm around her like they were married, the happy blacks at home, doing the happy black thing, in the middle of Civil Rights. So there's Momma with a broken back and he's squeezing her until she cries. But she can't move away. You hear? Her back's broken and a goddamn doctor's hurting her because he's gotta make black folks and white folks believe that Momma married a black man, and that pretty black little Kayla Reeves's not biracial. See? He buys all that shit. Your white shit. He buys it and Momma and I pay the bill. Which is why Momma's fired up, in her way, and putting up with me being fired up, but too nice to do anything useful—" She interrupted herself, shook her head. "You don't want to know."

He didn't, she was right. They sat there awhile, a long time for Kayla to sit, Ray believed. "What do you think I should do?"

She smiled. He had honored her by asking. "Move."

"No, really."

"Well, if it's Palmer, then you should move."

Ray looked at her. Palmer?

"With a 'P,' P-a-l-m-e-r. That's the boy. Jimmy. That's your boy."

My boy? Oh god. "How do you know?"

"Know? I went to school with his older sister. You fired her."

"How do you know that?"

Kayla's jaw tightened. "Small town."

"Oh," Ray said. And then: "Fuck it. I'm here," Ray said. "I'm not going anywhere." He hadn't meant to say any of that.

"You're dumb," Kayla said. "You shouldn't take this. You've got to leave. You're the wrong man."

There was light coming in the window and shining on a butter dish. It was a ceramic butter dish with a chipped lid. Ray thought about the butter dish, and then he thought about Kayla's earrings. He thought about her breasts, in a matter-of-fact way. She had a nice figure, round and fun to watch. She had been wearing her work clothes, pants and crisp white shirt, but the blouse from the closet looked nicer, better curves.

The day was disappearing. Night. He thought about his napkin in shreds.

"Want some Advil with your caffeine?" She wasn't smiling.

"Yes, please. But I'm ready to switch to something harder." And then: "I didn't take this. But now I'm choosing it. There's a difference. I mean"—and he didn't know what he meant—"I don't think that anything happens except we choose it. People look at us differently, sure. But we choose."

She was nodding her head as she handed him his Advil. Her eyes were shining. "That's right," she said. "Mm, aren't you the philosopher."

"So I'm here, right? And if this—if Palmer is it, the problem, then I'm doing something about it. About him. I choose to."

Kayla looked at him, and then away. "You're trouble," she said. "You're the wrong man, hear? And you're not talking to the police, because you've got to keep your job."

There was a long silence. Then Ray had a funny thought; he let himself smile: "Maybe . . . I'm not talking to the police. But maybe you are?"

She was stunned. She turned away—what was that look on her face? Kayla's expression was screwy, two or three expressions together. "You're trouble," she said. "But that might work," she admitted. "Jesus, you're trouble with a capital T."

Ray had to smile: "That's me. Mr. T."

She threw her hands up in the air. "Oh, fuck," she said. "Mr. T," she smiled. "Fuck you, Ray. . . . You just take your painkillers. Here. Take extra. I think you just might need them."

CHAPTER 6

"Do you know any black people?"

They were driving through the car wash, the soapy canvas strips slapping the car. Kayla had insisted: we're going out, you've been in the house too long, c'mon, a week's plenty. Get off your ass.

"You're not one of those pink white guys, complexion-wise. Does that matter to you?"

"When you see four black teens in a car, what do you think?"

"Have you ever hired a black woman? I know that you fire people, but have you ever replaced a white guy with a black woman?"

The soap was done, the canvas strips retreated to their corner of the ceiling. Rinse. A conical spray pounded Kayla's car, the jets twisting in their tracks, at last the sound too loud to talk over, what a relief. When he was a toddler, Tommy had been scared of these car washes, Ray thought.

And what was Ray scared of? He had to think. Public embarrassment, big snakes, the prospect of losing a child, pain. It was probably a fairly boring list.

The car wash ended with a sputter, and dripped slowly. Kayla began again: "Have you ever kissed a black person on the lips?"

"Have black people cleaned your house?"

"Did you have a black 'mother's helper' growing up?"

"Do you think the policies of the United States government are racist?"

"What do you think of financial incentives for minorities who finish high school? College?"

"What do you think of affirmative action?"

She was rattling her questions off a list she had prepared in advance, pulled from the pocket of a sundress. Big red flowers. Ray didn't know what to say. "It's not like I live in a bubble, you know." That was something to say, and useless.

Kayla laughed. "Okay," she said, putting the car in gear. "You're right," she said. Then she reached across the stick shift and gave his shoulder a little smack. "Don't answer the questions."

"Okay."

She hadn't been playing fair, Ray thought later, as they shopped for a few staples, plus fruit and veggies. Perhaps she did live in a world Ray couldn't fathom, fraught with Dr. Gates and Palmer and whomever, but that wasn't the same as two people talking. Just people, he wanted to say to Kayla. He wanted to slap her shoulder back, just you and me; just people.

The clerk was scanning their stuff, some pimply kid who had scratched out one letter on his nametag, to see if anyone would notice. "Hell, my name is Greg," said his pin. Kayla rummaged in her purse for her wallet, her head down, as Ray bagged the produce first. Here came the eggs, Greg handing them carefully to Ray, with a wink.

What the hell? Oh shit, Ray thought. A wink between guys. Ray didn't like it. "So, Greg," Ray said. "Got a high school degree?"

Kayla looked up.

"You bet," Greg said.

"And I'm sure they taught you good, in high school." Ray laughed so that Greg would laugh, which worked. "How are you on Malcolm X?"

"Ray!" Kayla hissed.

"Huh?" Greg said. He accepted Kayla's frequent shopper card.

"You know, Malcolm X. That guy in the movie?"

"Oh yeah," Greg said. "The wrestler. He's cool."

"Right," Ray said. "The wrestler. Didja know that . . . there's a scandal going on, something about wrestling fans being gay and all?"

Greg blushed. "Thank you, ma'am," he said to Kayla, as he tore off her receipt and handed it over. "Didn't hear that," he said. "Please sign here."

"If I were you, Greggie, I'd watch out. Won't wanna watch too much wrestling, you know." And then Ray winked back, to seal it, a wink that could mean anything.

"What the hell was that about? You were torturing that poor kid. Just because I put you on the spot, doesn't mean—"

"Hold on, hold on." Ray laid a bag of groceries in Kayla's trunk. Oh no, he thought. The supermarket parking lot. The three guys. "The kid had it coming. He was making faces."

Kayla looked at Ray. "Faces."

"You know." Ray was embarrassed. One more bag of groceries, there.

"Faces?"

"Faces," he repeated. "C'mon, Kayla. He was making faces. You, me, white guy with a black chick faces."

Kayla was amazed. "You're kidding." She slammed the trunk.

"I'm not." Ray walked around to his side, talking over the roof of the car. "I'm in Human Resources. I know faces."

"I see," Kayla shook her head as she settled into the driver's seat. "Ray knows faces."

CHAPTER 7

They had driven back by way of Ray's house; he had gone in to collect some clothes, a few papers and notes, his briefcase. Being in the house seemed a reminder: GOT YA. Then they had stopped for takeout, burgers and fries from a place Ray didn't know, Kayla ordering inside while he found himself slouched in the passenger seat. Was he scared? He couldn't really say. Freaked out, sort of, by his own behavior and by what still remained, the three little shits, still out there. Palmer, if that was the right guy.

Dinner, just the two of them. A reasonably tasty burger and good fries, but mustard on the burger, which Ray didn't like much. Ray ate the burger anyway.

"I still can't believe you," she had said, wiping her face with a napkin.

"Me either," he admitted. "That wasn't like me."

"Hm." She got up. "I've got it." She waved away his assistance, collected their Styrofoam containers and napkins, cleared the table. "What is like you?"

He thought about her question, one that, Ray had to admit, he had been considering for a little while. She was on target, this Kayla. "I guess . . . ," he stalled. "You know, I've got this job here, right? It's not an easy job." Uh-oh, he covered his mouth and burped. "Excuse me. . . . It's like . . . a lot of people are involved, and some may well lose their jobs." He was understating the truth, but felt a need. "I guess . . . because my job's hard, from a people point of view, I've got to believe that it's right. You know what I mean? That if I do this the right way, the plant's going to survive and even do better, which means the town does better, and the people who live here prosper. Not everyone, of course—"

"Because you fire people," she said.

"Yes, that's right. But BPR's a long-term thing, an investment. Management wouldn't have hired us if they weren't invested in making this work, in turning Windy Oaks around. It's a bottom-line issue, of course. My job has a lot to do with the bottom line, but I'm the one who sees the people affected, you know?"

He thought about what he was saying. Made sense, Ray thought.

"And . . . ?"

"And that kid in the store, that was a long-term thing. Okay, so I fucked with him and I'm sorry—yes, Mae, sorry about the language—"

Kayla laughed at Ray's invocation of the absent Mae.

"But you know," Ray came back to the issue. "It wasn't that different, kind of. I saw the face he made, and . . ."

Kayla was doing the dishes. "It was different, Ray. You're not telling the truth," she said, to the window she faced. Then she wiped her chin on her left shoulder, her hands still in the soapy water, looked at him. What was she washing?

"You're right," he said, before he could think too much. "It was different. It was the first time I've been out of the house, really, and . . . I . . ." He what? He was fucking angry, that's what he was. Ray exhaled. "I'm just so fucking angry sometimes," he said. "I get so fucking angry. But it felt good to be doing something about it."

"Right on," Kayla said. "That's it. Now you're telling the truth."

There was a long pause.

"And . . . ?" Kayla asked.

"And," Ray said. "And my thoughts . . . I feel like I'm playing word association, or something. My thoughts . . . it's hard to describe them as thoughts, really."

Kayla nodded. She didn't understand.

"So," Ray said. Uh-oh: he was about to make a bad decision. "So."

"So, so. So I think that we better do something else, and soon, before my anger wears off. Don't you?"

How Ray found himself in a small town named Brighton, in the middle of Nowhere as though Nowhere might have a middle, hunched as he leaned from a parked, borrowed car—the back door open, the dome light off—soaking rags with kerosene, confused even Ray. It was Thursday night, late, three or four in the morning; Friday, really, two weeks after Ray had been rolled from a pickup. It had been years since he had liked being awake this late. Kayla was in the driver's seat; her face shone with the unnatural, reflected light of too many surfaces: the humid air, the windshield, a Cleveland Indians cap, her eyes. It was three or four in the morning on a quiet Thursday night on a white trash street in a dinky neighborhood in a no-good town in the middle of nowhere, Ohio, the United States, North America, planet Earth, the Universe, and Ray Stanton and Kayla Reeves were about to burn a cross on Jimmy Palmer, Jr.'s front lawn. Jimmy Palmer, Jr., had poured beer up Ray's nose. And if Ray had cared to admit it, he would probably have acknowledged, yes, he imagined so, burning the cross had been his idea.

He and Kayla had talked and talked: what to do to a racist? What's the worst thing to do to a bully? How to get Palmer into trouble that wouldn't implicate Ray, or Windy Oaks? What was a guy like Palmer like? How to mess him up? He wasn't Klan, but he acted like it.

So there's a better question: how to nail a punk who acts like he's a member of the Klan? And the answer: make his friends hate him. How to do that? Make him seem . . . enlightened. Right, Ray had thought, getting somewhere—or so it seemed to Ray, talking and talking with Kayla. Ray, who had nothing else to do. Ray, a rookie, a guy who wasn't allowed to go to work, who had become a criminal.

Then the idea: what if we burn a cross on his lawn, will his friends think that the Klan did it, and that Palmer's . . . what? One of us, Kayla had laughed. But she had shaken her head. Don't know, Ray. A black woman burning a cross? Maybe I'll help, but you'd have to do the work.

Okay, he had said, out of his mind, insane. Taking charge, and acting. Okay, I'll do it and you help. It was an insane idea, but he had already talked himself into believing that sanity wouldn't matter. Sanity wasn't the issue: Ray had to do something, to fix himself.

The dogs hadn't started barking yet. Ray knew that there were dogs in a run to the left of Palmer's house, two or three hounds just waiting to bay. He had seen them on a drive-by, as he cased the block. Cased the block? What the hell was he doing? For chrissakes.

"C'mon," hissed Kayla. "Ray—"

"Almost there."

Kayla's head bobbed: no earrings, too shiny. "Park it!"

The makeshift cross lay in the trunk, a cross nailed together at the center, wrapped with rags, tied with string, sharpened at the base, ugly enough to burn. Kayla would carry the sledge-hammer, Ray the Strike-Anywhere matches. His hands would smell of kerosene, he suspected, for days.

Kayla slid across the front seat to the passenger side. She swiveled, to make eye contact. "Now?" she asked, her voice full of doubt.

"Might as well," Ray said.

"Might as well," Kayla said.

Neither moved.

"This is it, you and me," Kayla said.

"Yep," said Ray.

"If we're gonna . . ."

"Might as well," said Ray.

In Ray's senses, their hushed voices seemed to merge with the stink of the kerosene. He had a lot to be sorry for, but not this, yet. Not for another five minutes, and then his life would be different, again.

"Okay!" Kayla hissed. "We're moving." She slid from her seat. Ray was glad she had gone first. "Tag. We're it."

They walked, they didn't run. This they had planned, too, that the whole scene would be played at normal speed. It won't be an act of fear, Ray had insisted. Right, Kayla had said. It'll be vengeance. We're getting even. So no running? Ray had asked, his eyebrows raised. No running, Kayla had agreed. We're in charge, Ray had added. Taking charge.

He accepted the sledgehammer from Kayla, and began to pound the cross. The top had been wrapped with rags, too, to muffle the sound. A cross faces a lot of directions at once, Ray thought. No, just two. His shoulder hurt.

"You . . ." She was handing him the matches.

"Yes," Ray whispered. It was his job to light the match, and haul the sledgehammer back to the car, where Kayla would be waiting. It was his job to rattle the bars of his soul with a sharpened spoon. Now where did that thought come from? Ray took a deep breath, then exhaled silently. As he crossed the street to the car, he glanced at the sky. A cloudy night, just as predicted. He and Kayla had wanted a cloudy night.

"No dogs," Ray said to Kayla as they started to drive away.

Kayla didn't answer. Her eyes were wide, she looked happy, or petrified, or both.

"No dogs," Ray shrugged to himself.

"You did it," Kayla said. "I can't believe . . ."

Ray didn't hear the rest of what she said. He was driving away, three miles an hour below the municipal speed limit, his hands reeking of kerosene and his mirrors filled with flames. In the moment when he had tossed the match to the base of the cross and the cross had ignited, Ray had heard a new sound, or at least, a sound new to him, and his mind was full of this sound. Not the *Fooh!* of ignition, which might have been a kind of exaggerated barbecue noise; not the sizzle of combustion, nor the steady crackle of a steady flame; neither the *Whump!* of an explosion nor the reverberations that followed. In fact, Ray thought, the sound had been sort of bodily, human-made—and foreign too, as though it didn't belong.

Something else had made a sound, something inside Ray. It had sounded almost like air escaping. A shell kicked out of a rifle, and the little sucking sound the chamber makes? No, too Clint Eastwood. How about a vacuum tube popping, or one of those long fluorescent lightbulbs? Closer. A sound from the computer, when it won't do what you want? Not quite.

A last gasp, smiled Ray to himself.

"You're smiling," said Kayla. She had been squeezing his fingers too hard, which hurt. When they both noticed, at the same time, she let go.

"I guess I am."

"I can't believe we did it. Wow, is this ever gonna fuck him up."

Ray laughed. There was ugliness in the laugh: he liked it. You're fired, he told the rearview mirror.

Kayla bounced up and down. "His friends'll kill him!"

"Maybe."

"Oh Ray . . ." She was bouncing and bouncing, and shaking his hand again. "Shit, I'm pumped."

Pumped? He was a forty-one-year-old business process re-engineer on his first solo project, and she was a thirty-six-year-old army vet and restaurant manager, and he felt pumped, too, even though it couldn't mean to Kayla what it meant to Ray. Or vice versa, he supposed.

"C'mon, Uncle Ray. Tell it to me."

"I'm pumped!" Ray yelled. BPR, slash and burn.

"Pumped!" Kayla hollered out the window.

They were silent for a bit. Ray drove. The car was to be returned to its garage, to sit for a week or so, until Reggie came back to town. It was Reggie's car, a Chevy or something. It was an old car with wide, banquette-style seats. Reggie was Kayla's friend from work, a short-order cook. He would never know that the car had been borrowed; Kayla had been given the keys, for some unexplainable reason. She and Ray had even covered up the license plates with rags.

But first Ray needed to drive; they had planned to drive out of town, circle south, and enter Brighton from another direction, all before daylight.

"I should lie down," Ray admitted, almost in the instant the thought occurred to him.

"Oh, Ray," Kayla smiled. "Violence and sex?"

Ray didn't know how to take her comment. They were silent some more, except for that rattling heartbeat of Ray's, the blood drumming in his inner ear. Damn heartbeat. Ray checked his side-view mirror. No flames. Just his heartbeat, steadily hammering his life flat, thinner and thinner, until he could see through who he was, until Ray wasn't there. He supposed that he might be able to see through his own chest, right now, if he were looking in a mirror. And then the impression was gone, never having happened.

"Here," Kayla pointed. "That driveway."

He had a sense of the flames, even though the flames seemed to occupy a part of him other than his memory. Like a feeling does. The flames were like a feeling, overwhelming and unforgettable and physical. A slightly metallic taste left on the tip of his tongue, an adrenal surge and wham, nothing. *Fooh!*

What the hell? Ray thought. Now his senses weren't making any sense. He stepped from the Chevy, turned and closed the door. He was carrying the sledgehammer, dragging its leaden head. He half-expected to see the flames still in the mirror, or reflected in the back window, as he glanced over his shoulder at Reggie's car, just as Kayla shut the garage door. Or the flames could be engulfing the house in front of him. That house, there.

No, Ray thought, relieved.

"What?" whispered Kayla.

"Nothing," Ray answered. "I didn't say anything," he added, although he was unsure.

They walked the two blocks to where they had left Kayla's car, quiet in each other's company. Ray wanted to talk, or so he thought. Kayla must want to talk, he reasoned. Ray thought more about Jimmy Palmer, Jr., and two weeks ago. In the course of those cruel, unnatural events, Palmer had said something unbelievable. The other two guys had been holding Ray down and Palmer had been pressing a beer bottle hard against Ray's nose, almost up his nostril, and the kid had quoted John Lennon. Please stop, Ray had said. Aw don't be like that, the kid had said. Give peace a chance. Oh no, Ray had said, as the kid pushed the bottle harder. Harder. All we are saying, Ray had sputtered, trying anything, the beer pouring up his nose and down his neck. That's it, the kid had said. *Doo-doo-ba-doo-doo*, the kid had sung, and then he had added: shit, don't get beer on my shoes, asshole. Leave me alone, Ray had pleaded, leave me alone, leave me alone, leave me alone.

Maybe he should sing. Jesus, Palmer had liked that, Ray almost singing the song to keep from drowning in beer. But Ray had begun to need Palmer to like whatever Ray did, to approve. Ray had arrived at that moment in the night when all he wanted was for Palmer, the one in charge, to like something, anything; when Ray's willingness to please overwhelmed all else he might have been feeling. That had been the torture. The boys had stripped and abused him, but no physical distress could match the realization that Ray in that moment had become nobody and had no reason to ask for mercy, and he had asked anyway and no one had cared. Worse, Palmer had known the truth: when Ray had begun to beg, the kid had tightened those whitish-pink sunburned lips and pulled the bottle away, beer pouring slowly down Ray's chest. "Fff," Palmer had said, sneering as he had squinted into the emptiness of Ray's soul, and Ray had heard the Gates of Heaven clang shut behind that inarticulate, judgmental sniff. Don't do it again, Palmer had said.

Do what? Fire Palmer's sister? It couldn't be that. But Palmer was the guy, no doubt, Ray had even seen him, just a few nights ago, Palmer in his driveway as Ray and Kayla drove by. A drive-by, Ray slouched yet again in the passenger seat, terrified and furious.

When Ray thought about it, and when he and Kayla had talked about it, he still couldn't believe that firing Palmer's sister was the issue—nor did it make sense in connection with the other guy, Nathan what's-his-name. Ray hadn't done anything. Only seven people had been displaced so far, and they were all in middle management; seven supervisors sitting on their hands, four of whom were imminent retirees gazing out the window of fifty-nine-plus, three more recent promotions, last in, first out. These kids wouldn't care, Ray knew.

Whatever Ray hadn't done didn't compare to what he was supposed to do. Windy Oaks would change, and people would lose jobs, Ray knew, for that was the modernization plan, that's how his job was supposed to work; to save the plant and its remaining 475 employees, and to make production competitive once more. But no one knew all of the details of the reorganization plan, aside from Ray and Mr. Rivers and Anderson in HR. Goddamnit, no one knew!

When he closed his eyes, Ray could see flames. He couldn't decide how he felt about revenge.

The sledgehammer went into Kayla's trunk. An hour before, driving through the country, looping around the Little Big River, they had already stopped and changed, although the stink on Ray's hands remained. They had dumped their clothes, Ray's old dark blue Pepsi sweatshirt and torn black jeans; then they had tossed the can of kerosene—wiped clean of fingerprints—into a roadside ditch a few miles away from their clothes.

Kayla pulled her car into the driveway behind her building. "Breakfast?" Ray offered.

Kayla smiled. "You buying?"

"Better," Ray answered. "I'm cooking."

She looked pleased, sad. "I'd like a shower first."

"You bet." Ray had to stop thinking too much when he was this tired.

She showered. In her kitchen, he made scrambled eggs, bacon. He nuked two frozen sticky buns: Time, 3, o, Power. Beep, beep, beep, the sticky buns were ready. A big pot of coffee, of course.

"Mmm, coffee," Kayla giggled. She leaned her head into a towel, drying her hair—and there was Jilly in Ray's memory, her robe falling open. Her legs, her nudity. She was laughing. He surprised himself, to remember her laughing. Few of those memories remained.

"Righto," Ray blinked away the image of his ex.

Kayla pulled out a chair, sat. "Righto?"

"Hey. I'm tired, okay?"

"Righto?" Kayla repeated. "Mmm," she bit into a bun.

They ate in silence, hungry. A nerve in Ray's right eyelid decided to twitch. A thumper, Jilly would call it.

Done eating, Kayla looked at Ray: "Can I tell you a story?"

"Sure," Ray said.

She was folding her napkin. "Righto," she exhaled, making fun of him. "A story," Kayla smiled. "Let's see . . . Oh yeah. One Sunday night almost thirty-three years ago, a black woman named Mae was driving home to Brighton from a weekend visit with her sister in Lakecrest. Miss Mae wasn't alone; she had her daughter with her, a toddler. Mae had the music on, the kid was asleep, I think. At the Jefferson overpass, just as Mae approached, she saw a car spin out and ram the guardrail. The sparks must have been something. Then the rail sheared and the car went through. Mae pulled over, of course. The car had landed ten feet or so down, stuck in some small trees or underbrush. The driver must have been incredibly lucky not to have gone a bit further on the road, and then gone off the overpass. . . . Mae could see someone waving."

Kayla took a sip of coffee. "It was raining, of course."

"Course."

Kayla looked up from her cup. Ray watched her check the tone of his voice in his facial expression. He smiled a comforting smile.

"Course," she said, which meant Shut up, Ray. "So the car's not on fire, and no one's really in danger. Mae climbs down the hill and up into the tree and helps the driver unbuckle—a white woman in her thirties, might be drunk but who could tell right away—and then sees a kid in the back, kind of bloody. Who knows, but the kid looks to be hurt badly. Before car seats, right? So maybe the car's shifting, about to fall or something. Whatever. Mae gets the kid—yeah, she decides to move him. She's not very big, but she's always been fit, and she delivers the mail, you know, so she's in shape. Somehow she carries the kid down the tree and back up the slope just as a VW bus arrives, parks behind her on the shoulder, to help too. Mae steps over the guardrail. And she remembers thinking—and she's only said this to me once—that the VW guy should have his lights on, his flashers or something. Then she makes her mistake, and she walks the wrong way around her car—"

"Oh god," said Ray.

Kayla waited. "Before the pickup hit her, she threw the kid onto the hood of her car. Which was weird, you know. The kid was nine, and not small. And I think she must have thrown him backwards, over her shoulder, you know, like how you cup your hands and flip a kid in a swimming pool. Over the shoulder."

"Jesus," Ray breathed.

"Right," said Kayla. "Righto."

"Her back?"

"Both legs, her back, her collarbone. Most of the right side of her face has been rebuilt. Her sinuses are pretty much made of plastic. A coma." Kayla looked clear-eyed.

"That's a terrible story."

"It is. But it's not the end. See, I was three and my dad was in the service. And his white parents wouldn't take their black grandkid, even while Mom was in the hospital for four months. So we stopped talking to them, and then to him. Or maybe to him first. I don't know which."

Ray waited. There was a sticky blob on the table. Sugar? It was a good time not to go get a sponge.

"That's the end, except for Dr. Andy Gates, which I told you already. But he's only one guy and there are other people in this tiny town."

Ray considered what she meant. "Others?"

"It's hard to explain, Ray. It's black folks hurting each other." More silence.

"Your mom saw the pickup coming?"

"She must have." And then Kayla seemed a little surprised, as though the idea were new: "She's never said."

"Awful." He shook his head. His hands didn't know what to do with themselves. "There's been no contact with your dad?"

Kayla looked at him. Her look was her answer.

"Right," Ray agreed. "Course not."

"Your turn," said Kayla. "Got a story? How 'bout the one with the black girl and the white guy, you know, the one where they're Bonnie and Clyde." She giggled as she leaned back from the table, away. She didn't look like she wanted to giggle, but she giggled.

Kayla was good at making that face, the one where her voice or her laugh didn't jibe with what she had just said, or was saying, or thought, or might think. Bonnie and Clyde? Ray considered the comparison, the game. Okay, it was a game they were playing. Ray's turn. "Oh yeah," he smiled. "They drive around the countryside and every once in a while they burn something."

"That's it. A cross burned by a black girl on a white guy's lawn—I mean, Jesus!"

Her mouth was open slightly; she quickly clamped her teeth together. "You're crazy, Uncle Ray."

"What? Me? I am not. And I don't know if I like being 'Uncle Ray.'"

She tilted her head, just a bit. Her earring, a large silver loop, swayed like a swing. Kayla was looking at Ray.

"I . . . ," he tried.

She smiled.

"Um . . ."

Her smile grew.

"Oh hell."

"You're too easy, Uncle Ray. You're just such a pushover." She began to laugh, a small laugh.

"Cut it out. You're fired," Ray said to Kayla.

"I'm what?"

Ray was embarrassed. He looked down; there were his hands. "It's what I say. To myself. Don't you say something to yourself?" He wouldn't sneak a peek at her.

"I do. I say . . . I tell myself to manage. You know, a job thing, like yours. But a mantra, kind of. A pep talk." He had to see her expression: her eyes had widened. Then she blinked quickly, even more serious. "I'm shaking," she said. "See? I'm a little scared, Ray."

"Me too," Ray said. "But it feels different. Good."

CHAPTER 8

Before burning the cross with Kayla, Ray had been doing well all week, if doing well is what one does by healing physically. He had mostly stayed in bed, and begun to resent the unrelenting boredom. One afternoon, he had thrown a jar of jam into the alleyway behind Kayla's apartment, to hear the glass explode. He had little idea why he had done this, truly; it was unlike him. But Ray had found himself suddenly enraged by something on TV, which seemed logical, in an irrational way. Then he had gone out to replace the jam, and returned quickly.

Another time, he had made himself go out for a drink; the night that Kayla went to her accounting class, Ray had visited the bar around the corner. A quick drink, and then he had thought there was a cop lurking in a doorway—so Ray had hurried back to the apartment, after going around the block and making two purposeful wrong turns. He hadn't been followed, he thought.

But then he could have kicked himself. Shaw knew where Ray was. Why did Ray bother trying to shake a cop who might be offering some kind of protection? Stupid.

He had arranged for the leased car to be towed, and to pick up another car next week. The office had called to say that the insurance adjuster would be in touch—Riggs International had always taken out extra coverage, amen—and that they had found his wallet, and would he come get it? He hadn't asked about the groceries in the trunk, and simply assumed they had been discarded. As Kayla had been at work, Mae had brought him to the dealership. The wallet was there, the cards were all there. The photos.

Afterward, he had lunched with Mae, at her house, in a kitchen that could have been the kitchen of his house next door, laid out identically. Ham sandwiches. Pepperidge Farm cookies. Mae and Ray had enjoyed each other's company, quietly. Looking around her kitchen, he had decided he would put his toaster oven in a spot different from where she kept hers, on the far counter, away from the sink. More counter space, that way.

There had been one remarkable exchange with Mae, one that Ray had continued to consider. They had just finished eating. "You know," Ray had offered. "She does seem like an 'April.'"

Mae had laughed. "I know."

Neither had spoken. Then Mae had said softly, "But Lord help me if she couldn't use her brain once in a while."

"Beg your pardon?" Ray had wanted to understand.

Mae had taken her time. "Oh . . . nothing . . . But don't you listen to everything she says. Listen to what she means. She's a good girl."

"Yes, I'm sure—"

"She's just . . . Well, you know how some people itch and some people don't?"

"I think so."

"That's what I mean. She's just itchy." Mae had turned back around, a one-quarter turn away from Ray. "She's just itchy, that's all."

Itchy? The word had made him think of someone out of Dick Tracy, like Mumbles or someone. Kayla did seem uncomfortable; if that's what Mae had been saying, or warning him about, then yes, Ray got the message. He had smiled to himself: what a mom thing to say. "So are you having me to lunch because of her?" Ray had asked.

Mae had turned to look at him again. There had been an awful lot of meaning in her look: squinting and assessing, a sadness that Ray hadn't understood. She hadn't responded further.

He had called Anderson at the plant, to extend the medical leave. Yes, Mr. Rivers had told Anderson that Ray had had an accident—but now Ray was just calling to say that the doctor advised continued bed rest. Yes, Ray would take care of himself, yes, he was staying locally, yes, he thought it would be another ten days before he could return, but he might stop by and pick up some papers, do some work lying down once the headaches abated. Yes, he was more shaken up than he had first realized, you know, a concussion had to be taken seriously. Yes, he was thinking that he'd certainly be back around the Fourth, but if it could be earlier, sure, he'd try. Laughing for no reason. No, he didn't think that the Windy Oaks reorganization would suffer; the techs were in training on the sample comber and winder, and in truth, it would be two weeks before they learned the manuals. So some jobs were still safe, for now, Ray had told himself.

He had called Jilly, to keep the kids away. Their conversation was brisk, Hello, I'm all tied up here, may I talk to Jeannie and Tom? Jilly had been her cool ex-self, once she had determined that he sounded fine.

He wasn't fine, but he hadn't told Jilly that. Had she noticed?

Good-bye. I'll let you know when the situation changes.

He and Kayla had talked whenever they were together, or so it seemed. He had found out about her army career—a few years of ordered discomfort, stuff only to write home about, no combat, some leadership skills, and a government-funded education; and the number of years after, including a time when she did some stuff she didn't like, before moving back to Brighton three years ago. She had been married for eighteen months when she first got out of the service; the guy hadn't even warranted a name, in her retelling. And Ray had told Kayla about his kids, Tommy's being a little kid until recently, Jeannie harder to peg, a teen; and more about his work, of course, as Windy Oaks was on his mind, always there. He usually felt okay about his job, and while the Windy Oaks project would be an enormous challenge, he wasn't thrilled with the prospect of firing so many people, which he hadn't done before, at least not by himself. But the concept of the well-run, modernized and solvent company, and the subsequent benefits reaped by its employees, appealed to Ray, satisfied some sense of making things right. He could make other people's bad decisions for them, and make the same decisions work. His job was one that required skillful foresight. His background, in psych and industrial relations, prepared him well to make these decisions. Plus, he had begun to think of the assignment as a way to measure himself, or measure up to something.

Windy Oaks wouldn't be easy, Ray knew. Nevertheless, he had already begun to trim the most conspicuous excess—the middle management pencil pushers who always seemed to be in the way, like the supervisor at the DMV when you tried to get a license, who insisted that you had misspelled your own name, the person looking over the shoulder of the person trying to do the real work. So the retooling of Windy Oaks had begun. Employee severance had been arranged for the salaried folks about to be displaced; capital had been freed for reinvestment and technology. The shop floor would be safer, when everything was done. But Ray's job was about to include firing a lot of people, soon, and that part of the job, firing good people who weren't helping, continued to trouble him, had always troubled him when he had seen others have to do so, and he had always refused to let it trouble him just as it always had, his actions somehow possible despite contradictions, the emotional conundrum, residual ethics. You're fired.

Windy Oaks could be profitable, a 3 percent yield on the gross would be achieved, because Ray had a personal and professional investment in making it so. Not to mention that streamlining this particular workforce would require only a 32 percent displacement, of which close to 8 percent would constitute golden handshakes, and another 17 percent could be considered immediately reemployable, even if they had to move. Those were damn good figures and facts.

But before Windy Oaks was fixed, Ray had a cross to burn.

My god, Ray thought. It had been his idea and insane and they had done it. Holy shit. Kayla had loved it, Ray could tell. He had done it.

Why did so many enormous life events seem to happen all at once? Ray had no explanations. So what did he have? A dead alcoholic father, a happy mother living in a golf course retirement home and engaged to be married, a dysfunctional sister left of her own New Age center, no religious persuasion of his own, two great kids (one temporarily un-great, her teen years a kind of disease), and a soul the size of a BB pellet.

Ray was more confused than not. Souls probably don't come in sizes, Ray supposed. But with or without a tiny soul, Ray was sure of the changes the past two weeks had wrought: he was acting rather than reacting, burning rather than waiting to be burned. He was being a reckless coward.

Kayla had gone shopping; she was so excited by their lawlessness, she couldn't sleep. Too jangly, she had squeaked. If you go out, leave a note. In his borrowed bed in Kayla's guest room, Ray also felt all his nerve endings, like some sort of sea creature. A captured underwater freak, dumped into an unfamiliar lagoon. He had seen those creatures once before, on his honeymoon in the islands, when Ray and Jilly had taken a glass-bottomed ketch to a reef, and then snorkeled through schools of unreal neon fish and the occasional startlingly knobby monster.

He remembered the day distinctly: the whole experience had been like swimming through someone's mind, like God's mind, if Ray believed, which he didn't. He remembered how Jilly, her hair floating, and with the crooked, exaggerated smile and bubbled eyes of the diver, had seemed like an alien. He could still picture her in the water above him, how she shimmered. Ray remembered thinking that she wasn't there to save him, she was just lost. Then later, back at the hokey bar on the beach, he had heard a cigar-chomping auto exec—from Indianapolis?

How did Ray remember that? Damn—sneer that all the locals stole fish from each other's reefs, so their tourists could gawk at something. Ray had been infuriated: it was supposed to be a wonder, wasn't it? For chrissakes. Leave wonders alone.

Thinking about that day also meant thinking about Jilly's body, later, the specifics of which, even after all these years and not even liking her anymore, he remembered. They both had been so turned on: in the bed, then taking a bath, and then on the balcony. On the balcony. Jilly had insisted that Ray take her outside and hoist her up on the railing, her legs propped and spread on his shoulders. He had licked her, his mouth wide and his tongue flat against her, and she had poured all over his face, until her voice rose to its quiet, rhythmic moan, and then her little "ooh" squeal. Carry me, she had panted afterwards, giggling. I want . . . water. With her bare heels gleefully giddyapping against the sweaty small of his back, as they both began to laugh, Ray had carried her inside to the bedside night table—where she had reached down, grabbed a pitcher of ice water and poured it first on her new husband's head and then on her own. Ahhh! he had roared. I love you, Jilly had roared back.

It occurred to Ray that his emotions felt closer to the surface than usual: this was recovery, he told himself. Post-traumatic stress syndrome, like the vets had. Or maybe not. Because he was thinking about sex with Jilly because he was thinking about Kayla, Ray had to admit. Her body was becoming more important to him, as he had found himself increasingly aware of the nearness of her curves. He chuckled, uneasy: so his dick was confused. Which wasn't possible, of course—because while Ray might be confused, his dick was sure. After all, it had been Kayla who had taken his hand as they drove into the night, the burning cross sizzling in the car's mirrors.

Violence and sex, Ray said to himself. Uncle Ray.

CHAPTER 9

Ray crossed the street at Fifth, two blocks from the center of Brighton. Ahead he could see the light turn red on 17, the main thoroughfare, and the first rows of parking meters that announced the downtown shopping district, a business center crisscrossed by those meters, lines of little municipal men marching in place, good civil servants.

Only two blocks from downtown, Ray was still in a neighborhood. Here on this side of 17, the houses were mostly duplexes with the occasional older single-family home and apartment complex. Maybe Brighton was gray on principle, or seemed so from Kayla's window, but walking in Ohio in the springtime was polychromatic: broad canopies of elms and odd, oak-shaded irregular sidewalks, the concrete buckled from beneath, the driveways tarred, a tricycle temporarily abandoned in Mrs. Somebody's flowers. A few different greens, and purples underneath the shade trees.

The neighborhood wasn't poor, Ray realized as he walked. There were vans parked, one every three or four two-family; a delivery guy home for lunch, a contractor between remodelings. People worked here, Ray thought. They had real jobs. There was that smell, too, the one he remembered. Not sour, not rotten, but close to both. He would ask Kayla.

The cars were mostly American-made. Ray counted: Chevy, Olds, Chevy, Ford truck, Ford truck, Toyota, Ford truck. People with real jobs, working second shift at Windy Oaks, or working in towns twenty miles away, people with union jobs—a union that was anathema to people like Ray and Management, because a union shop would wildcat before people like Ray could get a chance to do their real jobs.

Ray slowly walked south and east, angled toward his leased home, the Hills, the Little Big River—and toward the Windy Oaks shirt factory, a little farther south, cradled in the river's southern spur. He walked McKinley Boulevard past McKinley High and signs for the prom, PAL camp, last week's musical revue ("A Spring Medley from *South Pacific*"); then he turned, and walked away from Brighton Estates, the wealthier part of town, where white money became small-town chauvinism and senseless pride. Now that was a Kayla thought, he realized.

He knew what he was doing, or thought he knew, a survivor opting to survive. Ray had chosen to leave Kayla's apartment, lock the door, and step into the lovely spring afternoon; purposefully, he walked back into the open arms that had welcomed him so viciously to small-town life. Come and get it, Ray thought, teeth ground together, tight. Black and blue, fresh shirt, pocketful of change. Uncle Ray, no one's pal. A cross burner.

He was three blocks from the factory. Here the two-family houses were more run-down; Ray saw another derelict tricycle, but mostly dead cars parked in small fenced yards. He saw black people and white people, older people on porches. The smell was more noticeable: Windy Oaks.

Coming toward him was a young woman pushing an umbrella stroller, heavy plastic bags—canned goods?—dangling from each arm, a toddler in tow. The day was warm, warmer the more Ray walked; the little boy or girl dragged a sweater or a blanket. The kid's face was dirty, orange from something. As she came close enough, Ray spoke: "Um, excuse me. The sweater . . ." Ray gestured.

She looked down at the child. "Oh. Thanks. Can you pick that up, please, Willie?" She smiled over her shoulder, maybe, as she passed. The kid did nothing; the sweater continued to slither along the sidewalk.

Ray crossed again, this time at Belleview. One more street to cross and then a right; two blocks to the factory, and then one step for mankind. It occurred to him that he had meddled with that mom and probably made her feel bad. She had known the sweater was dragging; Ray had only interfered. No one wanted to hear what Ray had to say. He paused at the corner of Corson Boulevard and Highway 17, one hand on the pole of a stop sign, from his vista on a hill in sight of the Windy Oaks factory, where the full parking lot and the factory windows below shone and reflected, all afternoon sunlight and chrome and fresh paint and glass and our daily bread. Brighton was a pretty little town, in its way, an impression he had first had last year, when he had started to visit Windy Oaks and begun his assessments. Back on Main Street the Park Cinema had stayed in business, amazingly, despite the neighboring town's sixplex, at the mall down 21; Binder's Pharmacy continued to be owned and run by a Binder, and even delivered after hours: the air here was breathed the same way it had always been breathed since the 1920s, when the mill had opened; the same air.

But as he stood on the corner—between steps and decisions—Ray knew himself to be more apart from these strangers and their lives, this town, than he had ever been from anyone or anywhere. Ray was standing in his own future, holding theirs, and he was alone.

"Hey." A car was idling alongside, an unmarked car driven by Detective Shaw. "Hey," Shaw repeated. He accelerated and then pulled over, ahead forty feet or so, maybe three car lengths, and idled there, waited for Ray.

Every gesture of Shaw's seemed part of a little game: Ray considered how Shaw had parked, and how Ray was supposed to heed, heel, approach the car.

Ray bent to tie his shoe. Oops, sandals.

Shaw honked. Ray looked up, didn't stand yet. Standing quickly would hurt, Ray thought. When he did look up, Ray saw that the police detective had gotten out of the car, and was leaning against the driver's door, arms crossed, in an official pose from the patrolmen's handbook, SOP, the same pose from their little drive two weeks or so ago to see nothing.

Now, Ray thought. He stood up. He waved. Fortunately, to enter the plant grounds, Ray needed to cross the street. "Gotta go," Ray called. "Late." He moved to cross the street, behind the police car.

"Ray," the detective said, his voice even.

Mr. Stanton, Ray thought. He kept walking.

"Ray!" The detective raised his voice. "Mr. Stanton," he insisted.

That was it, Ray thought. Respect. From a few feet off the curb, standing in the street, he turned back, victorious. "Detective," Ray said. He walked up to the car. Now he saw it clearly, an unmarked police vehicle, complete with all the latest wires and doodads.

"Mr. Stanton. Want a mint?" The cop held out a tin of Altoids.

"Sure," Ray said. "Thanks." The mints were powerful, as advertised. Damn game, Ray thought.

"Got some questions," the detective announced. He was dressed in khakis and a turquoise polo shirt, very golf club. His chin was pointed, his hair predictable, neatly combed, recently cut.

"Shoot," Ray said. Oops. Don't say "shoot" to a cop. He sucked on his mint.

The cop either ignored or missed the humor: "I'm curious . . . ," he said. "Do you know what you're doing?"

Ray's hands were tucked into the back pockets of his jeans. He kept his hands there, considered. " 'Bout what?"

"You know."

Yes, Ray knew. "No . . . can't say I do." Again: " 'Bout what?"

"Now Mr. Stanton," the police detective said. "I'm asking you a general question, to get you to admit something—just like the TV law enforcement officers do, since that's your frame of reference. There are all sorts of crimes in Brighton for which I could charge you. But I thought you might want to take your pick."

Under other circumstances, Detective Shaw's little speech might have been funny; instead, Ray was livid. The rage felt good, in a way, but too physical, somehow—in the jaw, in the hands curling into fists, in the shift of weight onto the left leg, in a narrowing of the gaze. Ray's body was angry, Ray wasn't. So he wasn't sure how to control himself.

"Hmm . . .?" The detective interrupted Ray's furious reverie.

"I don't know what you're talking about." There. A firm denial.

The police officer paused, looked closely at Ray, and then pushed off the car—so quickly and close to Ray as to make him flinch. The cop smiled, but his smile didn't mean that he was happy. He looked to be rolling the last of an Altoid around in his mouth.

"Okay, Ray. That's okay. You don't have to know anything today. It's much too nice a day, isn't it?" The question hung in the air. "Ray . . . I know it's not easy being you right now. But I can help; you'll see," he seemed to say to himself. And then: "Going to work?" Detective Shaw gestured with his detective-ish chin. "I'm sure they missed you." He leaned around Ray, too close, and then, as he opened the back door: "Get in, Ray. I'll drive you down the hill. Make an impression."

"No . . ." Ray's hand was available. "No, thanks," he waved stiffly. That's the last thing Jim Rivers wanted.

"Yes, thanks," Detective Shaw said. "I wasn't asking."

They drove wordlessly down the hill, Ray again in the back-seat. Jesus, Ray thought. For chrissakes, how obvious a signal could the cop send? Protective custody, Jesus. A ride to work.

By Admin, the police car idling loudly in the fire lane, Ray got out, stepped onto the walk.

"Hey," Shaw called, his elbow resting out the window. "I wanna tell you something."

"Mm?" Ray made a noise.

"Just a little-known fact. Got a guy here in town, not so smart a guy. Been in a little trouble, likes his bottom-shelf booze, getting liquored up, and you know, maybe he's headed for lockup some day, probably do hard time eventually. You know the type. But the guy's got a brother nine, ten years older, who's kind of—what is it called—challenged? Yeah, that's it. And the guy takes care of his brother like you wouldn't believe. Loves him, you know? Like a son.

"You got kids, Ray?" The cop waited. Ray didn't answer. "Oh sure you do. Right. A girl, Jeannie, and a boy, Tom. Tommy. And I hear that your mom's marrying a heckuva fellow. Anyway, this guy—his name's Palmer—once beat up a teacher because the teacher said something bad about this big brother."

A woman came out of the building, one of the HR secretaries. "Hi, Mr. Stanton," she said. "Paul," she said to the cop.

"Hi," the cop said.

"Hi," Ray said.

She had gone to the parking lot. Ray didn't speak. Shaw seemed to know everything anyway.

"You know what, Mr. Stanton?" The police detective didn't want an answer. "You should go to work. You're needed in there. You've got a lot of people to make unhappy." But when Ray turned his body, before he could step away, the cop added: "You know what else, Mr. Stanton. That's not a true story, what I just told you. I made it up. I don't even know a guy named Palmer, do you?"

The cop had not mentioned the cross, not once: Detective Shaw knew, of course, but he hadn't said.

As Ray reached Admin, and pulled open the screen, his gaze came to rest on the reddish-brown door. He could see the flames, again. There, without even having to close his eyes. Flames.

More than seven hundred people worked at Windy Oaks, running two shifts. The plant was integrated, which meant that product didn't have to be outsourced—or tossed to Mexico or the Far East, into the boon of NAFTA cheap labor. As usual for this sort of industrial profile, Windy Oaks was top-heavy at the supervisory levels, and packed with wage earners—the hourly folks there for twenty years, from McKinley High to combing cotton, still waving their diplomas, people responsible at the lowest levels for maintaining product flow, the critical path. Ray had seen the scenario, most recently at the Hansen Mills plant in Phillipsburg down south, where to run full bore and retool at the same time had meant holding on to all the wage earners until the last possible second, and then displacing just under 50 percent of the workforce (48 percent, precisely). Bo Jin had been in charge at Hansen Mills, a good man and a good re-engineer, but he hadn't seen it coming: the plant had struck. Then Bo Jin had been stared down at the table, had flinched, and had been made to negotiate with labor, which hadn't even been union. Ultimately, so many people had received golden handshakes at Hansen Mills that Dave Peterson had begun to call Bo Jin "King Midas."

That wouldn't happen here, and not to Ray.

"Afternoon, Mr. Stanton. Good to see you."

"And you, Doris," Ray acknowledged the Admin reception-ist, his feet moving. She would comment about his eye.

"Mr. Stanton?" she called after him. "Sorry about your accident."

The Admin hallways, industrial beige with an ageless, once-orange carpet, had been cut in the 1960s from a retired section of the power plant. As a result, the ceilings were low—not up to safety regs—and the area wasn't hard hat. So the building had to stand apart from the plant, OSHA said.

There were turns to make. His office wasn't easy to reach, which he usually didn't mind. No one in Accounting. Fillipi and his son, Fillipi, must be lunching late. No one in Sales? No, wait. Ray could hear the jangly hum of voices in the conference room, at the long board table that—apocryphally—had had to be cut into pieces to be moved through the narrow halls. What time was it? Damn, he wasn't wearing his watch. He didn't even have his briefcase. And no cell phone. Naked, again.

The smell here was more musty than sour, which meant that the neighborhood smell was probably off-product, Ray realized. Better have someone check Environmentals. Those codes were unforgiving.

One more turn. There. In his office, a square little room dominated by plug-and-play technology—computer, fax, telephone, clock, coffee pot—Ray closed the door, stumbled forward, leaned against the desk. Something fell. He didn't care. He couldn't breathe. He was gulping.

When he pictured the flames, they packed more than his mind's eye. From his jaw, on each side, the flames filled Ray's skull, licking upwards, inside.

Was there a knocking? Someone was there. Ray was gulping for air. Breathe, Ray, he told himself. He calmed himself down by opening his eyes. No flames here. Had the knocking gone away?

His cheek was resting directly on the desktop, right where the blotter had been until, with one of his first Windy Oaks reassessments, Ray had thrown out the absurdly obsolete thing. Folded easily, the cardboard and fake-leather blotter had stuck out conspicuously from the hallway trash can, which had not upset Ray, to be sure. Let them see it, he had concluded.

He had yet to lift his head, but he was breathing. He just wasn't ready to be here. What was he doing? He couldn't imagine— if this were his reaction to his own office—being on the plant floor. He would probably curl into a whimpering, fetal ball, out there. Someday, he knew, Ray would have to choose to do something, go somewhere. The thought made him smile. Better, he said to himself.

What had the cop said? It was hard to be Ray these days, or something like that. Go away, he told anyone, even though the knocking—had there been knocking, or was that Ray's heart?— had apparently stopped. Ray was still hugging his desk, his heart thumping, and the flames ... there was a connection between the flames and his heart thumping. If he could only think, he would be able to figure it out. He should go somewhere else. Not back to the apartment yet. Somewhere to be alone in public, in a crowd. Ray wasn't ready to be here. Which here? Windy Oaks? Brighton? Ray didn't know, but facedown on his desk sure wasn't anywhere.

CHAPTER 10

At approximately 5:45 in the afternoon on a Friday, the T.L.C. Family Restaurant on Main Street—a fifteen-minute walk from the plant, Bye, Doris, have a good weekend—bustled, thick with burgers and BLTs and mismatched sections of *USA Today.* "Special, side of toast," yelled a young waitress, as she pulled a bill from an apron pocket, her body moving in two directions at once. "Hi," she said to Ray. "Anywhere's fine." She slipped a pen into her hair as she rang a check. "Nine-seventy-three-nice-day-don't-you-think," she rattled off—and even before she had taken the ten from her customer, the register had delivered its change down a slide into a well-worn cup.

Ray had eaten here before, it hadn't been terrible, and he had come again tonight, on purpose, to exorcise something he was just beginning to understand, some element of his feelings that demanded action, even if that action consisted of merely sitting some place in public. Or burning a cross with Kayla.

He was sweaty. He could sit anywhere, just like anyone. On a red leatherette stool at the marbled Formica counter, Ray squeezed between a guy in cutoffs and a guy in cowboy boots and a blue suit. "Excuse me," Ray said to either of them, or both, easing his way. "Sure," he said to the offer of coffee from a guy in short-order whites. "Please," Ray added.

Kayla was shopping, Ray reminded himself. He'd catch up with her later: he had left a note. GOT YA, his note hadn't said. Earlier, he had been fantasizing about her, which wasn't difficult to recall.

From his stool at the counter, Ray watched the T.L.C. TV. One television station covered local and regional news that included Brighton; two news anchors, a sports guy, and a weather girl. One roving reporter, fresh out of a Dunkin' Donuts apron, still smelling of powdered sugar, her prom corsage barely dry between the pages of her yearbook. Miss Most Likely to Succeed, the daughter of the Buick dealer. The niece of some guy in middle management at Windy Oaks, some sixteen-year, veteran pencil pusher sure to be let go by Ray. She covered the stockyards, the Strawberry Days Festival, a human interest story about the church bazaar, the canned goods drive to aid victims of the spring floods. Ray liked to think that he could tell whenever she drifted from her script, but in truth, she might always be that way. Brunette, blue-eyed, smiling and unfocused. She would be the one to cover the story, Ray imagined. It probably wouldn't merit more. *Action News* headlines on Channel 6 mostly featured sound bites on violent weather, high school no-hitters, and urban crime, of which only the sports managed to be more than a network feed. She might be the one who covered the layoffs at the plant, the one who started to cry on camera.

The cook filled a ceramic cup, wiped the counter and then tossed a rolled setup on a paper placemat; almost as though in response, coffee splashed onto the saucer when he set down the cup.

Ray felt himself to be hiding. He toyed with the little tab from someone else's emptied half-and-half, and all the while Ray's head was lowered, eyes averted. He was incognito—but as what? He couldn't pretend to be anything or anyone, since most of these people might know him, or at least might have heard of him. But Ray hadn't even looked the hostess in the eye; he had chosen to stare down the cash register instead. This wouldn't do. Ray was scared to be sitting at this fucking stupid little counter, as though someone might come along and beat him again, here, in public.

Ray looked up, catching his own glance in the mirror, framed by the Marnis milk dispenser and a wire rack of single-portion

Post cereals, guilty of nothing but so guilty all the same. He looked like a criminal: for once, looks might not deceive. He read the milk dispenser again. Marnis.

"Ready, sir?"

She was a black lady in her fifties, her hair smeared some awful coppery brown. He hadn't noticed her before; he was glad to see her now. Ray closed his menu. "You bet. I'd like—"

"Oh hi, Mister, um, what was it again? I met you . . . now where was that?" She smiled. "I believe I've lost my mind. You're that new fellow, aren't you? At the plant . . .?"

Oh god, he thought. Oh no, oh god. Ray either didn't remember her—Gladys, Your Waitress, her nametag said—or he was too flustered to think clearly. But she knew him. Oh god.

"C'mon, help me out here, Mister! You're someone I've seen."

"Ray," he said, as he extended his hand. "Stanton?"

"Nope! That's not it!" She laughed as she shook his hand, and all of her seemed to shake too. "I mean, you're someone all right. That's you probably. Oh diddles," she said. "What'll it be, Roy?"

"Ray," he corrected her.

"Ray! That's it!" She chewed the corner of her lower lip. She paused. She had lipstick on her teeth. Someone should tell her. "So what'll it be today?"

"Um, I'd like the country-fried steak—"

"Fries or baked?"

"Baked."

"Red, white, or blue?"

"Sorry?"

Gladys laughed. "Oh shoot, Ray-Roy! You have to choose a color. This is America, and the Fourth of July's coming before you know."

"Why?" Ray asked. And then he gave in: "Blue," Ray said. "Definitely. Blue."

Gladys laughed again. "Steak, baked," she hollered into the open service window. She winked at him: "Blue!" she yelled.

"Blue!" Came a response from the back.

"Blue!" yelled the short-order cook.

For chrissakes. Ray reminded himself to breathe. Ray made himself smile at no one. He, the smiling guy sitting right here at the T.L.C. diner, had burned a cross on Jimmy Palmer's lawn. *Fooh!*

Jimmy Palmer did or didn't have a big brother.

When the waitress returned, Ray asked her to turn up the sound. News at six o'clock on 6. No problem. From a jukebox across the T.L.C., Burton Cummings bellowed *I got, got, got no time*—which probably meant that Ray wouldn't be able to hear the news. He edged closer. The anchorman appeared. The Guess Who continued to blather on, drowning out the news.

Ray almost panicked: there was the burning cross. The TV people must have arrived quickly, since the footage had captured the cross still burning. Or maybe the scene was shot by a neighbor, Ray couldn't tell by the quality of the image— or maybe they had reignited the sucker, to get it all on tape, live at six. He wasn't going to hear unless the volume was turned up.

The two waitresses stopped talking. They were watching. Gladys shook her head. "Ugh," she said. Then she elbowed the other lightly: "Will you look at that."

"Tt, tt." The younger woman shook her head, the noise between her tongue and her teeth.

"Some people," Ray offered. "You'd think they would've learned."

"Wouldn't you," said Gladys.

"Was that here?" asked the second woman.

"Think so," said the guy in the boots, next to Ray. The younger waitress turned away, her pen above her right ear. She had a mole above her lip.

Gladys said, "As if—"

"Tt, tt, tt," said her friend, her back to the TV.

"I'd kick their ass," said the guy in the boots. And then: "Pardon me, ladies."

Gladys turned up the sound. ". . . investigating," said the TV anchorman. "In other news—"

Gladys turned the sound back down.

"Tt, tt, tt," said the other waitress, drifting away.

"—like we didn't fight the Civil War." Gladys finished her sentence. Ray hadn't understood, or heard, the beginning of what she had said.

Until his dinner arrived, Ray thought about nothing: nothing, nothing, nothing, nothing, he thought, as slowly as he could, focused on nothing. No flames, no wars. Then he tried to read the Entertainment section of the paper; Ray stared at page C1 for too long, then turned to C2.

"Here's the blue," Gladys had said when she delivered his meal—and there, wrapped in blue foil, was his dinner roll. In plenty of time for the Fourth of July. Oh good, a holiday. Ray picked up his silverware, and began to eat the gluey meat.

"Twins, you know," said the guy in the boots, in the middle of a conversation.

"No!"

"One's bigger by half—"

"Gonna watch the game?" That must have been the cook. Ray peered to his left: yes, the cook, elbows on the countertop. The country-fried steak was terrible; it even tasted a little off, maybe.

"Damn."

"Boys. . . ." Gladys zipped by, her reprimand neatly delivered. For swearing?

"You'd say so too, if you'd been there."

"If it ain't tonight, there go the states."

"Damn."

"Gladys? More water, please." Ray tapped the rim of his glass; he'd try to drown his dinner.

"Sure thing, honey."

"Ray, is it?" The fellow in the suit and boots spun Ray's way. "Name's Hank. Hank Williams. Like the singer, only I can't." They shook hands, hard. "What brings you, Ray?"

Oh god, Ray thought. Here we go. "Well, it's a long story . . ."

"That must have been some nasty shiner. You woulda looked like one of the Flintstones—"

Gladys laughed, as she cruised by again.

"Like Barney. You know. In that one where Fred pegs Barney with the Bronco-saurus burger! And then Barney won't talk to Fred. . . ."

This time the guy on Ray's left, in a denim shirt and a loud tie, laughed. "Thanks, Hank," Denim Shirt added.

When had he replaced the guy in cutoffs? And why was he thanking Hank?

Hank rocked back a bit on his stool. "You in sales, Ray?"

Ray's lie, when it came, felt good. "I am."

"So what do you sell?"

"Insurance."

"I got me some of that. In case of a terrorist attack." He elbowed Ray.

"You're Stanton." Denim Shirt was talking. Oh god, oh god, oh god, oh god.

Ray spun slowly to face this neighbor. "I am."

"You're not in insurance. You're the guy at the plant."

"Well . . . sort of. That's me, anyway," Ray said. And then to his other neighbor, Hank whatever, and trying to guess right: "From the Puzzle Palace."

"Say, Ray," smiled Denim Shirt. "Did your friends catch up with you?"

With a chuck of his chin, Denim Shirt indicated a booth in the back. Four people were there, a woman, two little kids, and—oh god—one of the punks. One of them. Not Palmer himself, but the big kid, the other one, dabbing his mouth with a napkin. The one who had punched Ray in the eye.

The punk looked up: he waved.

CHAPTER 11

Once he had finished vomiting into the T.L.C. Family Restaurant toilet, patting his forehead with cool water, drying off, and then blowing his nose with a wad of t.p., Ray examined his face in the bathroom mirror. Gut check. His bruise had lightened to a combination of faded violet and myrtle, with light yellowish-green rings down the cheekbone; his hair a little ragged, his face clean shaven. His eyes looked kind of wild, or a little tired. But then, just for a moment, for a squirt of a second, Ray had thought he was looking at someone else. Someone else's face, with the occasional single, tough white hair sprouting at the sideburns, through the brown; someone else's watery eyes, someone else's problems. Who? It was a sensation he had experienced before, especially when too little sleep or the early stages of flu flattened his gaze, but never to this extreme. Who's that guy in the mirror?

Fear had turned his stomach inside out. After the punk had waved, Ray had felt the bile rise and mumbled an excuse, clumping down the narrow stairs to the john—just in time, as the sour mess spewed powerfully into the toilet, the lid mercifully left up. He looked again at the tiny mirror. Nothing but Ray. He stepped back into the hallway, flipping off the light but leaving the exhaust chugging.

"Hey. Y'all okay?"

It was Hank Williams. "Yeah," Ray lied.

"Toss your fries?"

"Mm."

"Tough night?"

"You could say that." Ray sat heavily in a broken cane chair underneath a pay phone. He sighed. Sitting was good. But don't order the country-fried steak, he thought.

"Boy. Potatoes do me in on that kind of stomach."

"Mm." He gulped a little, and then again. On the wall, in red, someone had written Lucy Goosey. And a phone number.

"You'd have thought the guy in the corner said something . . ." Hank continued: "You'd have thought there was something to say. That fellow in the booth knew you."

"I don't know what you mean." Ray looked up at Hank Williams. The guy leaned against the banister, one dumb hick, suit and boots and all, as he blocked the hallway. "Unless you mean to tell me," Ray added.

"Oh. Yeah. What's it about?"

The guy was fishing; he didn't know anything. "You tell me," Ray said.

"Well . . ." The word seemed to drag a smile across his face. "Could be some fellows were looking for you."

Ray waited. The guy was probably a fool. Let a fool talk, Dad liked to say.

"Could be you need looking for," Hank drawled.

What did that mean? The guy knew shit, and Ray wasn't in the mood to wait: "Could be a guy's got a big, fucking nose for someone else's business."

"Hey! I didn't . . ."

"Right." And then, as Ray stood up, close enough to spit his consonants, an inch or so taller than Hank-in-boots, too close, smelling his own breath and Hank's Old Spice instead of Altoids, and trying not to gag, Ray added: "Get the fuck out of my way."

They stared at each other: Hank straightened, thought about it, thought again, then slid his heels backward to let Ray pass. Ray could almost see each of Hank's tiny thoughts flicker across his face. Ray's heart had stopped. "You saying something, Hank?"

The man shook his head.

"That's right. You're not. Nothing. Sayonara," Ray fairly spat.

Hank had been bluffing and Ray had bluffed back, but even as he left his tip, paid his bill, and stepped back onto the busy sidewalk, the adrenaline continued to roar in Ray's ears. The punk had apparently left—but would he be waiting for Ray? Fuck the punk and the horse he rode in on. Horse, you're fired.

The sun shone brilliantly, never-ending. Fuck the day. Ray trudged forward, always forward, aware without being mindful of the glances of passersby. He moved from object to object, seeking cover. He leaned against a parking meter, pushed on, then against another meter. Another. So that's what parking meters were for, to lean on, in case of country-fried steak. Be calm, Ray-Roy.

"Hey, watch—"

He had walked right into someone, bam, kicked her in the shin.

"Ow, ow, ow, ow, ow."

"Um, sorry," Ray said. Her hand was on his shoulder. She was a frosted blond. She was hopping a bit. Ray was nauseous again.

"Bud!"

Without lifting his head, Ray looked sideways. Hank.

"You!" From thirty or so feet away, as he jogged toward Ray, Hank waved. "Glad I got ya."

Ray said nothing: nothing was all. GOT YA, he thought.

"Hey, bud. Ma'am."

The blond glared at Hank. "Hi, Hank."

"Ma'am?" And then Hank knew her. "Hey. Hi." Hank didn't know her name.

"Sorry," Ray said to her. She was angry.

"That's all right," she said. "Could have happened to anyone." She looked at Ray. "You're . . ."

He was dizzy. He blinked. He was going down. What the—

"Easy, buddy," Hank said. "I've got him," Hank told the woman.

"He doesn't look too good."

"Oh him? He's always this ugly," Hank laughed.

Shit, Ray thought, his head swimming. He leaned against a meter.

After making sure that Ray was okay, or asking at least, the woman left. It all seemed wrong, like everything else in this damn town: he kicks her, and she has to take care of him. Jesus. Welcome to Brighton.

"Sorry about that, back there. If I'd have known . . ." Hank shoved his hand toward Ray. "No hard feelings?"

Slowly, propped up by the ticking meter, twenty meter minutes left in units of five, but six o'clock come and gone, Ray reached forward and shook Hank's hand. Be gentle, Hank.

"Okay." Hank smiled. "Okay!" Hank said.

His inner ear pounding, all Ray could do was squint.

"Where y'all headed? You look a little shaky on your sticks. Got a car? Need a ride? How about I give you a lift?"

Ray wanted to say no: "Fine," he whispered, nauseous again.

"Okay!" Hank's grip was firm, Ray's left elbow in Hank's small palm. "I'm over here just a little."

"I . . ."

"Now don't you talk. You save it."

Ray nodded. He didn't want to need a ride.

"And don't you mind what I say." Hank's tone became serious as he aimed Ray left at the corner, gently, by the elbow. "It's not so often a guy's as talkative as me, I know, or so nosy. Matter of fact, I'm sure if you asked folks, they'd say, 'That Hank sure can go on' and then they'd say, 'That Hank sure is nosy' or whatever, but it probably wouldn't be nearly that polite, seeing how people don't take much to a guy being talkative and nosy, if you know what I mean, but if I was a girl—"

"Hank," Ray breathed.

"Pardon?"

Ray stopped. What he wanted to say needed a smile that Hank could see. "Please shut up."

"Oh, sure! Sure thing! I was going to! Don't you kick me, now, too."

"Thanks." He bent over again; something down there didn't feel right.

"I'm just past the dry cleaner's . . ."

The passenger door of the pickup unlocked, with a helping hand up and a foot on a running board, Ray launched himself into the cab of Hank Williams's truck, a Ford or a Chevy or whatever. Maps and catalogues littered the seat, but Ray didn't care, he had to rest. He hadn't felt this bad since . . .

Some sort of tiny compass or gyroscope, mounted on the dash, rocked gently in its plastic holder. It would be good not to stare at that, Ray realized. Don't look, he told himself, as the blurry white letters or numbers spun. Whoa.

"You okay?" Hank had climbed in, started the engine, and turned to check over his shoulder. "Seatbelt," he instructed Ray.

"Mm."

"You want to go somewhere? The hospital?"

"Been there," whispered Ray.

"Done that," added Hank, smiling quickly.

"I'm not far. East Bine," Ray said. And in that moment, he had made another decision. Ray was done staying with Kayla. He would go make his leased home his home. East Bine. Uh-oh, he gulped. Country-fried steak.

"Cool," said Hank. "Let's get you to the ranch and the señora and throw you in bed and let her—hell, that's not what I mean—"

"Thanks." Ray's head felt like a brick. Whoa, again. "And I'm sorry about the diner. I didn't—"

"Hey!" Hank waved his hand, then laid into his horn: somewhere very close, a car honked back. "Hoosier!"

"Really," Ray closed his eyes.

"Shit," Hank said. "Happens all the time."

The truck jerked. Ray's fingers began to whiten at the knuckles as he gripped the armrest tighter. The truck jerked again, and another horn sounded. Fuck. Hank couldn't drive. But if a man's going to die, he might as well watch. Ray opened his eyes again.

"Sorry," Hank said, as he mostly blew a stop sign. "Tranny needs work."

There was another pickup and—"Look out!" Ray yelled.

"Dang," Hank huffed. "You're tense."

The compass spun, Hank rode the clutch. Ray tried not to grind his teeth. "This left."

"Here?"

"Mm."

The next one-half block went by uneventfully. Unbelievable, thought Ray. "That one. With the trim," Ray pointed.

"Here we go. . . ."

Hank pulled into Ray's drive, the truck sagging low and hard on tormented struts. Ray hadn't had the time to vomit again, given how quickly the blocks had passed, and how terrifyingly. "Thanks," he said. "Heaps."

"Oh, sure."

They looked at each other. "You know—" Ray started to say something, stopped.

"I didn't—"

Hank laughed.

"Thanks again." Ray reached across his body to shake Hank's hand.

"You're welcome."

"See you," said Ray.

"Sure," said Hank.

Ray began to ease his way down from the cab, sliding along his backside.

"Say Roy—" Hank leaned over. "Catch a beer? I mean, not now, of course. Maybe later? After?"

Ray didn't know what to say. After what? Did the fucking guy know he was fucking insane?

"I feel I owe you."

So that was it. With one hand on the door handle, and another propping up the rest of his body, Ray rested. "Okay," he said. "Later. If I'm standing," which wasn't the plan.

Hank's smile was too bright to watch. "Great! Let's go to Dooley's. Say, eight?"

Dooley's? Dooley's, Dooley's, Dooley's, Dooley's, he muttered, to mutter something.

"Eight?" Hank asked again.

"Yeah, sure—"

"I'll pick you up—"

"No, no, no. That's all right. I'll meet you."

Hank laughed. "You like my driving, huh? Everybody does," he laughed again. "Eight, then. And if you don't make it, don't worry. I'm there most nights."

"Fine."

"Fine."

Ray wanted to leave; would Hank ever let anyone leave? "Eight, then." He shut the door, and steered himself up the walk. Next door, Mae waved from her living room window. A little wave. Ray tried a smile. Forward, march. Hank hit his horn, twice, two blasts that rang through Ray.

Another good-bye, Ray thought. Nothing like a good sick to get a guy all messy; Ray should know. But he felt worse than sick—guilty. Guilty and dizzy. All his feelings were more than one feeling, physical and confused. Scared.

Without turning around, Ray waved back, over a shoulder, almost: then, with careful movements, carefully, carefully, he unlocked his front door, stepped inside the house, and sank down onto the cool checkered tile of the vestibule, his stomach gurgling, his legs shaking. A friend, Ray thought. Another goddamn friend.

Something seemed to be hammering in Ray's head, behind his left ear. If only he could move faster, he could run away, his steps in time to the rhythm of the hammering.

CHAPTER 12

Days and nights and days and nights, and only Ray to speak to Ray. He was in his house, alone, hiding and reading the paper and watching TV, the cross still burning. He might have described himself as happy, so long as no one asked. He was feeling better, he liked to think.

Kayla and he had talked twice each day. You're staying there? For security purposes, he had told her, which might have been the truth. Okay, she had said, not believing him. I'll bring over your stuff. She had done so; their conversation at his front door had been awkward. Ray had been careful not to step too close. He had missed talking to her, he had told himself.

He had called his kids, chatted with Jeannie, a better conversation. She was pleased with a poster she had hung over her bed, sooooo cooooollll, another generic boy toy. When did she start liking boys? Ray couldn't really remember; she had always seemed ready. Tommy had been out, at a sleepover.

He had called Fran, his sister, left a message.

At one point, hanging up the phone, he had thought that he was calling everyone, and saying good-bye. Nah, he thought. That's just ridiculous.

Tonight, Kayla planned to drop by her mom's after nine; she had called Ray from the King's Plate, just after the lunch rush, to see if he might be available. He was available: knock, knock, knock, Ray knocked on Mae's screen door, knowing that he had done this before, knocking on her door after dark. He felt ashamed.

"Coming . . ." She smiled as she dried her hands on a dish-towel. "Come in, come in."

"Thanks."

Mae was wearing the pink tracksuit again, the one she had worn years ago, that night. "Coffee? I've just put a pot up."

"Please," Ray said.

"Help yourself," Mae said, as she poured cream into her mug. "Sugar's in the bowl."

Ray didn't want coffee, and something was wrong: she would never let Ray help himself, not Mrs. Reeves in Mrs. Mae Reeves's kitchen. Plus she was humming, and it sounded wrong.

"Now where's that child?" Mae looked at the clock. She didn't look at Ray. She looked at the clock as though the time might change if she looked hard enough. "She's stopping by after work," Mae told the clock. Mae hummed something tuneless. "Oh heavens!" she piped.

"Mae . . . ?"

"Yes?"

"Mae . . . can we have this conversation aloud?"

"Oh my," said Mae Reeves. "Well. It's just that I received a card. A disturbing card." She reached into the pocket of her sweats. "He wants to see me. On his next leave."

Ray studied the postcard. Brandenburg Tor, an old photo. But the troops were long gone from Berlin. The card was signed "William," the signature careful. "Do you want to see him?"

"That's just it," Mae said.

"What?" Ray asked. He handed the card back to Mae.

"I've never seen him. I mean, I've seen him. . . ."

"Oh," said Ray.

"It's Jack's brother, William. Jack's twin. Little April's Uncle Bill. Her real uncle," Mae added as she widened her eyes meaningfully at Ray.

So Kayla had called him "Uncle Ray" to Mae. "And?" Ray asked, not following.

"And he and I have written for years, so that I could keep track of Jackie—"

"Kayla's father?"

"Right. But it would be like seeing a dead person. They're twins . . ."

"So don't see him."

"Oh," Mae sighed. "But he's awfully sweet."

"So see him."

"There." Mae patted Ray's shoulder as she stepped to the table. "I knew you'd understand."

"Any time," Ray chuckled. Then Ray asked, "Mae? Are you feeling all right? Is something else the matter?"

She didn't turn, but met his gaze sidelong. "I'm sure I . . . it's probably the medication. For my back," she said. "I'm not supposed to drive," she giggled.

"I see," said Ray. "You're doped."

"Doped?" squeaked Mae. "Well I suppose I am. I'm doped." She giggled again. "I only took the pills."

"Ah," Ray said.

"When I do too much, the scar tissue becomes a problem—"

"Ouch," Ray said.

"I beg your pardon?" Mae hadn't heard.

"That sounds painful."

"Yes," Mae agreed. "It does. It's my lumbosacrum." She sipped. "Don't you just love a good cup of coffee? This is Maxwell House. Or maybe it's Brim."

Ray smiled. Was Brim still available?

"Are you laughing at me, Mr. Stanton?"

"Oh no," Ray answered, still smiling.

"The medicine makes me a little light-headed. . . ." Mae eased herself into a chair, lowering her body as though something might break; even though she didn't wince, Ray could see the pain.

He had risen from his seat, halfway: "Can I get you anything?"

"No, no, I'm fine. . . . Well, if you don't mind . . . there's a neck pillow upstairs. I forgot to bring it down. On my bed. It looks like a bridge."

"A bridge?"

"You know, like this." She laced her fingers together and curled her arms into a painful hoop. "Mh," she grimaced, her teeth gritted. "If it's not on the bed it's on the recliner."

"No problem."

"You know, you . . . oh never mind."

Ray walked through the living room, where the TV blared with the canned laughter from some replacement sitcom, too loud, of course. Mae must have taken a whopper of a painkiller—and even still, she seemed to be in agony. Ray went to get her pillow, pausing only to peek at the family photos in the upstairs hallway, photos similar to Kayla's, two sets of prints with every roll.

There. Mae with Jack. He had been a good-looking guy. Funny how knowing the name somehow changed Ray's sense of things; of the photo, the relationship, the past. Jack Reeves, the neighbor's ex. Mae Reeves, Kayla Reeves. White, black, and Kayla. And Jimmy Palmer, on whose lawn Ray had burned a cross, on purpose, with his accomplice, a young black woman. What the hell.

No, that wasn't right. Jimmy Palmer wouldn't be in any of these photos.

Another shot of Kayla; Ray found himself looking more closely. She might have been in her midtwenties in the picture, maybe after the service. She was wearing a skirt, nice and short, and a kind of wide-brimmed hat. A formal photo, with a lot of leg. Nice.

Uh-oh. He was keeping Mae waiting. Not nice.

When he returned with the neck pillow, Mae was still in her chair. Her face turned toward the light as Ray came into the kitchen; her eyes seemed glassy and dazed, wet and dry, somehow. "I think I'm stuck," she giggled, a little embarrassed. "I'd like to stand up when Kayla. . . . To be standing—"

"You got it," Ray said. He put the pillow on the counter, stepped behind Mae, and eased her up, his hands underneath her arms.

"Whew," she sighed.

"Where do you want the pillow?"

"Oh," Mae gave a nonanswer and a tiny flick of her hand. "Have you ever noticed how much someone weighs when they can't move?"

"Yes," Ray smiled.

"It's remarkable, isn't it?"

"I suppose—"

"And all those bodies that detectives and murderers have to haul around just weigh so much, you'd think that once someone's been murdered they'd be left there." She pursed her lips. "Hiding a body must be hard."

There was a flyer on the table: Dollar Days at ValuLand. Deep discounts. Maybe he didn't need the pills to think like Mae—maybe he just needed to be rolled from a pickup, and then all of his nice and orderly thoughts would go to hell.

"How much is your head supposed to weigh? Isn't it some enormous percentage of the body's total weight?" Mae touched her hand to her hair. "Oh dear," she said. "I'm babbling."

"That's fine." Ray made himself chuckle. "Now, Mrs. Reeves, I'm going to ask you your PIN. And then I'd like you to sign all your checks over to me."

"Don't be silly," Mae said. "Just hand me that cup."

Ray did.

"I hope you don't mind decaf," Mae said. "Caffeine . . ." She smiled at Ray, helplessly.

"Right. Not a good idea."

"Uh-uh."

"Right," Ray said. There was no need to tell Mae that he didn't care for a cup right now. Was he being patient? He thought so: he was learning new types of patience, one of which was doing nothing, choosing a lack of action. Waiting as action. He guessed it was Zen or something.

By the time Kayla arrived at twenty minutes after nine, Mae's demeanor had changed from giggly to slightly sad, then contemplative, then sad again. She would make some sense, and then none. Whatever she was on seemed to inspire tiny mood swings as well as clusters of non sequiturs. But the pain never went away.

"Momma?"

"Yes, dear."

"You're not feeling too well, are you?" It had taken Kayla five seconds to notice. Maybe the pillow on the counter gave Mae away. "Did you take a pill?"

"Mm."

Kayla looked at Ray. "How many?"

"Two," Mae answered just as Ray shrugged.

"Oh," Kayla rolled her eyes slightly. Her earrings tinkled, chandelier-style silver earrings.

"Your mom's been interesting—"

"I bet."

"I'm interesting," Mae said. And then: "I think I should probably go to bed. Will you come with me?"

"Good idea," Kayla agreed, taking her mother's arm. "Will you excuse us? I'm gonna help her upstairs."

"Of course," said Ray. "Goodnight. . . ."

"Goodnight, Ray." Mae smiled weakly. "Sorry," she added. And then to her daughter: "You know, it's not so bad. . . ."

It didn't take long. Upon her return, Kayla seconded Mae's apology. "Momma's not feeling well," Kayla explained. "She's not so smart about the pain, sometimes. She waits too long, and then she takes too much."

Ray nodded his head. He understood.

She razzed her lips, to no one.

"She's okay though?"

"Oh yeah," Kayla answered. "In a day or two she'll be okay. If you call a 'chronic disability' okay, or a metal bar in your back, welded to your spine." She razzed her lips again, blowing out tension. "I'd love a drink," she said, as she glanced down at her blouse, where some sort of mustard stain seemed to be pooled above her left breast. "You wanna drink?"

"Sure," Ray sighed.

"Gin all right?"

"It's good. Will she sleep?"

"Hard. But the headache tomorrow'll be bad. The drugs give her a hangover."

"Poor thing," said Ray, sounding like his own mom. Mom's getting married, Ray thought. Cool. Phone home, E.T., thought Ray.

Kayla slopped two fingers of gin each into a pair of rock glasses. Ice cubes. "Tonic?"

"Please."

"How about the sunroom?"

"That'd be nice," Ray answered.

Once there, in Mae's solarium, Kayla wedged off her shoes, unbuttoned the collar of her shirt, and flopped herself onto a chaise lounge, its vinyl pink-and-gray slats sure to stick to bare skin, if you were in shorts. Ray chose a wicker chair, his drink on a cork coaster. Kayla and Ray drank, quietly; a leaf clicked and fluttered off a ficus. Ray turned to look at the plant. Dollar Days at ValuLand, he told himself, for no reason.

Kayla was looking at him. "How come you moved?"

Ray had expected her to ask: "Dunno, really."

"They know you're here."

"Yep."

"You're more scared of me than of Palmer," Kayla announced with a smile.

Ray said nothing. He didn't think she was right.

"I used to drink gin all the time," Kayla said. "And then I got sick on it, and then I stopped liking it. And now I like it again."

"Juniper berries," Ray said.

"That's right."

They both fell silent again. No one needed to talk. Ray finished his drink.

"So how was your day? Anything interesting happen?" She was back, revitalized. "Who's the guy outside?"

"What guy?"

"Big. Farm boy, crew cut, you know . . . Oh my god!" Kayla squealed. "I know who he is! He must've just gotten out. . . ."

"What?"

"It must be Harold. And he must have just gotten out."

"What the—?"

"You know." Kayla's jaw was set firmly. "From the Big House." She scratched her cheek with her right index finger, some sort of knowing gesture, shhh, let's keep this a secret.

"You're kidding. From the Big House . . ." Ray couldn't finish the thought.

The silence made Ray gulp. Ray's breathing wasn't right. The Big House. Silence filled with fear. She looked at him. She was scowling. Then, almost without changing her expression, Kayla began to laugh. "You're too much," Kayla squeaked. Her earrings clinked as she shook her head.

"I am—?"

"The Big House," Kayla squealed.

"Right. I get it. Push the button."

"Tee hee," she said. "Tee hee, Uncle Ray."

"Tee hee. Uncle Ray's button." Ray had worked his cocktail napkin into an anxiety-cruller. Twist, twist.

"Sorry," Kayla batted her eyelashes at him. "Well, not really," she tittered. "I've missed you; you're such an easy mark."

"Very funny. So who's Harold?"

"Don't know," Kayla answered. "Some name for some white jerk."

"Right," said Ray. "Another white jerk."

"Now c'mon, Ray-man. Don't be like that."

"Fine," Ray said. He didn't like her little trick. "Look, I don't know what I feel about all this. I mean, shit, I'm in the middle of some race war, which . . . I don't know . . . it's become personal." He lifted his gaze, met hers. "You fight your own goddamn battle with your own goddamn father."

"Fuck you," she blazed.

"You wish."

They stared at each other. Furious. Kayla started to cry. "There's no reason for you to say that." She might have been crying, but her voice was steady. No quivers. So she wasn't crying. He didn't know how to read Kayla's reactions, or her emotions. But she had said that she missed him, which he appreciated.

"Okay. I'm sorry."

"You're not."

"I am," Ray said, and he was.

Kayla seemed sad. Her face was grim. "Look, Ray. Don't take swipes at me because you've been bad and you don't know what it feels like. Or because you panicked and moved back here, where of course it's soooo safe. . . . Oh, Christ. Make me another drink," she said.

On the way back to the kitchen, it occurred again to Ray that maybe she had actually started to cry. Smoke or fire? He mixed them each another drink. He had gone too far, but she was tough, that one. She was tougher than Mae knew. Trouble. In the army, a lieutenant or something, her uniform wrapped in dry cleaner's plastic in a hall closet. She wouldn't take his wishy-washy panicked bullshit. Neither would he, Ray thought. Enough.

When he returned to the solarium, Kayla was misting a flat of seedlings, parsley and something else. *Ffft.* He liked this room; he liked seeing it lit up from his empty house next door, and he liked being here. *Fffft.*

"You think you know," she said, her back to him.

"No. I don't know . . ."

Ffft. She put down the mister, turned and accepted her g-and-t. "You could be right just like you could be wrong."

What did that mean? Ray sipped his drink.

"I like men," she said.

"I know," Ray said. "I mean I thought so." What?

"Fine," Kayla narrowed her eyes at him. "Sit down, hero." There was a pinch of respect in her voice. Ray sat. She had called him a hero, but she probably hadn't meant it. "I'm not some neat little equation you plug into your Human Resources computer: bad dad, plus the history of slavery, equals hatred of whites, and a confused biracial chick. I'm not an equation."

"I didn't think you were," Ray lied.

Kayla thought for a moment. Her skin shone in the wash from a fluorescent Gro-Lite. "Now what are you going to do? Here?" She meant at his house.

"I . . ." Ray didn't know. He thought for a while. "Palmer knows who I am, where I live. But I've got to live somewhere, no matter what that punk knows."

"Punk? That's a word . . . " With her free hand, Kayla smoothed her hair, smooth already. "Maybe it doesn't matter," she acknowledged, nodded. "But asking for it, putting out a sign . . . you're smarter than this," Kayla said.

"Maybe I used to be," Ray admitted.

They sipped their drinks. His was working fine.

"Bad childhood? Trouble at home?" Kayla's expression resisted him. She might have been joking.

"Both," Ray said.

"It's your feeling-state that's out of whack. You need to find a place in yourself that's at peace."

"Wow," Ray smiled. "That sounds like crap."

"It would be if it weren't true."

Ray didn't know what to think. He let the idea slide. "And what about your feeling-state?"

"Oh I don't have one," she smiled. "Surgery." Her right hand massaged the back of her neck. She was tired. The silence

seemed comfortable. The plants filled the window; Ray and
Kayla sat in their separate chairs. It was a long silence, relaxed.
Last night, today, the evening, years ago—just two drinks, and
the whole jumble began to untangle. Ray could imagine a long
piece of string, and the knots in a row loosening, even the terror
unknotted, his muscles loosened into a natural state of slack
tranquility, as everything should be at the end of a day. It was
good gin, he thought. Something else, too.

From the outside, he guessed all those plants must make
Mae's window look like the inside of the house was outside.
He liked that idea.

Kayla smiled. "I guess we're not going to plan our next raid
on account of whatever."

"Guess not."

Ray sipped. An ice cube clicked against his incisor. "I
should get some sleep," Ray said.

Kayla considered the idea. "Right, then. I'll walk you out."

She had taken off an earring and now she put it back in,
quickly. They stepped to the door together. "After you."

"No, no, after you." Laughing.

Against the doorjamb. Her eyes open even wider, if possible,
his empty drink in his right hand. She put her palm on Ray's
chest, pushed him. Against the doorjamb. They kissed. On the
lips. He kissed her this time, again. He saw the corner of her left
eye. The jangling earring. She licked her dry lips, kissed him. He
didn't think. Her tongue found his. The feeling warm, cool. The
taste. His hand down the small of her back, he pulled her against
him. Her smallness. There. He knew what he was doing.

What was he doing? He pulled back, his head against the
doorjamb. He looked at her. Kayla's lips were parted, the lower
lip wet from their kiss. Lovely. She wasn't smiling. She pressed
against him. "Shut up," she said, before he could say anything.
Her hand slid down Ray's chest to his waist, to his hip; Kayla
pulled on Ray's hip, playful, her groin rubbing against his. He
was hard.

Ray put his hand on her ass.

"Mm," she said. She licked his neck. Lightly. She looked up.

His tongue found hers: the firmly teasing tip, the full flat tongue. Her tongue in his mouth. He knew what he wanted. Or not: what was he doing?

She made herself taller, then bit his ear. A good nip. Playful.

Slowly, he told himself. Go slow. He squeezed her ass, made his hand wide there.

"Mm," she said again, more of a grunt than a word.

He nuzzled her neck, her earring. The silvered strands spread against his cheek, his mouth.

She had lifted one leg, on tiptoe, to rub against him. Pressure. Stroking his crotch with hers. "Yeah," she said. "Like that," she added, when his hand squeezed her ass again.

"Good," Ray said.

"Shhh," she said. "Don't talk."

Her weight was too much in his one hand, so he put the other hand on Kayla's ass too. They rocked a bit, together. Rubbed together. He wanted all of it. He hoped she had a condom.

His tongue in her mouth.

She dropped her leg, for leverage. Pressed into him. Stopped. Flicked her tongue against his. Stepped back. "Okay," she said. "Phew," she exhaled.

Ray breathed hard.

"You're still married," she said.

He scowled. "Oh, c'mon."

"This is your decision," she said. "You."

For chrissakes.

She smiled. "I could take off my clothes." She lowered her hand, wiggled her fingers on the way down. She almost touched him. "You think about it." There was a rhythm to her movements, a fluidity. Kayla leaned back, looked at him. "You surprised me. I missed you," she said, as she stepped into the sunroom once again, turned off the lights, reached for her drink. She hadn't sat down.

Ray wiped his mouth. "I'm not drunk," he said. The truth.

She stood there. No smoke, just fire. Ray hadn't seen it coming, although maybe he should have. "You surprise me too," he said. "I've missed you too . . . I mean . . . Right. My decision." Ray stepped into the solarium, closer to Kayla. She turned around, her back to him, looked out the window. He could hold her hips, from behind, press against her. He could walk away.

His decision. Ray took a step. Another. His decision.

They were almost touching. He reached around, his hand in front, put his palm against her from the front.

"Hmph," she said, her voice deep. She rubbed her ass on his groin.

"More," he said.

"Shh," she said. "I'll talk. I like to talk."

He closed his eyes. He opened his eyes. He would keep his eyes open; he wanted to see what he was doing.

They had gone next door to his house, upstairs to the bedroom. She had condoms in her purse, which made him raise an eyebrow briefly. The sex had been lustful, nothing unbelievably athletic, yet aggressiveness and her dirty talk made their lovemaking fun. Come on. Come. Fuck me. Ray on his back, Kayla holding his shoulders, screwing. When he came, she came, her hand helping. He had wanted to feel more, but hadn't.

It occurred to Ray that the booze might have been in the way. Or something else had worked on him somehow, taken an edge off the eroticism.

Kayla had long silky legs, which Ray hadn't known. Her body was taut.

She lay on her side, her arm flopped over her head. He loved that part of a woman's body, the line from the elbow, down the biceps, down the underarm, to the side of the breast. He reached forward, cupped the curve of her breast. The soft weight.

He had last slept with someone just a few months or so ago, Dina, the woman he had met at the coffee place; he had had an affair five years ago, his last affair. He had slept with Jilly, his wife. Ex.

He had never slept with a black woman.

He had never been kidnapped and tortured. Or burned a cross with the help of his lover, a black woman.

"Again?" She smiled lazily.

Ray stirred. "I'm not sure."

"Mm," she said. "In a while. . . ."

He dozed. When he awoke, he could hear the shower. Down the hall, Kayla had left the bathroom door open, which he took to be an invitation. He didn't accept. Instead, naked under his light cotton robe, Ray padded around the house, going downstairs quietly. Then he opened the kitchen door and sat on the chaise lounge out back, the night air cool and humid, nursing his confusion, staring. A nice night, really. Stars. Her skin had been so amazing; he wished that she had left the lights on, so that he might have seen more. He was a dope. What was he doing? His shoulder ached.

"Hi."

He turned and smiled a small smile. "Hi." She was wrapped in a bath sheet, his green one. One of the few things he had unpacked in the house full of boxes. She was resourceful, of course. He knew that.

"Feel good?" she asked.

"Yes," Ray answered.

"Truth?"

"Truth." And it was the truth, sort of: there were too many feelings for Ray to say that he had any one feeling, except for the slow burn of his anger. Even now? Damn, Ray thought. But feeling good was one of the feelings he felt now.

"Will we do this again?" Her voice was small.

Ray looked at Kayla. He could see her fairly well, in the light from the kitchen window. "Sure," he nodded. "If you want."

"Okay!" She unwrapped the towel. She stood there naked. Very nice.

"Can we talk a little?" Ray asked. "For a little while."

Kayla stepped closer to where Ray sat, stopped, took his face in her hand, his head against her thigh. When he looked up, her eyes were shining down at him. "Whatever," she managed.

"Good," said Ray.

She stepped back for a moment, found the towel, wrapped herself up again as she sat on the edge of the chair, between his feet. Her back was to him. Ray had liked Kayla's back to him, upstairs. Her hips were full.

"I'm not going back to my wife—"

"Don't tell me," she interrupted. "I don't want to hear your fucking guilt, or how your marriage is over. Don't tell me you don't love your fucking wife, either."

"Whoa," Ray said.

"Right, Uncle Ray. Whoa. I'm your lover. Grow up."

He exhaled. She had said all that without turning around. A few drops of water fell on his ankle, from her hair or her arm. Cool water that was probably salty. Or a little soapy. Clean. Ray looked at the back of Kayla's head, her shoulders. He was tired. "That was fun," Ray said.

She turned her head and upper body to face Ray. "Think so?"

"Yes."

"I . . . um." Kayla fell silent. "I usually need to hear that. After. I don't know why." She looked down.

"I liked when you were on top."

She giggled, almost inaudibly. "Me too."

Ray was becoming aroused again. "And from behind." There was silence as they both remembered, or so Ray thought.

"What do you want to talk about?"

"Don't know," Ray admitted.

"Oh."

She shifted her butt sideways, threw one leg over his. He had an erection that he hoped she would or wouldn't notice. Small engine repair, Ray told himself. Mom and Dad, he told himself. He started talking about nothing: "I've got a sister.

Fran. She's married to this boring guy. You know, the kind who manages to say the emptiest things when the going's tough? Anyway, I don't think he's the point. Fran and I are pretty close—or at least, I'm close to her. I don't really tell her stuff. She's in AA.

"When we were kids she used to make me do things. She's four years older. Like she made a hat out of newspaper and then snuck dog shit in it. And she made me try it on."

Kayla smiled. "That's not true."

Was it? Ray thought so. He was very tired.

"But it's funny. Do you want me to put dog shit on your head? Is that why you're telling me?"

"Stop," Ray said.

Kayla stroked his leg. Just her middle finger, as though she were checking for dust. Oh that's a nice idea: a white glove test. He was not letting go. Let go of it, he told himself. So what if she's black.

"Fran's got a way of talking that reminds me a little of your mom."

"Really."

"Yep."

Ray put his hand on Kayla's back. He pressed in with his palm, near her scapula, until she arched into the pressure, her chin tilted up, slightly. In the open fall of the towel, he could see her right breast. Her nipple. Tell the story. "I remember once when Fran and I ran away, into the woods behind our house. I must have been five or six. Maybe seven? We packed our lunchboxes with food—like macaroni and cans of soup, like we would cook when we got there—and brought our kiddie sleeping bags. My dad must have been out; I think we wouldn't have if he was home. He used to want to be a pilot, just to fly, you know the era, when he grew up and all, but he didn't have the eyesight. So he worked for a freight company pushing paper until they were bought out, and then for a taxi and limo outfit, in dispatch ... sometimes nights.... Did I tell you that already? Anyway, we really intended to sleep in the woods, and build a tree house. She wanted to sleep in a tree house."

"Cute."

"Mm." Ray thought it over; Ray tried to remember.

"So what happened?"

"I fell," he lied. "I broke my arm and Fran had to leave me in the woods and go get Mom. I think I fell on a rock or a root."

The whole story had become a lie, thanks to one small embellishment. That's how easy it was to lie, or to change your life. Too easy? Ray wasn't sure why he had lied.

"That's terrible. Were you alone for a long—"

"An hour, I think."

"God."

"It hurt like hell."

"Poor you. . . ."

Ray waited and waited. Then he smiled. "I made that up."

"What?"

"I made it up," he said. And then he thought: just like the cop's little story. Detective Shaw. "The stuff about my dad, that's true. And we did hit the woods, but we got hungry so we came home," he admitted, smiled. "I've never broken my arm, only my leg. And my nose."

"And your nose again—"

Kayla threw her body onto his: she lay sideways, as she clenched Ray's wrist in her hand, and her hip pushed between his legs, leaning in. There he was. "Hey," she said.

"Sorry," he smiled. He wasn't.

"The condoms are upstairs," she said. Then her hand slipped inside his robe. She was moving slowly. She touched him.

"Mm."

Would the lie have been better if Ray hadn't admitted to it? The thought made sense—then, as she grabbed him, hard, thinking went away. "Like that?"

"Hey!" Ray opened his eyes. "That's a little much."

"Yes," Kayla said. "You deserve it. Liar."

"Is this what you like?"

"Oh no." Kayla let go. "I like to play with knives."

"Funny," Ray said. Kayla would say anything.

"Yeah, sure . . ." She wrapped his penis in the fabric of the robe and scooted herself up, toward him. The towel was draped over her shoulders. His erection was between her legs. Rubbing. "Can we talk a little?" Kayla touched herself with him. "For a little while?"

"Are you making fun of me?"

"Yes."

"Good." He closed his eyes. "There."

"And there—" She caressed his hand, then moved it between her legs, leaning back so that he could reach her, all of her, open her and touch her. She was wet.

"Wait," Ray said. Bad shoulder. He switched hands. "Better."

Kayla slid the fabric of the robe across Ray's penis, then uncovered him. They stroked each other.

"We should go inside," Kayla said. "You should be inside."

"How about here? Or in the creek. . . ."

Kayla stopped touching him. "I don't do fantasies, Ray."

"I . . ."

"Get it. This is real life. We make love to each other, or we don't make love."

"Fine," Ray said. He had been kidding. "I was kidding."

"Fine."

Was the moment gone? He couldn't tell. His erection had only barely eased. They were silent. Then she cupped her breast. "Men like my breasts," she said. "And they like my legs. I have nice legs," Kayla said. She pointed her toes.

"You do. You have great legs."

"Thanks. . . . So you don't like my breasts?" She smiled.

Ray shivered. He was cold, or tired. Both. "I think I need to go inside. Do you want—"

"Mm," Kayla said. "Shut up." She reached down between her legs, and touched herself. Ray watched the slick motion, the circle. He watched as she moved against her own hand. He liked watching what she was doing.

"Fuck," Kayla said, her voice deep. She moved her hand between his legs, found his penis and slid herself up on his lap. "Now," she said. She pulled him into her.

"Wuh," Ray gasped.

"Now." Kayla grabbed him.

The condoms were upstairs: Ray thrust his hips against hers. She was breathing hard, exhaling through her nose.

The condoms were upstairs.

"There!" Kayla raised herself up, off. There was sweat on her lip. She smiled a big smile, her front teeth shone. "You're fired."

"Very funny," Ray said. But what was he doing? Maybe Ray did know what he was doing: he was betting against himself, and losing. For chrissakes. A lose-lose proposition. He had burned a cross, seen his torturer in a diner, fucked without a condom.

War is hell, Ray thought. "Wanna go upstairs?" he asked Kayla.

"Okay!" she said brightly.

Ray got it. "You're making fun of me again."

"That's it, Uncle Ray. This be the girl."

Kayla was erratic as well as particular in her strangeness: Kayla had her rules, a few of which she announced but most of which Ray discovered only once he had broken them, with the subsequent instantaneous moodiness and recrimination his lesson. Still he found the fiery behavior a bit of a disguise, something Kayla wore rather than something she was. As a lover, at least the two times they had made love thus far, Kayla liked to be coddled just as she wanted to assert her control. She was in charge, her actions said: she could allow or deny. So the rules were there to test him, in a way, which Ray found immature for a woman in her thirties, insecure really—but not so difficult to deal with or understand. He even liked proving himself. Or he liked it now.

Her unpredictability allowed him the same. He could be who he wanted. Or he could just be. And Kayla had made love with Ray, and then again; she had wanted it again. He was pleased. A woman he had feelings for, more than just sexual feelings, had feelings for him.

Once Kayla had left, to go home, Ray had gone to sleep on his couch downstairs. Or tried to go to sleep, because his exhaustion wouldn't let him. Ray was wired. He could hear his pulse in his left ear, along his jaw, reverberating through his sinuses, an echo of what it was like to be alive. He considered his actions. Kayla had told him to grow up, and maybe she wasn't wrong. Hot, yes; wrong, no. So he wasn't allowed to invent guilt, or to punish himself for doing nothing wrong. Which didn't mean, he knew, that he had been acquitted in advance of all bad behavior: Ray would continue to be responsible for his actions, right and wrong and both, just as he would accept the judgments of others, the tyranny of the Golden Rule, the tricks of his conscience. For chrissakes, was that last idea a bucketful of bullshit, as his dad liked to say. Dad, who knew every plane in the air, and ended up sending cabbies to the airport until the cancer got him.

But Ray could hope that having a relationship with this thirty-six-year-old black woman was a good idea. Ray wouldn't lie to her, he decided, which was more of a commitment than he had made in his marriage; and if Kayla were willing, Ray believed that their getting together could mean more than the sex. Hey. Why not be appreciated. Why not appreciate someone.

He was a bit of an asshole, still, he knew. Brighton had done this to him: Jimmy Palmer, Detective Shaw, and Mae, and even Kayla. In such a simple world, where everyone saw life in terms of pairs—black and white, us and them, good and bad, full and empty—morality seemed somehow more complicated rather than less, even though everyone Ray had met behaved as though life here were simple. But the smallness of the town wouldn't let life be that way, as everything everyone did echoed through everyone else. Jimmy Palmer had dropped a big rock in Ray's pond, and the rippling wash had affected Kayla and Mae. Maybe Brighton was just a small pond, Ray thought, where everyone kept chucking stones into everyone else's lives, the ripples crazy, the waves messy. That was right. Regardless, Ray told himself the truth as he went to get some water, if he were an asshole now, he had always been an asshole. Brighton had only shown him the truth.

Water in a Dixie cup. Ripples. What ripples would his relationship with Kayla make? What would happen tomorrow?

He was happy, sort of. Having had sex with Kayla had given him something. In his mind or his soul, or with his dick, or with all of the above, Ray thought, he had regained an ounce of self-respect. Or maybe just an ounce of self: there was a Ray here, where in the past there had only been words, or things to do. He had been a man living in response to everyone else's life, an effect to their causes, Mr. Circumstance, Daddy Wait-and-See, Mr. Clean Up, Mr. Slash-and-Burn. Now he could do, be the asshole he was. Wrong and right, here was Ray, attractive to an attractive young black woman, thinking deeper than ever, singing "Getting to Know You" to himself. Plus this Ray was capable of anything, not to be trusted, glad to be angry.

Could he learn to be trustworthy? Or to be a nice guy? Ray hoped so, maybe.

He finally began to drift off to sleep, and as he did, Ray had a most unusual thought: if someone didn't believe in God already, Brighton wasn't a place to start. God had enough trouble being God, after all. And then another thought: you're fired, Ray sleepily told the old Ray.

CHAPTER 13

While the shower heated up, as the bathroom lacked a fan or a vent, Ray opened the tiny frosted window. Right. The screen was missing; he'd have to call the agent, what's her name, the nicer one. With the enormous briefcase? He couldn't remember her name. Outside, above the treetops, Ray could see the top of the lighting stanchion at the Sunset Park ball field, where the Pony Leaguers or the Bambinos or whoever would try to hammer hanging curveballs over a twenty-foot-high outfield fence. Gone, good-bye. Beyond that fence ran the Little Big, its swelled waters muddy with June rains and field runoff from upstream. If only the world hadn't changed: twenty days ago Ray could have walked to the park and watched the game, sitting in the stands like any other anonymous guy. He could have chosen a team to root for and watched them lose, and then as the players lined up to exchange high fives on the mound, Ray could have walked home to his boxed belongings, where packed somewhere lay an unread copy of *The Natural*, a gift from Bruce, who read a lot. Ray might not read the book, he knew, and he had to call Bruce about their trip, a call Ray kept putting off, but not for any reason he could identify. . . . But the point was that Ray couldn't bring any book to the bleachers: he couldn't be out there in the world, walking around, catching a game, innocent. No one was innocent, not anymore; or maybe no one had ever been innocent.

Ray was feeling cynical, yessir, which usually meant that he was upset with something he had done. His cynicism, as his charming soon-to-be-ex-wife liked to point out, mostly served as an idiot light for his conscience—which was a Stanton trait, since Fran had it bad. It's not a habit, Ray would tell Jilly, if she ever said so again; it's just in my wiring.

It was 11 a.m., the morning after, and Ray hadn't slept enough. He peed, and waited to flush in order to keep the shower temperature steady—the seat left up as a reminder to himself—and stepped into the shower stall. Jilly had run out of answers. But Fran was always a good example, when Ray and Jilly argued, of what Ray had managed not to become.

Although he had not turned on the caddy radio, forgotten really, Ray's shower was over, his hair shampooed and conditioned, his body soaped and rinsed, his ears scrubbed with a washcloth. The ritual had reassured, the same gestures in the same order. Do this. Do that. Do this. Thoughts about last night, a surge of feeling in his groin. Do that. Kayla.

He pulled back the curtain and reached for his oversized bath towel, one of the Stantons' older ones that had made the move to Brighton, just like the one Kayla had borrowed. Kayla. There was a flutter. A tiny, animal noise. Ray blinked, then wiped the dripping water from his eyes. Something was in the bathroom, something alive. What the—? A bird. Oh shit. No, a bat!

Ray wrapped the towel around his waist and motored to the door. The bat was shut safely behind him, caught in the bathroom. Ray wasn't scared, no, not Ray, but he had no experience with bats. Weren't they photosensitive? It was morning; what was the damn thing doing awake? He was sure that he didn't want the bat buzzing around the house later—do bats even buzz? Ray thought they made more of a chirping noise—but he didn't know what to do next. The whole thing seemed so fucking ridiculous, another fucking ridiculous thing happening to Ray, and while weeks ago he might have laughed, and even now he recognized the comedy, Ray found himself gritting his teeth, hard; more fucking anger. He probably needed to go get a broom or something. The bat seemed like another insult.

He trudged off to find some clothes, his wet bare feet leaving dark little puddles in the plush carpet pile. Then, dry and dressed, broom fetched from the closet, his hair messily matted because his comb and brush lay on the goddamn bathroom sink, and still needing a shave, he marched back down the hall toward the trapped bat.

There were his footprints. Ray was here. Killroy, Kill Ray.

Ray was infuriated. His face was probably red from the shower and the rage, both, red as marinara, with the possible exception of his black eye, now mostly light green. The image seemed funny. Ray had to smile, which surprised him. Funny colors.

Now to it: he would carefully shoo the thing out the window, and if Ray were lucky, he would be able to do so without hurting the bat, himself, or any of the bathroom fixtures. Bye-bye bat, Ray muttered. A-one and a-two and a-three . . .

As he stepped into the steamed bathroom, Ray wanted four hands: one to flash the light, two to swing the broom and one to keep hold of the doorknob, just in case. Are bats ever rabid? How could he tell? Where was it hiding? Ray closed the door and leaned back, one arm tucked behind him, and clutched the knob. He waited. Nothing. No fanged flying rodent, no screeching, no wings flapping madly. And then: there. The bat was curled up, partially obscured as it hid within a dark little fold of the shower curtain, six inches or so above Ray's head, two feet that way.

Ray exhaled softly. It was only a bat. But nothing would ever be what it seemed. Nothing was only itself in Brighton. Nevertheless, whatever the bat was or wasn't, Ray thought he should reconsider, and devise a better plan.

Stepping softly, Ray edged to the vanity and then opened the cabinet; he reached for a quart-sized take-out container he had used for cleaning, placed its worn scrub brush on the sink, and turned again to face the shower curtain, the broom in one hand and the plastic tub in the other. Ray would be gentle—he promised the bat. He would sweep the bat into the container, slap the broom on top as a lid, and then go downstairs and outside to release the little sucker. He could do this, his plan could work, if he made no sudden movements, every gesture believable to the bat, nothing too scary.

What was a bat used to? Maybe Ray's broom would scare the poor thing; maybe the broom would appear to be a predator or something. What animals eat bats? Ray waited. Let the bat get acclimated. But Jesus, acclimated? Be real. Ray moved toward the bat, and held the broom aloft, getting there, slowly. Take-out container in one hand and broom in the other, Ray felt a bit like a little kid, playing knight of the Round Table. Ridiculous, really.

The little creature's head couldn't be seen, tucked under its wing or nestled in the folds of the curtain. This could work. *Shhh*, Ray told himself. "Shhhhhhh," he told the bat. Still, he had to unfold the curtain just a bit, in order to sweep the bat down into the makeshift bat trap. Would the animal panic? Just smack the stupid thing into the wonton soup container and be done.

Ray rolled the broom handle slightly, working the bristles closer to the curtain, and then pushed the fold of the fabric open as he rolled the broom back again, turning the flat of the broom horizontal. The bat fluttered slightly, or shuddered, just as Ray swept the animal down into the cup and . . .

He clapped the broom atop, shut. Caught you! Amazing!

The thing wasn't happy, beating its wings against the gray curved walls of its plastic prison. But it wasn't a bat, it was a bird. A pretty small sparrow. And Ray was happy.

On the way downstairs, he raised the container to eye level, checking out his new friend. Hello, little bird. It was beating its wings, flying nowhere in the plastic container, but it was about to feel much better, released from Ray's bathroom and house to fly back to the woods or wherever, to its mate or its mom. Where would the bird need to go? Don't hurt yourself, little bird.

Ray opened the door, stepped out into his front yard, placed the cup down in the dry grass, and then inched backward as he kept hold of the broom until his hand held the end of the handle. It was almost noon, hot. From two feet away he lifted the broom from the container: the bird inched upwards until it perched on the cup, which began to tip, and then the tiny thing flew. It was fast; it had been ready to go. It was gone.

"You catch that?"

Ray turned around, startled: some kid a few years younger than Tom was standing on the walk, hair tousled and jaw pointed. "Yeah," said Ray.

"It bite you?"

"No," said Ray. What the hell? "It was only a little bird."

The kid sipped soda through a straw. He looked at Ray. "You live here?"

"Yes."

"I live there. The green house. The creek goes through our yard."

Ray stood there. The boy stood there. "I'm Mr. Stanton," said Ray.

"I know," said the kid. "You're the one got shot."

It made sense that Ray's other neighbors needed some lurid rumor to explain the predawn arrival of police car and ambulance, and that according to Brighton gossip his hysterical and disheveled appearance had been caused by a bullet wound. Nonetheless Ray was surprised by the kid's remark, and by how quickly the light from an emergency vehicle bred sensationalism. Brighton was small enough to create its own news—and Ray would probably be smart to remember that fact. Everything everyone did belonged to her or his neighbors; each act became a larger act in the retelling, which was a good reminder to Ray, in terms of Windy Oaks too. Something Rivers understood, of course.

But maybe they should have looked at the weekly *News and Gazette*, which was lying on the walk: on the front page, a cross was aflame on a racist hick's lawn. He dangled the paper in its baggie as he gathered his birding equipment and headed back indoors. Shot? Sort of, Ray mused. That wasn't so far off.

Back inside, Ray read the article three times, no news really, they didn't know a thing, and then he clipped it out, as though it were a coupon. He used a magnet from two dentists ago and tacked the article on the fridge. It was something to do: there might be more, a scrapbook.

Palmer must be twice as pissed, even though you couldn't see his house in the photo. And while the article identified the street, and not the address, Brighton was too small a town for the site to remain a secret. Palmer would be three times as pissed.

Let's see, Ray said. Rummaging in his Welcome Wagon plastic bag, Ray found the Brighton phone book, a dinky little multicolored thing, and looked up Palmer. Anson. Bob. Charlie Palmer, Contracting. Frieda and Morris with separate numbers at the same address, James, James Jr., Kyle, M., Walter and Mary. James Jr., 1612 S. 1st Avenue, Apt. B. And a number. Ray copied the information onto a Post-it. He picked up the telephone and dialed.

Three rings. Ray wanted to hang up. Four. Five. What time was it? Noon.

"Yeah."

The voice. Ray stopped breathing.

"Hello," said the voice. "Hello?"

Ray steadied himself against a cardboard box.

"Well fuck you too," the voice laughed. Click.

Staring at the dead receiver, Ray waited. He let himself breathe. He hung up, he picked up the phone again. Dial tone, dialing.

"What!"

Ray said nothing.

"It's okay, baby. I'm here all alone," the voice whispered.

What the hell did that mean? Ray hung up, and then Ray smiled to the boxes in his kitchen. It would seem that Mr. James Palmer, Jr., had a secret; it would seem that Ray had discovered

Mr. James Palmer, Jr.'s secret. Ray sat down, pulled his knees to his chest. This news changed things. Hey. The mostly healed bad scratch across his chest persisted in its discomfort, especially near the armpit where the scratched skin felt tight.

Maybe Jimmy Palmer's secret hadn't changed anything, since the odds remained far from even. A man like that, unpredictably capable of extreme violence, would always be a threat—whereas Ray's rage and cross burning hadn't made him dangerous, only unpredictable, and stupid. So Palmer was cheating on someone, so what. In a town the size of Brighton, his wife or girlfriend probably knew already: god, she probably wanted Palmer to cheat rather than come home, and who could blame her.

Still there was something powerful about having the phone number to go with the street address. If Ray were having trouble sleeping, he could call Palmer in the middle of the night, hang up, fluff a pillow, not disturb Kayla, roll over and go back to sleep. Ray could clip little letters from a magazine, glue together an anonymous note, wipe his prints clean, and let the mailman do the rest: we know who you are. Don't use the side door. Get out of town. You're finished. Fired.

In a previous life, none of these possibilities would have seemed Ray's style, but now he wasn't so sure. As the events of the past three weeks had already taught Ray more about himself than he had cared previously to acknowledge—was that true? oh shit—and he knew that he had changed, Ray couldn't say what the new Ray's style might be. Plus revenge had always seemed such an ego trip. Strutting around, all preening and self-satisfaction. But maybe this guy named Ray needed some of that, just a little more vanity. Or maybe laughing over Jimmy Palmer's naked body wouldn't mean anything to Ray. . . . That seemed more likely. Jimmy Palmer, Jimmy Palmer. Ray chanted the name to himself, everyone terrorizing everyone else. Very Middle East.

What did Ray want? Kayla, and Kayla. Maybe, too, to separate Kayla and whatever was going to happen with her from this crap, from Brighton and hate crimes and Palmer's fucked-up little world. When they got down to it, after all, race wasn't what brought Ray and Kayla together—criminal activity had, first Palmer's and then their own.

More of the same: Ray dialed again, let the phone ring once, then hung up. "Ffff," Palmer had said, the beer splashing on Ray's chest like cold piss.

He needed to calm down, to chill, as his daughter liked to say. Ray had been acting on adrenaline, working himself into a fury: he needed to do something different, get his thoughts going in another direction, start over. Stop calling, Ray told himself. Get a grip. What was Kayla doing now? The thought gave him the beginnings of an erection, images of last night's encounter freshly available. Her legs opening. Ray took a deep breath, held it, exhaled. Okay, he told himself. Fine. "Fine," he said aloud.

Then the phone rang. Oh god. Ray made the mistake of picking up.

"Ray! It's Jim."

"Jim?"

"Jim. Jim. Jim Rivers."

Right. Rivers. "Hi, Jim."

"Hiya. I was just wondering about you, you know? Just sitting here and thinking that Ray Stanton might want to come have drinks with me and Mrs. Jim and some folks at the club, maybe bring a friend, if you like. . . ."

A friend? What did Rivers know?

". . . so how about Monday the twenty-ninth in the p.m., say, five? Casual, of course."

"Thanks, Jim. I'd love to—" Ray lied.

"That's the twenty-ninth. And Ray . . . just one more thing. You keep your head down, hear?"

Oh god.

"Ray?"

"I hear you, Jim. Head down."

By late in the afternoon of what had become a hot day, although he didn't know the exact time, because Ray had made himself not check, he had accomplished quite a bit. The floor of the front closet had been vacuumed, the shelves had been wiped, three protruding nails had been hammered flat, and the pull chain on the light had been replaced. Ray's hiking boots now adorned a shoe rack, and the hideous ceramic French umbrella pot now stood sentinel in the vestibule, each letter of *Parapluie* visible except for the final "e." Upstairs, one room had been vacuumed and a dresser assembled (the latter task proving more complicated than the directions on the box had allowed, especially when Ray had realized that the hardware package had come incomplete, and two essential wood screws had been omitted).

He had been very sweaty, all afternoon. He had kept a rag nearby, to wipe his face periodically. He had drunk a lot of water. Ray unpacked, arrived. The urge to call Palmer had abated.

He could live here in Brighton, he supposed, so long as he didn't leave the house. He could unpack, clean, cook; he could lounge in the backyard, or fix up the stone barbecue, which looked pretty crumbly. He could do his job, or maybe another job, once Rivers called Head Office, and Ray was fired. He could bring Kayla, his "friend," to drinks at the club, and get himself fired faster.

Or maybe he should be sensible, and just do some work. He didn't like not working, which left him alone too much, thinking more stupid thoughts and placing phony phone calls. Well, except for Kayla; being available was fun.

But who was Ray Stanton when he wasn't working? Good question.

There was enough paperwork in his office at the plant— work he could bring back to the house, and do here. *Yeah, yeah, yeah,* he sang some Beatles to himself. He should work out of the house for a while, have Kayla come over to play every night, call Palmer now and then from various pay phones around town, find the woman he had kicked and buy her a diamond, make nicey-nice with Hank Williams and teach the greasy red-neck how to drive.

He dialed Palmer again. How many times had he done this? Four, five?

"Hello?" A woman's voice this time.

Ray waited, surprised. His hand was cupped over the mouthpiece of the phone.

"Oh c'mon . . ." The woman's voice faded, she hung up.

Ray should hang up. He looked at his hand. His knuckles were white, his grip tighter than he wanted it to be. He had no idea what the hell he was doing.

CHAPTER 14

When Ray stepped out of his leased house the next Sunday, with nothing adventurous in mind but pretty sure that he would finally sneak into the office, pick up some papers, and make the big money in the name of fatherhood, the day was already done. He stood in his driveway, briefcase in hand, brown-bag supper in the briefcase. A bump on a log in a hole in the bottom of the sea, he said to himself. He looked at the white pickup truck parked in the street in front of his house. Leaning against the truck was Detective Shaw.

Ray refused to recognize him. If no one sees him, he doesn't exist, Ray reasoned.

Had Ray forgotten something? He thought that now would be a good time to remember whatever he had forgotten. His ham sandwich could use a pickle. Ray turned and went back into his house.

Through a crack in the venetian blinds, Ray's least favorite kind of window treatment, an attitude inherited directly from his mother, he peeked. Damn. People who have venetian blinds, his mom would say, cover their living room furniture with shrink wrap, and only unwrap for funerals. Or christenings, Ray thought to add. No, funerals and christenings, on the same day, to save money on the catering. Now that would be a party.

This was ridiculous. The cop wasn't going anywhere, and Ray wasn't solving anything, or fooling anyone. But his body had gone back inside, slipped into its little snail house. Escargot, Ray thought. Shrink wrap.

He went back outside, approached the cop. "Hello, Officer. May I help you with something?"

"Mr. Stanton." Detective Shaw nodded his head. If he had been wearing a cap, he probably would have tipped it. Goddamn cliché.

"I said, what are you doing here, Detective?" Ray's left hand was in its pocket; in his right he held his briefcase.

"Nope. That's not what you said, sir. You said 'May I help you with something?'"

For chrissakes. Ray's mouth was probably open. Catching flies.

"But I'm glad you asked, Mr. Stanton. I . . . I need your help with a small job. Want to help out a member of your local finest? I'm sure you do. I know it's a Sunday, but you haven't been at the plant much, so it's not like this is a day off, right? You know?" The police detective opened the passenger door of the truck. "Hop in."

This was the third vehicle Detective Shaw had used to drive Ray around, wasn't it—how big could the Brighton police motor pool be? Instead of talking, or concentrating on his refusal to speak, Ray thought about Shaw and cars and the truck. Each of the vehicles had been fully loaded, maxed out with law enforcement gizmos—for which, Ray assumed, the force could probably thank Windy Oaks taxes. But this time, in this apparently brand-new unmarked police pickup, something smelled awful. Ray glanced around, as nonchalant as possible. The truck was clean, but something did smell terrible.

Ray had smelled terrible, he remembered. That night.

They drove in silence. The day was still hot, but the AC wasn't turned on, for which Shaw made no apology; the little sliding window between the cab and the truckbed was open— the smell, Ray thought, coming from back there. At least Ray wasn't being made to sit in the back again.

They drove alongside the river, the Little Big. A left up there, at the Sunoco sign, and they would be heading out of town. Ray was beginning to learn which roads led out of town, but no one was letting him leave. Not that he wanted to, really, because of Kayla. They had been having fun, squirreled away in Ray's house, having lots of sex. Yummy. Three nights out of the past four, and Ray was kind of worn out—although he could always go back to bed in the mornings, once she went to work, which certainly helped. She must be very tired, he realized.

Ray wasn't going to say anything. He wouldn't. They pulled into an alleyway, and then parked. They were behind the Brighton Town Hall. They were at the police station. Parked nearby was a large vehicle, a grader or a front-loader. One of those yellow jobbies, Ray thought, a real life Tonka. Now that would be a present for Tommy.

"Here," the policeman said. "This way, Mr. S."

Once inside, down a narrow corridor through two locked doors, past an attendant behind a glass partition who was working a switchboard and to whom Detective Shaw gave a cheery hello, they stopped at an unmarked door. No, wait. There was a tiny sign on the lintel. Lab.

"You'll want these." He handed Ray a pair of latex gloves. "Gloves," the policeman said.

They were standing next to a large black table, the kind high school chemistry classes used, complete with sunken sink and an n-loop faucet. On the table, a large object lay underneath a blue plastic sheet. Ray wasn't sure what the object was, or had been.

"The tests aren't done," Shaw said. "Forensic tests get more and more sophisticated all the time—you know, like on those TV shows. But once they get going, real experts can find anything they're looking for." He removed the sheet. It was the burned cross. "Give me a hand," Shaw said. "It's going over there, into that." With a chuck of his chin, he indicated a shipping crate on another table, plastic sheeting spread wide. "To the FBI," Shaw added.

Of course, the cross was small enough to be carried by one person, Ray knew, having helped to make it and then having hauled it around by himself. Now the charred wood and ash were well wrapped in a kind of greenish plastic, or it might have soiled Shaw's clothes, Ray reasoned. So yes, aside from the fucking irony and the fucking harassment, there was a fairly understandable reason for Ray's presence and assistance.

No, there wasn't. Ray was being played.

He took hold of the bottom as they slid the cross from the table. The two men carried the thing easily, put it where Shaw wanted, into its little packing coffin.

Why hadn't the damn thing burned to the ground? Everything in Brighton seemed unfinished.

His hands empty, his gaze unfocused, Ray found himself picturing his own body midair, as he was pushed from the back of Jimmy Palmer's truck. They had dumped him from a slowly moving vehicle. Everything unfinished was wrong. Ray focused again, came back to stare at Detective Shaw.

"Thanks, Mr. Stanton," the policeman said. He removed his gloves, looked at Ray. "Now then. Where you headed? Can I give you a lift? I'd offer you a snack, after all this hard work, but I'm sorry, I'm fresh out of donuts."

It was Sunday dinnertime, the plant was deserted, and even the skeletal clean-and-reload second shift had gone home. Sweaty from the drive, still speechless even after Shaw had dropped him off, Ray used his key card at the gate and then into Admin. His office door was opened more conventionally, simply by turning a knob. At least the AC was on, as usual—if only at maintenance levels, so that bringing the plant back online didn't require cooling the whole place down completely.

That was the thing with the new technologies, Ray had noticed. Everything worked better if it was left to run all the time. That's another reason why technological advances seem so inhuman, he supposed, even though they were imagined and implemented by people. But oh my, running Windy Oaks lights out, every human presence gone, would be quite a technological accomplishment, wouldn't it? Some factories in Europe—with the German and Italian robotics and computers so damn advanced—ran lights out. Amazing.

Of course, that wasn't an option here, and not just because of the capital investment. People, Ray thought. Brighton.

Goddamn Shaw, Ray swore to himself. For Christ's sake.

Ray would work. The cop didn't know everything, he couldn't have, or he would have arrested Ray. To hell with him, Ray thought. Goddamn Shaw. But Ray needed to act, to control something, to change the pace of the events; he knew this mood, fidgety and irritable. He needed to work. He sat at his desk, shuffled some papers, began to check his e-mail.

He had been away too long, 132 messages worth reading, the rest to trash. He was happy with the prospect of all those messages. Ray worked. It took him almost two hours to read through, backing up the important memos with hard copy, forwarding with and without comment, trashing and emptying trash.

It felt good to work. He liked it. He thought only about work. But deciding to think only about work was acknowledging that he was thinking about other stuff, wasn't it? Damn. What time was it? Almost nine. His sandwich had long since been devoured. He would try to reach Kayla soon, although he had left a note for her on his back door, in case she happened by. He had to tell her about Shaw.

What time was it? Ray let his body answer: it was time for a snack from the vending machine in the lounge. In his recommendations, he had already advocated keeping the vending machines. As is, the folks cutting and sewing and finishing, on piecework in this nonunion shop, put in twelve-hour days and took their lunch and breaks on the run; the vending machines saw a lot of action, which wouldn't change.

He walked out of Admin, made a left at the loading dock. The forklifts were parked, the lights and the klaxons and the ordered chaos of Receiving all in stasis, waiting for people. Just inside, the bales were there for tomorrow, graded and bar-coded, the foreseeable future.

Ray knew more about making shirts than he had ever known, even though shirt making wasn't his area, nor would it need to be, really. Technology investiture, resource management, and personnel coordination were Ray's métier, business process re-engineering; what he had learned about shirt making he could plan to forget, once his job here was done. Making thread and yarn, weaving and dyeing, cutting and sewing and finishing, all of it, in order, would be forgotten—unless he received another shirt factory assignment, which was unlikely. Dave Peterson didn't work that way: he wanted his team to be versatile, and he believed that learning a business from the ground up helped his people see the situation clearly. Ray supposed that Dave might be right.

There was a noise near one of the parked Caterpillar lifts. Ray heard the noise, stopped, and then decided not to hear it again. He took the long corridor past the nurse's station, past the IEs' offices, past the bathrooms. The corridor was long, tonight.

Behind him, a light went out. He glanced back. Yes, a light had burned out.

He was on the floor, at the yarn bins. He could see the lay-downs, the enormous machines that smoothed the cotton and then sucked it into air ducts. Here, the technology was fairly recent.

Another light went out. Shaw again? Damn Shaw.

Ray was almost on the main floor. There were double doors ahead. He somehow knew that he wouldn't reach the doors. Okay, Ray supposed. If that's it, okay. He turned.

"Hey, shithead," Jimmy Palmer said. "Good to see you."

Ray didn't answer.

"I said, 'hey.' You having trouble listening?" The guy was dressed in cutoffs and some heavy metal band T-shirt. Brown boots, the same ones.

Ray's right fist was balled. "I'm listening."

"I don't think so. I think you need help listening."

They looked at each other. Ray tried to breathe.

"So," Palmer smiled. "You having fun with the niggers?"

Oh god. There it was. Oh god. Neither one moved. That was fine with Ray. Then, "You're trespassing," Ray said, without thinking.

Palmer laughed. He took one step forward, looked down, smiled up at Ray. "I'm gonna kick your ass," Palmer said.

"Why?"

Palmer laughed again.

Ray's best escape route would be to turn and run, through the double doors, onto the factory floor. The combers were there, sixty yards of enormous, obsolete machinery behind which Ray could cower. Good thing that the Schlafhorst shipment hadn't arrived. The new machines were smaller.

Ray watched Palmer take another step. Ray turned and ran. He assumed he would be followed onto the floor, and he was right. What he hadn't considered was Palmer's preparedness: as Ray ran, the shop floor lighted by low-glow Exit signs and the occasional blue-light emergency phone, he could hear the whiz and smash of objects being thrown and banging against the machines, until something hard hit him in the back—a rock? Was Palmer throwing rocks? Ouch. Palmer had come with rocks to throw.

Actually, it hadn't hurt that much. Not a rock. Palmer was throwing other stuff.

Ray ducked under the strings of a comber, dodged between the green barrels of yarn waiting to be krilled. Between more barrels, left—something thrown smashed somewhere over there, to his right—and then he ran left again, into the darkness.

He wouldn't fit in an empty barrel, but he could crouch behind one. Although, if Palmer had a flashlight, Ray was dead, and if Palmer hit the floor lights, Ray was dead.

Ray tried to quiet his breathing: impossible.

Another sound, an object thrown, farther away. Another, close by again.

Time slowed.

Ray was squatting. Perspiration stung his eyes. Ten minutes, five years, no difference, Ray thought. His right calf began to cramp. He would stay still. Squat here. A smash. Something sounded like it had exploded, or popped.

Years again. Minutes.

He massaged the cramp in his calf, shifted weight so that his right heel touched the floor. Maybe he should start wearing his running shoes instead of his Rio sandals, whenever he went out, just in case. Another little explosion. Not a rock but something. Ray reached around: his shirt felt damp, slimy. Was Palmer throwing raw eggs? Good thing the polo shirt was yellow, Ray thought.

Palmer must have decided to sit somewhere. To throw an egg occasionally until Ray ran again.

Ray stood up: he didn't know why. He walked out from among the barrels, ducked under the threading arms of a machine. "Palmer," Ray said. And then louder: "Palmer! Palmer, you're—"

There he was. Near the plastic crating. He turned. "Can I help you?" It was a maintenance guy in coveralls. A black guy surprised and not smiling.

"I . . ."

"You got an ID?"

"Yes," Ray said. "Um . . ." His wallet? Yes. In his back pocket. He stepped forward, showed the guy his card. Ray could see the guy stiffen with recognition, a big boss.

"Okay," the guy said, smiling quickly, one hand on the handle of a garbage cart. "Yessir."

Ray made himself smile, then he turned toward the long corridor, egg on his back, and walked toward his office.

How long had he crouched behind those barrels? How many years? But Ray had reached some sort of limit, and he had stepped forward from hiding. He had been purposeful, foolhardy, stand-up. A man.

A man about to get his ass kicked. Is that what a man is, not someone brave, but someone willing to get his ass kicked? Maybe God did this, Ray thought. Maybe God kicked our asses, and if we were willing . . . What? Ray was furious again, with Palmer and Shaw and Kayla and everyone else. He could feel the rage rise in waves of bile, a crashing, blinding surf. Wave within wave. It was Jilly's fault, he told himself for no reason, which almost made him smile. Everything was.

He was standing in his office; he was looking around at the blank walls and the computer and the desk and the telephone. He wanted to destroy something. There was nothing. So he sat at his desk. In the drawer, he found an outdated datebook, a cigarette lighter, some Bics, a Baggie of loose change, all left by whoever used the desk before.

Ray's hands were shaking: better stop that. He set fire to the hard copy of an e-mailed memo, something from Anderson about an EOC addendum that required semi-immediate attention. Fucking Palmer, fucking Shaw. They could open the door; at any moment, they could step into Ray's office, Ray sitting here burning e-mail.

The page burned quickly: the heat moved toward Ray's hand. He wasn't going to move. He dropped the burning paper onto the cement floor, stamped out the flames. A test. Palmer wasn't finished, but neither was Ray. Let someone open the goddamned door.

He lit another memo: apparently, his office lacked a smoke alarm. This time, when the flames came close, Ray changed his mind, dropped the burning document, watched the curl of the paper's consumption, made another stand-up decision, as bad as all the others, and let the paper burn itself out.

Between burning memos, there was sadness.

Methodically, carefully, Ray lit another memo without glancing at the contents—that was three memos now, all in a row— and let the document burn out by itself on his office floor.

Rivers would have to be stroked, Ray decided. And now Kayla could talk to Shaw, and share. Shaw would want to help—and if Kayla did the talking, Ray might be able to keep his job. But Palmer could be outside the plant, waiting, or at Ray's house, or somewhere else in town, at any moment, behind a tree, vicious and dangerous. Ray would have to be prepared, or even more so, to be ready to act as soon as Palmer showed, even before Palmer could do more harm.

Okay, if that's that. Okay. Ray would buy a gun. He had fired a gun a few times, one day in the woods, as a teenager, with Bobby Simpkins. They had shot at birds with Bobby's father's rifle, and hit nothing, thank god.

The third memo smoldered: he leaned over, put out his hand, palm up, passed his hand through the shapeless gray-blue smoke. Again. His hand moving . . . Steady, steady, he told himself. Ray didn't recognize his own behavior; he had never done this before. And he might not be sane, or sure of his actions, but here he was, ready or not.

He set fire to a fourth e-mail. He licked the tip of his forefinger. G. Gordon Liddy, Ray thought. A test. He leaned over. Slowly, he put his wet finger to the flame.

CHAPTER 15

He was making himself not shake as she wrapped his burn in gauze and taped the finger. He had gone right to her apartment.

"Nigger? He used that word?"

"Yes."

"Woooh," she exhaled. Kayla was quiet, serious. Ray had seen her be talkative and serious, in fact she tended to talk at her most serious, but this was different because she was scared. He watched, learning. He told her everything he could remember, beginning with Shaw, the cross at the police station, and then the details of the incident at Windy Oaks. He saw Kayla's surprise register, her eyes sparkle. Eye contact. She gave his shoulder a small, consoling stroke. "Okay, so what happened to your finger?"

Ray looked down. His finger hurt.

Kayla cleared her throat, a noise. "Yoo-hoo. Hero?" Her mood had shifted. "You were saying . . ."

"I wasn't saying. Let's call it an accident."

"An accident."

He stood up. "Yeah."

"Well it's an accident, then. Like a kid you didn't plan to have."

He stepped to the fridge, to get himself a beer. Anything. He didn't like how well she could read him. "I don't always think you're funny," Ray said. There was nothing in the fridge he wanted; he closed the door.

Kayla smiled. "You're not supposed to." She stopped putting away the first-aid kit on the counter, turned, and approached, pinned him to the kitchen counter, pressed herself against him. "But I'm going to call the cops. Right now."

Ray didn't respond at first. There, he responded. He really liked her body. "Well . . . maybe not *right* now. . . ."

"Later," Kayla said.

"If that's okay," Ray said.

"Fine by me," Kayla smiled, grinding against him. And then: "Is it later? How about now? How do you feel? Can I call him now?"

Ray felt tired, helpless and enraged, affectionate, sad, pained. He told her so: it was the first time in his life, Ray thought, that he had answered that question so honestly.

Kayla exhaled. She leaned her upper body back, kept her torso pinned to his.

"You asked," Ray said. He felt kind of pleased with himself. He also felt aroused.

"So what am I saying to the man in blue?" she asked.

"I don't know," Ray conceded.

"Wanna have sex, and then decide?" Kayla reached around him to grab a glass of water, and flattened her body against his, her fun, curvaceous body.

Ray wanted to have sex, yes please, but he wanted badly to leave. He wanted to pack up, or not even bother, jump the all-night Greyhound west to another town, another and another; sleep on a bench in the buzzing fluorescence of the Farm Belt, sing hokey folk songs in his dreams, Woody Guthrie and all that, be a bum. The next morning he'd dress in the Men's, cheap jeans in a gym bag; then, over gray coffee and floppy toast with mixed-berry jelly, among the other exiles and parolees at Bob's Big Boy or Stuckey's or HoJo's, he would fit in, belong. He wanted to move on, out, be gone, see ya; find an all-white town and live there for a year, the happy idiot cutting lawns, reaming gutters, odd jobs for minimum wage; then send for Kayla and the kids, have a life. He wondered if Mom and Randall would buy an RV, hit the road, and come for a long weekend.

The fantasy was a cliché, let's go somewhere where no one knows us, too much driving and nasty food. Popping speed or sucking caffeine to keep the highway in focus, like on some kind of college road trip, going to see the Kinks in a forgettable arena two hundred miles away. He'd rather have sex, Ray knew. He was too much a grown-up to do a road trip.

"Okay," Ray said. "I mean 'no,' not now," he lied. "We've got to call Shaw. You do. Then we can have sex."

She laughed. "Now that's romantic. Your foreplay gets better and better."

"Thanks," Ray said, as he slid to his right, out of her delicious grasp. "I've been reading *Cosmo*." Let's stay here, Ray thought. He felt better. "And *Cosmo* says that to keep your man happy, you need to know when he's only aroused physically."

"I see," Kayla said. "Tired?"

"Tired."

"Got it."

They called him at home, ten-thirty on a Sunday night. "Hi, Paul? This is Kayla Reeves." Listening in on the other phone, Ray liked Kayla's telephone voice. Paul? Kayla knew his first name?

"Kayla, hey, how are you? How's your mom doing?"

"Oh, you know. . . . She's okay mostly, and then she does something she shouldn't. Like always."

The police officer laughed.

"How's Trina?"

"She's good," Shaw said. "She's got a new puppy that eats sneakers. A Lab. She's one happy kid."

Now Kayla laughed. Ray felt like her new puppy. Then there was a pause. Sit, Ray. He sat on the edge of her bed. Lie down. He lay down.

"Hey, I'm sorry to bother you at home, and to call this late, but it's kind of important."

"Figured," Shaw said. Ray could picture the police officer doing a jigsaw puzzle at a table, his hair neat. "So what can I do for you?"

"Well, that's a funny question, because I'm not sure . . . I'm calling to be a good citizen and all, but also to ask for your help. My friend needs your help. But he's in a bad place, and he can't ask himself. . . ."

Kayla told Shaw about Palmer, and the egg throwing, and Ray could almost hear the detective taking notes. "My friend," she called Ray. As she talked, Ray closed his eyes. He was incredibly tired. A breeze blew through the window, across his face, then stopped blowing. If only he could lie here for just a moment, and not sleep. His finger hurt. Stupid fuck, Ray told himself.

"So you see, he's in a predicament."

"I see," Shaw said. "But let me get this right. Your friend can't talk to me himself—why?"

"Thought you'd ask. He was told not to."

"By his friend?"

Kayla laughed. She had a great laugh. "Well, if your boss is your friend, then maybe."

"Aha, I see," Shaw said again. "Okay." Ray could hear him think. "Without more to go on, though, I mean information that comes directly and formally from your friend, I'm kinda powerless. At least, legally."

Right. And extralegally?

"I know," Kayla said. "So I'm just calling to keep you informed. A citizen's duty."

Shaw didn't laugh. "I'll see what I can do, and I'll certainly be around. Just tell your friend . . . not to do anything stupid. No more stupid tricks, no funny business. And tell him to tell his friend too. She wouldn't want to make a mess of a molehill."

CHAPTER 16

When he woke up, she was gone. He lay in bed for a long time, read some useless magazine until he really had to pee. He actually felt all right, not bad. What time was it? He couldn't remember if Kayla had to work today or not.

"Oops, sorry." She was peeing; he had walked in on her, forgotten to knock.

"It's okay, I'm done." She wiped and flushed. "Next?"

Sure, Ray thought. He peed, Kayla in the bathroom.

Behind the door was a full-length mirror. She had put her right foot on a little step stool, and was looking at the inside of her thigh, or maybe her labia, in the mirror. Her towel lay on the floor. Ray washed his hands, and stepped next to her, to the towel rack.

"Okay." She was done. She straightened. "Good morning. There's coffee."

"Good morning," he said, pecked her cheek. "Thanks. I'll find it."

They stood side by side, looking in the mirror, naked. She smiled. "How tall are you?"

"Five eleven. You?"

"Five five."

"Lotta legs," he said. He needed a shower, a shave, and to do about a thousand crunches. "You work out," he said.

"Yup. I don't mind the machines. But I've got a high waist," she said. "Not much butt. . . . My breasts could be bigger, don't you think. . . . Why isn't there hair on the inside of your thighs?" She gestured.

"Don't know," he said, looking. "Or on my knees. And it stops at my ankles," he pointed.

"I see that. Nice dick," she said.

"Thanks," Ray smiled. "You're okay, too," he said. "You know what I mean. You're beautiful," he said, gesturing.

"Beautiful," Kayla repeated. "Thanks."

They stood there, looking at each other. He wondered why she was sleeping with him. "Why are you sleeping with me?" he asked.

"Mmm?"

"I said, why are we together? You know, how come? What's in it for you?"

"I think . . . ," she began, and then nothing. She reached across her body, lifted her left breast slightly, a self-exam or a different gesture, he wasn't sure. "It's not about what's in it for me—but you didn't mean that, did you, because you asked three different questions." Kayla didn't wait: "You're attractive. You've got really sexy hands—" she looked away, a little embarrassed. There was a long silence. "But it's more than that, not just the physical. You're wrong so often about so many things . . ." She smiled. "So am I. But I guess . . . what I think is cool . . . I guess that aside from the talking—" Her face became more animated. "I mean, it's not aside from the talking. You know, you stayed here for two weeks, and all we did was talk. Almost nonstop from the beginning."

Ray knew, but he hadn't realized.

"It was the longest fucking first date I ever had."

He grinned. Made sense.

"And there's more. You're so wrong, and yet you're not willing . . . to just be wrong. I mean, you're trying. Like that stupid stuff you did to that kid at Frankel's."

"Huh?"

"You remember. That grocery clerk. The checkout line, how you messed with that clerk because you thought he was being racist. You're stand-up, Ray."

The kid with the face—what was his name?—who *was* being racist. Right. Ray considered what she had said. "Thanks," he murmured.

"Now you," she said.

"Mm-hm," he agreed. And then, without thinking, "You're totally sexy. Your ears and your lips and your legs—you have great legs, you know?" He gestured toward the mirror. "But you've got this . . . I don't know, passion? It's something. You feel so big—" She lifted her gaze, surprised, ready to be insulted. "No, no, no, no, no." He waved his hand. "That's not what I mean. I mean, you've got such big feelings. Your feelings are so important. And you honor them, too, you go with what you're feeling, which makes you, I don't know—"

"Unpredictable?"

"Yeah," Ray admitted. "But that's not it, either. My feelings are so complicated . . . they're . . . so new. It's like I have baby feelings."

"You surprise me, too," Kayla said sweetly, her hand moving to his chest, a caress.

"So . . ." Ray didn't like needing a shave, but he had more to say: "I feel like when I talk with you, I'm really talking, and getting a real person's response. That's how I want to be."

"Thanks. Are you done?"

Ray nodded.

"Okay, Ray." Kayla giggled. "You know, I gotta tell you this. Your hair . . ."

He looked in the mirror, and raised his hand to his head. Kayla was right: Ray's bed-head was doing something bizarre. "Um, do you have a comb or brush I could—"

"You know," Kayla giggled. "You look like—who's that guy, the one on *News Six*?"

Ray thought he knew. "The anchor guy? The big chin—"

"No, no," she laughed. "The weather guy."

"Oh damn." That guy. "All right, all right. I look like some weatherman and my hair's—"

"Nappy." Kayla lost it. "You've got nappy hair."

"Yeah, yeah. Aren't you funny." What did nappy mean?

"Are you always this grumpy before sex?" And then: "Oh damn," Kayla added affectionately. She sidled closer, her hip against him.

There was a pause as Ray tried to smooth his hair. What a pair they made. "You know, I've been thinking," he scratched his head. "I don't like you very much."

Kayla burst into laughter again, hopping a little, foot to foot. "Damn, damn, damn." Kayla's joyfulness rumbled in the back of her throat. "Oh . . . You don't like me . . . Oh man, you don't . . ." She laughed for a long time, and well.

Ray harumphed. She sure was easy to like. His finger throbbed dully.

It was fun watching a naked woman laugh, how her body moved. His lover. They were both still naked, and he stirred. Her breasts, his dick—and then she noticed. "Hey," she said, as she reached for his unburned hand, and then placed it back on her waist, moved into it. She was alive and zippy, and Ray smiled a big smile. "Wanna go back to bed?"

Ray looked down, and in the mirror, Kayla followed his gaze. "Yes," Kayla said. "You do."

The sex was slow, meaningful. She talked a little less, seemed a little less pushy, but was just as aggressive, in a way. And very bouncy. On top, too soon, Ray had only his gauzed, throbbing finger to consider, to slow himself down, wait for Kayla. The finger hurt when held aloft. To hell with them all.

She was cuddling in the crook of Ray's arm, amidst pillow talk and laziness in the sweet after-tang of their bodies. He might have drowsed. He wanted to take a shower.

"Ray-man?"

"Mm."

"I like this."

He smiled.

"But we've got to clean it up, you know?"

He knew.

"I mean, Palmer's dangerous, just left alone. We've got to do something, to get him to stop."

"We do?" Ray wasn't so sure.

"Think about it." Kayla rolled onto an elbow, propped herself up. "Shaw's gonna be watching your back, but we're just where we are, unless we do something."

She was right, but Ray didn't like it. "I don't like it," he said.

"Me either."

They were silent for a while—and then Kayla wasn't, bopping up, sitting, and shaking Ray's shoulder. "Oh, Jesus Christ, Ray! I've got it! How about . . . oh my god, it's so much the wrong move, and just genius. I rock!

"Listen to this, Uncle Bunny. So Shaw's been called, and Palmer thinks he's got you, right? How about we do another nighttime raid, something a teensie bit less illegal, and make Palmer so mad that he blows so he gets himself arrested? I mean, Shaw's got your back, and we'll be careful. What do you say, Rain Man? Palmer's gotta take himself out of commission, right? Why don't we help?"

Her eyes shone. What could she be thinking? Kayla was out of her mind. Whatever the idea was, Ray knew he would hate it—too dangerous. His burned finger throbbed, his hand by his side. More sex and violence, he thought. What a concept.

And so, he agreed: "Absolutely," he said. "It's just genius." He imitated her voice a little. "I'm in."

CHAPTER 17

They were together again in Reggie's car, Ray and Kayla's getaway car. It was late, again, four or so in the morning, they were both scrunched down, watching Palmer's house. Ray had a crazy thought: if only Reggie would come home, all this would be over.

Palmer's truck was parked in the driveway. The dogs next door were barking. The lights of the houses stayed off. If those dogs didn't shut up, Ray and Kayla wouldn't be able to do anything.

They had waited. Then, two days ago, they had written a letter to the *News and Gazette*, signed the letter James Palmer, Jr., dropped the envelope into the Mail slot of the newspaper's office. The letter had complained about Windy Oaks's racial insensitivity, about white management's trumpeting of the Fourth of July. How the plant closed down for the day, for a company picnic and softball game, and gave out door prizes, the winning tickets taped to the bottom of folding chairs set up at the Grove. How the same white management did nothing on Martin Luther King, Jr., Day, which was just another twelve-hour workday, on the clock.

It was almost the Fourth; the paper would surely run the letter.

They had giggled as they had written it, at Kayla's kitchen table like two kids. They had wiped the envelope clean of prints. Now they had cans of spray paint ready. Red, white, and blue, of course, cans of spray paint they had found in Reggie's workshop.

How had Kayla known the paint would be there? Ray hadn't asked.

What's the difference between what a man does, and what the situation makes a man do? Is there any? Ray had begun to chew on this question. He knew that he was being stupid, and that he shouldn't provoke the psychopathic James Palmer, Jr. But the situation: Ray and Kayla. The relationship, this high. What was Ray doing?

And then the dogs quieted, and Ray and Kayla slid from their getaway car and went to work. Palmer's truck had been backed into his driveway, which couldn't have been better. On the passenger side, away from the front door so that he wouldn't notice when he got in and drove away, they painted "Boycott the Forth," the same phrase they had used twice in the letter, the same spelling. Maybe the paper wouldn't correct the spelling, they had hoped.

Ray's heart was filling his senses; he could almost taste the blood pumping as he finished painting. "There," he stage-whispered.

Kayla couldn't contain herself, she was laughing so hard. "Oh, oh, oh," she sputtered. "Let's go." She grabbed her chest as she ran back to Reggie's car. "Oh god." And then back in the car and driving away, just as slowly as last time: "You're the man, Uncle Ray. I love it. You're the shit."

What time was it? Time to get a new life. The day had begun late at night in Palmer's driveway, and now it was daytime once more. It occurred to Ray that without a steady job, he tended to do most of his living after dark, like a college student. That could confuse a guy.

College. Just like the classroom Industrial Relations models predicted, Ray could see a crisis coming. He didn't need Croninger's *Group Dynamics* to identify the impending flash-point, nor did Ray have to consult his old IR journals to read up on statistical anomalies and their recurrence. The situation looked like a classic inversion, the unpredictable populace ready to burn down the house. So if Ray needed to read up, maybe it should be in the want ads—but that was a different matter.

Burning down the house, the Talking Heads song began to thump in his head, *fight fire with fire . . .* Was he behaving himself? Did he care? He was letting his fun be fun, Ray thought. A man is the situation he's in, after all. There was no Ray without the people in his life, his job, his feelings.

Oh god. C'mon, he told himself. There's a difference between having misgivings and feeling guilty. Or being guilty. And part of the difference, Ray thought, as he wiped his hands on his shorts, and stepped out into the bright sunshine, or maybe one big difference . . . was that this time he was being honest. Okay, well, maybe he was being honestly stupid, and breaking the law, and threatening his financial security, and maybe even doing stuff that he himself would not have approved of two months ago. But he had his reasons. Kayla herself was beginning to be all his reasons. No, that wasn't true: Ray was just trying to be honest, live honestly. His feelings for Kayla were part of that.

He was standing in his backyard, later that same life. What was going on? There were noises out front, which had risen in volume and tone; the noises were laced with emotions. Ray had stepped outside, and now he walked the flagstone path from his patio to the side of the house. He looped his thumbs in his front pockets. Wrong, too hick. He inserted both hands—all but the thumbs—in his back pockets. That would look more relaxed, better. He turned the corner, coming out from between his house and Mae's, ducking under the branch of a tree. He was neighborly, Ray was here.

Palmer's truck was parked across the street. Palmer had gotten out: across the street, a group of kids sat by their bikes, which had been dumped in various sprawls on a scraggly lawn. Two other kids, younger kids, straddled their bikes, leaned on their handlebars. Palmer was arguing with a kid, a young teenager, who knows how old.

The kid saw Ray, pointed.

Palmer turned—"You shithead"—Palmer shouted, coming toward Ray.

There was another car, a police car. "Hey, Jimmy." Detective Shaw had stopped his car in the middle of the street and rolled down the window. "Whatcha doing?"

"Nothing," Palmer said. He stopped walking, but not seething. He glared at Ray.

"Good," said the cop. "Shoot. What happened to your truck?"

On Palmer's nice blue truck, there was a swath of shoddy white paint slathered across the side, atop Kayla and Ray's patriotic handiwork. Ray wondered if there were blood vessels popping, at that moment, somewhere in Palmer's head, a thought Ray liked. He stepped forward, out into the street; he looked both ways before crossing. Ray didn't want to, but he was standing next to Palmer. "Hey," Ray said. "What's up?"

One arm dangling out the window, was Shaw trying not to smile? The two men watched Palmer. Palmer was bigger than Ray, younger, more sunburned. A farmer tan, Ray supposed. Palmer didn't seem particularly muscular, but he didn't need to.

A minivan had pulled up behind the cruiser, and was waved around.

"I . . . ," Palmer said. And then, as he and Ray stepped back, away from the police car, he turned to Ray: "Be seeing you," he said.

"I don't think that would be so smart," the policeman offered.

As Palmer left, Ray exhaled. Jesus. Time to sit down. Ray moved to his made-in-America Toyota; one arm touched the hot hood, whoa, too hot. He stepped toward his leased house, by way of his leased front path, and sat on his leased front steps. Detective Shaw was standing there, two steps from Ray's stoop. There was an almost perfectly oval blob of dried ketchup or something on Shaw's shirt; Ray took some pleasure in that fact, as though it mattered. Ray also took pleasure in the hour, which was almost absurd, almost even a cliché, ten in the morning on a Saturday, a week before the Fourth of July. Palmer had come by and Shaw had been there at this most suburban of hours and days, the kids across the street easeful and lazy on their second weekend of summer fun.

The day was hot, or would be any second, worse than yesterday. The sun hurt: Ray hadn't slept enough, even though he had slept in his own bed, and Kayla had not stayed. Ray had slept here: Ray was here. Which had been fortuitous, too, for now Palmer would think that Ray was staying here, which might keep the shit away from Kayla.

Be careful, Ray told himself, considering the policeman standing there. "Mm," Ray waved half a hello. He cleared his throat. "Good morning."

"Shall we step inside, Mr. Stanton?"

No, Ray thought.

"Mr. Stanton?"

Ray ignored the question. "What can I do for you?"

"Would you have any coffee? I could sure use some coffee."

Damn Columbo, Ray thought. "Mm-mm," Ray answered. There was a pot of coffee on the kitchen counter. "No coffee."

"S'shame," Shaw said. "Well then."

"What can I do for you?"

"Okay, Mr. Stanton. Here is what we know . . ."

Ray leaned his chin into his hands. He waited.

"Sure about that coffee?"

"I'm sure," Ray said.

"Okay." Shaw gave up. Maybe.

Ray smiled. The detective didn't like that smile; he officiously opened a policeman's little notebook, slid the pencil from its place, just like a miniature billy club. Like that night. You're fired, Ray pictured himself telling someone, anyone, himself.

"Okay. . . . Let's try something. . . . You know, I'm confused, Ray. You see, I've got too many views of who you are. Too many scenarios, as they say. In one, you're the innocent who's got his nuts in the C-clamp. Your family's not here and . . . you know . . . a little of this, a little of that . . . but the clamp's tightening, you know what I mean? You're in it. And in another scenario, you're someone's uncle, which is damned implausible, if I say so myself, since you're having relations with your niece, and there's some confusion as to the, um, racialness of the situation. Plus she keeps calling me to make me believe that you want to be helpful, and that you're just some kind of helpless victim."

Detective Shaw stopped. He was waiting for a response to what was supposed to be a bombshell. "And in another, you're acting like you're the new Klan, here to take care of your own. To get the little shits lined up, everybody in their bedsheets. Which makes you the perp, as they say on TV. Then there's the fact that that paint job's just not Jimmy Palmer's style. I mean, it's not making him any friends, you see, which he's not so stupid not to have known. He might be a moron but he's not stupid. He's also been going around denying it mightily, which makes sense to me. With or without the cross on his lawn, which I don't see for real, if you know what I mean.

"But it doesn't make sense, Ray. I'm not getting the whole picture. And I want to get it, I sure do." He paused. "How about you help me understand? How about that, Ray? If you're not going to give me some coffee, how about you clear up this fucking mess for me and then go home."

The last sentence had been drawn out, drawled, mock-hick, just for Ray. "There's something on your shirt," Ray said. "Right there."

Detective Shaw looked down. "Thanks," he said, despite himself. He scratched at the food blob, although a small crusty stain persisted. "Breakfast."

Ray looked at the detective. The stoop was as good a place as any—and breakfast meant that Shaw had had his coffee already, and was only playing a game, to get inside to make Ray uncomfortable. Ray had figured Shaw out, this time: one point for Ray. He almost smiled. He could have stood in front of Detective Shaw, pointed at the stain on his uniform, and then when the cop looked down, Ray could have flicked a finger to the cop's nose. Old trick.

Or Ray could seem to be more helpful: "I guess . . . sorry."

Shaw closed his notebook; the gesture was meant to inspire confidence.

"*Ahhem,*" Ray tried again, his throat cleared. "I guess you could say that I'm in the middle of other people's messes. At least everyone else thinks it's a mess," he conceded. "And I've got all sorts of reasons I can't talk to you, since I was told not to—"

Detective Shaw narrowed his gaze.

"—but if this is an official inquiry, or you're really questioning me, or you've got some business here, then I'm available. If not, right now, I'm going for a run."

Ray coughed. Detective Shaw looked down at Ray and Ray looked up at Detective Shaw. Change that, Ray the slash-and-burn guy thought: run the meeting. Ray stood. "I guess, Detective, that I'd better say, too, that unless there's some sort of crime you'd like to ask me about, I'd rather not talk to you." He put a hand on the doorknob, a signal: see, conversation over. "Isn't that what a witness or a suspect or just a plain ol' citizen can say? Something about a lawyer or something?"

"Ray—" The police officer interrupted himself. "Enough bullshit, okay?"

Ray didn't answer.

"Okay." Shaw held out his hand, waved. "If that's the way you want it. Allow me to say, however, that you're making a mistake. People are my business, not crime—and we've got more people in Brighton than criminals, by the way. I know people, you know? And I know that you're not up to this. You're out of your league, Ray. You're up to your ass in alligators, here." Detective Shaw rubbed his nose, angrily, a gesture that might have seemed comical, if he weren't so inflamed. Allergies? Shaw continued: "And let me also say, you little shit, that when I want to talk to you—or when I want you to talk—it'll happen."

"Maybe so," Ray agreed. He hadn't wanted to agree.

"Think about it," Shaw instructed. "Here's my card."

Ray accepted the business card. Detective Shaw tilted his head.

"Mr. Stanton, crimes have been committed. A cross burning—which I'm looking at as a federal civil rights offense—and two or three assaults and maybe a kidnapping. A man's property has been defaced. So don't fuck with me. Think hard about talking to me, and then make the right decision and give me a call."

Ray opened the screen door and then the front door. "I will," he said. He swallowed. Then he stepped inside and closed the door.

That, he realized, was the real Shaw. No coffee, just police work, protect and serve.

The doorbell rang. Ray jumped, and then threw open the door—but he knew, as soon as he opened the door, that he should have waited longer.

"Just checking," Detective Shaw said. He smiled a bad smile.

CHAPTER 18

The kids were still out front. Ray waited ten minutes, slow minutes, and then he stepped back outside. What was he doing? "Hi," Ray called out.

"Hey," one of the kids answered, as she sat up in the grass. A girl. The ringleader.

The kids stared at Ray. All of the kids were white, Ray realized. He stood there. When he didn't do anything interesting, the kids went back to their conversation. There were eight white kids, mostly twelve, thirteen, fourteen years old, maybe, and two who seemed much younger; it was easy for them to ignore a grown-up.

"Duh!" One of the kids called out, and they laughed.

"Retard," added the ringleader. The front of her shirt was incredibly dirty. How the hell did that happen? Like Tom, Ray thought; just like Tom. A few of the kids seemed to be chewing long pieces of grass, fake cigarettes, happy to be thirteen, and cool. He wanted to know what the kids had been talking about with Palmer. Ray would act normal, he would just sit on the stoop for a while, and then maybe go over there.

For something to do, he opened his wallet and looked at the plastic card and photo section. His driver's license. There, where once was a picture of Jilly in a big hat, in a hotel lobby, along with Ray on a business trip, he had put a picture clipped from a magazine, a photo of a grass hut in Bali or somewhere, from which a long dock stuck way out, forty or fifty feet above spectacularly clear green water.

Ray didn't need to see the picture of his ex to remember. Jilly's chin was tilted to the right, her jaw less strong than usual, which was why she liked the shot, probably, and why she had the wallet-sized reprint made for Ray.

Another photo: Jean and Tom a few years ago, in one of those mall portraits, a very little Tom in a bowtie, Jeannie in a green turtleneck.

Another: Mom and Dad, years ago, posed in front of the house in Newton, awkward. Ray's father had never looked comfortable in photos, but his mother had always smiled. In every photo she was smiling, the smile somehow less pained than Ray imagined it felt. There had been good moments, Ray told himself. Growing up could have been worse.

Another: Fran and Larry's wedding shot, Fran in an evening gown, above-the-elbow gloves. A goofy pillbox hat and veil. Her Jackie O, she had called it. Larry in a wide-lapelled suit and a yellow power tie—two years after wide lapels were out and yellow had stopped being a power color. On that subject, Ray had been bemused, but Jilly had been merciless: come on, she had hissed to Ray, as they had walked from the ceremony to the reception. The guy looks like he just got out of jail. Ray looked at the photo closely; Jilly had a point, which was kind of funny.

The Jackie O line had been pretty funny too, typical of Fran's acerbic wit. Her second marriage, her Ari Onassis. Larry the Good, Larry the milquetoast, who couldn't hold a conversation without resorting to platitudes, but wasn't mean to her, a hell of an improvement over Husband #1, the unmentionable Whatshisname, or most of the boyfriends between. Larry, whom Fran had dumped after just a few years, too boring.

Ray's sister had forever attracted double the trouble, and it had always been that way, even when they were kids. In the house, from their father, she had suffered from being the eldest and a girl. Not a boy. Dad had been . . . Dad, a guy who grew up between wars in the U. S. of A., who loved planes and never got to fly one, which he would have done with all the courage he didn't have at home. Dad . . . disappointed, drinking, and Fran had somehow seemed his reminder, as though a kid could represent a parent's failure, walking around the house, the embodiment of her father's aspirations. Fran had been the one he had blamed, Fran and Mom. So of course Fran had gotten out early and then married the same kind of guy right away, which hadn't worked at all. Drinking is punishment, she would say. And so is your taste in men, Ray had once made the mistake of adding— but it had been late, a phone call, and she had been too much of a mess to remember Ray's meanness, or too hurt to mention it again.

Ray looked up: the kids across the street were going. In a swirl of bikes and helmets, sneakers, jeans, like a parody of the motorcycle gang they would someday join, the kids peeled out, as Ray used to call it when he was twelve. They hopped curbs and practiced braking into skids; they circled a trash can, closing in for the kill.

Ray was the trash can. They were showing Ray. So this was paranoia. No more, he told himself. Not on your life: Ray got up, stuffed the wallet back into his pocket. "Hey," he called out. "Someone want to make some money?"

They were kids, so they wanted to make money. They skidded, turned, looped around, rode right up to Ray. "How?" the ringleader asked. She would be pretty some day, this girl-thug.

"Yeah, how?" a littler kid asked. A bigger kid hit the littler kid, not hard.

"Shut up."

"Ow."

"How, and how much?" she asked.

The kids waited for Ray. He had had experience with kids. He pretended to think. "Good money," he said.

"How much?"

"Yeah, how much?"

"Shut up—"

"Ten dollars, easy money."

The little kids were impressed. Now it was her turn. "What for?"

"Well, first I'll give you"—he pointed at the sweatshirted early teen who had been talking with Palmer—"ten bucks right now to tell me what that guy wanted."

The kid hung his head. There were nervous giggles. "That's Jimmy," the kid said. "He used to like my sister but now she's married. And I used to spy on 'em."

More laughter. Some of the nervousness abated.

"I get it," Ray said. "Spying on them . . . you were going to tell."

Some of the kids liked that line, and laughed. Ray felt happy to be with kids. "Okay," Ray continued. "Did he say anything else?"

The kid smiled. "Yeah. Jimmy wanted to know about you. I told him that you got shot. Jimmy's an asshole," the kid added. He toyed with his earring.

More giggles. Asshole was a big word to use in front of an adult, and—"Pay up," the girl said.

"Okay," Ray waved. The burned finger on his waving hand had finally begun to heal. He dug into his wallet, paid, his last ten.

"Now . . . ," he said, to take the moment back from the girl. Crap, he realized, this was just like a management meeting. He looked at their faces: you're fired, you're fired, you're fired, you're fired. But she stays. Ray came back, to focus: "Now for ten more bucks I want to know every time Jimmy Palmer comes near here. I want you to call two telephone numbers if Jimmy drives onto this street. I'll pay ten dollars for each time he does, and for each time you call both numbers."

The kids were impressed. "Twenty," the girl said.

"Fifteen," said Ray. "But I'm not paying each of you. You split it."

"Deal," the girl said. "Ten down."

Ray looked at her: she was good. "Deal," he said. "Let me get the cash."

Once they had peeled out, the street seemed safe again. Ray was standing on his front walk, his wallet open in his hand, Fran and Larry smiling. Ray knew that simply because Fran could do better didn't mean that she would—or he had come to the insight now, long after the fact. Ray also knew that Kayla was right, that Palmer had to be stopped, and that they had to let him stop himself. It was crazy, but probably right. This would work.

He closed his wallet. The leather at the fold had worn thin, the edging slightly frayed. He thought about Jilly: something had changed. Maybe he hadn't forgiven himself, and maybe he wouldn't, ever, but he felt like he had forgiven her, for all her meanness to him, their rejection of each other. Or he didn't want to have these feelings anymore, to think badly of her, and so he wouldn't. It felt like a change in how Ray felt about Jilly . . . because of Kayla.

He looked around, it was time to do something, the sun was beginning to sizzle. Ray knew that he was groping, but he was a guy, thank you, and how he liked to think of himself, what he wanted to believe about himself as a man, had been challenged. Ray had not been brave, and his own lack of bravery had shocked him. He was shocked, too, to discover that he actually believed some of the bullshit: when a man is not brave, a man is a coward. The issue was black and white, Ray thought, and smiled. He had begged them to stop, he had cried out, and Palmer had known what Ray was made of—nothing, on that night.

But plenty, now. The front door was unlocked, Ray stepped inside, closed the door. On the wall to his right, by the stairs, some sort of blue light and shadow shimmered. Cool. The sun shone through the blue blades of his Lasko oscillating fan, which stood on a box; the blue light on the wall had been filtered and cast through the front window and then through the plastic blades of the fan. Ray understood what he was seeing. The image on the wall, although no more than six or so inches of fake light refracted through fake stained glass, was pretty.

Fake and pretty: we believe about ourselves what we need to believe. Ray climbed the stairs, stopped, and put his hand in the light, passed the shapeless blue shadow over the back of his hand. Again. His hand all blue . . .

This was light, and not fire. There was a difference: he was done hurting himself.

Ray decided to go for his run.

He stretched in his backyard, pushing off the oak tree and the crumbling cement barbecue, his right quad a little tight, an extra stretch there. He ran along the river, when he could, maybe two miles, then back. The mist had become haze: it was damn hot. The ground was worn, a path along the bank. Occasionally, a tree limb hung down, menacingly. His lungs ached.

At his turn-around point, where Ray pulled up to a standing jog, a teenager fished under a trestle bridge, a milk crate full of tackle, a radio mounted on the handlebars of a ten-speed. Ray waved from across the river. No response.

Ray turned and came back. At Sunrise Park, a block from the house, Ray stopped at a water fountain behind the ballfield. Sunrise Park, he told himself as he read the sign. Not Sunset.

A Little League game was just ending and another one starting, boys and girls, T-ball. Moving his feet, knees pumping just a bit, cooling down, Ray stood behind the chain-link fence and watched.

It wasn't the game that interested him exactly. It was neither the sight of the kids—cute, sure, but fierce too, this is baseball, Dad—nor the hurry-up holiday parenting, complete with Norman Rockwell and all that 1930s small-town mediocrity, with the exception of the father pacing behind second base and sputtering excitedly into a cell phone. No, what interested Ray was how faded the experience seemed, and somehow how immediate. He was overheated and a bit fuzzy and taking it all in: the bleachers had peeled long before Ray decided to sit there, for a little while, jiggling the muscles in his legs, toes pointed;

savoring the fullness of the day in deep breaths of blue, green, white; the day, the complex smells and sounds. A car door, people yelling, a dog barking as a ground ball found its way through the whole team and skittered into the outfield. The dog running onto the field, chasing the ball, chased off, then leashed to the backstop, gagging against its collar. Stay, said a serious little boy, #16 on the True Value Hardware team. The dog's tongue lolling, lapping mud from around the water fountain.

The dog chasing the ball; Ray was the ball.

Now with runners on second and third, one out or two, Ray hadn't been counting, a solid little girl approached the plate, dragging the bat upside down. The handle squiggled a line in the dirt. Among the kids in the field, parents practiced being helpful.

Don't forget this, Ray told himself. Pay attention to each feeling.

But he wasn't afraid, which felt like a feeling he was glad not to have. Ray had gone for a run, truly without thinking, just choosing to do so. Sweats, running shoes, stretches—and out into the world, as though a man could head out somewhere, anywhere, waving hello as he passed James Palmer, Jr.; to work, to the T.L.C. Family Restaurant, to the police station to report a crime, or simply to run, the day exploding gloriously in his senses. He closed his eyes: the Little Big River stank a little, the grass had been freshly mown, he could taste his sweat, smell his own smells. Ray had decided nothing, but being alive had found him again.

His body was sore but not in pain. A few rounds of bouncy sex, a run, the Tylenol waiting in the kitchen cupboard, Ray had regained his body. Thanks, Kayla.

The fat girl was somehow standing on third base, all the parents cheering, four or five kids running uncontrollably in kid circles, one doing an airplane, kid squeals rising to a collective childhood shriek. What had happened? And then to himself: eyes open, stand up. "Way to go!" he shouted.

He climbed down, clumping from the bleachers, went back to the water fountain, pursed his lips, and let the water course down his chin and chest. If death wasn't what scared him, then what? Give peace a chance, Ray almost hummed.

"Hey mister."

"Mmp," Ray glanced to his left, gulped a sip. The kid was thirsty too. "Sorry."

As he wandered away from the game, Ray tried to picture himself in ten years: more gray, older kids, a job as . . . what? He would have his own firm, and he would specialize in . . . local business, BPR on a small scale, the good fight to keep Mom-and-Pop industries alive. Okay, so the idea wasn't particularly plausible, but hey, why not dream? In ten years, Jeannie would be twenty-five, Tommy eighteen—wow, what would they be like? As of last year, Jeannie wanted to be a fashion designer, and she drew pretty well and she liked colors, so who knows, maybe? In ten years, Ray would be fifty-one, if he lived that long.

Thinking about the future brought to mind an interview he had seen recently on TV, Barbara Walters or somebody else chatting with the latest Hollywood starlet, horses cantering playfully in the background, another Hollywood day, more Hollywood weather. The actress had had a pushy mom, Ray remembered. Worse, the mom used to ask her little girl: when are you going to get married? And the actress, not even a teenager yet, would say: when I'm thirty-five. Then the mom would ask: when are you going to die? And the little girl would say: when I'm thirty-five. Ray shook his head. Awful.

When would Ray die? Not yet.

The answer made him pause. He was just down the street; he could almost see Mae's place, the leased car, the Cheez Whiz sheen of the leased house, its blue shutters. The lawn needed cutting, but hey, Ray had been busy being kidnapped and tortured, burning crosses, sucking face, writing letters and spray-painting cars, going for a run.

He had decided something. Although it might not have seemed the most profound decision to anyone else, Ray had decided something. It was his decision. He wasn't going to die yet.

Home, he showered, shaved, dressed. Shorts and a T-shirt, bare feet. He was different: he felt different. Throughout his leased house, Ray wandered without purpose, his thoughts collecting. There, at the edges, were pieces of a dream from last night: a pair of sunglasses, one lens missing, a skyline seen in the missing lens. He had no idea what the dream meant, or how the partial scenes added up; he wasn't very good at understanding his own dreams, and the increasing frequency of their disturbing imagery these last few weeks in Brighton, how close to the surface everything had become, didn't help, as all the dreams seemed to blur together even more than usual.

So what? he asked himself. Ray entered the kitchen. A second glass of OJ, a brief escapade chasing a sprightly, enormous fly up the kitchen window, the flyswatter a surprisingly gratifying object to hold. To have, Ray thought. To wield with a resounding smack. He felt uncertain and powerful, one emotion fueling the other: to be uncertain is to have the power to choose, he thought. Choosing. This was living, Ray thought.

A fly was dead and Ray was not.

CHAPTER 19

Happy hour at Dooley's Bar and Grill, dollar shots, beer nuts and Channel 6. At the end of the bar, two women sat drinking gin and tonics, their hair piled up in matching piles, top-knotted and overflowing. Lots of rings, both. Ray stood behind them; the woman to his right glanced back, smiled, said hello.

"Hi."

She returned to her friend, sister, coworker, all of the above. Maybe they took night courses in real estate. Maybe not. It occurred to Ray that they were here to meet men like him.

The news began, Ray couldn't hear it. The clips were of a river, the closed captioning too small to read from where he stood. There would be a local crime report later, he knew, in about eight minutes. Around here, Ray sniffed, a bar was probably the scene of the crime anyway. Probably the scene of every crime, if not the source.

The bar looked like it should, dark and well used. It was crowded, permanently smoky. Men and women, some white collar, a few black faces; four TVs, two over the bar and one in each corner. A steam table along the wall offered complimentary wings; hand-printed signs read Hot, More Hot, Blast Off. A black-and-white P.O.W. flag hung above the register. Behind the rows of grade B liquor, a leaded-glass mirror had mostly yielded to a jigsaw puzzle of postcards: Erin Go Bragh, Love from Scenic Donegal, The Wearing O' the Green. A jukebox stuttered *Buh, buh, buh, Bennie and the Jets*. It could be 1978. Along the far wall, a beer can collection gathered dust; there were probably even some pop-tops.

What if Palmer's here? Ray thought. And then: Oh fuck it. Ray hadn't told Kayla where he'd be, and he hadn't told himself why he was here. "Beer," Ray said to the bartender. Right. Slide onto the seat and don't order an import. Put your money on the bar.

The two women were turning. Eye contact. "Hi," the first said. She stuck out her hand. "Phyllis."

Ray shook it. "Ray," he said. He knew her from somewhere.

The second woman smiled. "Sally," she nodded. Then "Sal," she confessed.

"Ray."

The bartender slid their way, alerted by the introductions. Of course, Ray thought. The woman he had kicked in the shin. Damn town, Ray thought. Damn tiny little fucking universe.

He would buy her a drink, as an apology. No harm in that. Ray raised his free hand, two fingers in the air, waving. A peace sign. Give peace a chance. "Two more here, please. My treat. And I'll take another beer."

"How nice!" chirped Sal. "A gentleman."

"Thank you, Ray," smiled Phyllis.

"My pleasure," said Ray.

"Charrrrmed," Sal trilled.

"Truly," said Phyllis.

"Really," said Ray. "It's the least I could do."

"You didn't have to," added Phyllis.

"That's the truth." Sal shook her head.

"I—"

"Stop!" yelled Phyllis. And then everyone laughed.

"A tab?" asked the bartender, furthering the cause.

Ray looked to Phyllis, who smiled. "Why not," he answered. A drink or two meant he was legitimately sorry.

Phyllis was smiling more. She felt pretty tonight, Ray thought. Behave, he told himself. Curiosity, he told himself. That's all, nothing more.

For a noticeable moment, no one spoke. Then Ray and Phyllis together said "So—"

Sal giggled, sipped, giggled. Phyllis tilted her head, a coy tilt.

"So," Ray tried again. There, on the news, was a video replay of a cross burning. Ray's cross. Again? He indicated, with a tilt of his chin, the TV. "This stuff happen here a lot?"

"Drinks?" asked Sal. She was confused. "It's a bar."

Oh no. Ray kept a straight face, turned to Phyllis; he hoped she could hold her liquor better than her friend. "You know, the Klan."

"That's something," Sal clucked.

"Not that I've heard," said Phyllis. "Except lots of people don't get along, like anywhere."

"Right," said Ray.

"Where you from?" asked Sal, brightly.

"Oh," Ray laughed. "Same as you. You know."

She looked at him. "I'm from here," she smiled.

Ray smiled along: "Well, me too!"

Ouch. Phyllis had given Ray's biceps a pinch. "We're just having our drinkies, right, Sal?"

Sal giggled.

Graciously, he hoped, Ray took the pinch as a hint, and he turned back to Phyllis. He was sorry; he wouldn't make fun of Sal. "Sorry," he said softly. The jukebox was playing very early U2. The music hammered at him: three chords and some clever anger. "What do you ladies do?"

Sal tilted her head, her hair flopped to one side. "I work at the high school," she said. "Level 4 secretary. I'm Math/ Science—"

Phyllis hadn't answered. She looked down.

"And she's at the plant. Phyllis is a super," Sal said. "Super duper."

Oh hell, Ray thought. Kicked and then fired. Phyllis was still looking down at her hand, her rings. "I'm in management," Ray said, as plainly as possible.

Everyone sipped. No one wanted to discuss what they did, or who they were, not with drinkies at Dooley's. Sidelong, Ray looked more closely at Phyllis. She might have been blond, but the hair was so dyed or frosted he couldn't tell. She was wearing slacks, a white sleeveless blouse. She was nice looking, not slim, maybe in her midthirties. Maybe younger. She had a mole or a birthmark on her left cheek—he couldn't tell without staring rudely—rings even on her thumbs, and long nails. Ray couldn't see her right earring, but her left looked to be a little guy in a red necktie, like some sort of business voodoo. Maybe someone from work, or her ex, strung up. She had a nice neck. In fact, it was her nicest visible feature. She had a very nice neck.

He was embarrassed: he hadn't put on a good shirt. He hadn't been ready to think about looking nice. "You know," Ray began to lie. "When I was in high school there was an incident like this one, right on my block." He nodded at the TV. "Afterward, the people moved. Pleasant folks, two kids. A girl—if I remember correctly—she wanted to be a violinist or something. She was sort of a prodigy."

"What did they do?"

"You mean where'd they go? I'm not sure. Or what did they do—"

"I mean, what started it?" asked Phyllis. She was back in the conversation, apparently, having decided something.

"Don't know," Ray pretended to admit. "Probably no one could say."

Phyllis thought about that. Ray's left hand jingled the change in his pocket. His shoulder throbbed dully. Then he had a stupid, grim realization: maybe lying made his body hurt more. Oh great. At this rate, he'd be struck by lightning any day now.

No way, Ray decided. Lame.

"It's like those feuds," Phyllis said. "I was just reading something in *Newsweek* or somewhere, about two Hispanic families . . . in New York? They used to be friends, godparents, the whole deal, and now they're killing each other. And no one knows what started it."

"Hillbillies," Sal added.

"Or something," Phyllis agreed.

Ray pushed on: "But it's different when it's racial, right? I mean, don't you think?"

"No difference to me," Phyllis said. "Sal will tell you. We've had our share at the high school, and there's no difference. It's either a girl dating the wrong guy or the boys' soccer team all carried away with themselves, thinking that swastikas don't mean anything. Or sucked into the violence and all that. Sometimes it looks racial, but there's no difference really."

"Do the kids hang together?"

"You mean blacks and whites?" Sal asked. "Be real."

Phyllis slid a silver ring from her right index finger, then rubbed the ring on her palm. "But where do they? They don't want to."

Ray had no answer. Phyllis seemed to have answers.

"You're downers," said Sal. "Get happy."

Both Ray and Phyllis smiled tightly. Both women knew a lot, had seen plenty, chosen to be who they were. In Ray's estimation, they probably knew more than he ever would about race—even though they were white, as Kayla would be quick to point out, which meant that to Phyllis and Sal racism only existed when it made the news.

Phyllis would never understand Kayla. Would Ray? He thought about her. She and Ray had made the news. The cross had burned brightly, Channel 6, in every home.

"You're just visiting," Sal declared.

"What makes you say that?"

"Well . . ." She laughed, and Phyllis laughed along. "This isn't that big a place. And if you had come here, we would've checked you out," Sal said.

Ray raised his eyebrows. "Oh?" he asked, pleased.

Sal blushed. "You know," she said to her drink.

"But I do know you," Phyllis said. "You're—"

"Yeah, yeah. That guy at the plant." He wanted to change the subject.

"Well, that's where Phyllis works!" And then: "Bet you're married," Sal said.

"Separated. Filing," he offered.

"Kids?"

"Girl and a boy."

They were all three glancing at each other intermittently. Nerves.

"I've got a kid," offered Sal. "Phyl's got two, too. Two, too," she giggled to Phyllis.

"How you folks doing?" asked the bartender. "How's my gal, Sal?"

"Medium-rare," said Sal. She was pleased with her joke; her body jiggled a bit, left-right, left-right.

Phyllis looked at Ray.

"Anyone want anything?"

"Fine here," answered Phyllis, looking at her watch. "We've gotta—"

"Oh poop," said Sal.

Phyllis reached in front of Ray, put her hand on her friend's shoulder. "We should be—"

"And you, bud?"

Had he just been offered a beer? "Sure thing," said Ray. "If the ladies . . ."

Phyllis smiled at Ray. What did he think he was doing?

"C'mon, Cupcakes."

Phyllis snorted, flushed.

Sal turned to Ray. "I'm not supposed to call her that."

"Cupcakes?"

"It's an old, boring story."

Ray extended his hand, maître d'-style, and spoke in a funny voice: "You first, Madame, tell me your boring story. And then"—he winked—"I'll show you my moonwalk."

"Your French accent sucks," grumbled Phyllis. "Okay . . ." She turned to the bartender. "One more for the toad. And I'll tell my dumb story."

"The toad!" Sal shrieked. "One more for the toad!" Her face changed: "Oh I gotta go wee."

"I'll join you," Phyllis chimed. "Ray, do you think you could find us a table?"

He craned his neck. "Looks possible."

"Great," said Phyllis.

"You're wonderful," said Sal.

Three beers were usually Ray's limit, Ray remembered as he carried his fourth beer and the ladies' drinks to a free table. Ray and the Three Beers, he told himself. Yessir. He was a bit buzzed.

By the time Sal and Phyllis had returned, Ray had fixed a plate of wings for the table; wet wipes and extra napkins, celery sticks and blue cheese in Dixie cups. Or ranch dressing? He couldn't tell. The jar behind the bar probably said dressing.

He was going to regret something, he realized, and it would most likely be the food, which seemed to glisten with a sort of Day-Glo sauce, safety orange. No nukes. He took a bite—hot, hot—slurped his beer, swabbed his chin. Rinse and repeat.

"My favorite," Phyllis said. She helped herself, Sal.

"Wuh." Sal waved a hand in front of her face. "Hot, hot, hot." She waved faster.

They ate, in a chorus of smacking lips, clinking glasses, giggles, like teenagers. Like Jeannie and her friends. Milkshakes and french fries, the sophomore class meal. Coffee and extra-strength painkillers tomorrow, Ray shook his head.

Sal cupped her hand, leaned toward Ray, as though to whisper. "Shhh," she said loudly. "You're cute."

For chrissakes. "You too," Ray said, although he meant to say thanks. Uh-oh. Time to hit the can. Kick the can? And then: "If you ladies will excuse me . . ."

"My!" Sal chortled.

"Of course," Phyllis added.

In the Men's, not sure how he had gotten there, Ray peed, his forehead resting on the cool tile wall above the urinal, one hand raised, the other on himself, aiming, waiting to shake. He would have read the graffiti, if only he could open his eyes. Better yet, Ray would have written something. Did he have a pen? What a long piss. His lips were kind of numb. Come on, Ray. Four beers? Wuss.

There were no paper towels but Ray didn't care. He gave the faucet a quick punch, turning on the cold, then splashed his face, ran his wet hand along the back of his neck. Bluhhh. The water stopped. He punched the tap with his palm again. He looked up. If the mirror had been a TV, it would have been filled with flames.

Instead, there was Hank Williams.

"Hey," said Ray. "How—"

"Gary!" said Hank.

"Ray," said Ray. "It's Ray."

"What the fuck!" laughed Hank. "It's Ray!"

Oh man, thought Ray. Who's the designated driver?

"Let me give you a hand, Ray-gun. You got—hey, no towels—I guess it's a blowjob or the t.p., if you know what I mean. I mean, excuse the Franglais. There's the blower if you wanna put your face in it, not that I'd recommend that, it's like too quick a tan, if you ask me. Might as well boil if off. But a man's gotta do what—"

"I'm fine." Ray wiped his face with his hands, dried his hands on his pants.

"Sure you are."

Ray snorted, rubbed his nose. "Come join us."

"Us?" asked Hank. "Ooh boy. Well I just happen to be alone. Nice shirt."

Again, across the crowded room, steady, steady, hand on a chair, almost there. The girls had cleaned up; the chicken bones and napkins and wipes had all disappeared, presto, pronto. Ray's mug was full, his head clouded. Chance of thunderstorms, later, maybe. "Think it's going to rain?" he asked the girls.

"Nope," said Phyllis. "Not—"

"Hey Sal," said Hank.

"Hankie," Sal keened.

"Hank Williams, just like the singer. Only I'm not."

"Phyllis Herman. We've met," she added. They shook hands.

"Hankie's from around," offered Sal.

"It's a pleasure," Hank smiled. "Like I was just telling Ray here, Dooley's is for people you want to know, in my book. So you go to Dooley's and people are there and you meet them. That's what Dooley's is for."

Ray tried not to make a face. Hank and Sal deserved each other, fine. So who did Ray deserve? Or what? He had come here . . . why?

"Let me buy y'all something. What'll it be?"

"What'll I feel like, Phyl?"

"You feel like going home—"

Hank objected: "Hey! I'm only just arrived. Let a working man buy a lady a Harvey Wallbanger or two."

Sal laughed deeply, in the back of her throat, in her chest, a smoker's laugh. Phyllis rolled her eyes, for Ray. And then: "Ray? You okay?"

Ray drank, nodded. "Hank owes me a drink. How about it, girls?"

"That's the spirit, Ray-gun!" Hank said.

Sal was agreeing, her face aglow. Soon enough, Phyllis would have to relax, thought Ray. She's had her few.

"Draft for me," said Ray.

"Gin and tonic," Sal raised her hand.

Phyllis smiled. It was a big smile and Ray liked to see it happen. Kayla had a great smile. "White wine spritzer for me, and for Sal. That's what she's drinking."

"Oooh—"

"Now don't mope."

"Look. See my lip? I'm moping. Who's going to help me?"

Hank laughed. "Stay out of this, Ray. If you know what's good for you."

Ray chuckled. The room had seemed a little fuzzy for a second. All right. The food was helping. Had Phyllis done something different with her hair while Ray was in the bathroom?

It looked different. He sipped his beer. Sal and Phyllis saw a guy they knew, waved, talked about him, not unkindly. Ray half-listened. The Miller clock said 7:12 in big red letters. Or was it numbers? He didn't know the song on the jukebox, a country tune. Like someone being pinched while she sang. Ray had been pinched by Phyllis, once, recently, but not since.

"Here we go. . . ." Hank had the four drinks squeezed together, to carry them in one trip.

"Thank you, sir," smiled Phyllis. Another big smile.

"Thanks, Hankie." Sal began to laugh. "Thankie, Hankie . . ."

"Is this it? We even, Ray?"

He laughed. "Even up."

"Amen," hollered Hank.

"There you go," Ray said to no one.

"So you see the news? The Klan came and burned a cross on J. T.'s lawn!"

"The Klan!"

"Junior or senior?" asked Phyllis.

"Junior," said Hank. He took a slug of his beer. "Holy shit, that's something," he concluded.

Ray was going to vomit. The Klan was here: right here in River City.

"Hasn't happened in ten, twelve years," offered Hank. "Last time was that Wilkerson family, when the fight at the old tool-and-die went ugly—"

"Really?" said Sal. She didn't seem to care. "Mm."

"Anyone know why?" There. He had asked. He could function.

"Well, the Wilkersons weren't like us, if—"

"No," Ray cut in. Was that too loud? Concentrate: be sober. Breathe. Breathe. Okay, now say it: "I mean. . . . Palmer's?"

"Haven't heard. Now that Wilkerson thing's funny, if you think about it. You ask me . . ."

Ray tuned out. His eye was watering; quick, someone might see. Sal was watching Hank, Phyllis was watching Sal, Ray was watching everyone. Good. He was okay. As long as he didn't try to stand. Breathe, and don't stand up.

"—thought I recognized the house," Phyllis was saying. "I know his sister from work."

"My wine's got water in it," Sal complained.

"Now, now." Hank's hand was on hers.

"So where you been, Hankie?"

Phyllis was looking at Ray. Her face was close. "You're awful quiet. Anybody home?"

"Sure. I just—"

"Tell her, Ray! Women live longer, right?" Hank was insane.

"That's right." Ray licked his lips.

"Well I knew that," Sal cooed. "It's because we drink more than you do—"

"Oh ho!"

"And we're better at sex."

"Whoa there, honey! You're what?" Hank had nearly spit.

"You heard me. Isn't that right, Phyllis?" Her friend's name had been tough to say. Sal giggled. "And it wasn't women burning that cross. I'll bet you my Saturday panties."

"Shit!" Hank guffawed. "Shit, shit, shit, shit, shit!"

Phyllis was beaming, laughing so hard she twisted in her chair. Hank began to bang his head on the table, in fun. Sal gave Ray a tiny, triumphant smile.

"Damn," said Phyllis. "I lost a lens."

On his knees, crawling among his drunken compatriots, Ray knew that he would never find the missing contact lens. It was too small, he was too big. For chrissakes, now what was Hank doing? He had started to crawl underneath the next table. Sal had followed. A crawling conga line, great. No way he would—

"Hey." Ray held up his hand. "This it?"

"Wow," Phyllis exhaled. "You found it." The tops of their heads pushed at the underside of the table. She lightly touched the faded bruise on his face, his eye, then she kissed Ray softly, tongue. "Thanks."

A kiss? She was kissing him, so Ray kissed back. Tongue? Okay, Ray responded. Tongue.

Oh, was he going to hurt tomorrow. In the cab going home, Phyllis's hand stroking his thigh, his thigh not objecting, Ray could dimly make out the next day's hangover. Bluh. Was it foggy out? He hoped so: real fog would help explain what Ray saw when he looked out his window, and why there were no flames outside, and none shimmering in the reflected glass. He turned back to Phyllis, who was very good at demanding attention. With his hips, he moved against her hand, toward her hand, there.

"I'm not coming in," she murmured. "Can't. The kids . . . But you can call me."

Kayla, Ray thought, as he nodded. He had half-expected her to say that, even though he didn't want her to come in, mostly. "You sure?" he asked.

"Mm," she said, her mouth finding his.

Then he pulled back. "I'm sorry," he said. "You're very attractive."

"That's nice," she smiled.

"No," Ray said. "I mean yes. But also about the other day. I didn't mean to. . . ."

Phyllis cocked her head. "What are you talking about."

"About the other day. You know. I didn't mean to kick you like that."

"Kick me?" she laughed. "When did you kick me?"

Ray looked at her, as best he could. "I . . . "

"Ray," Phyllis was still laughing. "You're confused. We met at the plant. The supervisor's meeting?"

"Right," Ray said. He would believe her. He was drunk and he hadn't kicked her.

"East Bine," the cabbie said.

"Right," said Ray. Nothing was right. He straightened up. "That one."

"The blue—"

"No, next. The yellow." What time was it? What day?

"I'm in the book. Phyllis Herman. One 'n.' "

"Check," Ray said. "I'll remember." The cab pulled into the driveway. "She's going on," Ray said, giving the driver a five and some ones. "Keep it."

"You're not going to call," Phyllis said.

Ray looked at her. She was probably right. "I—"

"Company," said the cabbie.

Ray turned his head, saw the streetlight and the first sliver of the rising moon competing in his window; he saw Mae's flowers like glowing coals. Rooms were beginning to be lighted, lives ignited. A high-pitched laugh spilled through a screen door, as though it had happened years ago. The street seemed full of sound and movement and memory, the night turned inside out, its guts exposed, and everything was just beyond his focus, something to come to, later, or maybe not at all. A different life, Phyllis squeezing his hand where it lay on the seat, her hair different, she had definitely done something. But the blue shutters of his house weren't blue, this wasn't his house anyway, why had the cab stopped here? Nothing was burning here, Ray thought, which was good.

"Ray . . . "

He made his eyes work. Mae was walking toward him, toward the cab. Ray got out of the cab. He stood: he was standing.

"Who's that?" Mae asked. She was not smiling.

The cab door was closed. Ray looked at Phyllis. "I don't know," he admitted. "I'm drunk," Ray tried to whisper.

"I noticed," Mae said. "Kayla's inside. Let's hope she didn't see."

CHAPTER 20

They had talked for an hour or so, pouring too much coffee, Ray's body still overwhelmed by the beer, confused and drunk. Then, at one point, Mae had discovered a stain on her slacks and gone upstairs to change. Kayla had stepped to Ray, touched his hair, laid his left hand on her shirt, her breast, said nothing. If she had seen, she would have said. She was Kayla, he told himself. But she said nothing: she hadn't seen. She didn't ask where he had been, or why he was drunk.

The night was going nowhere, the talking felt good, saying nothing important about nothing pressing. They had discussed the news, but without specifics—especially since neither Kayla nor Ray would reveal to Mae their roles in the cross burning, the car painting, the letter writing.

Ray was finally sober. His head ached. He regretted Phyllis. Stupid, Ray thought. What a gargantuan mess he had almost made of an enormous mess. He wondered, uncharitably, if she had been trying to save her job, which seemed possible, unfortunately. What he would have said if Kayla had asked who Phyllis was.

When Mae returned, she separated the lovers with a polite clearing of her throat. "Well," Mae said.

"Yes," Ray agreed.

"My turn. Going potty," Kayla threw up her hands, left the kitchen, shaking her head side to side, girlishly, as she pushed through the double doors into the living room. A moment later she called from the other room, calmly: "Ray? I think there's a police car out front."

"Oh dear," said Mae.

Both Ray and Mae stood.

"Come look," Kayla urged, as Mae and Ray entered the room, crossed to the front window, peeked through the drapes. "That one. Just behind the Jeep. It's unmarked."

"There? But somebody's in it," Mae said.

"That's right," Ray explained. "Surveillance. Stakeout."

Kayla's glance caught Ray's. "Cool," she chirped.

"What?" Mae's hand partially covered her mouth. "Oh no. How awful."

"Maybe not," Kayla offered. "Maybe he's watching to keep us safe."

"Oh? I see. Of course."

Did Mae see? She seemed not to know what was happening.

"Momma? The police are probably here to make sure nothing happens to Ray." Again, Kayla looked toward Ray, communicating: she had noticed her mother's confusion too. "Momma? Are you okay? Should we take a break? How about bedtime."

"I beg your pardon?" Mae was genuinely surprised. "You think I'm some sort of invalid. Or incapable? Baby Girl, this better be a moment you regret. 'Bedtime.' So you two can—" She stopped herself. Her gaze dropped to her hands, palms up, rolled over, there were her cuticles, and then palms up again.

Ray watched Mae lose the argument she was having with herself.

"Sorry. I'm sorry, honey. I do feel a bit out of sorts. I think I will go lie down. It's been a long day, hasn't it? All this trouble, and we're involved. That's right." She turned to Ray. "If you'll excuse me, then?"

"Of course," Ray smiled. "And thank you, Mae."

"Pardon me?"

"Yes," Ray said. "Thanks. I'm the one in the middle, and really, you're my Good Samaritan, so now you're involved. I'm sorry about that, but I appreciate your support. The company—" he added stupidly.

Mae smiled. "I see. You're welcome."

Back toward the kitchen, as Mae trudged upstairs, Kayla pushed Ray, until Ray stopped at the double doors. Her hand was on his back, she pushed again, harder.

"Hey!"

Her hand slipped lower, grabbed him, goosed him. Ray squirmed away, into the kitchen. She followed, grabbed him again, reaching, firmly.

"Kayla!" Ray had used her name; it had sounded strange aloud. If he hollers, Ray thought.

"'The company . . . ,'" she snorted.

"I know," Ray said. "Dumb, dumb, dumb."

"C'mere," she gritted her teeth playfully.

Her smile became suggestive, her hips did a little horny dance backwards. "Bring it here," Kayla whispered loudly.

"Here?" Ray arrived, leaned into her against the counter, his hand cupping, between her legs. "Like this?"

"Sh," Kayla said. "You'll wake the baby." She grabbed him. "Like this," she said. She bit his ear.

"Mm."

"Mmmmm." Her stroking broadened, fingertips spread to a widened palm. "We can't," Kayla said. "Not here. It's too dangerous," Kayla breathed. Then she slid her body against his, up and down.

Something she learned from the movies, Ray thought. More, Ray thought.

"Let's go to your place," she whispered.

"But what about the police?" Kayla put her hands inside his pants, almost on his butt, and pulled Ray closer—any closer and Ray would be inside her, it seemed, which is what he wanted. "Hmm?" he asked again. His head ached a little.

"I'm thinking," she said.

"You're not thinking; your eyes are closed."

In a slow, fun circle Kayla licked Ray's upper lip and lower lip. Her tongue was remarkably pink. "So?"

"So what about Paul Shaw?"

"He's not invited."

"Kayla . . ." He had said her name again, slower.

"Fine." She pushed him away. She half-meant it. "You go out the front door, since he knows you're here and he's probably watching you, and I'll go out the back. Same time. But take your time outside. Distract the poor public servant. Show him your, um, thing." Then she began to sing: "*Would it be my fault if I could turn you on. . . .*" She spun away. "*Would I be so bad if I could turn you on!*" She stopped singing. "Do you remember that song?" And then: "Your place in five minutes? I'll meet you on the kitchen floor. You'll be able to recognize me, no problemo, Tío Blanco: I'll be the one with the carnation between my legs."

Ray smiled. Who wouldn't like this? He left Kayla in the kitchen and peeked out the front door of Mae's house. Once he heard the back door open, he stepped outside, pretended to catch his sleeve on an invisible sharp thing, said "Ouch," and dropped his keys on purpose, in clear view, he hoped, of Shaw. Ray would stall. He fumbled around, took his time, opened Mae's door again, peered inside, turned around. He picked up his keys, looked at them, jangled. He rubbed his arm. Was he taking enough time? He scratched his nose.

Ray was standing on the stoop, nonchalant, in front of Mae's house, when Jimmy Palmer, Jr., drove by in a beat-up old two-toned car, not in his truck, a hat screwed down on his head, looked up, pointed a finger—*Pow!*—at Ray.

Down the block, the unmarked police car pulled into the street and approached slowly.

A cab pulled into Ray's driveway.

The outside light on his house flashed on and off, twice. Kayla.

Phyllis was standing next to the cab. Jesus!

The police car sped up, screeched to a stop, at a ridiculous angle, in front of the house.

Kayla was naked, Ray was sure.

Phyllis hadn't seen him. She must have already paid the fare.

From inside his house, Kayla pulled open the front door halfway.

Detective Shaw stepped from the car. Engine running. A plastic bag in his hand.

Phyllis slipped her purse down her arm, caught the strap. She looked surprised.

Detective Shaw said something to Phyllis, then stepped past her to Ray's house. The cop knocked on the screen door.

From behind him, Ray heard his name. Mae Reeves was standing there in her own doorway, quizzical.

He must have turned, to see Mae.

Phyllis saw him. She gave a little confused wave. She held something aloft.

Kayla had stepped outside, in front of Ray's house. She was wearing a towel or one of his shirts—how? so quickly?—which covered her just as it announced that she was naked underneath. It was probably unbuttoned, by the way she held it closed, sexy.

Ray was pointing up the street, where Palmer had gone.

Detective Shaw also pointed up the street, where Palmer had gone. The cop seemed to be asking a question. He had put down his garbage bag.

Phyllis was saying something.

Mae said Ray's name again.

Mae called to Kayla, said Kayla's name.

Kayla called to Ray.

In this kind of situation, Kayla was capable of—what?

Ray stepped toward Phyllis, Kayla, Shaw. This wasn't happening.

"Mr. Stanton," someone was saying.

"Ray?" someone was saying.

"Mr. Stanton, I'm sorry, but I must have a word. Could we step inside?"

"Ray?"

"Mr. Stanton? Are these your clothes?" Detective Shaw showed Ray the open bag. "Mr. Stanton, I asked you a question. Are these your clothes?"

"Ray?" Phyllis was asking. "Is this your wallet?"

"Ray?"

"Mr. Stanton, I have some news that might interest you. Mr. Stanton? How about a word?"

"Ray?"

Shaw had his notebook open: "Mr. Stanton, do you know a Nathan Mapes?"

From behind the screen door, Kayla said, "I do. What's happened?"

"Nathan Mapes . . ." Detective Shaw was watching Ray. "Was just released from the hospital. He was beaten. And—"

"Oh no," said Kayla. She opened the door. "Is he—"

"Ray?" said Phyllis. "I should probably go."

Four people stood there: Ray and three people who don't go together. His lover, a local law enforcement officer, and a woman he had kissed but not kicked. Plus Mae in her doorway, a Good Samaritan on disability, his lover-in-law. They had his clothes and his wallet.

People were talking around him.

"He'll be okay. But something strange about it . . . Ray's name. Mr. Stanton? Your name was written on Nathan's arm. His attackers wrote your name on his arm."

CHAPTER 21

The cop had gone and Phyllis with him. Mae was back inside. Kayla had slipped on shorts, her earrings dangling, her mood apparently connected to her choice of earrings, the hoops on a happy day, the jingly silver ones when she wanted something—or maybe these were her nighttime earrings. Ray and Kayla sat on Ray's patio drinking a drink Ray didn't notice. A wet glassful of a wet drink. Kayla was still wearing Ray's shirt, the light yellow button-down with the bleach stains, the shirt he wore to unpack boxes. Ray and Kayla on a Saturday night in Brighton, Ohio.

The introduction hadn't exactly won anyone over: Kayla, this is Phyllis. From the plant. Phyllis, this is Kayla. Um. Kayla . . . Reeves. Pleased to meet you, they both had said at once. Then Kayla had gone back inside, politely.

A few minutes later, after Shaw had finished asking Ray a number of questions, the cop had offered Phyllis a ride. But first, standing on his front walk, Phyllis had reached to touch Ray's face, his bad eye. Before her hand could get there, Ray had turned away, touched the cheekbone himself, testing. You're fired, Ray had told himself.

Everyone else gone, Ray and Kayla sat out on Ray's back patio. They had had sex on that chaise lounge, right over there.

"So. What do we do?" Ray was at a loss.

"Do?"

"You know. Do. I'm just asking."

Kayla didn't look at him. "Want a cigarette?" she offered. "Or does Phyllis not smoke."

"You don't smoke. I don't smoke. Phyllis . . ."

"I used to smoke," Kayla said. "Who's Phyllis?" Kayla had a pack of cigarettes. She lit one.

Ray didn't know what to say. "We shared a cab," he offered. "I must have left my wallet on the seat."

"Do you want me to believe that?"

"It's the truth."

"Fine. Then that's what I'll believe."

They were silent. Ray could make a list of the subjects they weren't discussing.

"Yes. Yes, please. I would like one."

She looked at him. "What?"

"A cigarette."

She complied. They sat for a while. They smoked. The cigarette tasted like a memory: Thursday night poker games, laundry quarters in a pile, years ago, in college, before the world had ended. Maybe he would join Bruce's weekly game, back in Medford.

"I'm different," he said.

"You're not kidding," Kayla agreed. "But I'm still Kayla. Don't ever call me Phyllis."

"Ha ha," Ray said. "Funny."

There was more to say; he tried again: "It's not that I'm confused, though. It's not like I don't know who I am." He faltered. The night was out there, just beyond the light spilling onto the back lawn from the kitchen window. "Three weeks ago this might have made me cry. When you were out. By the way, you work too hard," he said.

"Really."

"That's right," he told himself. He waited for his heart rate to slow. There. And one, and two: lub-dub, lub-dub, lub-dub, lub-dub. He slowed his heart rate. Good. "—I knew already," he continued an unfinished thought. "I mean, it's not like I didn't suspect that . . . this . . . I thought about you, you know."

"I don't understand," Kayla said. "Knew what? When? What are you talkin' about?"

Ray rolled the tip of his cigarette ash against the concrete. "Nothing. I mean, I knew what I knew already. About myself. But I guess what I'm trying to say is that I've been thinking about you pretty much non-stop. When I'm not being scared." He thought about Nathan. Oh shit.

She had sprawled on the chaise lounge, and Ray could see the curve of her hip where the shirt hiked. Where the shorts began, and then fun. He made himself not look.

"And . . ."

"No," he answered. "I mean, there's no more. You're having a good influence. I feel . . ."

"Oh lord," Kayla giggled. "He's got a hard-on."

Ray didn't answer, he didn't have to: he stood up and approached Kayla, then half lay next to her, one foot still on the patio. Wasn't that some screwy tradition, one foot on the floor to keep from getting too frisky? He couldn't remember. It had been in one of Tom's books. Was that recently? Oh hell.

"Uncle Ray?"

"April Mae?"

She moved to slap him, turned the gesture into a caress. His thigh. "What are we doing?" She was wide-eyed. "I mean, I think I know what I'm doing. I'm in a relationship. . . . I guess what I'm asking is what are you doing? This is what you want, right?"

Ray started to stand, changed his mind. Goddamn roller coaster wouldn't stop, would it. He eased his weight onto his butt again, one hip leaning into Kayla. Her skin was underneath her clothes. He knew what to say: "I'm in a relationship too. It's what I want."

"Good," she said.

"You think so?" Ray's voice had squeaked slightly.

"Mm-hm," she giggled.

"And—"

She took over: "And I don't know what's going to happen, or how it's going to go. Or end. But I want to be with you. . . . If that changes, I'll let you know."

"Me too," Ray answered her look.

"Good," she said again. "Wanna do it?"

"Like you wouldn't believe," Ray said. "Let's." He touched her face. They kissed.

"Okay!" Kayla sat up. "Be right back."

He liked her.

"Ray?" Kayla had turned around; she was backlit against the kitchen light.

"Yes."

"Maybe . . . I think we should talk to Nathan instead."

Ray considered the suggestion. "Yeah, probably right." he said.

"Good," Kayla said. "How's now? I'll give him a call. And Ray. . . ?"

"Yeah?"

"I need to trust you. I'm trusting you."

They took Kayla's car, Ray in the passenger seat. As they drove, Ray recounted his conversation with Detective Shaw. The cop had asked the usual: a certain Nathan Mapes had been assaulted, did Ray know him? Would Ray have any idea why his name might be linked with Nathan Mapes's name? Did Ray know anything about the assault? Would Mr. Stanton care to comment on why his name had been written on the wrist of the victim's fractured arm? Just for the record, what was Mr. Stanton's relationship to the victim?

It seemed like Shaw had asked questions to which he already knew the answers, mostly, a tactic Ray recognized from work, how to manage an unpredictable and thus potentially dangerous team member. How did Mr. Stanton know one James Palmer, Jr.? When did they first meet? Just for the record, what was Mr. Stanton's relationship to Mr. James Palmer, Jr.? To the Palmer family? Was Mr. Stanton a member of a fraternal organization? Was he a church-going man? Did Mr. Stanton have a criminal record? Where was he three Tuesdays ago, say, between 2 and 5 a.m.? And during the same time period two Thursdays ago? Could he confirm his whereabouts during the times in question, on those particular dates; was there anyone who could corroborate his account of his whereabouts? As a small matter, what was Mr. Stanton's occupation? His date of birth? His military record? Was Mr. Stanton planning on staying long in Brighton?

Kayla had responded with a strange smirk to the retelling of Shaw's inquiry, her mouth in a small grimace that might actually have been called amusement.

The car radio, playing softly, crackled with lightning from somewhere else, far away, overwhelming the local AM station. With the sound of each sizzle, Ray searched what he could see of the sky, pinched as it was by the short buildings of Brighton. Nothing. It was almost eleven and the heat hadn't broken, or even promised to break. Ray realized that he and Kayla had not spoken for a few minutes. He liked that.

Promised to break? Since when did the weather, or whatever or who, make promises.

He caught sight of a sign: Reston and Fourth. They were driving out toward the Hills, in the direction of the Windy Oaks factory. This was the third time in recent memory that Ray had driven late at night. Fourth, if he counted that night. His senses flooded with the memory: Palmer, the other guy in the hat, the other other guy; the damp, dank night; the foul ditch and the gleaming eyes of some animal. The animal was Ray, probably. The night shone like a dark mirror.

Ray sighed as quietly as he could. No need for Kayla to notice. He made himself breathe naturally, again, once again. Breathe. Maybe he was having panic attacks: they felt like little bursts of emotional artillery. He and Kayla were going to meet Nathan, after all, whose arm was broken on account of Kayla and Ray's stupidity.

Kayla parked. "It's around the corner," she said. "We're a little late."

The bar might have been a grocery once, or a dry cleaners. On the corner of Third Avenue and Oliver, just a block from where Highway 17 spun off and around the river and passed the plant, the bar still had a plate-glass frontage reminiscent of goods on display. Not a grocery . . . maybe a stationery store? Some place where an old guy ran the numbers from behind the counter, where Mama's little boy was sent to see if Mama had won; where a hand-rolled cigar could be purchased, a single, or a bottle of hooch; where the day's gossip played off the preacher's sermon from the previous Sunday, everybody gussied up, scrubbed and shining and absolved. Ray knew that he was buying into his own ignorance. He looked at the Budweiser sign blinking in the window, knew what he was doing was wrong, and did it anyway. He was a racist: he should probably admit that.

"It's a bar," Kayla said to Ray.

"I know," he answered.

They took a booth along the wall, red vinyl benches and a wooden top varnished so many times the varnish had become the top. Someone's initials had been drilled with a penknife into the wood, angrily, maybe, an "L" and an "O." Ray slid in first, Kayla next to him so she could see the door. Two beers. Ray didn't know what to think, so he just looked: a few people in fancy clothes, coming from or going to another get-together, a flash of green rayon or silk, somebody laughing. Could he be a white guy and just look at black people? Was it always racist to think of them as "black people"? Perhaps it was, but unless he asked Kayla, how would Ray ever know? At the bar, a row of serious drinkers slumped into their drinks. Ray recognized that slump and its various stages: slump, slide, fall. Unconsciousness. Those were drinkers, he knew. That was what it meant to drink. Dad drank. Fran drank.

Ray was okay. Two bars on the same night, but he was okay. A little wide-eyed.

There was a certain utility to the bar that Ray recognized. Even the decorations—a plastic bulldog draped in Christmas lights, a smoky mirror, a flock of faded Little League pennants, photos of someone's dead relatives—each had a purpose. Or added up: to drink. Ray smiled to himself, just a little smile. He was projecting. Still he wanted to drink more than he wanted to be seen looking around. On the wall near the front door hung a nifty Cassius Clay promo poster, definitely a reprint.

Of course, Ray knew without thinking, he would be the only white person here. This wasn't Dooley's, where Kayla would probably never go.

Kayla smiled at Ray.

Ray smiled at Kayla because she had a nice smile. He turned around, checked out the room. A white couple with a young black man were seated at a table, squeezed together at a table meant for two. So much for knowing, Ray told himself. So much for feeling white and set up. Well, maybe he still felt manipulated, but mostly by himself, his stereotypes—and by his own definition of happiness, for other people and for himself.

Kayla put her hand on his arm, then back on the table. Ray was beginning to wonder what they were waiting for—not whom, he realized, but what. What would happen tonight to change all this, turn off the sound in his head? What would he do? What was he capable of? They had lured Palmer out of hiding, as planned. Now what? Poor Nathan.

Kayla was jittery too. He reached across the table to take a cigarette, touched one finger to the back of her hand. She attempted to smile again.

"It's a bar," Ray said.

"Oh, that's nothing," Kayla smiled. "I've been to lots of bars. There they are," said Kayla. She half-stood.

Ray took a drag, blew out the match, stood, all at once. He didn't know whether to be pleased with himself, horrified, terrified, vindicated, or what. He was everything combined, no one response sufficient. How was he doing? Ray couldn't have said. Guilty as charged. You're fired.

Nathan Mapes, stooped and too thin, had his arm in a cast and a sling. He wasn't smiling. He had stopped just inside the door. There were two women with him, both a little older than he appeared to be.

"They who—?"

"Nathan and Lu." Kayla waved. "And Sylvie."

He leaned over, tapped the ash of his cigarette in the plastic ashtray, no ash really. He didn't know how to smoke. Right, he reminded himself. Quit smoking.

"Hi, Nathan, Lu. Sylvie." Kayla hip-checked Ray over, made room. He sat. "Slide in, pull up a chair."

"Hello," said Nathan.

"Hiya," said Lu.

"Hello, my dear," Sylvie said. Everyone sat.

"Beer?" asked Kayla.

"Okay," said Lu. Nathan nodded. Sylvie nodded.

"Another for me," Ray added. It wasn't his voice, but a squeezed sound.

"Right," said Kayla. She stood again, sidled out. "Ray? Why don't I do the honors." Kayla removed her wallet from her purse, and turned. "I'll get this one. . . . Nathan," Kayla said, standing. "This is Ray. This is Nathan, Lu, and Sylvie."

"How'd you do."

"Hiya," said Lu.

"Hello," said Sylvie.

The honors? Ray half-smiled at Nathan. He tried to smile better at Sylvie, but she was busy clicking "Hello"—more of a little cluck, really—to a woman across the room, a woman who couldn't hear the sound, no way, not at this distance. But the other woman smiled broadly, a woman in jeans and some kind of uniform top. She liked Sylvie, Ray thought. They liked each other. In a different universe, or in someone else's nightmare, Ray could buy them drinks, hang out, complain together about bosses, the weather, what was the world coming to? Too damn hot, don't you think? And how. All week, they say. Really?

I better buy that window fan I saw today. Hey, a fan? Good price? Pretty good: want me to pick one up for you? Why that would be nice of you, real nice.

Lu was wearing some sort of perfume. It didn't smell good, to Ray. She had on a T-shirt. Nathan was wearing jeans and a T-shirt. Sylvie was looking at Ray, so he looked away. Kayla was standing at the bar. He liked what he saw: one foot raised on the footrest of a barstool, her hip cocked, her head tilted, an easy laugh as she handed the bartender a ten. If Ray could stay focused, then liking Kayla might see him through.

He checked out his lover: he was content, for a millisecond.

"Here we are," said Kayla. She had carried a cocktail tray expertly, leaned over, balanced, to serve their drinks. "So," said Kayla, as she sat again.

Ray steadied his voice before he spoke. "We heard about your trouble," he said to Nathan. Ray could run a meeting.

"Mm-hm," said Lu.

"Same boys?" asked Kayla.

"I didn't know them once," Nathan said. "Didn't know them again."

"But there's more—" Ray stopped himself.

"And we heard about yours," Sylvie said.

"That's it," said Lu. She might have been Nathan's sister, her face shared his thin, lost look. But she wasn't his sister.

Nathan sipped his beer awkwardly, his hand curled at a strange angle. Ray understood, as his breath caught. They had broken a right-handed man's right arm. Goddamnit. Ray and Kayla had done this to Nathan. "Did they sing?" Ray made himself ask.

"Mm?"

There was silence.

"You know, did they sing when they were—"

"Your name was written on me," Nathan said. He held up his arm, which was in a cast and a sling. "They broke my arm. They used a bat."

"Oh shit," said Kayla. "I'm so sorry . . ."

"Wasn't you that did it," said Lu.

Ray had been shaking his head; he stopped, he looked at Nathan and Lu. At Sylvie. In the woods again, Ray thought. Stolen overalls, floppy boots. Keep the eyes open, Ray told himself. Keep going, he told himself. Then Ray made himself ask: "Did they say anything? You know, about me?"

"It's okay," Kayla said to Ray. "We're okay," she told Lu.

"No, sir. But they knew they was going to do it. They talked about it."

Ray was confused. The whole thing seemed like a play, everyone sitting at a table on a stage. And Nathan seemed always to have the wrong lines. Kayla gave Ray a look, her hand slightly aloft, cautionary, which said *Shhh*, as she indicated that she'd handle things.

Maybe the fire department will arrive, Ray thought for no reason.

"Nathan . . ." Kayla smiled, began again. "I'm having trouble following. Did they say anything about Ray here?"

"Not exactly," Nathan said. "They just wrote and one of them yelled at me—"

"Wrote what?" Kayla asked. She had taken another cigarette; her hand was remarkably steady.

"You can tell them, Nathan."

That was Sylvie. A woman about Ray's age, dressed in a red sleeveless top and dark shorts. A perfectly reasonable-looking person.

"Yes ma'am," Nathan said. "They wrote 'Uncle Ray' on my arm."

Kayla's head jerked quickly from her beer. "'Uncle Ray'? You sure?"

"Was his arm, he'd remember."

Everyone looked at Sylvie. Of course, Ray thought. There was a drop of sweat on Nathan's lip—no, two, three drops. Where had all the air gone? "They know," Ray said.

"They know what?" Kayla's voice had begun to rise, her words more punched than spoken. "It's okay," Kayla said again, to anyone.

"You're the uncle, isn't that right?" asked Sylvie.

She had stopped the conversation again. Who was she? Ray took too large a swig of his beer; hesitated, swallowed twice. "Right," he said as he stared down at his hands. "I'm Kayla's uncle."

"You don't act like an uncle," Lu said. She was pleased, her arms crossed. What a detective.

"I—"

Kayla waved her hand, cut him off. "We're just saying that, honey. It's just something to say, you know? It's a small town."

Sylvie and Kayla looked at each other—too long, Ray thought—until Sylvie smiled.

"Mmm. I had an uncle once." Lu giggled, and then she chucked Nathan under the chin; he responded shyly. They were cute, Ray thought. Are we? Across the bar, the woman in green was laughing loudly. She was happy.

"They . . . they know. About us. Uncle Ray." Kayla didn't seem upset.

"I know," Ray said. "They know about you."

"Course we do," said Nathan. "Everyone knows Kayla and Mae."

"That's right," Sylvie said. "Everyone knows the Reeves."

"Twice." Kayla raised an eyebrow. Her right hand was on Ray's knee; with her other hand she drove. "Damn," she said. "They hurt him twice. I can't believe that," she shook her head. "It's our fault."

"Maybe he thinks I really am your uncle? Small town," Ray said. Neither of them believed what he said. Oh well. He was sweating again, the night still hot. "Mm," Ray said. "So who's Sylvie?" he managed.

Kayla's eyes shone. "Now that's more complicated." They were stopped at a red light. Theirs was the only car on the road. "I'll try to explain," Kayla began. "Do you know how there's always someone at church who tells the minister very politely that his sermon was no good? That's Sylvie. Self-appointed. And she seems to have taken an interest in you. She's just paid a house call, after all. She's mean, at heart—even if Momma doesn't think so. That's Sylvie. So if she's interested, it also means that she's doing things. That's her way. Pardon me, but that woman's a bitch. Got 'em everywhere."

Ray gave Kayla a smile and then turned back around to face forward. Ahead, through the windshield, the sky was a strange color, the kind of red when red is almost orange. Pollution or rain or both.

"I'm not sorry," Ray said. "Who cares about her. Fuck her."

Kayla laughed hard, at Ray. "Easy, Ranger Ray. You shouldn't say that." She laughed, turned the car left onto East Bine. Home.

"Oh no? Well fuck you, then. And your mother."

"Oh damn," Kayla said to the rearview mirror, her laugh out of control. "Damn, Ray. You're killing me."

He was killing someone, in his own way. Ray was managing Palmer's violence, getting the guy to go break an arm here, write a name there. Throwing eggs. It was Ray's fault, and now he didn't know what to do. "Palmer's done," Ray said. "I've had enough of the little shit."

They arrived, parked in his driveway. Kayla's expression shifted into something else, watchful. She snapped her fingers. "Ain't you've been gone a long time, Uncle Ray. You different. You growed up. You the man."

CHAPTER 22

Ray and God, alone together in Ray's bed. Kayla in the bathroom getting naked, ready. Ray and God, and Ray didn't know what to say. Should Ray not do what he was about to do? Should he apologize in advance? Ray was hard already; Kayla had seen to that, grabbing him on the way upstairs, and to a swift completion of all conversation, after her little black self-parody. You must be tired, she had said. Gonna hit the hay? Kayla had added in a white girl voice. Ray had heard that voice before, it was the one that called him Uncle Ray.

Ray and God and Ray's erection. A glass of water on the nightstand, a box of tissues. What was God doing here anyway? Where had He been when Ray had needed Him, called; in the woods, on the road, in the ditch, twice on Palmer's front lawn, at the T.L.C. Family Restaurant, who was He fooling with all His indifference? What was God doing for Nathan Mapes? God wasn't here, Ray decided. There's no God here.

"What?" asked Kayla. The bathroom door was partially open.

"Nothing."

"You said something—"

"Did I?"

She stepped into the half-light of the room, brushing her teeth. Naked, comfortable.

Ray was hard. "You look nice," he said.

"Thanks," she said.

No apologies, nothing from or for God. When Ray and Kayla had come back to the house and closed the door, he had been in the middle of asking her something, but the conversation had faltered, nothing more to say. Just lovers. Ray felt like it was all he could do, be Kayla's lover. It was the only thing going right—and if God had a plan He must have forgotten it. And yet, Ray felt something different, a feeling he liked. Stand up, Ray thought.

She stopped brushing, returned to the bathroom, rinsed. "Oooh," she said. The ceiling fan was on, the sheet their only cover. Had he turned off the light in the kitchen? He had forgotten to turn off the light in the kitchen.

"Mmm," Ray said.

"Gimme," Kayla said.

It all seemed so domestic, so matter-of-fact. In the master bedroom of a three-bedroom house, Ray and Kayla having sex. Ray on top, Kayla on the bottom. On their sides, from behind. Not much talking. Very sweaty sex, the sheet quickly tossed away.

"Yeah," Kayla had half-moaned. She was closer. "Yeah," she had said again.

His sweat and her sweat. Nice. So Ray had stopped, a tease.

"I want it," Kayla had said. And then: "Wait. Don't move."

Ray waited. He liked this part, as he tried not to think about what they were doing, or touch himself.

She was back. She was holding some kind of small toy, with soft bristles. "I'll show you," Kayla said. "Me first," she smiled.

Once he was back inside her, she reached down and moved his hand. The toy. She wanted it in her ass, the soft bristles first. She moved against it. Ray kept his hand there. Until he didn't want to, or couldn't anymore.

"What are you doing?" Kayla asked.

"I . . ."

She slid him out of her. "Why'd you stop?"

"I don't know. It . . . "

"Too weird, lover? Got a problem?" Kayla grabbed the toy, tossed it; then she rolled over, put the flat of her hand against Ray's chest and pushed him, hard. He was on his back. "What makes you so middle-of-the-road?" She sat on him. Grabbed him. Pulled him back inside, the condom making a little squishing noise. "You like it hard? Rough sex, Ray?" She was gritting her teeth. She was bucking on him. She was grinding on him, grabbing at herself, wanting to come.

The angle hurt a little. He didn't have a problem with the toy.

"Like this?" She leaned back, reached around, grabbed his balls. "Arrr," she growled. She rode him, she squeezed hard. She was leaning back too far.

"Like this. Yeah, yeah, yeah, yeah, yeah . . ."

More than the angle hurt. Ray didn't want to be hurt. He came. He came so quickly, he didn't have time to hold back.

She was coming. Her body shook and shook; Ray was done, but he didn't mind. He could stay inside her, lie there. Not moving was better than moving. . . . Kayla bent to him, took his lower lip in her teeth. Gently, she chewed just a little. She leaned back, put her finger on his lip, then in his mouth. They both were covered in sweat, wet skin on skin. "Not bad," she said.

Not bad, he thought. Complicated. He might have said so, but her finger was in his mouth. Then it slid out.

"Did you like that?"

Ray wanted to say yes: "No."

"Mm," she said. She slid off, and then lay down on him. Only then did she realize what he had said: "No? You're lying."

"I am," Ray said. Ray held her.

"I think my mom must have heard," Kayla giggled.

"Probably," Ray answered, made himself giggle a little. Kayla might have wanted Mae to hear.

He had dozed, then awakened abruptly either from a dream or in a dream. In the dream, at least just beyond the end of the dream, he had sat up, right there, Kayla next to him. What else? He took a sip of water.

In the dream, there was a woman: she was sexy, although not naked. What did she have on? More, Ray said or didn't say, to no one, in the dream. Then, aroused completely, Ray had awakened.

He tried to lean over to the nightstand—he couldn't reach—he wanted a sip of water.

"What is it?"

"Just a dream," Ray answered. He breathed out, huffed.

"Mmm," Kayla had said.

She curled toward him, her thigh crossed his, her skin hot. Ray shifted his weight so his penis wouldn't touch Kayla. He was still hard from the dream. It was uncomfortable, his penis pushing awkwardly against the bottom sheet, Ray's hips shifting slightly, then again. He was sweating, but that could have been from the heat—the bedroom was very hot, the air closer.

"I had long hair," Ray said.

"Oh no," Kayla said. Her voice sounded small and kind of adorable.

"And I was flying. And I think I was in Cleveland, like when the river there caught fire and burned—was that in the seventies?"

"Mmm . . ."

"In the seventies? God, I can't remember when that happened," Ray said. Kayla had fallen asleep again. "When was that?"

"Ray," Kayla said in her sleep.

He lay back. The top sheet was bunched at their feet, in a sinewy knot across his ankles; Ray knew that he couldn't get out of bed without waking Kayla again. He propped up his head a little by scrunching the pillow: one elbow had almost nestled between Kayla's breasts, her right breast resting mostly on Ray's forearm, his hips and his torso a bit too angled, askew, so as to keep his hard-on from touching her. The moonlight was half-bright, the walls stained with it. The bedroom was too hot, the ceiling fan helped, but not enough. Another awfully hot day tomorrow.

Ray doubted whether he could fall asleep quickly. He really wanted that sip of water. But what was the name of that river? Was it . . . ? Oh hell. Ohio. Fire.

He considered where he was, stuck. There were worse places to be stuck. Ray thought about being single: it hadn't happened in almost twenty years, and a year later he was already entwined in a relationship he liked. Not to mention Phyllis? No, Phyllis didn't fit. That was just booze and other stuff, and his own stupidity. But he knew, too, that his success rate—whatever the hell that phrase meant—wouldn't remain so high. He just wasn't the kind of man to be lucky in love.

He thought about Kayla. She was his lover. Tangled awkwardly, his head slightly above his torso, Ray could only look. His face was a foot or so away from Kayla's right breast, her nipple. A sheen of sweat on her skin had dried, leaving another kind of sheen. Slightly chalky without being chalk, of course, her nipple was more purple in this light than brown or black, Ray thought. Just like the black-purple of her labia, before he saw pink. But black too. Vulva

With the sensuous weight of Kayla's breast on his arm, Ray had difficulty concentrating on not-concentrating, which was his usual method of combating sleeplessness. Thinking his mind blank, his body empty. Be in a room, the mind empty; think of it emptying. But now, with a woman's breast on his arm, the breast dark brown and purple and lying on him, available and sexual, Ray had a hard-on he wanted to make go away. It wouldn't, he knew, or it would once he fell asleep. He was happy. She might be wet still or easily again—he could wake her. He wasn't in the most comfortable position to sleep.

He was happy. Shit.

More dreams: something mostly irretrievable about an animal, an enormous deer or an antelope. Concentric circles in the sand, seen from above. Heel-to-toe, heel-to-toe, walking. But a place not for him. Heel-to-toe, heel-to-toe.

Then the most powerful, the fear, the terror: his feet were too small, Ray looked down and saw his feet one-third their usual size. That's not going to work, he knew, falling over. The falling was too far, catch the branches, the roots, the—wind? Hanging from wind, somehow. Doesn't hurt, he thought. Except for the sores.

He woke again, anxious. Those sores had been awful, each one a needle full of pain. God. But they didn't hurt too; they were just a dream. Dream sores.

Kayla was snoring slightly. She might not be beautiful, but she looked beautiful.

How could he have felt the pain of the dreamed sores so acutely? Man, the mind was a screwy thing. Ray looked at the clock, got out of bed, stretched. It was later than he thought. He had actually slept, he realized as he trudged down the hall. He suspected that he might be awake for hours, having slept some.

Ray stepped into his kitchen. Kayla was upstairs, Mae was next door, Jilly and the kids were in Medford. Who else? Fran was a phone call away, Mom was in Florida with a guy named Randall, Dad was dead. The next-door Russells, Ray and Jilly's Medford friends, were traveling somewhere in Italy: he had even received a postcard from them, mailed here to Brighton, an Ugly American cartoon of some fat guy in Bermudas attempting to straighten the Tower of Pisa. It hadn't been funny, except that it probably jibed with the millions of euros Sally Russell had spent already in Tuscany, shopping her way into the hearts of sales-help everywhere. Ray and Jilly had tried that; four years ago, when their marriage had seemed ready to unravel, they had taken a tour with some guy who called himself "Captain Italy." Each minute planned: a bus, a church, lunch in the piazza, a bus to the catacombs, a tour of the frescoes. A nap, then pasta alfresco and too much Chianti. Every expense itemized on the pretrip itinerary, even the negligible tips for meals, Captain Italy taking care of all the details. Someone else to do the thinking, which had seemed to both Jilly and Ray a good idea.

They had fought through Italy. They had had a fight at St. Peter's in Rome, of all places, hissing at each other in the underground tomb of the popes. They had had great make-up sex too. Where was that? Right. In that hotel in Venice, the city on the water. Whoa, Ray thought. He lifted his cup of water, a silent toast to Jilly. "Marco," Ray said aloud. Polo, his sister Fran would have answered if she had heard, playing their childhood game.

Ray's muscles ached, his run and sex and laziness, he realized, as he reached for the Tylenol on the counter. Wasn't it just a few years ago when some maniac had poisoned Tylenol? Ray remembered. He and Jilly had come home from the movies to the bottle of pills open on the countertop, Tom couldn't have been more than a year or two old but he wasn't in the playpen, the newspaper listing the lethal lot numbers, the babysitter gone, the TV blaring. Where are they, Ray, where are they? I don't know!, he had yelled back. Ray running through the apartment, hollering Bets? Betsy? Betsy? It wasn't that big a place. Betsy! And Jilly yelling too, until they both had arrived in the bedroom, caught the light from under the door, threw open the closet. Sixteen-year-old Betsy, eighteen-month-old Tom in a nest of blankets, a flashlight to read by, Curious George or Babar or some other animal who would have been terrified to have been in that closet. Tom giggling, his eyes wide to what the darkness held. Jilly crying soundlessly.

Jeannie must have been at a friend's house that night, a sleepover or something. Had she been old enough? Ray started to count on his fingers. Now his Jeannie was sixteen.

Cheer up, Ray told himself. Don't be such a maudlin sonofabitch. Or do, Ray reconsidered. Go ahead, revel in it. Somehow all of the memories felt bigger tonight, to match Ray's new life—but no matter what Ray felt, being maudlin or not wouldn't matter, because moping or smiling wouldn't change the fact that Palmer had come again, and Ray was next.

Only this time, tomorrow or whenever, Ray could respond: he would lead Detective Shaw to the scene of the crime, their roles reversed. Look, Officer, it's a lot of lives here, not some

TV show. These are real people, and they don't behave according to plan. Ray was here to do a job, save Windy Oaks and all that, which might include being fair to good and bad people. All without—what had Shaw called it?—racialness. So here's Palmer; take him away.

Racialness was the least of it, Ray thought, except maybe not for Kayla. Okay, once more over the top: Ray would try not to think for the women in his life, a habit he shared with every man he had ever known, and probably a fatal flaw inherited from his dad. How the hell could Ray know what Kayla thought or wanted? Kayla's actions were usually inscrutable—especially in relation to the warmth Ray now felt from her, most of the time.

Yeah, right, he told himself, Kayla loves Ray. Because as everyone knows, feeling warmly toward someone, which Ray did toward Kayla, usually meant that the other person felt the same, and that equaled being loved. . . . If you're sixteen, maybe. Come on, Ray. Remember not to lie to yourself, he almost said aloud. "Dummy," he did say aloud.

But her behavior was also beginning to seem knowable to him, in a way; she was beginning to make more sense. And with that knowledge was a serious danger: Ray had come to understand that Kayla's worldview was so informed by race that he was starting to see himself not as her lover, but as her white lover. She was his black lover and he was her white lover. Which meant that they were together, in an odd way, because of racism rather than in spite of it. Fuck. The opposite was true too; in spite of racism could be seen as because of racism. Affirmative action, no kidding.

Was this more thinking for her? Was she sleeping with Ray because she wanted to, or with a white guy? What did he feel, for chrissakes?

When Ray opened the front door of his house, he did so for no conscious reason—until, just as he did so, he realized what he was wearing. He expected to see no one. He was right. He saw no one, and no sign of God, just moonlight on the Toyota. East Bine as an otherworldly, weirdly lit, fucked-up little street. It was good to have his expectations met.

Ray stood on his front stoop for what seemed a very long time, naked, doing nothing.

CHAPTER 23

The sun had begun to sizzle on the asphalt, the morning dew or mist or humidity still patchy on his parched lawn, his neighbors', Brighton and beyond. All over. With the temperature this hot already, and soon to be hotter, thinking about places beyond Brighton became more difficult than usual; there was something about heat that brought the immediate even closer, the visible world the only world there could be. A property of heat, he thought; something fourth dimensional, or sci-fi.

Palmer had broken Nathan's arm: Ray and Kayla had stirred a violent man into further violence. Which meant that Ray and Kayla had done this to Nathan, and not so indirectly—a fact that had kept Ray from sleeping. They should have realized that Palmer would respond violently when actually provoked.

"Morning, Ray."

"Morning."

Mae was in a short-sleeved flowered jumpsuit, a yellowed print with yellow and pink flowers. It reminded Ray of her sweats, the morning after, in her bathroom, May 22 not circled on Ray's calendar, years ago. But almost everything Mae did reminded him of that night.

She stood up carefully, then called out, across their yards: "Do you like flowers, Ray?"

"I do," he called back. He had just taken a shower, his first of the day. "Don't know much about them, but I do."

"I love flowers," she said more softly, drawing him closer.

His answer hadn't mattered. Ray crossed the lawn, approached. "Tell me about these, they're azaleas—"

Mae's smile interrupted him: but it wasn't until she had smiled that Ray realized that she hadn't smiled yet. "I'd like to," Mae said. "Some other time maybe . . ." She was tugging at the plastic or rubber tip of her gardening glove, her pruning shears tucked under one arm, her plastic sun visor shading her face. "Church in an hour or so and . . . well, you know."

"Church?" Ray wanted to touch her shoulder. He did.

"Yes. I volunteer."

He thought about that. "I know this must be difficult for you," Ray said.

"Difficult?"

"You know. Me."

She gave a laugh. "You think you're difficult. Maybe you think so," she said. "But you'd be wrong." She couldn't resist, even with the gloves off; Mae clipped a twig at the V, where it began. "The difficult part is wondering when she's going to stop hurting herself, and then, if she does that, wondering what she'll do with all that pain she's got. Because I gave her this"— she pointed with the shears, taking in everything—"and you're just . . . oh I don't know."

"Just visiting?"

Mae looked at Ray, hard. The plastic visor cast a green shadow across her forehead, her head was thrown back, her throat was bare except for an enormous strand of faux blue pearls, blue as blueberries. The nice clothing and the jewelry were for church, but she must have wanted to garden first, before her back collapsed for the day. Ray watched Mae's neck- lace bob as she breathed; she was still looking at him, so it was a good place to keep his gaze.

"I hope you think more of her than that."

"I didn't mean—"

"No, of course you didn't." She waved her hand. "That's okay."

Quick, change the subject: "I didn't know you volunteered, Mae."

She smiled. "I do. Kayla sometimes does too, at the community center. But it's only for me," Mae admitted. She waited. "Are you a church-going man?"

"I'm not," Ray said. "My dad wouldn't."

"I didn't think you would be." Mae moved, a bit stiffly.

"Are you uncomfortable? I could—"

"No thank you. I'm fine," she added.

"Please just say so," Ray said. "I can—"

"Ray," Mae spoke sharply. "I live with this."

"Right."

She took off the visor, puffed her hair, put the visor on again. "Do you mind if I say something?"

"Please."

"You know I've got a bad back. My sense of it . . . I mean, how I live with it . . . is with God's love. I understand that the rules aren't ones I've made. Do you see?" Her right hand fluttered. "And you . . ." She looked away. "You don't seem to get it. For once the rules aren't ones you made. Do you understand? You're a victim."

Ray thought about that. "Of what?"

"Racism, terror, violence, suspicion." She paused. "Sex."

There was a long silence, as Ray thought some more. Politics too, he thought. "So what do I do?" he asked, which seemed polite. Nappy hair, Ray thought, for no reason.

"Stop victimizing yourself. Stop victimizing others." Now she was looking him in the eye.

"I'm not—"

"If you're the victim, you're the oppressor. Like the good book says, 'Can a man take fire in his bosom and his clothes not be burned?'" She seemed thoughtful, then flashed a very small grin. "Proverbs 6:27."

Ray smiled back, despite himself. "The good book doesn't mean much to me," he said. "Got anything else?"

"Okay," Mae answered. "How's this: you've made your luck, now change it."

"That's better," Ray said. "I see what you mean." And then: "But Mae . . . are you telling me all this to keep me from seeing Kayla? Because if you are—"

She interrupted his sentence. "No . . . That's not for me to do. Or say."

"Is that the truth? I don't think so. I mean, I'm not saying you're lying, but that's not the truth either. You don't want me with her, and she's obviously not going to listen to you on the subject, so you're telling me."

"Fair enough," Mae said. "You caught me."

"That's okay, Mom," Ray smiled, and immediately regretted what he had said. "I mean, you're a good mom with a good kid—"

"Thank you."

"—but I've got to say that this is between Kayla and me, now. We're not children, neither of us. We're not twenty-two—we're not even thirty-two. We're adults. So while I appreciate your concern, she and I need to figure out what to figure out. . . . Sorry if that doesn't make any sense."

"No. It does."

"But you don't like it." Ray could tell he was right.

Mae nodded her head, up and down; it looked like yes but it meant no.

"Sorry."

"Don't apologize."

"I'm not," Ray said. "I'm expressing regret. I'm sorry that you won't like the results."

"Ray . . ." Mae was taking her turn. She held out her hand, he put his hand in hers, she covered his hand with her two hands, safe, reassuring, a harbinger of doom, ready to deliver even worse news. "Let's go inside."

Through the front door, the same front door as his, then through the house and into her kitchen. Coffee? No, thank you.

Here, sit. Ray's chair. Mae began to wash up, her back to him, and then she began again: "I think you're a nice man, Ray. Really. I even like you. But you've known us what, a month, not even? And in that time you've also been through what may be the most traumatic event of your life, at least it seems so to me. And it seems so to Kayla. She told me . . . Okay . . . let's see, how can I put this? Maybe she's confused. But you're not in your right mind, whatever that may be when you're with your wife and the kids, just sitting around or going out to Burger King. This isn't you, Ray. It's like you've had a personality shift or something, because being a victim is new to you. It has touched you for the first time in your life—"

"I've been thinking that too—"

"Yes. And you need . . ."

Ray waited. Mae didn't know what he and Kayla had done to Palmer, only what Palmer had done. Did she know about Nathan's arm? Mae had only part of the story, as though she had been reading every other page of a book, or skipping some chapters—which is how most people work, he supposed. And how Ray, too, knew only part of anyone else's story.

She was staring at him. "I mean, I think it's done, don't you? Shouldn't you leave now?"

In her eyes, there was brown and a little green. Nice.

"Ray?"

He leaned back. Maybe it was time, Ray considered. But go where? He couldn't think of a place, and so he started to talk: "You know how when you were little and it was summertime and you got to play outside after dinner? I mean, did this happen to you? . . . When I was a kid, and school let out for the summer, we got to play outside late, and that was the best. You know how when the sun started to go down around eight or nine or whenever, it would go down for the longest time and then, *ping*, no more? Being in Brighton is like that. . . . I don't know what I'm saying anymore. . . . That's how old my son is, by the way. He's eight."

"I can see that you're confused." Mae said, laughing just a little. "So what next?" The question asked, she turned back toward the refrigerator.

"I just don't know. So maybe it hasn't even been a month, but since then I've been having trouble deciding what to do. In advance—know what I mean? Like I never know what I'm going to do until right before I do it, or as it happens. It's—"

"Foolhardy?"

"Could be," Ray admitted. "But it's better too. Before, I wouldn't decide until after. Which wasn't working. And sucked." He blushed. "Pardon me."

Mae ignored his vulgarity. "I can see why you would think that. But it's not better, if you don't mind my saying so. It's just foolhardy. You're an adult, and you're behaving like a teenager."

Maybe, Ray thought. "Maybe," Ray said. "Okay. But all of this has helped me understand myself much better. How often do you get such an opportunity in life?"

"Right," Mae said. "See? You're not searching for yourself, you've been shown. . . . It's still after the fact." She was done tidying, ready to leave. "But you'll need to think more clearly, Ray. Danger's a bad high."

"What do you mean?"

"Just look at Kayla. Danger twists you all around, makes every moment so important you forget what's really important, or why you've got to be careful, for the future. That there is a future."

He cut through the bushes in time to hear the phone ring. "G'morning," he said to Kayla in the kitchen as he picked up his pace, hurried through the back door.

"Good morning," Kayla said with a quick wave.

He was inside his own kitchen, same layout, Kayla at the kitchen table rather than Mae. She was sitting in the chair next to Ray's.

"Hi," she smiled. The phone rang again.

"Hi," he smiled back.

"I thought you should get the phone—"

The fourth ring: he thought so too. "Hello?"

"Hello," said the person on the other end, a voice Ray knew. "Is this Ray?"

"Sure is," Ray said to Anderson. "What's up, Steve? How's your weekend going?"

"Well," Anderson laughed. He seemed nervous. "I'm . . . I'm at home. Just thought I'd call to give you a heads-up."

Ray looked at Kayla, shrugged his shoulders. "Oh?"

"Yes. A heads-up. Mr. Rivers heard something last night. He's worried that you're involved in a mess of some kind. He's upset, you know? I think that's the real story. Anyway, he's placed a call to your main office. . . ."

Ray had nothing to say. The day wasn't too hot yet, he thought, sweating already.

"Ray?" Anderson asked. "You might even get a call from your people. Just to let you know. It's nothing, I'm sure."

It's nothing, Ray thought. "Oh . . ." He made himself laugh. "That's all? I'll be happy to talk to Mr. Rivers myself—"

"No, no, no. Don't do that. This is a heads-up call, you see?" Then, in a softer voice: "He doesn't know I'm calling. When you see him tomorrow, you can't say anything."

Tomorrow? Ray looked at the calendar on the wall. Oh god. Drinks at the club on the twenty-ninth. "Ah. Well, hell," he forced a chuckle. "Thanks, Steve. Stevie. Now I understand. And I'll be sure to be prepared when I see Larry tomorrow, and I'll act plenty surprised." He winked, which made Kayla smile. She was amused. Or maybe she was thinking about last night, Ray thought. Fun.

"That's the ticket," Anderson sighed. "Now you get it. Be the Boy Scout. So. Gotta run. Take care, Ray."

"You too, Steve. And thanks for the heads-up."

"Don't mention it," Steve Anderson said. "I mean—" he laughed. "Really. It would be better that way."

Some days turn into the next day, simple as that. Wired, sleepless, testy, Ray and Kayla had sparred a bit, then she had left. Nathan Mapes had a broken arm—the fact loomed over all that Ray and Kayla did and said. They should spend some time apart, Ray reasoned, once she had left. He had not told her of his conversation with Mae, why bother.

He slept, ate, slept; those were the highlights. He fretted. Then it was Monday morning, Kayla off work but still at her place. A quick call—you okay? Sure. You? You bet—and then it was Monday afternoon, and they were alone together in Kayla's car. She had arrived unannounced, wanted to take a drive, just the two of them, to go somewhere; she had wanted to show him something.

What? he had asked.

You'll see.

Going for another ride, Ray had thought—and even though it would be with Kayla, he had bristled. Not in Reggie's car? A good sign. Do we have to today? How long do you— She had interrupted him: just an hour, what's the matter with you? The expression on her face had changed to quizzical, bemused, sad, all together. Then only sad.

Now in the passenger seat of Kayla's car, Ray paying little attention to the road, the day too hot, the AC roaring and fluttering, he had relaxed. Or caught himself relaxing, which wasn't quite the same, but a beginning. Conversation had been breezy: in fact, Ray realized, conversation had been so light that he could participate without thinking. Almost relaxed, he told himself, gabbing away with Kayla, more talking than thinking.

More conversation. Ray was learning about the food industry, tight margins and an itinerant workforce. Kayla was interested in the business: she wanted to manage a nicer place, although she didn't want to get her Hotel and Restaurants degree. She felt too old for school. Owning a place was an option, and while she didn't have the cash, she had some savings—she'd need a backer, probably, to cut a deal that included equity and a buy-in schedule.

They were out of town, south on Highway 17, then elsewhere, east. In the countryside, the cows, the summer crops; the stunning, occasional poverty. A roadside farmhouse, barn and garden all in shades of green and yellow as though neatly quilted together—maybe that's why farmers' wives made quilts, as replicas or maps? Ray knew it wasn't why, but he liked the idea, as though one could check out a quilt to see where the Lower Forty ended.

His gaze had returned to the scenery: a stand of trees looming over a mailbox. He rolled up the window—at a smell—then down again a half-mile later, the smell gone. Natural selection, Ray thought, for no reason. The HMS *Beagle*.

They came to an intersection, stopped at the stop sign. Kayla turned to her right to look for traffic, smiled at Ray. She had been talking about her mom delivering the mail, how Mae had really liked the job, all the people, how once she had been bitten by a toy poodle, who hadn't been quite big enough to bite her. Mae could tell great stories, Kayla said.

Kayla made a left onto a gravel road. The steady *pink-pink-pink-pink* of gravel on the underbelly of the car. A significant cloud of dust behind them, following them, their own dust, Ray and Kayla followed everywhere they went by who they were.

A stand of poplars on one side of the road, a farmers' market on the other. They stopped, got out. Ray walked slowly, aware that he had not walked slowly in days. He enjoyed his walk. At the fruit stand, flats of strawberries had been laid out, the early pickings. It was Monday afternoon, but no one was here. A sign said "2 for $1.00," a plastic bucket held a dollar or two in change. The Strawberry Family wasn't home.

The heat had thickened. Ray and Kayla were eating chemically sprayed strawberries, two dollars in the bucket, who cares about anything, their car parked along the gravel road, doors open, surrounded by a hazy horizon. Nothing to see. Chatting or not. Someone made this up, Ray thought. Someone thought of this and presto. But he hadn't meant God, Ray knew that: God was volunteering in church with Mae, setting up the barbecue. Not here. God eating barbecue.

"There's nothing to see," he told Kayla.

She smiled, a strawberry half-eaten in her left hand. "What do you mean?"

He shook his finger at her. "I mean you don't have anything to show me. This isn't why we came," he insisted.

"What could you mean, Boy Toy? Of course this is it."

Ray laughed. It was a new laugh, just born. And then: "So how many strawberries is enough?"

She hesitated. "That's a mighty tall question . . ."

"Yes, it is," he agreed.

"What do you think?"

"Well . . ." Ray stalled. "Let's see. Rather than turn this into a silly little conversation about lovers and sex, and when is enough enough, how about we think about strawberries really?"

"Fine," Kayla said. "If you'd like."

"Okay," Ray agreed.

They were silent some more. "I think," Ray began, "that now I should tell you some sort of story about strawberries, something true, like how my mom made strawberry shortcake or once my dad covered the kitchen table in strawberries, and when we woke up, there they were like Christmas in June."

"You are a strange man."

"True. But my dad was an alcoholic, and no fun for a lot of years. I have none of those stories." Kayla was waiting for him to say more. He didn't. Now she wanted to tell him something. Ray smiled to encourage her.

"You're in a strange mood."

"I am," he agreed.

"I need to tell you something," she said. "It's not good."

"I figured."

"This is hard for me." Kayla frowned.

"Yes."

"I . . ."

"Kayla!"

She laughed at herself, just a little. "Okay," she breathed deeply. "Here it is: my mom called Jilly."

"She what—? Oh Christ. Why would she do that?" Ray said. And then he laughed.

"That's funny?"

He laughed and then he laughed some more. When he stopped, the grass and the fields were right there, so Ray looked at them. The road, the heat, the fields of whatever the fuck that was. Lives ending.

"Are you okay?"

"No," he said, but he was. He was shading his eyes, trying to see what that speck was. What was that speck? If only he could make out what it was. Kayla was next to him. "It's over, it's long over between us, but . . . I never—" He stopped himself. What could he say? "I mean . . . I never wanted to parade myself, you know. There's no reason to hurt her." He gestured with his hand, indicated to his right. "This is it? Jesus. Some view. You coulda showed me something better."

"Um . . . ," Kayla exhaled. "I don't understand what you're saying."

"It's wrong," Ray said, and it was. He chuckled again.

"What is?"

"Shit," Ray said. He hung his head. "It's not like she had any reason to know. She told her—right?—about us? That's why she called. Your mom called so that Jilly would know about us. And then Jilly would swoop in and carry me off, my true love, and you'd be saved from the badass white guy."

Kayla's silence was a confirmation.

Ray had paced away a bit, so he turned and looked back at her. Kayla didn't know what Ray had been thinking. "I'm sorry," Ray said.

"For what?"

"For what I just said. For everything. But it's kind of funny, too."

Kayla's eyes flared. "Don't you be damn sorry. Not for one minute. We're here because we want to be. Even here," she indicated the fields and sky.

"Right," Ray said. "Like you said the other day. The big picture." He was completely sorry. "Damn," Ray said.

"No doubt," Kayla said. "She's frightened."

"She is? She is?"

"Yes, she is."

The speck moved. A crow or something.

"She panics, always has. She's maternal and it gets in the way," Kayla the daughter announced.

Ray was sweating. Low-to-mid nineties. But being maternal didn't get in the way, it was the way. Ray had kids: he knew how it worked. "Still, it's like you're some goddamned second grader. It's so . . ."

Kayla was nodding her head. "You know, I think she even likes you. But you're not the point. Not to Miss Mae."

The crow had perched in a tree along the edge of a field. Kayla was watching the bird too, now. The bird seemed to be watching back. "I see," Ray said. He didn't. "Oh I don't know. She treats you like a child."

"I am her child," Kayla said. She looked away, over his shoulder somewhere. "I'm her only daughter. But let's go back a sec. Look at you. You're saying things to me—and expressing all these emotions—that you couldn't talk about before. Say to your wife. Don't you think if you could speak to your wife, now that you're really talking, that you could solve . . ." Her sentence drifted away.

Touché, Ray thought, nice try. "No," he said. "I don't think that. I told you, it's over. For me, it's been over for three years. If I were to talk with her, the way I talk with you, she wouldn't like it. She wouldn't know what to do with me, either. Plus, she and I . . . we don't like each other too much, deep down."

Kayla had been listening hard, her jaw set. "So tell me I'm right, and that this is good, you and I together, and I'll stop, right here. I mean, I'll stop worrying whether my mom is right and we'll keep going. Or admit that you think of me as . . . some black chick you're doing . . . and I'll be nice and cut you up and send you back in big pieces to your wife, FedEx, no hard feelings—"

What a choice. Ray smiled. "This is good," he said. "You and I."

"But crazy," Kayla said. "Fine."

"Crazy," Ray repeated, not that he thought so. "Not even crazy."

Kayla looked at Ray. "I'm still a black chick you're doing," Kayla said. "Sometimes, it's how I think of us. I can't help it."

Kayla had driven Ray out here to tell him what Mae had done, to have a real conversation together and let him decide, and discovered that the decision wasn't his alone anymore— a conclusion they both were pleased to reach. It was a very important event, he thought. They had made their first important decision together, Ray realized, as opposed to one of them deciding and the other agreeing. Still, there was more to say: "I'm not going to leave you because of your mom's call. Or even because of Palmer. You and I are not done."

"No, we're not." A tissue appeared—from where?—and then daubed a cheek. Crying didn't seem to slow Kayla down, Ray thought. Was that a woman thing? Ray knew very little about women.

"You're too good," Ray said.

Kayla sniffed, shrugged. "I'm not. You don't know. That's what people say of my mom, anyway, and not of me."

"She's not too good—" and she wasn't. He had proof. "But she's got a lot to be thankful for."

"Okay," Kayla said. She was done crying. "Let me have it."

"Hm?"

"I said, okay, Ray. Do the two-bit analysis of mom and daughter. But don't forget to consider the black angle. Because it all starts there, and you have no idea what you're talking about, honey."

"Whoa. . . ." And then: "I don't?"

"No."

"No," Ray said, annoyed with the banter. They were facing each other again. Ray's sadness and Kayla's sadness, a few feet apart. She couldn't have known, Ray thought, that being out here in the countryside, surrounded by all this space, made him feel trapped again, in all the openness.

"You look awful, you nice man. You can't imagine. You've got to get more sleep. . . . But you're also okay, which surprises me. It's very, um, surprising." Kayla peered at him, directly into the sunlight angling over his shoulder, her hand shielding her eyes, squinting. "You're a better man than most . . ."

"Of yours?"

She glared at him. "Yes. And most. Don't be such a jerk." She toyed with her right earring. "Do you like talking on the telephone? I mean . . ." She quickly tried to change what she had said. "I'm not suggesting that you leave, you understand, but I . . . it's just that I have a theory about people and phones. Sometimes if I pretend I'm talking on the phone I do better in person. Make sense to you?"

"I've never really thought about it."

"Oh. Do men do this at all?"

"Men?" Ray laughed. Laughing was good. "How the hell should I know? How about black restaurant managers?"

Kayla stared at him, shocked or pretending to be. "How should I know?"

"Right. My point exactly."

"You are trouble, Mr. Stanton. And trouble makes trouble, as my momma used to say."

"Did she? Probably still does," Ray smiled. "Guess that's it," Ray said. "Any more news?"

"No," Kayla smiled back. A real smile. "So what are we going to do?"

"We? We are going to go home and get fixed up, and go have drinks at the club with my boss, who plans to pull me aside and tell me that I'm fired. How's that."

"Oh my god. I forgot. The club? You're taking me to the Greenwood?" Kayla laughed. "Where did they dig you up?" She leaned into him, kissed the tip of his nose, just right.

Ray laughed too. "I think you're asking the wrong question, Baby Girl. I think that the real question is where are they gonna bury me."

Her hand on the ignition key. "Ready?" Kayla wasn't really asking.

On the way back, the car broiling with the AC cranked, after long silences and the occasional nicety, Kayla began to sing something softly. Her voice wasn't beautiful. Kayla couldn't sing, Ray acknowledged. Okay, he thought, some people can't sing. Some people can't sing, some people can't drive, some people can't decide; some people have all the luck, none of the clues, all of the money and they win the lottery anyway. Some people wait forever until life happens to them. Some people wait forever and nothing happens.

Ray wasn't waiting any more: he was sorry for Nathan and Jilly, Tom and Jeannie, Mae, Fran; furious at Palmer, happy with Kayla even when she was sad, or doubted him. He felt all of these emotions. But he wasn't furious with Mae. He thought that she had brought him into her kitchen this morning to tell him about the phone call, and that, once there, she couldn't bring herself to tell him. She was too embarrassed by her own behavior.

Ray could have talked about it, though; he could have looked her in the eye and said what he felt. He could have said: Jilly's my ex, our failed marriage predates all of this by years, and it's serious and permanent. And then he could have said, Mae Reeves, what you did was wrong. Just because she had seen Phyllis in the cab, Ray thought, and might have seen a kiss.

The car had cooled off, amen. Kayla was singing badly, but was comfortable enough to do so, to sing with Ray there. She was herself. Ray was himself, too, thanks to Kayla. Talking, and learning to talk. Ray was happy, and he was beginning to understand why—no matter the whims of an absentee landlord named God.

Life sucked and Ray was happy. You're fired, he said to Mae. And then it occurred to Ray that he was himself—feeling more comfortable to be Ray—thanks to Kayla. And thanks to Jimmy Palmer, too.

CHAPTER 24

The grounds of the Greenwood were immaculate and green but not wooded. Through the country club gates and up the winding lane Ray and Kayla drove, the lawns on both sides putting-green perfect. At last, one-half mile in, they reached the Palladian-style main building conspicuously decorated with sculptures and gas lamps; Ray slowed, then turned into a circular drive that curved beneath a portico, where parking valets lounged by the key hut, no one moving in the late afternoon heat. A pimply kid opened Kayla's door, and then came around to swap Ray's car for a piece of paper.

Kayla looked great. Smaller earrings, a little makeup, conservative shoes to go with her slacks and blouse. A handbag Ray had never seen. He wore a quiet shirt and tie, and a blue blazer with nautical insignias on the buttons, de rigueur, he thought. Loafers.

Early in the development of business process re-engineering, in the 1970s, Stevens and Osgoode had noted the need for public relations investiture. When changing the infrastructure of an organization, they argued, the BP engineer should consider altering the organization's appearance too. Important structural changes by themselves, ones that couldn't be seen, tended to make clients nervous; but a new logo and team colors, or even new offices, encouraged consumers to believe that all a firm's difficult decisions would be for the better.

Which is one way to tell that an organization's leadership might be stuck in the past; if appearances remained the same, Ray had come to think, an organization that claimed to have made structural changes probably had done so only as a result of external pressures, rather than as a result of any sort of leadership or vision. Forced to change, a reactionary management over-invested in a firm's traditions or history tended to start penny-pinching when it came to appearances. Just like a country club: no more lawn jockeys, but plenty of indications that the club hadn't changed on purpose, that the Board of Directors wanted it this way, and that the clientele wanted to be told what they wanted. A country club was an institution; the definition of "institution," as Ray had learned, is "that which does not change."

The bar was on the right. And the left. Were there two bars? One for whites and another for whites, Ray thought, grimly. What were they doing here? Left, he chose: blue, in honor of the Fourth. He approached a hostess, a high school girl in a white blouse and black skirt. "Hi," she said. "May I help you?"

"Hi," Ray smiled. "Yes, please. We're looking for Jim Rivers."

"Of course," she said. "He's in the Shack. Right this way." She grabbed a pad from her stand, turned, and walked through a dining room. Ray and Kayla were meant to follow.

Oak paneling, beige carpet, heavy wood tables, an elderly couple in matching wheelchairs. A bar in the middle of the room, stools that twirled, chits instead of cash, sign here. A man with a bright red face and a horrific green shirt nursed a triple something. The Shack wouldn't be a shack.

White people.

Through a very pretty, long room, a glassed-in patio that ran along the back of the building, down the hallway to another dining area and bar. There were Rivers and his wife, another couple, a third guy; only one other table occupied. The Shack had a dark, low-beamed ceiling. All the men stood when Ray and Kayla approached.

"Well, hi, Ray. Glad you could make it." Rivers shook Ray's hand. "And the lovely lady? I don't believe we've met. . . ."

"Kayla Reeves, Jim and Cindy Rivers."

How do you do, how do you do, these are the Carltons, this is Hap Singletary, Hap called Hap since he was a kid—since we all were kids, throwing rocks at the caddies on the fifth hole, and then we'd come back later and dive in the pond for the lost balls, sell 'em back to the duffers. How do you do, pleased to meet you.

The hostess handed her pad to Rivers, who scribbled his name and signed for his guests. More organizing, Rivers in charge: What'll it be? Janice, could you set us up? Beefeaters here, that's a g-and-t, Hap's a bourbon man, when he's not a scotch man or a rye man.

"Or grain alcohol," Hap huffed. "Hell, lighter fluid!"

Lots of laughter.

"Miss Reeves?"

"White wine, please," said Kayla. She was seated between Mrs. Carlton and Cindy Rivers.

"Bourbon for me," said Ray. "Rocks, please." Kayla was good, ordering the right drink, a white wine. He should thank Mae for Kayla's manners—or maybe for her savvy.

Chitchat, the weather, the Indians' chances, work being done on 21. Mrs. Carlton a bit slurred around her consonants, drinking. Hap Singletary, a name Ray knew, although he couldn't remember from where. Jim Rivers being nice, what a pleasant fellow. With a big smile, about to offer a handshake and a pink slip.

"And what do you do, Miss Reeves?"

Kayla smiled. "I'm in the food industry. Staff of twenty-two," she said.

Ray could love her, he thought.

"And whereabouts?"

"Here in town," she said.

"Don't I know your mother?" Hap asked.

"Probably," Kayla said, her earrings twinkling, side-to-side. "Mae Reeves?"

"Mae Reeves!" Mrs. Carlton exclaimed. "Why, she's a pip!"

A pip? Kayla agreed, and Ray had to as well. A pip.

"Didn't you just move back to town?"

"That's right . . ."

Three years ago, Ray thought.

More chatter, more nothing. Had Ray liked these kinds of gatherings? He had been to so many, he couldn't count. Keeping clients happy with small talk, everyone important. Ask them lots of questions about themselves, may I see pictures of the kids.

"Ray, let me borrow you a minute. . . ." Rivers rose, gestured.

"Sure," Ray said. "If you'll excuse me," he said to Kayla. He scraped his chair backwards, rose. Here goes, he thought.

They stepped outside, through a screened door to a patio, Rivers gesturing, this way. Across the garden, a small building. "That's the Shack, the real thing. Some say it was a moonshiner's." Rivers laughed.

Ray nodded.

"You know, Ray, I like you. I really do. You've got a great head on your shoulders, and your plan for us . . . well, it's a doozie. It's gonna work, by golly!" He clapped his hands together. "You're a different animal, you are—all that lateral thinking and re-engineering. I can see why you're skyrocketing, and I'll tell anyone the same.

"But it's like this. Brighton's Windy Oaks and Windy Oaks is Brighton. We share a heart, if you know what I mean. We're the same person. And something's not right, all this . . . I don't even know what to call it . . . unpleasantness? I'm at a loss, Ray, really I am. It's unhealthy, that's what it is."

They were strolling. If Rivers moved to put his arm around Ray, Ray might just bolt. Probably not, Ray thought, but he was tempted. Stay cool.

". . . I just think that would be best."

What? Ray had missed the verdict. "I'm sorry," Ray said. "Mr. Rivers? What did you say?"

"I said, Ray, that I think you need to move on. Know what I mean? We'll take it from here." He smiled wanly. "I've been reading our terms, and, you know, there's that out clause . . ."

Yes, Ray knew. Redress and recoup, the clause in the contract that allowed a client to terminate if public perception turned; a clause that required both the client and the Riggs rep to sign off, terms rarely invoked, necessary to include. Jim Rivers and Ray Stanton would each sign off: the BPR reorganization would formally terminate, Windy Oaks thrown back on its own devices. With a codicil: no further implementation of the BPR plan could transpire without additional settlement, "mutual satisfactions." Of course, if one side decided to break the contract unilaterally, that would be different, expensive and litigious.

Jim Rivers was still talking, and Ray didn't care. Racist shit, Ray thought. Where are all the black people, in the kitchen?

"So, here's my idea, Ray. I'd like to encourage you to sign off; to a tune, of course."

To a tune? "I beg your pardon?" Ray turned to look at Rivers.

The Windy Oaks CFO was embarrassed. "I think we can find a nice way to do this, Ray. I mean, I understand that things would change for you, at the home office, if you signed off."

"I see," Ray said. "But I'm not sure what you mean?"

"Well . . . what if we start with twenty, and then we . . . um . . . that is, you provide your notes for the short term, and we continue doing the good work you've done. Then another ten a month from now. August 1. That's when you'd sign off. See? I think the offer's generous."

Now Ray did see. Twenty thousand dollars in hush money, for his notes and projections—which Rivers and Windy Oaks would use, Ray's plan implemented—and then ten thousand dollars to close the matter by August 1, when Ray would sign off. A golden parachute. GOT YA.

"We'd also . . . the payments would be sheltered. You'd be okay."

Of course, Ray thought, they'd find a way to make the monies tax free. Gifts up to eleven thousand dollars, or a similar maneuver. Offshore or something in the islands. Greasing the palm of everyone but Uncle Sam.

"That's quite a proposal, Mr. Rivers."

"Jim, Ray. Call me Jim. We're family here."

"Jim, then. But I have to think about it."

"Sure, sure, I'm sure you do." Rivers put his arm around Ray's shoulder, gave a little squeeze. "You think about it. Just let me know after the holiday."

"Oh my god, that was unbelievable." Kayla seemed fired up, bouncy in the passenger seat.

"You're not kidding." Ray tried to smile. His jaw ached from gritting his teeth.

"So are you unemployed? Wanna wait tables at the King's Plate? You'd have to start in the dishroom, of course."

"I don't wash dishes," Ray grumbled. "Not for a living."

"Did you see those people playing croquet? I mean, oh my god!"

Ray hadn't. He was silent.

"Ray? You don't look so good."

"I'm fine," he said. "I'm just dandy."

"Ray? That's not a good face you're making. . . . What happened?"

"What happened? I'll tell you. No one could look me in the eye, because you're black. Hap Singletary, the car dealer?" Ray had remembered. "He's the one leasing Windy Oaks a parcel for one dollar a year, in perpetuity, and in exchange Jim Rivers and his family and who knows, even the fucking family dentist each has a Lexus. Goddamn mini-Mafioso, everybody in bed with everyone else. But that's not what happened, uh-unh. What happened is that jolly Jim took me on a stroll and offered me thirty thousand dollars to walk away from Windy Oaks by August 1. Probably away from my career, too."

"Oh fuck." She was suddenly less bouncy. "Wow. Thirty thousand dollars." She looked out her side window, then turned back to face him. "But you know, Ray, Greenwood's not that kind of place—Brighton's not like that, it's not how you think. I've got friends who are Greenwood members. Black folk. The chef's a friend too, trained at CIA, very talented guy. . . . So, on the surface, it's not like that." She touched his hand. "Sorry, boyfriend. . . . But don't you worry, you'll understand racism someday. Or maybe class conflict. . . ." She gave him three little maternal pats, and giggled. "Whatever. Whattaya gonna do?"

Beep. "This is Andrea from around the corner. At 11:15 today, Jimmy drove by your house. Thanks for the money. Leave it under the mat by your back door, and we'll get it."

Beep. No message.

Beep. "Uh, Ray? Could you give me a call? It's Mom."

Beep. No message.

Beep. No message.

Beep. No message.

Someone wasn't leaving a message, Ray thought, irritated.

Kayla had skipped upstairs to change. She was too fucking happy. Thirty grand? With that and severance, if Riggs International fired him. . . . No, it would be thirty grand and food stamps, each month's WIC allotment torn into thirds, one strip for Tom, one for Jeannie, one for Ray. He wouldn't be fired, he'd be "slid," the term used for someone demoted to a job that ultimately resulted in a resignation, something monotonous or demeaning.

Thirty grand wasn't enough. He couldn't leave with only thirty grand on the side, could he, not with any long-term security? He'd be unemployed, and all the rest of Ray's money would be tied up in the divorce, halfsies. He'd have thirty grand squirreled away, and nothing else. He couldn't afford to sign off, goddamnit.

Almost without thinking, he had called Mom. "Hi, Mom, it's Ray."

"Oh, hi, Ray. Thanks for calling back." She sounded better than her message. Phew. "Could you hold on a second—I'll have to skip next door. Randall would like a word."

What? He didn't have time to say anything; Mom was gone. He waited, tied to the wall in his kitchen, strung along by the phone, he thought. An umbilical cord, he thought.

"Ahheemm," Randall cleared his throat. "Raymond? This is Randall Fleer."

Oh shit. "Hi, Randall. Please, just Ray's fine."

"Ray, then. Much obliged. Ray. Well, Ray, I know that your mother has shared our happy tidings—"

"She certainly has, Randall. Congratulations. That's wonderful news."

"Well, thank you, thank you. She's quite a woman."

"That she is." What did Randall want? Ray was impatient.

"And she's awfully proud of you, Raymond. And she loves those grandkids."

Ray listened. Raymond.

"And . . . that is, Raymond? We'd be pleased as punch . . . I mean to say . . . your mother . . . ahhhemmm." Randall had to clear his throat again. "I'd prefer not to do this by phone, but I'd like to ask your permission. To marry your mother, that is."

Ray had to smile; he was charmed. "Of course," he said. "That's kind of you to ask, and completely unnecessary. She makes up her own mind," he added. "Always has."

"Well, I admire a man who minds his manners, I like to say. So I better mind mine!" Randall laughed.

Ray laughed too: it felt good. Thirty grand would make a hell of a wedding gift; he could send Randall and Mom around the world on a year-long adventure.

"And . . . Raymond? We would like for you to give her away, and for the kids to be in the wedding party, and for little Jean to be Maid of Honor? Do you think they'd like that? Could you ask them? Would you do that for your mother, Raymond?"

He didn't know what to say . . . he couldn't . . .

"Raymond?"

Ray was choked up.

"Raymond."

"Yes," he managed. "I'd be honored."

CHAPTER 25

Ray was trying to understand time. His job had become an extended hiatus; no daily schedule needed to be heeded, no Flintstone-style whistle blown to indicate the start of happy hour. He had just come from happy hour, but on someone else's time, and he wasn't happy about what had happened. But there was more: Mae called Jilly, Kayla took Ray for a drive, the Strawberry Family wasn't home, Jim bought Ray a drink, Randall got on the phone. Each of these discrete events seemed joined together, in a way, as part of some kind of momentum, time surging. And there was another period of time, a weekend: Nathan and Lu, Uncle Ray. Phyllis, Sal, and Hank. Sylvie. Time had surged then, too, and ebbed or eased or something, then surged again. It felt as though Ray's watch worked, and then stopped, and then sped up to catch up, and then stopped—and that the speeding up was becoming faster, the momentum more powerful.

When the phone rang again, Ray wasn't ready to talk—he had a mouthful of Coke, but really, he just wanted to be left alone. So he screened the call.

"You know who, you shit. Meet me at the plant."

Ray put out his hand, leaned against the counter. A meeting? Oh god. It seemed so TV that Palmer would want to meet Ray: it would be a trap and Ray would be prepared for the trap and his cell phone (which Ray would have to go buy) would be pre-programmed to 911 and Kayla would be perched in the rafters with her service revolver, just in case. Or maybe Palmer would just kick the shit out of Ray, and Ray could go back to work and see where he and Kayla were headed, and Brighton would be safe for democracy. Then he remembered: Kayla had gone out to pick up a pizza. Was she safe? He had no way of knowing. A service revolver? Yeah, right.

Ray was scared because he knew he would go to the meeting, and he would be at risk. Although with such a brazen invitation, Palmer had to figure that Ray would take precautions, and that no one would be able to hurt anyone else, right? That was an awful lot of sense to attribute to Palmer, Ray thought. What made Ray think that Palmer was capable of reason? There had been no evidence of reason in any of Palmer's actions.

So Ray should outthink the bastard; and Ray would go unarmed, because he didn't believe in violence. No, that was too TV. Ray would go unarmed, because he didn't own a gun, and wouldn't know what to do with one anyway, if . . . damn. He needed time to think. But he wasn't panicked, which surprised him, he was just too full of words.

Ray knew that going to meet Palmer—he'd leave in five minutes, okay, he said to the kitchen clock—might mean a conclusion to all this nonsense, or at least the prospect of a conclusion. Palmer would only want to talk, to negotiate a truce or something, or he wouldn't have arranged the meeting so that others might learn of it easily, and show up too. Ray considered Palmer so far: that night, the pain, GOT YA and the eggs and the pickup truck and *Pow!*, the drive-by. Each incident like a pin, being pricked all the time with a pin. He had to go, Ray thought, or this would never end. But a pin seemed the wrong instrument—it was beginning to feel more like a pointed hammer, a miner's tool or something, like a pickax.

His good running shoes and shorts and a T-shirt, all perfectly boring, the right clothes to wear to meet your maker. Yes, that's right, Ray thought, as he climbed into his breath-defying Toyota, a broiler. Look reasonable and be crazy. This could work, Ray thought, since acting crazy was often a good strategy, on TV. And of course, the situation wasn't TV, only life and time surging, but from TV Ray had learned what to do. Educational TV, Ray thought, bemused—and scared. He would go to the meeting. The meet? He was going to the meet. He had decided not to leave Kayla a note.

There was a two-toned beater parked poorly, at an odd angle, just outside the south fence. Palmer. "Beater," Ray said aloud. His dad's word for that kind of car. Where would Palmer be? Well, meetings take place in offices. Ray was purposeful, as he walked to his office, the second shift in full swing but all the administrative offices empty. No, wait: someone would have to be in Admin, Lopez, the night man.

Palmer was there. The cop was there, his feet on Ray's desk.

"Hiya, Mr. Stanton. Glad you could make it," Detective Shaw said. He slid his feet off Ray's desk. "You know Mr. Palmer, I'm sure. Mr. Palmer, I believe you have met Mr. Stanton."

Ray stood in the doorway.

"Oh now, c'mon in. Shut the door. Have a seat—" The policeman indicated the remaining unoccupied chair. "Welcome to today's show: Vigilante Justice, starring yours truly, Judge Shaw."

Ray sat in the chair people used when they were being fired or slid. "You're good," Ray said, thinking about taking the thirty thousand dollars.

"Why, thank you," said the policeman brightly. "Coming from you, that's a compliment. . . . Okay," said Shaw. "Who wants to go first? How about you, Mr. Palmer. Yes, I think that you should go first. At approximately 19:00 hours on the night of May 22, you and Johnny Bowers and a third party deliberately rammed Mr. Ray Stanton's rented car in the parking lot of the Food Town, after which you forcibly abducted Mr. Stanton and removed him to your vehicle, a blue Ford pickup bearing Ohio license plate Alpha, Niner, Niner, Zebra, Boy, Three. . . ."

The cop had begun without benefit of notepad. An impressive recitation, Ray thought.

"No. Wait. Let me stop here. J. T., maybe this would be better if you told me yourself? How about it? Story time? After that, maybe it will be nap time."

Ray smiled.

"What are you smiling about, Mr. Stanton?" The cop hadn't appeared to move, or to glance Ray's way. "Something funny?"

"I . . . No sir."

"Ooooh. 'Sir.' See, Jimmy? See what it means to be polite. How about you try."

"Fuck you," Jimmy Palmer said. "I want my lawyer."

Detective Shaw stood up, slowly. He came out from behind Ray's desk, stepped close to Jimmy Palmer, paused, and then drove his fist, swiftly and athletically, downwards into Palmer's stomach. The punch pushed Palmer deeper in his chair as he gasped for breath, the chair atilt. "You've got a lawyer, Jimmy; he's the guy who's gonna make sure you're convicted for assault. You shouldn't have done what you did to Mr. Mapes. . . . And as for tonight, I am your fucking lawyer, Jimmy. Don't forget it. 'Cause I'm also the hanging judge tonight."

Palmer was having trouble breathing. Ray watched. Palmer's breathing evened out, just a little. Okay.

"What about you, Mr. Stanton? Ray? Would you like your lawyer to be here?"

"No. No, sir."

"Good." The policeman sat down once more behind Ray's desk. "Now let's try again. . . ."

This time, Detective Shaw recited the facts—which he knew surprisingly well, although he didn't know everything. For instance, he knew all about that night, but he didn't know for sure who had been there with Palmer, who the third guy was; he knew about the cross burning and the truck, but he didn't know that Kayla had helped, Ray's coconspirator. And the police officer knew about Nathan, of course.

But Nathan's assault was the only crime Shaw could prove, Ray realized, which was why they all were here, why the meeting was set up so surreptitiously, not at the station house but at Windy Oaks on a Monday night, off the record. The cop didn't have anything, Ray thought—a thought as TV as all the rest. Be careful, Ray told himself.

What else didn't Shaw know? He didn't know that Ray had fired 7 white people, or that approximately 225 people, all told, were probably going to be displaced, whether Ray was in charge or Jim Rivers did the firing in Ray's name. Detective Shaw didn't know, or didn't mention if he knew, whether or not Palmer had been hired to do all this shit to Nathan and Ray—or just to Ray, a thought that had begun to bother him. Or maybe Shaw knew everything, and was only reciting select details, to keep control of the situation, to manipulate both Ray and Palmer.

Glancing sideways, toward Palmer, Ray realized that what he had presumed to be sunburn might be, instead, the man's color. Palmer was kind of rose-colored, maybe. A very pale-skinned guy who worked in the sun? Ray didn't let his expression change.

"So that's where we are, gentlemen. Right here. . . ." Detective Shaw grinned, a small almost furious grin. "Thank you, Your Honor. Now. May it please the court to find . . . ? No, you may not approach the bench. The Court finds both defendants guilty, and sentences them to . . ." Shaw paused; his gaze shifted from Palmer to Ray and back again. "Cease and desist. Even better, the Court decrees that the five-block radius around Mr. Stanton's residence be declared a Palmer-free zone, and that the five-block radius around Mr. Palmer's residence be declared a Stanton-free zone. Furthermore, the Court promises that its lawfully empowered detective Mr. Paul Shaw—that's me"—the policeman pointed to himself—"right? . . . that the lawfully empowered detective Mr. Paul Shaw shall hereby be granted the right to break one finger on each defendant's hand for every violation of said statute. So help me God." Shaw smiled seriously; the man wasn't joking.

"Oh. And a few more things, boys. Let me add that you each have work to do, if you want parole. You"—he pointed at

Palmer—"will do twenty hours' volunteer service at the new community center site. You'll help build the pool." Shaw gave a grim, deep chuckle, then stopped. "And you, Mr. Stanton, you'll do twenty hours' volunteer service at Morningside. D'ya know the place? The senior citizen home near the plant. Lots of Windy Oaks folks go there to die."

Shaw seemed finished. He stood up. "Now I'm going to trust you boys—I mean, I don't trust either of you, but I'm going to go wait in the hall, and I expect you boys to stay here in this office for five minutes, together, before you leave, and if either of you comes near the other"—Shaw cupped his hand to his mouth, to feign a whisper—"I'm going to break two fingers, one each, no matter who started it.

"And let me just add, gentlemen, that you're both fucking babies. Yes, babies. And I don't care if you are fucking babies, this is my town. If you make more trouble, you little fucking babies, I'll make you pay."

Shaw's face was flushed. Ray felt suddenly nauseous.

The police officer pushed his way out of the small office, hands up between Palmer and Ray. "The clock starts now."

They were alone together. The door was shut. "I'm gonna fucking kill you," Palmer said.

"No you won't," Ray said.

Palmer glared at Ray: "Am too. I'm gonna fucking kill you."

For chrissakes, think of something new to say. Then Ray couldn't resist, as all his self-control, his decency, and maybe even his prudence abandoned him. "So . . . did you like your truck?"

Palmer started up violently, stopped himself, settled down into his chair. The tendons—were those tendons?—in his neck bulged, taut. "You're dead."

Ray pointed his finger at Palmer, cocked the thumb. "Like this? *Pow.*"

They were still in their chairs. Good thing. Something shifted in Palmer, something major. He snorted, smiled.

"Shaw may be tough," Palmer said, apparently thinking aloud, "but I'll get him."

"Oh that's smart, Jimmy," Ray said. "You'll get the police detective."

Palmer was furious again: he glared at Ray. Jesus, Ray. Shut up, Ray.

"You're dead. You don't get it, man. You're dead."

"No," Ray said. "I'm not. Because I'm done with you and you're done, all by yourself. Because I live here with my girlfriend. Because you don't understand shit about me—especially now that you made me . . . " The thought trailed away. Why bother.

"Nigger lover. And your bitch too. You're dead."

"Watch your language," Ray said. Now he was pissed. "Get off it. You're some twenty-year-old prick and you're going to hurt me right in front of the cops so that you can go to jail forever. Brilliant. You're a fucking moron."

Palmer's mouth was open. Ray was tempted to ask Palmer if he had a tiny dick. "I'm done with you, Jimmy. I'm sure your friends loved your truck, and that you've paid your debt to society, thanks to me. So now—" Ray stood. Five minutes, ready or not. "Go fuck yourself." He stepped toward the door.

Palmer's mouth was still open; the boy seemed too angry to move. He was a boy, after all. But then he stood too, suddenly and violently, his chair falling over backwards. Ray was partially facing the door and partially turned, too, so that he could see Palmer, just in case. More stupid than insane, Ray thought. More cruel than stupid. Palmer advanced toward Ray . . . and the door was open. Detective Shaw stood there. "Here we are, gents. Step right this way, your vehicles await." He gave Palmer a little push, one finger to Palmer's shoulder, hard. "Jimmy. You look upset. Now don't be: until you go down for Nathan Mapes, you're out of jail free."

Ray rolled down all the windows and turned the air-conditioning on full blast. He watched Palmer drive off, watched Detective Shaw do a U-turn, swing around the lot, and pull up so that his driver's window faced Ray's.

They should exchange donuts, Ray thought.

"So, Ray, how would you like to swear out a complaint, and Jimmy goes away? Shall we finish this?"

Ray was thinking. He made a decision: "No thanks," Ray said. "Not guilty."

Shaw's gaze narrowed. "Okay, so that's what you want. Well, then, I've got more to say to you. First, Gracie Adams runs Morningside. Tell her I sent you. Second . . ." The policeman chewed his lip for a moment, plucked something from his mouth with his left hand, looked at the something quizzically. "Second . . . I think that you've been the victim of a violent crime, and Jimmy should go away for it. So you reconsider. Swear out a complaint, and this'll be done, and I'll even consider forgetting your junior high shit and all. Do you understand me? Jimmy's too stupid to listen to me for very long, but you're not— I know that about you. And I even . . . don't get me wrong . . . I even thought that some of your little games were kind of amusing. But not now, not after Nathan Mapes. I want you to swear out a complaint, and I'm not tolerating any more bullshit. Nothing. Zero tolerance. Which means you make one phone call, swear out a complaint, and this ends. That's the script."

Ray was sweating. Cool off, he told himself.

"Mr. Stanton. A couple more things. Think about it: Jimmy's up for Nathan Mapes, so your story will mean more. . . . And oh yeah, just in case you were getting all righteous and all, remember that little tale I told about our J. T. Palmer? Well, that was true. He's got that older brother, and he treats him nicely, and supports him. And not that I'm saying this to change things, because it doesn't, but Jimmy's got other eats on his plate, you hear?"

The cop paused. "Just so you know," he said. "He's making mistakes, and he's going to jail, but he's a person." The detective had a remarkable look in his eye; Ray didn't know what it meant. "Okay," Detective Shaw began again. "Now. One last little point. My offer ends this week. You don't call me by midnight Friday night, and you're on your own. Which means if you don't call, and Jimmy and you get into it, I won't be there to help you out, but the law will be, to clean up, and the law doesn't choose sides if both are dirty. So if you decide to fuck up too, you'll both go to jail. Promise."

Ray had heard this before from Detective Shaw, this one-time offer, only now the man seemed serious. What would Shaw really do? Ray had no idea. Shaw was too savvy to outguess; the detective had degrees of seriousness.

"Okay," Ray said. "I'll think about it."

"One more thing—"

"I said I'll think about it."

The policeman was surprised. "No," he said. "I was talking," he said. "One more one more thing. . . ."

"Yessir," Ray made himself say.

"Good. One more one more thing: go kiss your girlfriend, Mr. Stanton. She's worth a kiss."

CHAPTER 26

His leased house wasn't air-conditioned, of course; he'd have to buy a window unit or two. In the kitchen, the cupboards half-full with make-do dishes, Ray sat eating cold pizza, picking off the gray blobs of rubbery mushroom. He liked cold pizza, although even the mention of it used to horrify his mother. She was easy to horrify, Ray thought, and adept at feigning horror. She also liked to sit like this, alone. As her own marriage had faded, a marriage that ended only with the death of Dad—which, thank god, had come fairly quickly, once he took sick—Ray's mother would sit in her chair in the living room when the sun went down, and not turn on a light until everything around her had deepened from shadow into darkness, through each small stage of darkness until the night arrived. In her wing chair with the embroidered little white flowers, Dad at the Horse 'n Buggy or the Corner Pub.

Ray liked catching himself in moments like this, sitting alone as his mother used to sit while she waited or didn't wait for her husband to come home and drink before leaving again to go hit a bar, another day Dad deemed wasted, a day spent making trucks go places, when he still worked in freight. Ray liked coming upon something in himself, like this, that he had inherited from Mom—especially something nice, like how he also took comfort in sitting alone. He even believed, as a son and a father both, that these inheritances constituted a kind of love. How sitting here in this kitchen said something nice about his mother's life; how Ray's kids might do the same, how his son, Tom, might find himself sitting alone in a kitchen someday, and smile at the thought of Ray doing the same. Or maybe Tom would inherit Grandma's wing chair, the gift skipping a generation, like some sort of recessive gene.

Kayla had left him alone this morning, with the leftover cold pizza and his problems, to brood. Despite himself, he was getting better at brooding, if brooding meant being able to think for a long time about what to do. She would meet him later; she'd stop by her mom's. She had been awed by Detective Shaw's stage-managed showdown, and pleased with Ray. He had earned his kiss, Kayla had said. Now, will you make up your mind, and decide what to do? she had said.

"You have reached the Stanton residence. No one's—"

"Hello! Hold on! . . . the machine . . . hello?"

"Hi, pumpkin. How are you?"

"Oh hi, Daddy. I'm fine." Jean immediately sounded bored.

"Can I talk to Mom, please."

"Sure, Daddy. I'll—"

"Love you, pumpkin."

"Dad," his daughter whined.

Ray waited.

"Love-you-too-bye. Mom! Telephone!"

That's what he had wanted. Ray exhaled, his shoulder creaking a bit as he let the tension go. He rolled his head to the right, just a little, to crack his neck. No go. Ouch.

"Hello."

"Hi, Jilly."

There was silence, phone hiss, a pin not dropping; then: "You bastard."

Ray didn't answer.

"Did you hear me? You're a bastard."

"Maybe," Ray said. "But I'm sorry she called you, if that means anything." He pictured Jilly's face, the beautiful cut of her cheekbone when she wore her hair down. Jilly wouldn't want to cry, Ray knew. He waited. "Sorry," he offered again. "That didn't have to happen."

"It didn't. You . . ."

More silence, phone hiss. They had lost the ability to discuss anything, really, except for their arrangements for taking the kids, and perhaps each other's failings. This probably wouldn't be a real conversation, he said silently to himself, thinking about Kayla.

"Who is this woman you're seeing? No . . . I don't want to know . . . don't tell me. . . . You've got to talk to Jean," she said, changing the subject. "I had to ground her, but she's been really bitchy about it. She's trying to push me around. I . . . I would appreciate support."

"Sure," Ray said. "Let me talk to her. How about you put her back on?"

His daughter returned to the phone grudgingly. Ray listened to her whine, Mom this, Mom that. Then he asked Jean to put her mother back on, so that Jilly could recite the facts to Ray as Jeannie stood there.

"No," Ray said to Jean, back on the phone a third time.

"Oh, Dad," Jean whined. "Why?"

"You know why. You have four days left on the grounding, and that includes no overnights." Four days until Friday, and Shaw's deadline: nice coincidence, Ray thought, father and daughter both grounded.

Jean was getting worked up. "But I'll be grounded after, I promise. You can even tack on two extra nights. I won't care. Please?"

"Nice try, pumpkin." Ray shook his head at the telephone. "Mom's right. No dice." Ray easily imagined the look on her face.

But then Jean must have dropped the phone and stomped off, because he heard her yell from far away, "You don't care! Goddamn you! Shit!"

"Ray?" Jilly was back on the line. "Thanks."

"Sure."

"She's getting tougher, you know. Someday she won't listen at all."

"I know. I don't like it."

"Yeah," Jilly sighed. "You and me both. The cursing's bad."

Ray was sad. He told Jilly what he had to tell her, why he had called—that he would have to visit the kids in Medford this summer rather than have them come to Brighton. He didn't mention Kayla again, didn't say anything about Windy Oaks or Palmer or Detective Shaw.

The sadness was physical: his body was sad. Damn, Ray thought, as he got off the phone. Fuck. That's right, the cursing's bad. No surprise there, Jeannie's a Stanton, more like Fran than Ray, Grandpa than Grandma. Or maybe she was like Ray after all. Fuck it, he smiled. The cursing's bad.

He felt better, resolved. Not that Ray knew what he was going to do next, but with or without the thirty grand, he had decided to stay in Brighton longer. The one decision he had made was a decision to be with Kayla, and that was what he wanted. Good. As for the rest? Fuck it.

Of course, he could just stay on the job and not sign off, push forward with his assignment, damn the torpedoes. Palmer would definitely remain a problem—as Ray still didn't feel that he could come forward, given Rivers's warnings about unwanted publicity, etc. But if Palmer were out of the picture, then what? Best-case scenario: Windy Oaks would be reorganized and Ray would become the right bad guy once again in Brighton, doing his job the right way no matter what people thought, half-sure in his assurances that the plant would survive, the town wouldn't die, race wasn't an issue.

Or he could take the thirty thousand dollars and quit Riggs on August 1. He could use the money to . . . set up Kayla in her own restaurant? Not enough money. Set himself up in business? Doing what, in Brighton, within the limits of his expertise? Not enough opportunity. Just live here for a year? That seemed possible, although the support issues and the divorce would be tricky.

The pizza was gone, every slice. Sitting alone in his kitchen hadn't gotten Ray anywhere—just as it hadn't gotten his mom anywhere either, he knew. Palmer was still out there, and Ray was scared. Motivated, too, but to do what, he didn't know.

Ray was standing behind the screen door to Mae's kitchen, a door that was open for no good reason, given the heat. He was eavesdropping, and he shouldn't.

"Would you please put that plate in the dishwasher?" Mae was annoyed with Kayla—but Ray was annoyed with Mae. Seeing her had reminded him.

Wait. He checked: actually, he wasn't annoyed with her, he thought. Bizarre.

"Momma—"

"Mm-mm, you sure can talk."

"Momma, I'm . . ."

"You're what? Sorry?" Mae walked to the counter and with her right palm checked the temperature of the coffee pot. "Hand me a mug."

Kayla complied, and then: "No. I'm not sorry."

Ray should make a little noise to let them know he was here, clear his throat or something. He should knock.

"Mm-hm?"

"You don't get mad. You don't. . . . I refuse to be sorry for what I feel."

"Kayla . . . No one is saying that what you feel isn't right. But being right doesn't help . . . and feelings . . ." Her voice dropped. "Feelings end."

There was silence as Mae and Ray waited for Kayla to explode. She had turned away abruptly to look out toward the window, her hands flat on the counter: she saw Ray, her lover. She smiled at him, a good smile. She winked. Then she screwed her face into something angry again, pretending. "Momma. It's my life." She spun back around, to face Ray. "Hey. Come in. Look, Momma, it's Ray." Kayla opened the screen door, and stepped to Ray. "Hi." She kissed him.

"Hi." He kissed back, surprised, catching her only partially.

She wasn't smiling, not for her mother. Kayla was wearing jeans and a T-shirt; and now she was twinkling or fiery or both, her hand resting on the back of Ray's neck, which he liked. Goosebumps. She had kissed him, of course, for Mae to see.

"Hey, Ray, did you ever see *Jungle Fever*?"

"Kayla!" Mae's anger was immediate.

"Sorry." She shrugged. She wasn't.

Was that the one about the architect? He had seen the film. He had liked that film, although he mostly thought that Spike Lee was a blowhard. But Ray knew what jungle fever was.

"So what's up?" Kayla asked. And then, before Ray could answer, she said, "I'm wearing long pants to make Momma feel hot, so that she'll turn on her air-conditioning."

"So what's up?" Mae repeated. "A patrol car's been driving around the block every twenty minutes. That's what's up."

"I see," Ray said.

They chatted about nothing, about Uncle Billy, Kayla's real uncle, who had followed up his postcard by calling, his voice on the phone after all these years. Mae suspected that Jack, Kayla's permanently estranged father, had sent his twin brother to check on Mae. So what if Uncle Billy visits? Ray thought. Maybe he would invite Fran, and she and Billy could go out on a blind date. Or maybe Fran would like Detective Shaw, if he were single. The man's evenhandedness made him likeable, Ray thought, and he would be an interesting addition to the family, when all of this was over.

Would everything be over? What about Kayla? No, Ray thought, chatting along somehow, his mind doing too many things at once. That wasn't what he wanted. He wanted his job, his life. He felt like winking at Kayla. He waited for the conversation to turn, for Mae to look elsewhere. What were they talking about now? Oh yeah: Nathan and Lu.

There. Ray winked.

Kayla winked back. "Okay," she said. "What's up?"

"Um."

Kayla narrowed her gaze. "Spill," she said. "I know you."

"I had a talk . . ." Ray realized that he had to say something. "I spoke to my ex. I needed to." Ray waited; both women seemed remarkably interested. This was kind of fun. He waited some more. "So I told her the kids can't visit here, and I'll have to travel there to see them on weekends, every other weekend, I think. I'll probably go next weekend."

There was a whole lot of silence as Mae and Kayla both pursed their lips, mother and daughter expressions. They seemed to be trying not to exhale.

"That's wonderful," Kayla finally let loose, beaming. She understood, as he knew she would: Ray was staying.

Mae shook her head at Ray. "Would you like some pie?"

"No thanks," Ray said. "Got anything else? Something . . . cold?"

Mae's expression was impossible to decipher: "I think I've got some ice cream. Butter pecan, I think," she said, as she opened her freezer.

"Butter pecan ice cream? That's just about my favorite, ever, Mrs. Reeves. Wow, that cold air feels good. You should leave that freezer door open, it would be good for the room. Hey—" He smiled at Kayla. "You never offered me ice cream. Some hostess you are."

"Here it is," Mae held up a box of ice cream.

"No thanks," Ray smiled. He fanned a hand in front of his face. "Actually, I've changed my mind. Woooh," he huffed. "It's too hot in here for ice cream. Have you ever thought about air-conditioning?"

"Oh dear," Mae said. "You're insane. Baby Girl, he's insane. And rude."

"I know," said Kayla. "But you know me, it's how I like my men. Insane and rude." She stepped forward, kissed him again. This kiss Ray timed better: he had seen it coming. He was the guy she was talking about liking, after all.

CHAPTER 27

Ray was sitting out back, thinking about Palmer. Palmer hadn't spoken particularly well or clearly; his speech had rolled and gurgled, and his words had been swallowed just as they were pronounced. Eye contact had been a problem. Body language had indicated passive-aggressive resistance, trouble. He had slouched, he had drifted. He had rubbed an eye with the back of his dirty, chewed hand.

Ray thought about Palmer the way years on the job had taught Ray to consider people, with the sharp scrutiny of an employer. You're fired, Ray concluded. Sorry. But you just don't fit the plan, Jimmy.

The plan. Did the plan have one standard for whites and another for blacks? How did Kayla fit the plan? Even if race weren't an issue, Kayla would be in between; she didn't seem to fit, either, except maybe when he held her. That fit.

And how about Ray?

Neither management nor labor.

Neither married nor single.

Neither young nor old.

Neither peaceful nor violent.

Neither a criminal nor law abiding.

Neither at home nor on the road.

He felt a little bit like a teenager surrounded by adults, as though he and Kayla were sixteen, and were doing all they could to make the grown-ups unhappy. Not that Jeannie would appreciate the comparison, Ray thought, since teens think that they've cornered the market on alienation. Nevertheless, Brighton itself still seemed a mystery to him, so much a closed society and so small that he would never feel included. It was like a union, or a club for whites where he wasn't welcome anymore. Bad thought. Ray shook his head. Because there had to be a way to exist here, to be Ray Stanton and do the job and keep going with Kayla, and not have to hide.

He and Kayla were different. They behaved differently toward one another when in front of other people, in public. Once they were alone, they listened to each other; they were good listeners, together. As for the politics of it, shit: Ray had begun to think of the interracial stuff as a problem other people had, even though it was easy to go crazy, obsessing about how people like Palmer and Rivers and Detective Shaw were judging everything Ray and Kayla did because of their races. Race wasn't an issue for him, Ray thought—no, wait, that was bullshit, too. Palmer's racism was Palmer's problem, sure, but ignoring race had a habit of becoming racist in its way, too. Guilty as charged, he told himself.

Shortly after the two of them had slept together, one afternoon a month or so ago—was that right?—they had lunched at his house, Ray in his boxers and Kayla home to check on him, or to say hello, or some such excuse. She had kept up the pressure: squinting, flashing her danger smile, tapping her fingers, and always sliding an extra foot or two away, out of reach, teasing him. Uncle Ray, some more chicken? Iced tea, Uncle Ray? What are you doing, Uncle Ray? In Kayla's sexy tone Ray had heard only a smidgen of irony, but all that teasing had begun to irritate, too.

They had moved into the next room and settled down for a few minutes, Ray and Kayla sitting in his living room, each with a section of the *News and Gazette*; she had been sprawled on the sofa, feet dangling, toes almost angled to a point, in her blouse, black pants, and Reeboks. He had sat in a chair. Then he had folded the paper to follow an article, and had caught her looking out the window. She must have known he was looking at her, but she hadn't budged, or looked his way.

Something about the light through the window had changed how her face had looked, or maybe she had just been thinking and her expressions had changed with the quickness of her thoughts, but no matter the reason, she had looked different, in touch with something he hadn't understood. The light through the window had seemed a kind of spring bath, bright and even kind of green around the edges, like someone's skin on your own. Ray had thought, then, that he would never know her. He was tired of not knowing people, he had realized.

Hey, he had said.

What? Kayla hadn't moved when she answered.

I'd like you to stop treating me that way.

Hm?

You know. Gimme a break.

A break? Uncle Ray wants a break?

I'm not some fucking Uncle Tom.

That had turned Kayla, eyes wide: That's backwards, Mis—

And I'm not every fucking white man.

Eyes even wider, she had turned back around, away from him.

Silence. More silence.

Ray had waited.

I know, she had said. And then quietly: I know.

He had wondered if she would smile. Okay, she had said. If you do something, she had said. For me.

Sure, Ray had answered. I'll try.

Complain a little. Stop sucking it up. You let me in; you let me help.

Ray had thought that one over. Had he been rude? And then he had asked Kayla: Have I been too macho?

Kayla had sniffed, amused. D'you know what Mae Reeves said? My momma said—wait, let me get this right—"The man thinks he's fine."

He had immediately known it was true: as his ex had liked to say, Ray wasn't sharing. Fine, he had agreed. Okay, he had added more nicely.

But it's not because you're white, Kayla had said. You know. It's because you're a guy. Guys keep their doors locked.

Where'd you hear that? Ray had chuckled. Hell.

Who's it sound like, Colin Powell? Kayla had answered, then she had started to giggle. Oprah? W. E.—?

John Wayne, Ray had countered. Bill Clinton.

Ted Turner, Kayla had snorted. Roger Rabbit.

Donna Rice.

Who? Then Kayla had remembered the reference. Oh right. How 'bout—

Prince, he had said: or whoever he is.

Kayla had laughed hard, wiped her eye. Then she had tossed her earrings around as she sang: *I get de-lir-i-ous whenever you're near.*

Uh-oh, Ray had said, hands up. I give.

Uncle? Kayla had turned to smile at him.

Uncle.

You talk some shit. Kayla had stood up. You're worse than me.

Am I? I'm hoping it's temporary, he had admitted.

Mm, she had said. Mm-hm. Another great white hope.

"Ahem . . . excuse me? Mr. Stanton? Ray?"

Ray stood up. Little strips of bark fell from his lap—he had been peeling the stick—and what didn't fall he brushed away.

"Hello. How nice, um, it's . . . Phyllis, right?" The woman from the bar.

"Yes," she said. She was wearing a lot of makeup. Long shorts and a blouse.

"How nice to see you." Ray had stood; they shook hands. "What's going on—I mean, well, what can I do for you? Please." He indicated an available cast-iron chair.

"Thank you."

"Can I get you anything? Water? A Coke?" Ray was glad to be alone; good thing Kayla was inside.

"Well, a pop would be nice."

"Great. I'll be right back."

Ray turned and walked toward the house. Once inside, he stepped to the kitchen window, to take a peek. Would she still be there? Was she there at all? Something today about Phyllis seemed unreal, dollish and invented. Maybe it was her hair. Still, there she was. Here. Ray could see her in profile; despite her careful makeup, Phyllis looked like she hadn't slept. Could be she just wasn't a sleeper.

Two glasses, ice. He could hear the shower running upstairs, the water draining through a pipe in the wall, and Kayla singing badly again, which made him smile. He popped the Cokes, poured, then pushed open the screen door, butt first, backing out to the backyard. Let's do it.

"Here we are."

"That's awfully good of you. Thank you. It's been so hot."

"You're welcome."

They sat, Ray and Phyllis perched on their garden chairs. They sipped their sodas. Pop, he reminded himself. Ohio.

"That's nice. . . . I was just admiring your neighbor's garden. It's lovely—"

"Yes."

"My father's wife was a gardener. My stepmother. She had a greenhouse."

Ray waited.

"I . . . ," she said. The thought died.

"Yes?" Ray prompted.

"Yes," Phyllis repeated. She exhaled. "I need to tell you something."

"Mm." Ray was getting used to this.

"I . . ."

"Phyllis, please." He was getting irritated: why couldn't these people just speak their minds?

"Yes?"

"Please. Speak frankly."

"Okay." She took a breath. "Do you know the Palmers? Jimmy Palmer . . . he has a sister, Rita. Rita spends time at, um, Spot's, you know, the bar?"

"Yes?" He didn't. He could almost see Phyllis wrestling with herself, the struggle played out behind her eyes. He waited.

"Sometimes we drink at Spot's; it's a plant hangout. So a friend of mine was there last night, and she heard Rita talking. About you. She was drunk and she said things. Like her brother Jimmy was taking care of you. And . . ." Phyllis trailed off. "You know you fired Rita. And I think . . . the Palmers are trouble," Phyllis said quickly. "They hate a lot of people."

Of course Ray remembered Rita, and her file, although her last name wasn't Palmer but Woodley. She had been hired from the outside, having worked elsewhere, some place she had spent five good years and had three years off to have kids, and she had only been a shop super for eighteen months—which meant, all together, that she couldn't be offered a rollback, that there was no job on the floor to which she could return, last in, first out, because she had no seniority. She had seemed to take her dismissal well, Ray had thought at the time. Rita Woodley must be much older than J. T.

"Do they hate blacks?" asked Ray.

"Everyone—but blacks especially. Yes," said Phyllis. "They're country. Isn't that a terrible thing to say?"

Yes, Ray thought. "No," Ray said.

"She . . . uh . . . I thought I'd warn you that they're looking for you. And Rita said and 'your black bitch.' All they need is an excuse, those people . . . you know. They're going to do something. Bad."

"Yes," Ray exhaled. He knew this.

"So you take care."

"I will," Ray said. And then: "Phyllis? Thanks. I mean it."

"Oh, you're welcome," said Phyllis. "Those really are lovely roses. Are they dwarf?"

"I'm not sure."

"Lovely. I've gotta go."

Ray stood. They shook hands again. All the news was old news, the past repeating like a lousy meal.

"Mr. Stanton?" Phyllis had let go of his hand, no kiss good-bye. She had turned away; she was leaving. "I thought that you should know." She blushed. "You seemed nice," said Phyllis.

"I was," said Ray, and he meant it. He used to be nice, but now he was merely happy.

What kind of soldier would Ray have been, he wondered. Piss in the pants, refuse to leave the trench, shoot off a toe, frag an overzealous lieutenant in the back? Or lose it the other way, not care, go wacko in war paint and camouflage, harbor extra knives, secretively collect scalps and skulls? He couldn't say. He didn't know enough about that side of himself to say.

Hadn't that been a book, the scalps and stuff? No, wait. He had seen that in a movie about Vietnam, a good movie that Fran had recommended, even though it had seemed pretty exaggerated, or so he thought. That was the trouble with movies and even books about war—books which Ray liked to read, especially about Vietnam—they tended to embellish upon events. Then again, Ray knew that he was exaggerating too, in a way, imagining himself as a soldier; all this drama was making him feel important, Windy Oaks the front. Life in Brighton—burning crosses with Kayla and kissing single moms in a local dive—had become exaggerated, or at least bigger than his life usually was. His self, whatever that meant, felt bigger too. He was a veritable giant, right? Ray snickered, sipped his Coke. Except when he was being stripped, tortured, and tossed into a ditch from a speeding pickup. But maybe even then, too.

For chrissakes. Get off it, he told himself. Go do something. The pickup hadn't been speeding. Don't lie.

So he called his mom, checked in: yes, everything's fine, work's going well. He listened to her rave about her Randall, and how courtly his behavior was. But then, for the first time since the engagement, her tone switched back to a kind of whine. She complained about her wrist, where a cyst had developed and was "clicking painfully" when she played the piano. Mom loved the piano: at a local nursing home each Friday, she accompanied the sing-alongs. The piano and her sewing circle. She had turned into the woman she wanted to be, someone with limited needs who seemed, at last, happy, but being happy apparently still meant that she needed to complain to Ray.

Off the phone again, he returned to his chair outside, dragged the recliner into the shade, lay down. Just for a minute.

Buh, Ray shook his head. How long had he been sleeping? When he opened his eyes, the sun was mostly down, the day gone. He was drenched, the collar of his shirt a different weight and color. His back was soaked too. Ick. Ray rubbed his head and face with his hands. He had been dreaming. He couldn't remember his dream. What day was it? Oh yeah. It was almost the Fourth of July. The Fourth, Ray thought, which made him smile grimly. He was planning a boycott.

Kayla wanted pasta, which he made, just spaghetti and Ragu. Then she suggested a twilight walk, even though the heat was still incredibly oppressive—a walk, and who knows what might happen next, she said, snapping her fingers at him twice. In the kitchen, Kayla had leaned across his body and kissed Ray deeply, and then turned her body to him fully. Now with grinding. Ray had kissed back, with more grinding. He liked how easily their bodies met.

They left the house, locked the back door and came around the slate path to the front, Kayla and then Ray between Mae's house and his own. He watched her hips slide, thought more about the kiss, aroused. This way, she indicated with a chuck of her chin, and Ray agreed wordlessly. He reached down and took her hand.

"Sure?" she asked.

"What do you mean?"

"You know what I mean, boyfriend."

He did. "Yeah," he admitted, and then he added, "Yeah, I'm sure."

Holding hands for the first time, Ray and Kayla walked down East Bine and toward the park. They didn't have a lot to say to each other; the heat overwhelmed any need to speak, and holding hands seemed important enough to warrant silence. So they just walked into the park and around the duck pond, under the overpass, skirting the river. There was a playground: four little kids were climbing a jungle gym, moms watching, one little blond girl hanging upside down from the monkey bars, "Mommy, look at me." Ray and Kayla looked too. The girl didn't remind him of Jeannie at all, but she was a little girl, and that was enough.

Kayla might want kids, Ray realized. Did Ray want more kids? My god, not in Brighton. He should ask.

Their hands were sweaty. He let go, slowed to step around her, switched sides and took Kayla's other hand.

"Nice," she said. "Smooth."

"That's me," Ray said.

They walked until they both wanted to stop, a good walk in the nasty humidity. At home again, he watched her walk upstairs, to take another shower. They both were drenched, the night air close. As she disappeared at the top of the landing, Ray thought that he should wave. Bye, honey. Bye-bye. Have a good day. Don't forget to do the errands, pick up the dry cleaning.

He put the Parmesan away, which he had forgotten to do; the plastic container had a sheen of moisture. He washed the soaked sauce pot. So he would live in the house and he would visit his kids in Medford, and eventually, the kids would come to Brighton and visit him. But next to Mae? Why not. She would be their honorary black grandmother.

Ray wiped the sweat from his lip by scrunching up a shoulder and rubbing his chin, mouth, and nose on his T-shirt. Was that everything? He looked around. Nope. He still had to wash the bread knife and her iced-tea glass.

He tried again. So he would live on East Bine—or he would say fuck it, the project's off, get me out of here, David. And David, Ray's boss, no moral beacon himself, Ray supposed, would say sure, and then slide Ray into something meaningless, the arc of his career cast downward, for business reasons even Ray could understand. Despite a cool thirty thousand dollars on the side, Ray wouldn't like it. But he might be able to refashion his career at Riggs—wouldn't he? Except that to do so meant he would have to be in Medford, not Brighton. Kayla.

Ray dried his hands on a tea towel, hung the towel on its little hook. Everything in its place. Or everything just out of place, one place to the left, including Ray. He wasn't facing the issue, this Ray admitted to himself. The real question wasn't what would happen but what did Ray want? He wanted to finish the dishes, consider his options—burn a finger, sleep with Kayla, burn a cross, get drunk. Choose.

He had forgotten about the burn on his finger, which at the moment had a dishwater-soaked paleness to it. Okay, so Ray hadn't been the most rational man around, he admitted, despite having chosen to act, and having acted rather forcefully, Kayla at his side.

The dishes were done. Ray looked around for something else to do. Through the window again, he could still smell—or thought he could—something rank. Maybe the river?

"I've been waiting."

He hadn't heard her come into the kitchen. "Sorry," he smiled. Kayla had a T-shirt on, one of Ray's.

"Would you like to join me upstairs?"

He would. He turned off the light.

Another shower, and then to bed. Naked, facing one another, Ray and Kayla lay with the light on, still some sweat on his upper lip, more to come. She put her hand, her full palm, on the left side of his face. "Boyfriend," she said.

"Yeah," he replied. "Girlfriend."

Her eyes crinkled. "That was a good thing to do." She meant the walk, holding hands.

"I thought so. It was fun." His hand moved to her waist, rested there.

"What's going to happen to us?" she asked, her hand now on his hip.

"I don't know," he said. "What do you want?"

Her hand moved lower, found him and loosely held him. He stirred. "I want . . ." Kayla thought about it, smiled a dirty smile, her eyes twinkling. No earrings. "I want really slow sex."

"We can do that," Ray answered. He took the hint, and put his hand between her legs; she shifted her hip to accommodate him, as he cupped her, not moving, no pressure. "Then what do you want?"

"I don't know, Ray. But I like this. It's . . . mysterious. You know, I once heard someone define romance as mysterious. Not having all the facts, and wanting them—I think that's what he meant." She had begun to stroke him with her finger, up the length of his penis to stop at the tip. Just as she arrived there, she shifted her weight, left, right, left, to push herself against his cupped hand.

"Mm," he said.

"I mean . . . I know, it's kind of stupid and all, because you never have the facts, and you never really know if anyone's telling the truth—or, at least, it's possible to think that way, although I think it will fuck you up. If that's what you believe. But it's also . . ." She ran her finger down again. One finger. "I don't know. Look, I'm trying to have a real conversation here, and you're distracting me." She wrapped her hand around him, pulled upward slowly, gave his erection a little tug and then pulled down again, almost a full stroke.

"Mmmm," he said.

"See what I mean? You're distracting me. Like I want to say that I've got all these questions about you, and then you say something totally fucking brilliant, like "mmmm." Jesus, what's a girl to think?"

He gave a little nod and exhaled, a tiny laugh. She was in a talkative mood.

"Right," she said. "What do I want? Well . . ." She was stroking him, finally, but still slowly. He wondered if she were wet, and so he moved the fingers cupping her, just a little shuffle, as though playing a piano lightly. She responded, pushed back. "I don't think that Windy Oaks is going to let you stay, you know? Jim Rivers is pretty well known to be tough, quite a taskmaster. Boss man."

"Kayla," Ray said. "I . . ."

She stroked him fully, twice, her hand curled around him, up and then back down to the base. She was squeezing.

"Mmph."

"I know," she smiled. "You want to talk about what's going to happen *after* sex once it's *after* sex."

And so they stopped talking, and made love. They couldn't help but be incredibly sweaty, their skin sticking together and even making stuck skin sounds. From behind, as he held her hips and moved inside her, slowly and deeply, he could feel the perspiration down the middle of her back.

"Stop," she said, breathing hard.

He did. She reached down and used her fingers to open herself more, then pushed back onto him, deeper.

"That's deep," he kind of gasped.

"Right there," Kayla said. "Don't move. I'm ready . . ."

Ray didn't move. He was incredibly excited.

"After this . . . ," Kayla said softly, almost a purr. "I want more of this. Lovemaking," she said.

He pushed against her, just a fraction deeper, the condom tight but all the sensations just beyond it, too, which slowed him down. She gave a little moan.

"I'm going to touch myself," she said. "Don't go anywhere."

It wasn't much longer. When she started to come, she gripped him inside, and he started to come too. He held her hips and pumped; she bucked back on him, and moaned and even gave a little happy whine. She might have said his name, but he wasn't sure. His orgasm was strong, and afterwards, he felt tingly in various places; he realized he had been gritting his teeth, too, which he stopped doing. His jaw clicked. "That was good . . . ," he said. It was good.

"Yeah," she agreed. "We're getting better. Do you need to move?"

He was wearing a condom; he should move. He pulled out.

"Oh, Ray," she turned around very quickly, hugged him hard. Was she crying? "What's going to happen?"

He didn't know what to say. "I don't know," he said. "More lovemaking," he said.

CHAPTER 28

Again, she was gone when he awoke, to help her mom set up the church barbecue. Not because of church, she had said at one point during last night's walk, but because of Mom. To keep Mae Reeves from hurting her back.

I'm not talking to your mom, Ray had responded. As of now.

Kayla had laughed. You better be a better boyfriend than this, she had said, because so far you're not so great on your threats or promises. She had squeezed his hand affectionately, to let him know she had been kidding.

Last night, lying face to face, he had loved her body. She had a beautiful body—it was becoming more beautiful, to him, he realized, the more intimate they were. That meant something. He thought about when they were making love and she had pushed him lightly, to change positions, and he had slipped out of her, and she had laughed. She had a good laugh. She had thin arms, amazing legs.

He had very little food in the house, he saw. Would the stores be closed? No, wait, it was only July third. So he would think about buying groceries, and then go to the store. He would need another shower, too. The temperature must have been ninety already. Brighton was hot as hell, he thought, or hotter. Wear those sneakers, he told himself. Boy Scouts are always prepared.

East Bine to Sunrise Park, where it was too hot even for T-ball. Was this a heatwave? Seemed so. Right on Moseby, toward the Hills. A dogleg left, then right onto McKinley. A house across the street looked exactly like Ray's house, the same awful yellow, the shutters decorative and goofy. He wondered who lived there. Were they okay? Whoever had painted Ray's house must have painted that one—in fact, there might be many more of the same, identically ridiculous houses sprinkled throughout Brighton.

Someone called out: "Susie! Susie!"

Ray wanted to answer, to say anything. Susie lost her job, he wanted to shout. Stay under the radar.

He set a good pace, he would keep from meddling, he would look at nothing, he would walk. McKinley to Main, where the U-Shop was, a mom-and-pop grocery run by a haggard couple with too many children, an eight-year-old or one of his five little sisters always perched on a stool near the register, the two or three times Ray had been there. All the kids older, at their ages, than Ray had been when he was a kid. Was that so bad, for Ray to have grown up more slowly than kids were growing up today? Maybe that was his Jeannie's problem—and maybe that was his own problem, as a dad, that he expected Jean to grow up more slowly, at the speed at which he had grown up.

Brighton was quiet. He found it difficult to believe that the whole town wasn't on vacation, that people lived here at all. He shopped, the only customer in the store. He bought linguini, grapefruit juice, whole wheat bread. He bought condoms and *U.S.A. Today* and the *News and Gazette*. There was the letter to the editor, right on page ten, the spelling corrected but the signature, boom, right at the bottom where a signature goes. Oh man—Ray could only wonder what might happen next.

He bought cigarettes, as he had decided to start smoking, standing in the store, rereading the letter to the editor, and then looking up to see the racks of cigarettes. A box of Marlboro Lights, please. He wasn't sure he liked grapefruit juice very much, but Kayla did. Maybe he would try it.

On the walk home, Ray took off his shirt. The heat seemed to peel off the sidewalks in sheets, then hover. The morning had become afternoon. When had that happened? The heat wasn't going to break. Through the almost solid air, Ray wandered, slipped. The slipping through, rather than the being hammered: he felt more anonymous than ever. After all, no one had looked surprised by Kayla and Ray holding hands.

Didn't the elderly care too much about the weather? Ray thought so. Or maybe someone had once told him that, which let him think so. He wondered how many of his own ideas had been someone else's first.

Upon his return he ate a sandwich, lunch or something, and did nothing in the awful heat. Playing lots of solitaire, keeping score, and sitting right in front of the fan, as the occasional card fluttered off the table. He won. Vegas owed him $105.

The day was ending and he had just pushed himself away from the table, where he had been absentmindedly skimming the Entertainment section, when the phone rang. He let it ring. After the third ring, but never in the middle of the ring, he answered. "Hello." He was thinking that even the afternoon had gone somewhere—where the hell do days go?

"Ray," she whispered.

"Hi, Kayla," Ray said, happy.

"I need you." There was a long pause, kind of a scraping sound. "I've done something. . . . Please."

Action: "I'm there," Ray said. "Just tell me. What is it? Where are you?" He was standing up, looking for a shirt. "Are you all right?"

"It's . . . I'm at my place," she said. "But don't park nearby." Her voice had risen slightly with each syllable. She was terrified.

He would help, Ray knew. "Give me ten minutes. I'm—"

"Ray?"

"Yes."

"Come alone. No police. And don't tell April."

She hung up, and with that little click, the conversation was over. Oh god, Ray thought. Don't tell April? Kayla was April, so—oh god. She was saying something. It must be Palmer: Palmer had told her to call, and she had been smart enough to use a code word, and . . . Okay, okay. Should he call the police anyway? Should he have Mae call the police for him, say, in thirty minutes? Should he bring some sort of a weapon? He wasn't ready for this: he would never be ready. Going out, he told his empty house. Be back soon.

Ray was beginning to connect cars and violence, he thought, as he drove. Get there, get there, get there, get there. In the rearview mirror, Ray eyed the traffic behind him. He was glad not to see Detective Shaw, but still suspicious. Get there.

Maybe when this was over, Ray would tear up his driver's license—or not, since that would put him in everyone else's cars, with everyone else driving him where he didn't want to go. But when would this be over? How?

Two streets from Kayla's, in case anyone was watching. Get there, but be careful.

He parked. He was drenched again in sweat, as the AC hadn't had time to cool off the car. Ray walked along the sidewalk. The walk felt like walking in slow motion. Up the street, a group of kids rode their bikes crazily, zigging across each other's paths, bumping tires with an occasional squeal and high-pitched laugh, shorts and T-shirts, kids being kids, thrilled with the hot summer night so early in July. White kids, but not his pals, not the kids from his street. In the other direction, Ray counted four people gardening in front of four different houses, in gloves or not, on their knees in the dirt or the grass on a hot July dusk in the middle of their universe, in the middle of their lives. It was being in the middle, among others, that meant something, Ray thought. Family. Someone dragged a garbage can down a driveway, the rusted, misshapen metal scraping asphalt—then Ray noticed the other garbage out, garbage night. The trash cans go out, come back empty.

It couldn't be garbage night, Ray realized. No garbage collectors work on July 4. All the garbage cans were too early. So maybe they were getting ready for a block party: spiked watermelon and three-legged races down Main.

Why had his neighborhood been so deserted earlier? The heat.

He turned the corner. One short block to Kayla's street, nothing for mankind. Ray doing the walk, the same kind of walk he had walked a month or whenever ago, step, step, one foot and then the other foot, only today he was in a different neighborhood, in the middle of his own life at the beginning of middle age. The difference tonight, he realized, was all important: middle age, for Ray, might mean a chance to reconsider.

He reached Kayla's corner. He would walk up to the front door and ring the bell. Or no: he would knock lightly with a loose fist. With a loose fist. He liked that idea. No one gets hurt and no one backs down—and the whole disaster comes to an end. That would happen, and then he would not call Detective Shaw. Or maybe Ray would call, make a different decision, get out of this mess, leave.

A dog barked, staked to a tree. A dog of a breed Ray didn't recognize, although it clearly wasn't a mutt.

Detective Shaw: What breed of dog was it, Mr. Stanton?

Ray: It was . . .

Detective Shaw: I'm having trouble believing you, Mr. Stanton.

Ray, not answering.

Ray shaking his head. Clearing his thoughts, getting rid of Detective Shaw. And then Ray was standing at the front door of Kayla's building; Ray had arrived as nonchalantly as possible, turning up the walk where the walk was, a neat turn, keep off the grass, no need to make eye contact with anyone, or anything.

A steady gaze. A loose fist. Maybe he should take off his shoes. He climbed the three flights slowly and quietly. The door was partially open. It swung open farther, about a foot, as Ray put his hand on the handle. The door made a TV soundtrack squeaking sound as it swung. Be careful.

"Ray," she whispered. "Thank god. It's you."

"Can I come in?" he asked, which might have been the dumbest question he had ever asked.

Stay cool. Cool. He was inside, Kayla had opened the door for him. Her T-shirt was torn under her armpit, almost to her hip, he could see her black bra, her eye looked swollen. A chair was upended.

"Where is he?" Ray asked.

"In the kitchen."

She was walking with a limp. "You okay?" Ray asked.

"No," she answered. "But I will be."

What had Palmer done? And Kayla? Ray was scared.

In the kitchen, Jimmy Palmer was sitting in a chair in the middle of the room, his feet and his hands bound. A wide piece of masking tape was over his mouth.

"Here," said Kayla. As though giving Ray a present. Her eye looked bad.

"Kayla?" Ray asked.

She stumbled slightly, steadied herself on his arm. "Oh Ray . . ."

Ray had yet to look away from Palmer. Palmer's eyes were slits. Hatred. "Did he hurt you?" Ray asked.

"He grabbed me, he was waiting for me here. He was in the hallway and I . . ."

Palmer had begun to shake his head. Wildly. Was that blood on his scalp? "It's okay," Ray said. "Just catch your breath."

She was gulping air, and she gave a very quick grateful smile. She slowed herself down. "He made a mistake, Ray. He turned and I hit him. He fell. Then I tied him up."

"Did he hurt you?" Ray inched to his left, but no closer, checking out her eye.

"Not really. No. I'll be okay."

"Good," Ray said. And then to Palmer: "Hello, Jimmy." And then: "Christ, what did you hit him with, a tire iron?" She must have gone back to Basic Training, remembered how to kill. And then: "Did anyone see you?"

-264-

Kayla's jaw was set: "I don't think so. He surprised me. I hit him with the lamp. I broke it," she giggled, frightened.

Was Palmer smiling, was that the expression under the tape? Ray realized that Kayla had drawn the shades and left the light off, or turned it off, a good idea.

"I went out to call you. I didn't call from here. Ray?" Kayla seemed to draw herself up, breathing deeply. "Let's go in the other room—"

"Bring him?"

She nodded, no. "No. Let's go sit down for a minute."

Ray stared at Palmer. Palmer might have winked. "Okay," Ray said. Fine, Ray told himself. He tried to relax his shoulders, stop their slight shaking.

In the living room, he sat. She came to him, sat next to him on the sofa, their thighs touching. He held his hand out, palm up, an offer, and then she took his hand. "Kayla?" He was probably wide-eyed.

"Give me a minute. Shhh."

He waited for her. Then, "Please," he asked.

"Okay," she said.

"What do we—"

"We?" She leaned back, looked at him. "This isn't 'we,' Uncle Ray. I did this."

Ray had been wrong: she didn't see Palmer as a gift.

"Ray." She had turned down her little smile. "I . . ."

He waited, then he couldn't wait. "Yes?"

"Yes," Kayla told herself. Then she took a deep breath. "I . . . I'm not sure how to say this, so here goes: I need you to finish this. I hate him, and I'm not thinking and . . . I don't know what to do." She was crying.

"And I do?" Ray almost laughed.

Kayla backhanded a few tears away. "That's right. I need you to put an end. To this." She leaned to her left, then swung her body upward to the right. Ray saw pain on her face, scrunched up there, around her mouth and eyes. "Ray."

"Goddamn it, he hurt you." Ray was angry.

Kayla was standing. "I'm sorry, I didn't want to put you in this position. He did this to me. But it's nothing, really. I . . . I gotta go. You've got to help me. You're the only one. I'm sorry." She hung her head.

"I'm sorry too," he said. "Don't be sorry."

"Don't you understand?"

"No," he answered. He was lying.

She took Ray's cheeks in her hands, leaned, kissed: Kayla's tongue found his, fully, swirling slowly. A good kiss. She stopped kissing him. "I'm falling for you," she said. "That's not supposed to happen. But we've got to be . . . able. You know? I'd say free, but no one's free."

He didn't want to understand.

CHAPTER 29

He was sitting on Kayla's couch in Kayla's slowly darkening living room. In the other room, Palmer was tied up and gagged. Ray liked that.

Kayla had gone to lie down; the bedroom door closed quietly. Smart girl, that Kayla. He could think of so many reasons they shouldn't be together, courtesy of Mae and Ray's conscience; each reason, though, had already been rendered moot by what was happening between Ray and Kayla, the attraction, the sex and the fun—and even the specter of Jimmy Palmer somewhere out there, prowling as Ray and Kayla made love on his leased patio. And then: in truth, Ray admitted, there were no reasons for him and Kayla to have gotten together, which was why when they did get together, it felt honest, unfettered.

She was falling for him. Was he falling for her? In many small ways. Did he love her? He couldn't say. But he wanted to be with Kayla—a feeling that was only getting stronger. Plus she turned out to be smart, that Kayla. Smart and dangerous: to deliver Ray here, to a delivered Palmer. But bound and gagged? For chrissakes. The absurdity was so beyond Ray that he decided to ignore it. Just be, just Ray. No one was expected for dinner tonight, not to Kayla's.

Ray was still sitting on the couch. The light was ebbing. A night just like the rest, and the others that would follow. Then Ray was standing in the kitchen as the light there waned a little less quickly, the uncurtained window facing west, an alley and another building, everyone on top of everyone else. Armpit homes, Ray could almost hear Dad say.

Palmer had apparently tried to hop across the room, and had slipped to the floor not far from where he had started. He couldn't have fallen, Ray thought, because Ray would have heard something. Palmer lay on his right side, the tipped chair propping him up, one unbound bare foot wiggling a little, probably to retain circulation or maybe just because it could; and his face, which Ray needed to see, was reduced to a strip of masking tape, a profile, and a left eye wilder than it had been earlier. Not meaner, though. A little bit of light from the rest of the day shone across Palmer's waist and hip, across the upended seat of the chair, and stopped where Palmer would never see it, upon his shirt. A foot-long slice of light, lost on Palmer.

He had noticed Ray, and was making sounds. Ray leaned against a counter, shakier than he would have preferred. He would not take off Palmer's gag yet.

Okay, so give it time. Ray hopped up onto the counter, elbows and knees working. Kayla liked to sit on the counter, like this.

The day was ending but taking its time too, making time longer, the light shrinking where it fell on Palmer. Where Palmer had fallen. The day had gone quickly, and now was going slowly again.

Once Palmer had stopped making sounds, it might have been another twenty minutes of sitting wordlessly: Palmer bound and gagged, helpless on his side, the curious shaft of light on his torso shrinking into oblivion, the right side of his face pressed and probably sweat-stuck to the linoleum floor, his feet bare, the room shrinking too into its most simple shapes, two men and their hatreds, roundish lumps in a fuzzy place, everything and everyone defined by blurriness.

Ray's hands were fading in the last of the light, even as his eyes adjusted.

This was the most elemental Ray had ever been, filled with hatred. And the hatred surprised him, how it brimmed in his eyes, overflowed into the room, moved out from him like something alive, born of Ray, his hands not full of rage but enraged themselves.

He hated.

Palmer hadn't moved in a while. Good. Shut up, bastard. Ray tried to consider his hate, to reason his way back from danger. In the darkness of the room, at his feet, lay someone less than human, a thing. Could this be happening? Did a person become less than a person just because he was capable of hurting others? Was Palmer less than a person because he refused to think, and just hated instead?

Ray squinted into the gathered darkness. The shapelessness had resolved somewhat into small shapes, the dark side of the room more real, the sink and the piled dishes knowable in silhouette. The dishes were dirty, Ray thought, because Kayla had been spending so much time at Ray's, only coming home to change.

Six feet away, at most, Palmer was probably squinting too, one eye narrowed to make sense of his surroundings, of Ray's nonaction so far. So far. Ray would act, do something, decide to be. Okay, now what? He wanted to hurt Palmer, to draw on Palmer's arm, write Nathan Mapes on the skin of the animal. That was Ray's first choice, or almost: he wanted Palmer naked, first, one unbound hand covering his groin in terror, self-defense. Ray wanted Palmer to be in pain.

Ray would kick him. Or Ray would do something worse, with a—what? He knew. They were in the kitchen, where knives were. Ray's career might be in the crapper because of this bastard—a thought that was worth having, over and again, whenever calm resurfaced. Windy Oaks was a goner, and Ray's career too. Lots of folks, careers in the crapper.

There was something to say about the prospect of Ray acting rather than reacting, in spite of Palmer's whimpering—Palmer was whimpering. Ray heard the sound. Damn, Ray shook his head. Vengeance wasn't sweet, or sour, it was just good. No one goes home, Ray thought. He eased himself from the counter, and approached the prone, bound body. That's right, it's a body. Nothing more.

Palmer might have had a stroke, with only his one eye working. . . . None of that, Ray thought. And then, with his foot, Ray nudged Jimmy Palmer. Palmer's head whipped around as far as it could, bound as he was, in terror. Ray knew what that felt like. Good. Feel that.

Kayla was standing in the doorway, in light cast from the hall. She had cleaned up, Ray guessed, although he couldn't see her clearly. "What are you doing?" she asked. "Ray?"

"This." Once more, with his foot, Ray nudged Jimmy Palmer.

"Ray," Kayla said. "Think about it."

Okay, Ray reasoned. He stepped back. Think about it. What he wanted was not to lose: there were too many ways to make mistakes here, and most of them would be permanent. He had two kids to consider, a finished career, a new lover, a sister who would never understand herself (much less Ray), a mother engaged to a charming man, and a nice, untrustworthy woman living next door, with her nice azaleas and dwarf roses blooming nicely. And here was fucking Palmer.

Ray also had the law to think about, and the fact that standing where he was standing, with Palmer bound and gagged, was probably already a crime, and possibly even a serious one. Nonetheless, and perhaps most significantly at the moment, standing here enraged, Ray wanted to act, and that desire overwhelmed all else, at least any more rational thought. So he had nothing to consider, or lose, with the possible exception of his own integrity, whatever the hell that was.

It was a desire, wasn't it? It wasn't a decision. Screw it. He nudged Palmer again. "I thought about this," he told Kayla. Ray's foot pressed against Palmer's bare forearm.

No, no, no, no, no. Was that what Palmer was saying, or what Ray wanted Palmer to say? Or what Ray was saying?

He pulled his foot back again. Ray had touched Palmer and felt nothing. The physical contact had done nothing to or for Ray's hatred. Uncle Hate.

But there had to be a solution that would let Ray win. He wanted to win—which seemed like a first, to want to win so badly. Being alone with his enemy's body, itself pulsing with hatred and terror, Ray assumed, meant having an opportunity to act beyond the uselessness of the previous month, to come out of his terror. To stand up. Sure, maybe someone would say macho crap—Jilly would think so, definitely, not that he cared about her opinion one whit—but what would such a response mean? What could anyone else know of Ray's emptiness, and all he had learned as he stepped from the ditch by the Welcome to Brighton sign? He had learned how empty he was, had been, might be till death did him part. Uncle Empty.

But not anymore, Ray thought.

Then the telephone rang, and Ray didn't think. It rang four more times.

Kayla turned the stove light on. "Let it ring," she said, after the fact.

Palmer had somehow rolled over and pushed himself up, onto his knees, the chair tied across his back.

"Telephone," Ray said to Palmer. It was what, the second time Ray had addressed his captive? That's right, Ray thought. A captive. "Wanna get that?" Ray said. He waited. The telephone had already stopped ringing. "Oops," said Ray. "Too late."

Ray turned to Kayla. "Give me time," he said. "Me and him. I won't hurt him—" Ray smiled. "Maybe."

"What are you going to do?"

Ray didn't know. "I need time," he said firmly. "Please."

"Okay," she said. "I'll be in the other room if you . . . whatever. You know."

Kayla stepped toward Ray, bent toward her, and they kissed.

That one, Ray thought, was a kiss for Ray, not for Mae or for Palmer. He liked it. Soft lips.

Alone again with Palmer. And then: "Hey. Listen up. I'm going to talk to you. That's right, you bastard, no matter what the hell I say, you have to listen. How about that. Roll around on that one, you shit."

Damn it was hot. Ray was drenched. He should take off his shirt.

"Once upon a time . . ." Ray stopped. "Right. You've heard that one. Okay, let's try this: you know, I . . ." He what? What Ray had started to say shocked himself. Interesting.

Again, he spoke to Palmer: "You know, I've been meaning to thank you. I mean, for all the stuff you did to fuck with me—" His voice rose. Ray held up his hand, in the darkness, calm down, be cool. The guy's tied up. "I really did get a lot out of it. Like Kayla. Remember her? The girl who just left, who must have surprised the shit out of you, when she clocked you from behind with a lamp? Remember her, that chick who hit you on the head and tied you up? Anyway, where was I? Right. Kayla and I have had some great sex, and I wouldn't have had that sex if it hadn't been for you, now would I? Hm?"

When Ray stopped talking, there were no other sounds inside the room. Maybe Palmer wasn't breathing.

"Don't you think when I ask a question you should grunt or something? Or I should kick you if you don't? Or maybe I should just break your fucking face? Right? Right?!"

He had almost screamed. No, Ray thought. Stop, Ray thought. And then: leave me alone, leave me alone, leave me alone, leave me alone.

He could see Palmer's eyes, now and from that night, and the expressions were different. That night Palmer had been gleeful and perverse—but these were the eyes of a man bound and gagged. So it couldn't be the same, Ray told himself.

Then a bad thought: Ray had switched places with Palmer, filled himself with Palmer's hate, and lost.

No, not yet. Ray hadn't lost yet. But hatred poured out every time he opened his mouth, a feeling he couldn't seem to control.

What to do? Ray carefully paced the tiny kitchen. "Don't go any-where," he told his captive. "I'm gonna go watch some TV," Ray joked. He turned off the light above the stove.

How long had he been sitting on the kitchen counter? The clock on the stove wasn't visible from this angle. Ray had been sitting a long time, though, because his shorts were damp and he didn't usually sweat much under his shorts, which meant that he must have been sweating for a while.

Palmer had to be really hot, maybe even dangerously so. The air in the kitchen was considerably closer than the air in the liv-ing room. Ray had better check, since he didn't want the guy to die. If the guy were to die, Ray wouldn't win, he would just go to jail. And Jilly wouldn't let the kids visit him, and Mae wouldn't visit him either—but Kayla might. Probably would, Ray thought. He thought about Mae, kind, in her useless fashion, although now . . . maybe not so kind. Just well meaning.

It was remarkable how good Kayla seemed to be at being Kayla, just who she was, and especially in comparison to everyone else. Funny . . . No, it wasn't funny, it was amazing. Kayla was honest.

He had settled into the darkness. Above the sink, a white box fan was wedged under the weight of the window. Ray ran his hand along the cord until he found the plug, unplugged, then ran the cord up as he groped for the socket. There was a light switch. He stretched himself fully across the counter and turned on the light—flash, Palmer blinking, still on the floor; there was the socket, where Ray would remember it—then off again, into more darkness. His own eyes needed to adjust. He waited. Then, with some groping and a little planning, he plugged in the damn fan, turned it on, then turned himself around to face Palmer.

Ray in charge, the BPR expert choosing a setting, adjusting the environmental controls. He had done something planned. "Comfy?"

Could Palmer hear Ray? The fan was loud. "I said, 'comfy?'"

Silence.

"You better answer. Try 'no.'"

Palmer shook his head: no.

"Good," said Ray.

Oh god, they had communicated. The bastard, the bastard, the—

The hatred was there again, searing through his jawline like a little piece of aluminum foil ground between the teeth. And the muscles in Ray's arms had tensed by themselves. He looked down. One hand a fist, the other flexing. Stop, Ray thought. But it was unstoppable. You're okay, he tried to con himself. Don't stop.

What was the opposite of hate? What would a priest say to that? Ray had only known one priest, at least one with whom he had ever spoken, truly, who although clownish had been a reasonable guy. Old already, when Ray had met him, at a school function for Jeannie's kindergarten. A tag sale, or something, and then once or twice more at the PTA, at the school raffle, seated next to each other and across from the night's big winner. It had been sort of strange to talk to a priest just like a regular person: since Ray wasn't Catholic, he had thought of a priest as a kind of alien. Not human like us, Ray had concluded. But a nice guy.

So what was the opposite of hate? He couldn't ask a priest, despite Ray's belief that the Catholics were pretty good at categorizing sins, and hatred. No, Ray told himself. This wasn't about turning the other cheek, it couldn't be. This was about winning: Ray was going to win.

Could he hate so much his hate would disappear? Could he rid himself of it? What was on the other side of his feelings?

"What time is it?" he asked the gagged man. There should be a clock on the wall, right about there. Ray stood, took two steps, checked out the clock, focused carefully. 10:35. What the hell had Ray been doing? "Do you think the clock's right?" And then, before there was time to respond: "Don't answer."

Palmer was not a large man, and his mass seemed further reduced by being tied up, but where Ray was now, with Palmer's body between Ray and the fan, almost no breeze reached Ray. He could wipe a sweaty brow with a sweaty bicep, but what the hell did that do.

But then Ray realized: something was going to happen.

"You must be wondering what's going on," Ray said. "I'm waiting." There. That should confuse the bastard further. "It's past ten-thirty already," Ray added. "When it's time, you'll know. . . .Want something to eat?" he joked. "No? Oh right, you've got that masking tape problem, so you can't eat, can you? Bet you're hungry."

The joke had not been funny, even Ray knew that. Maybe he would wait another hour. Just sit here, sweating.

He did that, he sat there at least another full hour. Ray sat and sweated and watched Palmer shift occasionally, the man clearly uncomfortable, his circulation severely constricted by his restraints. Ray sat and thought, and every so often he didn't think too. The night, the pickup truck, the walk—and Kayla and burning the cross and Kayla. It must have been exhaustion, he reasoned, because sitting there he found a way to un-think, to see himself as though from a distance, participating and watching too. In the corridor with Kayla, her family pictures, Mae in the photo, in uniform, flowers blooming in her hand like a bomb, dusk filling the upstairs hallway, the air choked, the window cut into the shape of a—

He had been dreaming, sort of. "Brruuhh," he shook himself. Palmer was still there. Now what time was it? Was it time yet? Ray thought it was time. Ray stood, turned on the light, blinked in the glare, surprised by the time, 12:09 on the wall, Palmer sleeping or pretending to sleep, his one eye closed.

What would Ray do? While he hadn't lost his job, his career wouldn't be the same: his career with Riggs International would be compromised, with or without the Windy Oaks project. Would be? Had been already. He thought that his life would never recover—or maybe that thought belonged to weeks ago, before firing people meant firing a person, someone who cared so much that she would set her brother upon Ray.

Or maybe he should just do the fucking job, and then life would go on, and he would deal with Rivers and the repercussions. If Ray didn't sign off, the contract had to be honored, after all. He could just continue, which he was bound to do, contractually, and make more people unhappy and do the job right. Now that was a thought.

"What time is it?" Ray asked again.

And then Ray knew what to do.

"Now," Ray answered his own question. "It's the Fourth of July." Uncle Right.

Ray turned on the light, nudged Palmer. Palmer opened an eye: the eye widened, flared, then narrowed, wary, mean. "This is it," Ray said. His voice was gravelly.

"Hmmp," Palmer answered.

"No," Ray said. "You're not talking." Close to his captive, Ray crouched, lowered his face. An eye to an eye, he thought. "See?" Ray showed Palmer a fist. He paused. Palmer had the good sense not to talk, if that was what kept him quiet. Ray's pause became a silence, waiting.

This was all about waiting, and the ability to go somewhere, in himself, to wait. He was there, in himself; Ray had found a place Palmer had shown him. What kind of place was it? Maybe it was a place new to him, but Ray could wait there.

His knee itched, so Ray moved to scratch. Palmer flinched, then squirmed slightly, his fear obvious.

There, Ray thought. But was Ray's fear obvious? And then he was right, and he knew it, and he stood up, in his rightness. "You lose," Ray said to Jimmy Palmer. "Right now."

This was it: Palmer's eye widened.

Ray reached for the phone, picked it up, dialed 911, and asked for Detective Paul Shaw.

"Do you want to see a doctor?"

"No," she said. "I'll be okay."

Okay, he thought. "I . . . I'm done," Ray said.

She nodded, reached her hand out and touched his arm. "You used the phone?"

"Yep," Ray said. "Shaw wasn't in, no surprise. But they're sending a car . . . and maybe, before I change my mind, I should wait out front. Away from him—" He chucked his chin toward the kitchen. "Before I change my mind."

Kayla squeezed his arm. She smiled.

"But I've got a question for you . . . I . . ." Ray tried to smile in response. "I've been thinking of going home . . ."

Kayla wasn't moving: she might not be breathing.

He did smile, a real smile: "I'm going to go get my kids. Do you like kids? Mine are great, usually. But I might only be able to bring Tommy here, at first, since my daughter, Jeannie, she's a teenager, and her friends are really important right now. Not her dad. But I thought that next weekend I'd—"

She was kissing him, a sloppy kiss, and hugging him and flinching from pain and he was kissing her back.

They got their things. Denny's or some place might be open—maybe the T.L.C. diner, Ray thought—and they'd go there, and have an all-night breakfast. The King's Plate was closed on the Fourth, which saved Kayla from having to eat there. Although some day soon, Ray wanted to eat there.

They would leave the door of the apartment open, Palmer on the floor of the kitchen. She grabbed her backpack.

Had she known what would happen? Had he?

Ray opened the door of Kayla's apartment: there was Detective Shaw, seated on the floor, in the hallway. How long had Detective Shaw been there? He would get the message, the dispatch officer had said.

"Mr. Stanton. Ms. Reeves."

"Hi," Ray said. In his peripheral vision, Kayla looked ragged around the edges. They were holding hands.

"Pull up a seat," Shaw said.

"We were just going—" Kayla started to say.

"Sit," Shaw said.

Ray nodded to Kayla, it's okay. They sat, all three of them in the hallway outside Kayla's apartment, Ray and Kayla facing Shaw. It felt like being in a dorm again, late at night, a burning candle jammed in an empty wine bottle. Partying with friends.

A long silence ensued. Then Shaw began: "Goddamnit, I've got to say that I sympathize with you. You know, young love and a new life and all that bullshit, just like we like to believe in."

Ray waited. Kayla's hand gripped his.

"But I'm going to have to do some business." He turned to Ray. "Did you call me, Mr. Stanton?"

"Yes," Ray said. He was glad he had called.

"Just under the wire, I would think. Good job, Ray. Now, Miss Kayla. I'd like to know a few things, and we can discuss matters here or at the station—" Shaw wasn't smiling. "First, let's talk about Jimmy. Nice letter." He almost smiled. "But you know, Mr. Palmer's pickup probably isn't salvageable."

"What—?" Ray didn't want to ask.

"Oh, you didn't hear? Jimmy's truck burned. Big fireball out by Ace. Looks like someone set it on fire. No one told you?" He waited. "Miss Kayla, you and I go way back, but there's nothing bankable here, if you were involved. You know what I mean?"

Ray was silent. There were too many reasons to ask why.

"Ray." She was looking for eye contact, searching his face. "I . . . I didn't do anything. I wouldn't do this."

She might have been lying. He liked her an awful lot.

"Okay. So that's your statement."

"It is," Kayla said. She nodded at Shaw.

"Okay," said Detective Shaw. "Second. How about you make another statement, regarding what happened here tonight."

Kayla exhaled, a big sigh. "Jimmy Palmer hit me, and dragged me up the stairs. But he made a mistake, and . . . I hit him. I broke a lamp."

"I see," said the police officer. "That's certainly a start. We'll need you to fill out a complete report, of course, and the details will be important. But I'm pretty sure that something's going to work, here." Shaw paused. "And you, Mr. Stanton? Are you ready to talk to me?"

Kayla squeezed Ray's hand.

"Mine's a longer story—and I'm willing. But may I ask a question? Detective . . . how long have you been here . . . ?" No, wait. A different question. He turned to Kayla. "You called him too?"

Kayla smiled. Shaw smiled. "It's a small town," Kayla said. "Lots of people know lots of people's phone numbers."

Shaw nodded.

"I guess," Ray said. "And some people want to look out for some other people."

In the street, standing in front of Kayla's building as she clutched his hand, a police cruiser double-parked with a uniformed cop driving, Palmer in the back, Ray realized something else. The law might be blind, but Shaw wasn't. Shaw . . . he liked being in charge, being the law. Shaw liked being fair, too, but he chose what fair meant. So Palmer would be punished—and Kayla? Had she actually burned Palmer's truck? Her expression seemed to say yes, although Ray wasn't sure. Maybe Jimmy's friends had caught up with him. But if she had set fire to the truck, nothing would happen to her unless there were witnesses or evidence, and even then, she'd probably get a suspended sentence, Ray thought, knowing that the idea was pure TV.

TV or not, a suspended sentence seemed just right, precisely what Kayla and Ray had earned, a deferral rather than a judgment, a future contingent upon good behavior, lawful small-town manners, a certain position in the community, Ray's hard-won job at

Windy Oaks done well—and he would do it well, he had decided. The white guy and the black woman careful not to parade their affections, but holding hands in public.

To hell with that, Ray thought. It was about holding each other, later.

But it wasn't over, Ray knew. Job or no job, Palmer under arrest or out on bail or free, nothing had ended except something Ray had wanted to change. Something Palmer had shown him; something worth getting rid of, Ray thought.

Then he turned to face Kayla.

"Right," Ray said. "Breakfast."